THE ZERO GAME

more...

"PROVES MELTZER IS AT THE TOP OF HIS GAME...
[A] complex plot, breakneck pacing, well-drawn characters, and shocking twists."

—*Exclusive Magazine*

❏

"MELTZER WRITES LIKE A GRANDMASTER OF
MANY YEARS' EXPERIENCE...HE HAS FEW EQUALS
in his ability to ratchet the suspense level to new
highs...If you haven't reserved a bookshelf for him
yet, you will soon."

—**BookReporter.com**

❏

"ONE BUMPY ENTERTAINING RIDE! A fine political
adventure!"

—**RebeccasReads.com**

❏

"A GRIPPING STORY...Brad Meltzer gives his readers
an inside look at politics—a world where nothing is
real [and] power is the ultimate prize."

—**CurledUp.com**

Also by Brad Meltzer

BRAD

THE ZERO GAME

MELTZER

WARNER BOOKS

NEW YORK   BOSTON

Warner Books
Hachette Book Group USA
237 Park Avenue
New York, NY 10169
Visit our Web site at www.HachetteBookGroupUSA.com

Printed in the United States of America

Originally published in hardcover by Warner Books
First International Paperback Printing: August 2004
First United States Paperback Printing: February 2005
Reissued: May 2007

12 11 10 9 8 7 6 5 4 3

For Jonas,
my son,
who holds my hand,
tugs me along,
and takes me on the most
cherished adventure of all

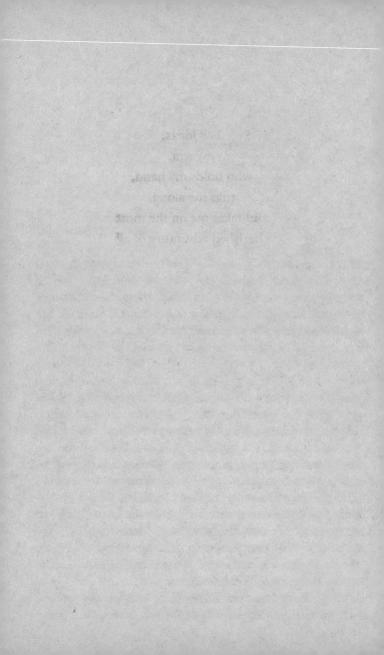

Acknowledgments

THERE'S ONE NAME on the cover of this book, but I've always maintained it takes far more than that to transform an imagined idea into reality. For that reason, I'd like to thank the following people: always first, my love Cori. To paraphrase someone far smarter than myself: The words aren't real until Cori reads them. She's always been my first editor and adviser, but for this book, in her real-world position as a lawyer in Congress, she was also my eyes and ears into the complex world of Capitol Hill. What she doesn't know is how humbled I was to watch her do her job. Forever the fighter of the good fight, she thought she was teaching me political mechanics. What she really did was remind me what idealism is all about. I love you for that and so much more. There are endless reasons I couldn't do this without you, C. Jill Kneerim, my agent and friend, whose insights and intuition challenge me to bring honesty to the forefront of my writing. Her guidance is among the first I seek, but it's her friendship that I treasure (even more than she knows). Elaine Rogers, for the amazing work she's done from the very start. Ike Williams, Hope Denekamp, Elizabeth Dane, Seana McInerney, and all the other incredibly nice people at the Kneerim & Williams Agency.

Now more than ever, I'd also like to thank my parents, whose unflinching love brought me here today. They keep me grounded, support me, and forever remind me where home really is. Everything I am, everything I have—it started with them. My sister Bari, one of the strongest people I know, for sharing that strength whenever I need it. Thanks, Bari, for everything you do. Dale and Adam Flam helped brainstorm the game, while Bobby Flam and Ami and Matt Kuttler read early drafts. Their love and support helped me throughout. Steve "Scoop" Cohen, fellow dreamer, brother in creativity, and all-around mad genius, for the eureka moment that led to this entire book. The ideas are fun; the friendship is far more valued. Thanks, Cheese! Noah Kuttler, without whose help I'd be insanely lost. Noah's the first sounding board I go to after my wife. He's that talented. He knows he's family—I just hope he realizes how blessed I feel to have him in my life. Ethan and Sarah Kline helped develop the game, and Ethan has fearlessly pushed me as a writer since my very first manuscript. Paul Brennan, Matt Oshinsky, Paulo Pacheco, Joel Rose, Chris Weiss, and Judd Winick, my alter egos, whose reactions and unwavering friendship are an endless source of inspiration.

In every novel, the goal is to make a complete fabrication sound like absolute fact. The only way to pull it off is to arm yourself with details. I owe the following people tremendous thank-yous for making those details available: Without question, when it came to explaining how the government actually works, Dave Watkins was my congressional sensei—an incredible teacher who was patient enough to answer all my inane questions. From initial brainstorming to final chapter gut-checking, I trusted him with every detail. He never let me down. Scott Strong was the Indiana Jones of the U.S. Capitol, guiding me through unexplored passageways and abandoned tunnels. His friendship and trust were indispensable to creating this reality. Tom Regan took me eight thousand feet beneath the earth's surface and reminded me exactly how this country was built. I just hope he knows what an impact his kindness had on me. Sean Dalton, for spending days explaining every tiny detail of the appropriations process, which is no small feat. His mastery of the minutiae was vital to this book. Andrea Cohen, Chris Guttman-McCabe, Elliot Kaye, Ben Lawsky, and Carmel Martin, for making themselves available whenever I needed them. The best part was, since they're among my closest friends, I could ask them the stupidest questions. Dick Baker is an institution unto himself. His generosity and historical insights brought the institution of the Capitol to life. Julian Epstein, Perry Apelbaum, Ted Kalo, Scott Deutchman, Sampak Garg, and everyone from the House Judiciary Committee are just the greatest. They made introductions, gave explanations, and came to my aid at every turn. Michone Johnson and Stephanie Peters, for being wonderful friends who helped bring Viv to life. Luke Albee, Marsha Berry, Martha Carucci, Jim Dyer, Dan Freeman, Charles Grizzle, Scott Lilly, Amy McKennis, Martin Paone, Pat Schroeder, Mark Schuermann, Will Smith, Debbie Weatherly, and Kathryn Weeden took me into their respective worlds and answered question upon question. Their help cannot be overstated. Congressman John Conyers, Congressman Harold Ford Jr., and Congressman Hal Rogers were generous enough to invite me inside—those were some of the best days of the process. Loretta Beaumont, Bruce Evans, Leif Fonnesbeck, Kathy Johnson, Joel Kaplan, Peter Kiefhaber, Brooke Livingston, and Chris Topik gave me a firsthand look at the incredible work that's done in Interior Appropriations. Mazen Basrawi, for letting me *see* through a blind man's eyes. Lee Alman, David Carle, Bruce Cohen, George Crawford, Jerry Gallegos, Jerry Hartz, Ken Kato, Keith Kennedy, David Safavian, Alex Sternhill, Will Stone, and Reid Stuntz for painting such realistic pictures of life on the Hill. Chris Gallagher, Rob Gustafson, Mark Laisch, William Minor, and Steve Perry were my experts in the art of lobbying. Michael Brown, Karl Burke, Steve Mitchell, and Ron Waterland of Barrick Gold, for all their help in getting me down into the mine. Michael Bowers, Stacie Hunhoff, Paul Ordal, Jason Recher, Elizabeth Roach, and Brooke Russ took me back to my youth and shared the excitement of being a page. Bill Allen, David Angier, Jamie Arbolino, Rich Doerner, and James Horning filled in the Capitol's physical details. David Beaver, Terry Catlain, Deborah Lanzone, John Leshy, Alan Septoff, and Lexi Shultz, for helping me with mining issues and land exchanges. Dr. Ronald K. Wright, for his always amazing forensic advice. Keith Nelson and Jerry Shaw taught me all the fighting skills. Dr. Ron Flam and Bernie Levin shared their hometown. Edna Farley, Kim from L.A., Jon Faust, Jo Ayn "Joey" Glanzer, Harvey Goldschmid, Bill Harlan, Paul Khoury, Daren Newfield, Susan Oshinsky, Adam Rosman, Mike Rotker, Greg Rucka, and Matthew Weiss, for walking me through the rest of the details. Brian Lipson, Phil Raskind, and Lou Pitt, whose hard work and friendship are immensely appreciated. Kathleen Kennedy, Donna Langley, Mary Parent, and Gary Ross, for their tremendous faith, sight unseen. Rob Weisbach, for being the first to say yes, and the rest of my family and friends, whose names forever inhabit these pages.

Finally, let me say thank you to everyone at Warner Books: Larry Kirshbaum, Maureen Egen, Tina Andreadis, Emi Battaglia, Karen Torres, Martha Otis, Chris Barba, the nicest and hardest-working sales force in show business, and all the other incredible people who make me feel like part of the family. They're the ones who do the heavy lifting, and they're the reason this book is in your hands. I also want to send a tremendous thank-you to my editor, Jamie Raab. From the moment we met, I've been under her care, but this is our first book where she's the sole editor. I'm the lucky one. Her insights about the characters forced me to delve deeper, and her suggestions left these pages far better than she found them. Every writer should be as blessed. Thanks again, Jamie, for your friendship, your endless enthusiasm, and most of all, your faith.

THE ZERO GAME

If the American people found out what was going on there, they would tear it down brick by brick.

Howard R. Ryland
Capitol police officer
On Congress

. . . the real problem is that government is boring.

P. J. O'Rourke

1

I DON'T BELONG HERE. I haven't for years. When I first came to Capitol Hill to work for Congressman Nelson Cordell, it was different. But even Mario Andretti eventually gets bored driving two hundred miles an hour every single day. Especially when you're going in a circle. I've been going in circles for eight years. Time to finally leave the loop.

"We shouldn't be here," I insist as I stand at the urinal.

"What're you talking about?" Harris asks, unzipping his fly at the urinal next to mine. He has to crane his neck up to see my full lanky frame. At six feet four inches, I'm built like a palm tree and staring straight down at the top of his messy black hair. He knows I'm agitated, but as always, he's the perfect calm in the storm. "C'mon, Matthew, no one cares about the sign out front."

He thinks I'm worried about the bathroom. For once, he's wrong. This may be the rest room right across from the Floor of the House of Representatives, and it may have a sign on the door that says, *Members Only*—as in *Members of Congress* . . . as in *them* . . . as in *not us*—but after all this time here, I'm well aware that even the most formal Members won't stop two staffers from taking a whiz.

"Forget the bathroom," I tell Harris. "I'm talking about the Capitol itself. We don't belong anymore. I mean, last week I celebrated eight years here, and what do I have to show for it? A shared office and a Congressman who, last week, pressed himself up against the Vice President to make sure he didn't get cropped out of the photo for the next day's newspaper. I'm thirty-two years old—it's just not fun anymore."

"Fun? You think this is about fun, Matthew? What would the Lorax say if he heard that?" he asks, motioning with his chin to the Dr. Seuss *Lorax* pin on the lapel of my navy blue suit. As usual, he knows just where the pressure points are. When I started doing environmental work for Congressman Cordell, my five-year-old nephew gave me the pin to let me know how proud he was. *I am the Lorax—I speak for the trees,* he kept saying, reciting from memory the book I used to read to him. My nephew's now thirteen. Dr. Seuss is just a writer of kids' books to him, but for me, even though it's just a trinket . . . when I look at the tiny orange Lorax with the fluffy blond mustache . . . some things still matter.

"That's right," Harris says. "The Lorax always fights the good fight. He speaks for the trees. Even when it's not fun."

"You of all people shouldn't start with that."

"That's not a very Lorax response," he adds in full singsong voice. "Don't you think, LaRue?" he says, turning to the older black man who's permanently stationed at the shoeshine chair right behind us.

"Never heard of the Lorax," LaRue responds, his eyes locked on the small TV that plays C-SPAN above the door. "Always been a *Horton Hears a Who* guy myself." He looks off in the distance. "Cute little elephant . . ."

Before Harris can add another mile to the guilt trip, the swinging doors to the rest room bang open, and a man with a gray suit and red bow tie storms inside. I recognize him instantly: Congressman William E. Enemark from Colorado—dean of the House, and Congress's longest-serving Member. Over the years, he's seen everything from desegregation and the Red Scare, to Vietnam and Watergate, to Lewinsky and Iraq. But as he hangs his jacket on the hand-carved coat-rack and rushes toward the wooden stall in back, he doesn't see us. And as we zip up our flies, Harris and I barely make an attempt to see him.

"That's my point," I whisper to Harris.

"What? Him?" he whispers back, motioning to Enemark's stall.

"The guy's a living legend, Harris. Y'know how jaded we must be to let him walk by without saying hello?"

"He's going to the can . . ."

"You can still say hello, right?"

Harris makes a face, then motions over to LaRue, who raises the volume on C-SPAN. Whatever Harris is about to say, he doesn't want it heard. "Matthew, I hate to break it to you, but the only reason you didn't throw him a *Hi, Congressman* is because you think his environmental record is crap."

It's hard to argue with that. Last year, Enemark was the number one recipient of campaign money from the timber, oil, *and* nuclear power industries. He'd clear-cut Oregon, hang billboards in the Grand Canyon, and vote to pave over his own garden with baby seal skins if he thought it'd get him some cash. "But even so, if I were a twenty-two-year-old just out of college, I still would've stuck my hand out for a quick *Hi, Congressman*. I'm telling you, Harris, eight years is enough—the fun's long gone."

Still standing at the urinal, Harris stops. His green eyes narrow, and he studies me with that same mischievous look that once got me thrown in the back of a police car when we were undergrads at Duke. "C'mon, Matthew, this is Washington, D.C.—fun and games are being played everywhere," he teases. "You just have to know where to find them."

Before I can react, his hand springs out and grabs the Lorax pin from my lapel. He glances at LaRue, then over to the Congressman's jacket on the coat-rack.

"What're you doing?"

"Cheering you up," he promises. "Trust me, you'll love it. No lie."

There it is. *No lie*. Harris's favorite turn of phrase— and the first sign of guaranteed trouble.

I flush my urinal with my elbow. Harris flushes his with a full-on grip. He's never been afraid to get his hands dirty. "How much will you give me if I put it on his lapel?" he whispers, holding up the Lorax and moving toward Enemark's coat.

"Harris, don't . . ." I hiss. "He'll kill you."

"Wanna bet?"

There's a hollow rumble of spinning toilet paper from within the stall. Enemark's almost finished.

As Harris shoots me a smile, I reach for his arm, but he sidesteps my grip with his usual perfect grace. It's how he operates in every political fight. Once he's focused on a goal, the man's unstoppable.

"I am the Lorax, Matthew. *I speak for the trees!*" He

laughs as he says the words. Watching him slowly tiptoe toward Enemark's jacket, I can't help but laugh with him. It's a dumb stunt, but if he pulls it off . . .

I take that back. Harris doesn't fail at anything. That's why, at twenty-nine years old, he was one of the youngest chiefs of staff ever hired by a Senator. And why, at thirty-five, there's no one—not even the older guys—who can touch him. I swear, he could charge for some of the stuff that comes out of his mouth. Lucky me, old college friends get it for free.

"How's the weather look, LaRue?" Harris calls to Mr. Shoeshine, who, from his seat near the tiled floor, has a better view of what's happening under the stall.

If it were anyone else, LaRue would tattle and run. But it isn't anyone else. It's Harris. "Bright and sunny," LaRue says as he ducks his head down toward the stall. "Though a storm's quickly approaching . . ."

Harris nods a thank-you and straightens his red tie, which I know he bought from the guy who sells them outside the subway. As chief of staff for Senator Paul Stevens, he should be wearing something nicer, but the way Harris works, he doesn't need to impress. "By the way, LaRue, what happened to your mustache?"

"Wife didn't like it—said it was too Burt Reynolds."

"I told you, you can't have the mustache *and* the Trans Am—it's one or the other," Harris adds.

LaRue laughs, and I shake my head. When the Founding Fathers set up the government, they split the legislative branch into two sides: the House and the Senate. I'm here in the House, which is in the south half of the Capitol. Harris works in the Senate, which is all the way over on the north. It's a whole different world over there, but somehow, Harris still remembers the latest update on *our* shoeshine guy's facial hair. I don't know why I'm surprised. Unlike the monsters who walk these halls, Harris doesn't talk to everyone as a political maneuver. He does it because that's his gift—as the son of a barber, he's got the gift of gab. And people love him for it. That's why, when he walks into a room, Senators casually flock around him, and when he walks into the cafeteria, the lunch lady gives him an extra ladle of chicken in his burrito.

Reaching Enemark's gray suit jacket, Harris pulls it from the coat-rack and fishes for the lapel. The toilet flushes behind us. We all spin back toward the stall. Harris is still holding the jacket. Before any of us can react, the door to the stall swings open.

If we were brand-new staffers, this is where we'd panic. Instead, I bite the inside of my cheek and take a deep gulp of Harris's calm. Old instincts kick in. As the door to the stall opens, I go to step in front of the Congressman. All I have to do is buy Harris a few seconds. The only problem is, Enemark's moving too quickly.

Sidestepping me without even looking up, Enemark is someone who avoids people for a living. Leaving the stall, he heads straight for the coat-rack. If Harris is caught with his jacket . . .

"Congressman . . . !" I call out. He doesn't slow down. I turn to follow, but just as I spin around, I'm surprised to see Enemark's gray coat hanging lifelessly on the coat-rack. There's a sound of running water on the right side of the room. Harris is washing his hands by the sink. Across from him, LaRue rests his chin in his palm, studying C-SPAN with his fingers covering his mouth. See no evil, hear no evil, speak no evil.

"Excuse me?" Enemark asks, taking his coat from the rack. The way it's draped over his forearm, I can't see the lapel. The pin's nowhere in sight.

I glance over at Harris, who's wearing a calm that's almost hypnotic. His green eyes disappear in a soft squint, and his dark black eyebrows seem to take over his face. Japanese is easier to read.

"Son, did you say something?" Enemark repeats.

"We just wanted to say hello, sir," Harris interrupts, leaping to my aid. "Really, it's an honor to meet you. Isn't that right, Matthew?"

"A-Absolutely," I say.

Enemark's chest rises at the compliment. "Much appreciated."

"I'm Harris . . . Harris Sandler . . ." he says, introducing himself even though Enemark didn't ask. Leaving the sink, Harris studies the Congressman like a chessboard. It's the only way to stay ten moves ahead.

The Congressman extends a handshake, but Harris pulls away. "Sorry . . . wet hands . . ." he explains. "By the way, Congressman, this is Matthew Mercer. He does Interior Approps for Congressman Cordell."

"Sorry to hear that," Enemark jabs with a fake laugh as he pumps my hand. Asshole. Without another word, he opens his coat and slides an arm into the sleeve. I check the lapel. There's nothing there.

"Have a good day, sir," Harris says as Enemark slides his other arm in. Enemark rotates his shoulder blades and pulls his suit jacket into place. When the other half of the jacket hits his chest, a tiny flash of light catches my eye. There . . . on his other lapel . . . there's a tiny American flag pin . . . a little triangle with an oil well on it . . . and the Lorax, whose big Dr. Seuss eyes smile at me.

I motion to Harris; he looks up and finally grins. When I was a freshman at Duke, Harris was a senior. He got me into the fraternity and, years later, got me my first job here on the Hill. Mentor then, hero now.

"Look at that," Harris says to the Congressman. "I see you're wearing the logging mascot."

I turn toward LaRue, but he's staring at the ground to keep himself from laughing.

"Yeah . . . I guess," Enemark barks, checking the Lorax out for himself. Anxious to be done with the small talk, the Congressman leaves the bathroom and heads across the hallway to the House Floor. None of us moves until the door closes.

"The *logging* mascot?" I finally blurt.

"I told you there's still fun going on," Harris says, looking up at the small TV and checking out C-SPAN. Just another day at work.

"I gotta tell Rosey this one . . ." LaRue says, rushing out of the room. "Harris, they're gonna catch you sooner or later."

"Only if they outthink us," Harris replies as the door again slams shut.

I continue to laugh. Harris continues to study C-SPAN. "You notice Enemark didn't wash his hands?" he asks. "Though that didn't stop him from shaking yours."

I look down at my own open palm and head for the sink.

"Here we go . . . Here's the clip for the highlight reel . . ." Harris calls out, pointing up at C-SPAN.

On-screen, Congressman Enemark approaches the podium with his usual old-cowboy swagger. But if you look real close—when the light hits him just right—the Lorax shines like a tiny star on his chest.

"I'm Congressman William Enemark, and I speak for the people of Colorado," he announces through the television.

"That's funny," I say. "I thought he spoke for the trees . . ."

To my surprise, Harris doesn't smile. He just scratches at the dimple in his chin. "Feeling better?" he asks.

"Of course—why?"

He leans against the inlaid mahogany wall and never takes his eyes off the TV. "I meant what I said before. There really are some great games being played here."

"You mean games like this?"

"Something like this." There's a brand-new tone in his voice. All serious.

"I don't understand."

"Oh, jeez, Matthew, it's right in front of your face," he says with a rare glimpse of rural Pennsylvania accent.

I give him a long, hard look and rub the back of my sandy-blond hair. I'm a full head taller than him. But he's still the only person I look up to in this place. "What're you saying, Harris?"

"You wanted to bring the fun back, right?"

"Depends what kinda fun you're talking about."

Pushing himself off the wall, Harris grins and heads for the door. "Trust me, it'll be more fun than you've had in your entire life. No lie."

2

Six Months Later

I USUALLY HATE SEPTEMBER. With the end of the August recess, the halls are once again crowded, the Members are frozen in preelection bad moods, and worst of all, with the October 1st deadline that's imposed on all Appropriations bills, we're clocking hours twice as grueling as any other time of the year. This September, though, I barely notice.

"Who wants to taste a food item less healthy than bacon?" I ask as I leave the polished institutional hallways of the Rayburn House Office Building and shove open the door to room B-308. The clocks on the wall shout back with two loud electronic buzzes. The signal for a vote on the House Floor. The vote's on. And so am I . . .

Wasting no time, I make a quick left at the hand-woven Sioux quilt that hangs on the wall and head straight for our receptionist, a black woman who always has at least one pencil sticking in the bun of her prematurely gray hair. "Here you go, Roxanne—lunch is served," I call out as I drop two wrapped hot dogs onto her paperwork-covered desk. As a professional staffer for the Appropriations Committee, I'm one of four people assigned to the subcommittee on Interior. And the only one, besides Roxanne, who eats meat.

"Where'd you get these?" she asks.

"Meat Association event. Didn't you say you were hungry?"

She looks down at the dogs, then up at me. "What's up with you lately? You on *nice* pills or something?"

I shrug my shoulders and stare at the small TV behind her desk. Like most TVs in the building, it's on C-SPAN for the vote. My eyes check the tally. Too early. No yeas, no nays.

Following my gaze, Roxanne turns around to the TV. I stop right there. No . . . there's no way. She can't possibly know.

"You okay?" she asks, reading my now-pale complexion.

"With all this dead cow in my gut? Absolutely," I say, patting my stomach. "So, is Trish here yet?"

"In the hearing room," Roxanne says. "But before you go in, someone's at your desk."

Crossing into the large suite that houses four separate desks, I'm thoroughly confused. Roxanne knows the rules: With all the paperwork lying around, no one's allowed in back, especially when we're in preconference— which means, whoever's back here is someone big . . .

"Matthew?" a voice calls out with a salty North Carolina tinge.

. . . or someone I know.

"Come give your favorite lobbyist a juicy hug," Barry Holcomb says from the chair next to my desk. As always, his blond hair is as perfectly cut as his pinstriped suit—both of which come courtesy of bigshot clients like the music industry, the big telecom boys, and, if I remember correctly, the Meat Association.

"I smell hot dogs," Barry teases, already one step ahead. "I'm telling you, free food always works."

In the world of Capitol Hill, there're two kinds of lobbyists: those who swoop in from the top and those who burrow in from below. If you swoop in from the top, it's because you have direct connections to the Members. If you burrow from below, it's because you're connected to staff—or in this case, because you went to the same college, celebrated your last two birthdays together, and tend to see each other out for a beer at least once a month. The odd thing is, since he's a few years older, Barry's always been more Harris's friend than mine—which means this call is more business than social.

"So what's happening?" he asks. There it is. As a lobbyist at Pasternak & Associates, Barry knows he's got two things to offer his clients: access and information. Access is why he's sitting here. Now he's focused on the latter.

"Everything's fine," I tell him.

"Any idea when you'll have the bill done?"

I look around at the three other desks in the room. All empty. It's a good thing. My other three office mates already have their own reasons to hate me—ever since Cordell took over the Interior Approps subcommittee and replaced their former colleague with me, I've been the odd man out. I don't need to add to it by letting them catch me back here with a lobbyist. Of course, Barry may be the sole exception.

Sitting just below the Grand Canyon lithograph that

hangs on my wall, Barry leans an elbow on my desk, which is packed with volcanoes of paperwork, including my Conference notes of all the projects we've funded so far. Barry's clients would pay thousands, maybe millions, for those. It's sitting four inches to Barry's left.

But Barry doesn't see it. He doesn't see anything. Justice is blind. And due to a case of congenital glaucoma, so is one of the Hill's best-known young lobbyists.

As I cross around to my desk, Barry's vacant blue eyes stare into the distance, but his head turns as he traces my steps. Trained since birth, he absorbs the sounds. My arms swinging against my body. The in-and-out of my breath. Even the crushed hush as my foot hits the carpet. In college, he had a golden retriever named Reagan, which was great for meeting girls. But on the Hill, after being slowed down by strangers who were constantly asking to pet the dog, Barry branched out on his own. These days, if it weren't for the white cane, he'd be just another guy in a snazzy suit. Or, as Barry likes to put it: Political vision has nothing to do with eyesight.

"We're hoping October first," I tell him. "We're almost done with the Park Service."

"How 'bout your office mates? They moving as happily along?"

What he really wants to know is, are the negotiations going just as well? Barry's no fool. The four of us who share this office divvy up all the accounts—or sections—of the Interior bill, each doing our own specialty. At last count, the bill had a budget of twenty-one *billion* dollars. When you divide it by four, that means we're in charge of spending over five billion dollars. Each. So why's Barry so interested? Because we control the purse strings. Indeed, the whole purpose of the Appropriations

Committee is to write the checks for all discretionary money spent by the government.

It's one of the dirtiest little secrets on Capitol Hill: Congressmen can pass a bill, but if it needs funding, it's not going anywhere without an Appropriator. Case in point: Last year, the President signed a bill that allows free immunizations for low-income children. But unless Appropriations sets aside money to pay for the vaccines, the President may've gotten a great media event, but no one's getting a single shot. And that, as the old joke goes, is why there're actually three parties in Congress: Democrats, Republicans, and Appropriators. Like I said, it's a dirty secret—but one Barry is all too aware of right about now.

"So everyone's good?" he asks.

"Why complain, right?"

Realizing the clock's ticking, I flip on the TV that sits on my filing cabinet. As C-SPAN blooms into view, Barry turns at the sound. I once again check the vote count.

"What's the tally?" he asks.

I spin around at the question. *"What'd you say?"*

Barry pauses. His left eye is glass; his right one is pale blue and completely foggy. The combination makes it near impossible to read his expression. But the tone in his voice is innocent enough. "The tally," he repeats. "What's the vote count?"

I smile to myself, still watching him closely. To be honest, if he were playing the game, I wouldn't be surprised. I take that back. I would be. Harris said you can only invite one other person in. Harris invited me. If Barry's in, someone else invited him.

Convinced it's just my imagination, I check the totals on

C-SPAN. All I care about are the yeas and nays. On-screen, the white letters are superimposed over a shot of the still mostly empty House Floor: thirty-one yeas, eight nays.

"Thirteen minutes left. Thirty-one to eight," I tell Barry. "It'll be a slaughter."

"No surprise," he says, focused on the TV. "Even a blind man could've seen that."

I laugh at the joke—one of Barry's old favorites. But I can't stop thinking about what Harris said. *It's the best part of the game—not knowing who else is playing.*

"Listen, Barry, can we catch up later?" I ask as I grab my conference notes. "I've got Trish waiting . . ."

"No stress," he says, never wanting to push. Good lobbyists know better than that. "I'll call you in an hour or so."

"That's fine—though I may still be in the meeting."

"Let's make it two hours. Does three o'clock work?"

Again, I take it back. Even when he doesn't want to, Barry can't help but push. It was the same way in college. Every time we'd get ready to go to a party, we'd get two calls from Barry. The first was to check what time we were leaving. The second was to recheck what time we were leaving. Harris always called it overcompensation for the blindness; I called it understandable insecurity. Whatever the real reason, Barry's always had to work a little harder to make sure he's not left out.

"So I'll speak to you at three," he says, hopping up and heading out. I tuck my notebooks under my arm like a football and plow toward the door that connects with the adjoining hearing room. Inside, my eyes skip past the enormous oval conference table and even the two black sofas against the back wall that we use for overflow. Instead, like before, I find the small TV in the back and—

"You're late," Trish interrupts from the conference table.

I spin midstep, almost forgetting why I'm here. "Would it help if I brought hot dogs?" I stutter.

"I'm a vegetarian."

Harris would have a great comeback. I offer an awkward grin.

Leaning back in her chair, she's got her arms crossed, completely uncharmed. At thirty-six years old, Trish Brennan has at least six years more experience than me, and is the type of person who says you're late even when she's early. Her reddish hair, dark green eyes, and light freckles give her an innocent look that's surprisingly attractive. Of course, right now, the hottest thing in the room is the small TV in the back. I have to squint to see it. Forty-two yeas, ten nays. Still looking good.

As I pull out the chair directly across from her at the conference table, the front door of the hearing room swings open and the last two staffers finally arrive. Georgia Rudd and Ezra Ben-Shmuel. Already prepped for battle, Ezra's got a sparse poor-man's-environmentalist beard (*my-first-beard,* Trish calls it), and a blue dress shirt rolled up to his elbows. Georgia's the exact opposite. Too much of a conformist to take chances, she's quiet, wears a standard navy interview suit, and is happy enough following Trish's lead.

Each armed with an oversized redwell accordion file, they quickly head to different sides of the table. Ezra on my side, Georgia next to Trish. All four horsemen are here. When it comes to Conference, I represent the House majority; Ezra does the House minority. Across the table, Trish and Georgia do the respective same for the Senate. And regardless of the fact that Ezra and I are in different political parties, even House Republicans and Democrats can set aside their differences for our common enemy: the Senate.

My pager vibrates in my pocket, and I pull it out to check the message. It's from Harris. *You watching?* he asks in digital black letters.

I glance over Trish's shoulder, toward the TV in the back. Eighty-four yeas, forty-one nays.

Crap. I need the *nays* to stay under 110. If they're at forty-one this early in the vote, we've got problems.

What do we do? I type back on the pager's tiny keyboard, hiding my hands under the desk so the Senate folks can't see what I'm doing. Before I can send it, my pager shakes with a new message.

Don't panic just yet, Harris insists. He knows me too well.

"Can we please get this going?" Trish asks. It's the sixth day in a row we've been trying to stomp each other into the ground, and Trish knows there's still plenty to go. "Now, where'd we leave off?"

"Cape Cod," Ezra says. Like speed-readers in a race, all four of us flip through the hundred-page documents in front of us that show the spending difference between the House and Senate bills. Last month, when the House passed its version of the bill, we allocated seven hundred thousand dollars to rehabilitate the Cape Cod Seashore; a week later, the Senate passed its version, which didn't allocate a dime. That's the point of Conference: finding the differences and reaching a compromise—item by item by item. When the two bills are merged, they go back to the House and Senate for final passage. When both bodies pass the same bill, that's when it goes to the White House to be signed into law.

"I'll give you three hundred and fifty thousand," Trish offers, hoping I'll be satisfied by half.

"Done," I tell her, grinning to myself. If she'd pushed, I would've settled for an even two hundred.

"The Chesapeake in Maryland," Trish adds, moving to the next item. I look down at the spreadsheet. Senate gave it six million for stabilization; we gave it nothing.

Trish smiles. That's why she was kissing tush on the last one. The six million in here was put there by her boss, Senator Ted Apelbaum, who also happens to be the Chairman of the subcommittee—the Senate equivalent of my boss, Cordell. In local slang, the Chairs are known as Cardinals. That's where the argument ends. What Cardinals want, Cardinals get.

In quiet rooms around the Capitol, the scene is the same. Forget the image of fat-cat Congressmen horse-trading in cigar-smoke-filled backrooms. *This* is how the sausage is made, and *this* is how America's bank account is actually spent: by four staffers sitting around a well-lit conference table without a Congressman in sight. Your tax dollars at work. Like Harris always says: The real shadow government is staff.

My pager again vibrates in my lap. Harris's message is simple: *Panic.*

I take another look at the TV. One hundred seventy-two yeas, sixty-four nays.

Sixty-four? I don't believe it. They're over halfway there.

How? I type back.

Maybe they have the votes, Harris replies almost instantly.

Can't be, I send back.

For the next two minutes, Trish lectures about why

seven million dollars is far too much to spend on Yellowstone National Park. I barely register a word. On C-SPAN, the nays go from sixty-four to eighty-one. It's impossible.

". . . don't you agree, Matthew?" Trish asks.

I stay locked on C-SPAN.

"Matthew!" Trish calls out. "You with us or not?"

"Wha?" I say, finally turning toward her.

Tracing my gaze back to its last location, Trish looks over her shoulder and spots the TV. "That's what you're so caught up in?" she asks. "Some lame vote for baseball?"

She doesn't get it. Sure, it's a vote for baseball, but it isn't just any vote. It actually dates back to 1922, when the Supreme Court ruled that baseball was a sport—not a business—and therefore was allowed a special exemption from antitrust rules. Football, basketball, all the rest have to comply—but baseball, the Supreme Court decided, was special. Today, Congress is trying to strengthen that exemption, giving owners more control over how big the league gets. For Congress, it's a relatively simple vote: If you're from a state with a baseball team, you vote for baseball (even the Reps from rural New York don't dare vote against the Yankees). If you're from a state without a team—or from a district that wants a team, like Charlotte or Jacksonville—you vote against it.

When you do the math—and account for political favors by powerful owners—that leaves a clear majority voting for the bill, and a maximum of 100 Members voting against it—105 if they're lucky. But right now, there's someone in the Capitol who thinks he can get 110 nays. There's no way, Harris and I decided. That's why we bet against it.

"We all ready to hit some issues?" Trish asks, still

plowing her way through the Conference list. In the next ten minutes, we allocate three million to repair the seawall on Ellis Island, two and a half million to renovate the steps on the Jefferson Memorial, and thirteen million to do a structural upgrade on the bicycle trail and recreation area next to the Golden Gate Bridge. No one puts up much of a fight. Like baseball—you don't vote against the good stuff.

My pager once again dances in my pocket. Like before, I read it under the table. *97*, Harris's message says.

I can't believe they're getting this far. Of course, that's the fun of playing the game.

In fact, as Harris explained it when he first extended the invitation, the game itself started years ago as a practical joke. As the story goes, a junior Senate staffer was bitching about picking up a Senator's dry cleaning, so to make him feel better, his buddy on staff snuck the words *dry cleaning* into a draft of the Senator's next speech: *... although sometimes regarded as dry, cleaning our environment should clearly be a top priority* ... It was always meant to be a cheap gag—something that'd be taken out before the speech was given. Then one of the staffers dared the other to keep it in.

"I'll do it," the staffer threatened.

"No, you won't," his friend shot back.

"Wanna bet?"

Right there, the game was born. And that afternoon, the distinguished Senator strolled onto C-SPAN and told the entire nation about the importance of "dry, cleaning."

In the beginning, they always kept it to small stuff: hidden phrases in an op-ed, an acronym in a commencement speech. Then it got bigger. A few years ago, on the Senate Floor, a Senator who was searching for his handkerchief reached into his jacket pocket and proceeded to wipe his forehead with a pair of women's silk panties. He quickly laughed it off as an honest mistake made by his laundry service. But it wasn't an accident.

That was the first time the game broke the envelope— and what caused the organizers to create the current rules. These days, it's simple: The bills we bet on are ones where the outcome's clearly decided. A few months back, the Clean Diamond Act passed by a vote of 408 to 6; last week, the Hurricane Shelters Act passed by 401 to 10; and today, the Baseball for America Act was expected to pass by approximately 300 to 100. A clear landslide. And the perfect bill to play on.

When I was in high school, we used to try to guess if Jennifer Luftig would be wearing a bra. In grad school, we made bingo cards with the names of the kids who talked the most, then waited for them to open their mouths. We've all played our games. Can you get twelve more votes? Can you get the Vermont Congressmen to vote against it? Can you get the nays up to 110, even when 100 is all that's reasonably possible? Politics has always been called a game for grown-ups. So why is anyone surprised people would gamble on it?

Naturally, I was skeptical at first, but then I realized just how innocent it really was. We don't change the laws, or pass bad legislation, or stroke our evil goatees and overthrow democracy as we know it. We play at the margins; that's where it's safe—and where it's fun. It's like sitting in a meeting and betting how many times the annoying guy in your office uses the word "I." You can goad him and make your best attempts to alter it, but in the end, the results are pretty much the same. In the world of Capitol Hill, even though we're split between Ds and

Rs, 99 percent of our legislation is passed by overwhelming majorities. It's only the few controversial bills that make the news. The result is a job that can easily lapse into a repetitive, monotonous grind—that is, unless you find a way to make it interesting.

My pager once again shudders in my fist. *103,* Harris sends.

"Okay, what about the White House?" Trish asks, still working her list. This is the one she's been saving for. In the House, we allocated seven million for structural improvements to the White House complex. The Senate—thanks to Trish's boss—zeroed the program out.

"C'mon, Trish," Ezra begs. "You can't just give 'em goose egg."

Trish raises an eyebrow. "We'll see . . ."

It's typical Senate. The only reason Trish's boss is playing the jerk is because the President has been pushing for a settlement in a racial discrimination lawsuit against the Library of Congress. Trish's boss, Senator Apelbaum, is one of the few people involved in the negotiation. This close to the elections, he'd rather stall, keep the lawsuit quiet, and keep it out of the press. This is the Senator's way of pushing back. And from the smug look on Trish's face, she's loving every minute of it.

"Why don't we just split the difference?" Ezra says, knowing our usual mode of compromise. "Give it three and a half million, and ask the President to bring his library card next time."

"Listen closely . . ." Trish warns, leaning into the table. "He's not getting a single muddy peso."

107, it says on my pager.

I have to smile as it inches closer. Whoever the organizers are—or, as we call them, the *dungeon-masters*—these guys know what they're doing. The bets can go from twice a week to once every few months, but when they identify an issue, they always set the game at the perfect level of difficulty. Two months ago, when the new Attorney General came to testify for the Senate Armed Services Committee, the bet was to get one of the Senators to ask the question, "How much of your success do you attribute to the support of your family?" A simple query for any witness, but when you add in the fact that a few days earlier, the Attorney General insisted that public figures should be able to keep their family lives private—well . . . now we had a horse race. Waiting for the words to be uttered, we watched that achingly boring Senate hearing as if it were the final round of *Rocky.* Today, I'm glued to a vote that was decided by a majority almost ten minutes ago. Even the baseball lobbyists have turned off their TVs. But I can't take my eyes off it. It's not the seventy-five dollars I've got riding on the outcome. It's the challenge. When Harris and I put our money down, we figured they'd never get near 110 votes. Whoever's on the other side obviously thinks they can. Right now they're at 107. No doubt, impressive . . . but it's the last three that are going to be like shoving a mountain.

108 blinks onto my pager.

A buzzer rings through the air. One more minute left on the official clock.

"So what's the count at?" Trish asks, swiveling at the sound, back toward the TV.

"Can we please not change the subject?" Ezra begs.

Trish doesn't care. She's still scanning the screen.

"Hundred and eight," I tell her as the C-SPAN number clicks into place.

"I'm impressed," she admits. "I didn't think they'd get this far."

The grin on my face spreads even wider. Could Trish be playing? Six months ago, Harris invited me in—and one day, I'll invite someone else. All you know are the two people you're directly connected to: one above, one below. In truth, it's purely for safety purposes—in case word gets out, you can't finger someone if you don't know who they are. Of course, it also brings new meaning to the term *anybody's game*.

I look around the room. All three of my colleagues take subtle glances at C-SPAN. Georgia's too quiet to be a player. Ezra and Trish are a whole different story.

On TV, Congressman Virgil Witt from Louisiana strolls across the screen. Ezra's boss. "There's your guy," Trish says.

"You're really serious about this Library thing?" Ezra shoots back. He doesn't care about seeing his boss on television. Around here, it happens every day.

109, my pager says.

On TV, Ezra's boss once again rushes across the screen.

Under the desk, I type in one last question: *How'd Witt vote?*

My eyes are on Ezra as the pager rumbles in my hand. Here comes Harris's answer.

Nay.

Before I can respond, the pager vibrates one last time: *110.*

Game over.

I laugh out loud. Seventy-five bucks in the toilet.

"What?" Georgia asks.

"Nothing," I say, slapping my pager against the top of the conference table. "Just a stupid E-mail."

"Actually, that reminds me . . ." Trish begins, pulling out her own pager and checking a quick message.

"Is anyone here *not* completely distracted?" Ezra asks. "Enough with the friggin' Blackberries; we've got a serious issue—if the White House gets zilched, you know they'll threaten a veto."

"No, they won't," Trish insists, clicking away on her pager without looking up. "Not this close to the election. They veto now and it'll look like they're holding up funding for the entire government just so they can get their driveway repaved."

Knowing she's right, Ezra falls unusually silent. I stare him down, searching for the tell. Nothing's there. If he is playing the game, the guy's a grandmaster.

"You okay?" he asks, catching my glance.

"Absolutely," I tell him. "Perfect." And for the past six months, it's been exactly that. Blood's pumping, adrenaline's raging, and I've got an in on the best secret in town. After eight years in the grind, I almost forgot what it felt like. Even losing doesn't matter. The thrill is in the play.

Like I said, the dungeon-masters know what they're doing. And lucky for me, they're about to do it again. Any minute now. I check the clock on the wall. Two o'clock. *Exactly at two.* That's what Harris said when I first asked him how we know when the next bet is.

"Don't worry," he had said calmly. "They'll send a signal."

"A signal? What kinda signal?"

"You'll see—a signal. That way, when instructions go out, you know to be in your office."

"But what if I don't see it? What if I'm on the Floor . . . or somewhere else in the Capitol? What if the signal goes out and I'm not here when they send it?"

"Trust me, this is one signal you won't miss," Harris insisted. "No matter where you are . . ."

Glancing back over Trish's shoulder, I eye the TV. Now that the vote's over, the camera goes back to the Speaker's rostrum—the multilevel platform the President uses to deliver his State of the Union address. Right now, though, I'm more focused on the small mahogany oval table that's just in front of it. Every day, the House stenographers sit there, clicking away. Every day, they keep track of everything uttered on the House Floor. And every day, like clockwork, the only objects on that desk are two empty water glasses and the two white coasters they rest on. For two hundred years—according to the rumor—Congress puts out two glasses, one for each side. Every single day. Today, however, is different. Today, if you count the glasses, there's just one. You can't miss it. One glass and one coaster.

There's our code. That's the signal. One empty water glass, broadcast all day long for the entire world to see.

There's a soft knock on the door, and all four of us turn at the sound. A young kid wearing gray slacks, a cheap navy blazer, and a blue-and-red-striped tie enters the room. He can't be more than sixteen, and if the uniform doesn't give him away, the rectangular nametag on his lapel does. Set off against a black background, the stark white letters read:

House of Representatives Page
Nathan Lagahit

He's one of a few dozen—a high school page who delivers mail and fetches water. The only person on the totem pole lower than an intern.

"I-I'm sorry . . ." he begins, realizing he's interrupting. "I'm looking for Matthew Mercer . . ."

"That's me," I say with a wave.

Rushing over, he barely makes eye contact as he hands me the sealed envelope. "Thanks," I tell him, but he's already out of the room.

Regular mail can be opened by a secretary. So can interoffice. FedEx requires a return address. And a messenger service would add up to a small fortune if you used it on a regular basis. But the House and Senate pages barely leave a footprint. They're here every single day, and while all they do is run errands back and forth, they're the easiest thing to miss. Ghosts in blue blazers. No one sees them come; no one sees them go. And best of all, since the pages get their instructions verbally, there's no physical record of where a particular package goes.

An empty water glass tells me to be at my desk. A sealed envelope carried by a page tells me what I'm doing next. Welcome to game day.

"Trish, can't you just meet us in the middle?" Ezra begs as Trish shakes her head.

Refusing to get into it, I angle my chair away from the group and examine the envelope. As always, it's blank. Not even my name or room number. And if I'd asked the page where he got it from, he'd say someone in the cloakroom asked him to do a favor. After six months, I'm done trying to figure out how the inner workings of the game happen.

Wedging my thumb under the flap of the envelope, I give it a sharp jab and tear it open. Inside, as usual, the notice is the same: a single sheet of paper with the royal blue letterhead of the CAG, the Coalition Against Gambling. The letterhead's an obvious joke, but it's the first reminder that this is purely for fun. Underneath, the letter begins, *Here are some upcoming issues we'd like to focus on* . . . Just below that is a numbered list of fifteen items that range from:

(3) Convince both Kentucky Senators to vote against Hesselbach's dairy compact bill to:

(12) Within the next seven days, replace Congressman Edward Berganza's suit jacket with a tuxedo jacket.

As usual, I go straight to the last item on the list. All the rest are bullshit—a way to throw people off in case a stranger gets his hands on it—but the last one on there . . . that's the one that actually counts.

As I read the words, my mouth tips open. I don't believe it.

"Everything alright?" Trish asks.

When I don't answer, all three of them turn my way. "Matthew, you still breathing over there?" she repeats.

"Y-Yeah . . . no . . . of course," I say with a laugh. "Just another note from Cordell."

My three colleagues instantly leap back to their verbal fistfight. I look down at the letter. And for the third time, I reread the words and try to contain my grin.

(15) Insert Congressman Richard Grayson's land sale project into the Interior House Appropriations bill.

An earmark. A single Interior earmark. I can actually feel the blood rushing to my cheeks. This isn't just any issue. It's *my* issue.

For once in my life, I can't lose.

3

So what do you think?" I ask as I rush into Harris's office on the fourth floor of the Russell Senate Office Building. With its arched windows and tall ceilings, it's nicer than the best office on the House side. The two branches of government are supposed to be equal. Welcome to the Senate.

"You tell me," Harris says, looking up from some paperwork. "Think you can really put the land sale into the bill?"

"Harris, it's what I do every day. We're talking a tiny ask for a project no one would ever possibly look at. Even Congressman Grayson, who made the original request, couldn't care less about it."

"Unless he's playing the game."

I roll my eyes. "Will you please stop with that?" Since the day he invited me in, it's been Harris's most recurring wet dream: that it's not just staff playing the game—it's the Members playing as well.

"It's possible," he insists.

"Actually, it's not. If you're a Member of Congress, you're not risking your credibility and entire political career for a few hundred bucks and a chess match."

"Are you joking? These guys get blow jobs in the bathroom of the Capitol Grille. I mean, when they go out for drinks, they have lobbyists trolling the bar and picking out girls so they can leave the place unescorted. You think a few of them wouldn't get in on the action? Think for a second, Matthew. Even Pete Rose bet on baseball."

"I don't care. Grayson's project isn't a four-star priority that reaches the Member level—it's grunt work. And since it's in my jurisdiction, it's not getting in there unless I see it. I promise you, Harris—I already checked it out. We're talking a teeny piece of land in the middle of South Dakota. Land rights belong to Uncle Sam; mineral rights below used to be owned by some long-defunct mining company."

"It's a coal mine?"

"This ain't Pennsylvania, bro. Out in South Dakota, they dig for gold—or at least they used to. The company had been digging the Homestead mine since 1876—true gold rush days. Over time, they applied for a patent to buy the land, but when they sucked out every last drop, the company went bankrupt and the land stayed with the government, which is still dealing with the environmental problems of shutting one of these suckers down. Anyway, a few years back, a company called Wendell Mining decides it can find more gold using newer technologies, so they buy the old company's claims out of bankruptcy, contact the Bureau of Land Management, and arrange to buy the land."

"Since when do we sell government land to private companies?"

"How do you think we settled the West, Kimosabe? Most of the time, we even gave it away for free. The problem here is, even though BLM has approved the sale, the Interior Department has them so buried in red tape, it'll take years to finalize unless they get a friendly congressional push."

"So Wendell Mining donated some money to local Congressman Grayson and asked him for a bump to the front of the line," Harris says.

"That's how it works."

"And we're sure about the land? I mean, we're not selling some nature preserve to some big company who wants to put a mall and a petting zoo on it, are we?"

"Suddenly you're back to being an idealist?"

"I never left, Matthew."

He believes what he's saying. He's always believed it. Growing up outside Gibsonia, Pennsylvania, Harris wasn't just the first in his family to go to college—he was the first in his whole town. As silly as it sounds, he came to Washington to change the world. The problem is, a decade later, the world changed him. As a result, he's the worst kind of cynic—the kind who doesn't know he's a cynic.

"If it makes you feel better, I vetted it last year and revetted it months ago," I tell him. "The gold mine's abandoned. This town's dying for Wendell Mining to take over. The town gets jobs, the company gets gold, and most important, once Wendell steps in, the company's responsible for the hardest part, which is the environmental cleanup. Win, win, win, all around."

Harris falls silent, picking up the tennis racket that he usually keeps leaning on the side of his desk. I've seen the town where Harris grew up. He'd never call himself poor. But I would. Needless to say, they don't play tennis in Gibsonia. That's a rich man's game—but the day Harris got to D.C., he made it his own. To no one's surprise, he was a complete natural. It's the same reason he was able to run the Marine Corps Marathon even though he barely trained. Mind over matter. He's almost there right now.

"So it all checks out?" he asks.

"Every last detail," I say as my voice picks up speed. "No lie."

For the first time since I entered his office, I see the quiet, charismatic grin in Harris's eyes. He knows we've got a winner here. A huge winner if we play it smart.

"Okay . . ." Harris says, bouncing the tennis racket against the palm of his hand. "How much you got in your bank account?"

4

AT EXACTLY 9:35 the following morning, I'm sitting alone at my desk, wondering why my delivery's late. On C-SPAN, a rabbi from Aventura, Florida, says a short prayer as everyone on the Speaker's rostrum bows his head. When he's done, the gavel bangs and the camera pulls out. On the stenographers' table, the two water glasses are back. Anyone on the Floor could've moved them. They're out there all day long. On my phone, I've got seven messages from lobbyists, fourteen from staff, and two from Members—all dying to know if we've funded their project. Everything's back to normal—or as normal as a day like this gets.

I pick up the phone and dial the five-digit extension for our receptionist out front. "Roxanne, if there're any packages that come in—"

"I heard you the first thirty-four times," she moans. "I'll send 'em right back. What're you waiting for anyway, pregnancy results?"

I don't bother to answer. "Just make sure—"

"Thirty-*five!* That's officially thirty-five times," she interrupts. "Don't worry, sweetie—I won't let you down."

Ten minutes later, she's good to her word. The door from reception opens, and a young female page sticks her head in. "I'm looking for—"

"That's me," I blurt.

Stepping into the room with her blue blazer and gray slacks, she hands me the sealed manila envelope—and checks out the office.

"That's not real, is it?" she asks, pointing to the stuffed ferret on a nearby bookcase.

"Thank the NRA lobbyists," I tell her. "Isn't it far more practical than sending flowers like everyone else?"

With a laugh, she heads for the door. I look down at the envelope. Yesterday was spent dealing the cards. Today it's time to ante up.

Ripping open the flap, I turn the envelope upside down and shake. Two dozen squares of paper rain down on my desk. *Taxi Receipt,* it reads in thick black letters across the top of each one. I shuffle the pile into a neat stack and make sure every one of them is blank. So far, so good.

Grabbing a pen, I eye the section marked *Cab Number* and quickly scribble the number *727* into the blank. Cab 727. That's my ID. After that, I put a single check mark in the top right-hand corner of the receipt. There's the ante: twenty-five dollars if you want to play. I don't just want to play, though. I want to win, which is why I start with a serious bet. In the blank marked *Fare,* I write *$10.00.* To the untrained eye, it's not much. But to those of us playing, well . . . that's why we add a zero. One dollar is ten dollars; five dollars is actually fifty. That's why they call it the Zero Game. In this case, ten bucks is a solid Benjamin Franklin—the opening bid in the auction.

Reaching into my top drawer, I pull out a fresh manila envelope, open the flap, and sweep the taxicab receipts inside. Time for some interoffice mail. On the front of the envelope, I write *Harris Sandler—427 Russell Bldg.* Next to the address, I add the word *Private,* just to be safe. Of course, even if Harris's assistant opens it—even if the Speaker of the House opens it—I'm not dropping a bead of sweat. I see a hundred-dollar bet. Anyone else sees a ten-dollar taxi receipt—nothing to look twice at.

Stepping into our reception area, I toss the envelope into the rusty metal basket we use as an Out box. Roxanne does most of our interoffice stuff herself. "Roxanne, can you make sure to take this out in the next batch?"

She nods as I turn back to my desk. Just another day.

"Is it there yet?" I ask twenty minutes later.

"Already gone," Harris answers. From the crackle in his voice, he's got me on speakerphone. I swear, he's not afraid of anything.

"You left it blank, right?" I ask.

"No, I ignored everything we discussed. Good-bye, Matthew. Call me when you have news."

As he's about to hang up, I hear a click in the background. Harris's door opening. "Courier's here," his assistant calls out.

With a slam, Harris is gone. And so are the taxi receipts. From me to my mentor, from Harris to his. Leaning back in my black vinyl rolling chair, I can't help but wonder who it is. Harris has been on the Hill since the day he graduated. If he's an expert at anything, it's making friends and connections. That narrows the list to a tidy few thousand. But if he's using a courier, he's going off campus. I stare out the window at a perfect view of the Capitol dome. The playing field expands before my eyes. Former staffers are everywhere in this town. Law firms . . . PR boutiques . . . and most of all . . .

My phone rings, and I check the digital screen for caller ID.

. . . lobbying shops.

"Hi, Barry," I say as I pick up the receiver.

"You're still standing?" he asks. "I heard you guys were negotiating till ten last night."

"It's that time of year," I tell him, wondering where he got the info. No one saw us leave last night. But that's Barry. No sight, but somehow he sees it all. "So what can I help you with?"

"Tickets, tickets, and more tickets. This Sunday— Redskins home opener. Wanna see 'em get trounced from insanely overpriced seats? I got the recording industry's private box. Me, you, Harris—we'll have ourselves a little reunion."

Barry hates football, and he can't see a single play, but that doesn't mean he doesn't like the private catering and the butler that come with those seats. Plus, it gives Barry the temporary upper hand in his ongoing race with Harris. Neither will admit it, but it's the unspoken game they've always played. And while Barry may get us the skybox, come game day, Harris will somehow find the best seat in it. It's classic Capitol Hill—too many student government presidents in one place.

"Actually, that sounds great. Did you tell Harris?"

"Already done." The answer doesn't surprise me. Barry's closer to Harris—he always calls him first. But that doesn't mean the reverse is true. In fact, when Harris needs a lobbyist, he sidesteps Barry and goes directly to the man on top.

"So how's Pasternak treating you?" I ask, referring to Barry's boss.

"How do you think I got the tickets?" Barry teases. It's not much of a joke. Especially to Barry. As the firm's hungriest associate, he's been trying to leap out from the pack for years, which is why he's always asking Harris to throw him a Milk-Bone. Last year, when Harris's boss changed his stance on telecom deregulation, Barry even asked if he could be the one to bring the news to the telecom companies. "Nothing personal," Harris had said, "but Pasternak gets it first." In politics, like the mob, the best presents have to start up top.

"God bless him, though," Barry adds about his boss. "The guy's an old master." There's no arguing with that. As the founding partner of Pasternak & Associates, Bud Pasternak is respected, connected, and truly one of the kindest guys on Capitol Hill. He's also Harris's first boss—back from the days when Harris was running the pen-signing machine—and the person who gave Harris his first big break: an early draft of a speech for the Senator's reelection bid. From there, Harris never touched the auto-pen again.

I study the arched windows on the side of the Capitol. Pasternak invited Harris; Harris invited me. It's gotta be, right?

I chat with Barry for another fifteen minutes to see if I hear a courier arrive in the background. His office is only a few blocks away. The courier never comes.

An hour and a half later, there's another knock on my door. The instant I see the blue blazer and gray slacks, I'm out of my seat.

"I take it you're Matthew," a page with black hair and an awkward underbite says.

"You got it," I say as he hands me the envelope.

As I rip it open, I take a quick survey of my three office mates, who are sitting at their respective desks. Roy and Connor are on my left. Dinah's on my right. All three of them are over forty years old—both men have professorship beards; Dinah's got an unapologetic fanny pack with the Smithsonian logo on it—professional staffers hired for their budget expertise.

Congressmen come and go. So do Democrats and Republicans. But these three stay forever. It's the same on all the Appropriations subcommittees. With all the different power shifts, no matter which party's in charge, someone has to know how to run the government. It's one of the few examples of nonpartisan trust in the entire Capitol. Naturally, my boss hates it. So when he took over the subcommittee, he put me in this position to look out for his best interests and keep an eye on them. But as I open my unmarked envelope, they're the ones who should be watching me.

Dumping the contents on my desk, I spot the expected pile of taxi receipts. This time, though, while most of the receipts are still blank, one's filled in. The handwriting's clearly male: tiny chicken scratch that doesn't lean left or right. The fare's listed at fifty bucks. Unreal. One round and we're already up to five hundred dollars. Fine by me.

Harris calls it the Congressional Pissing Contest. I call it Name That Tune. All across the Capitol, House and Senate pages deliver blank taxicab receipts to people around the Hill. We all put in our bids and pass them up to whoever invited us into the game, who then passes them to their sponsor, and so on. We've never figured out how far it goes, but we do know it's not a single straight line—that'd take too long. Instead, it's broken up into branches. I start our branch and pass it to Harris. Somewhere else, another player starts his branch. There could be four branches; there could be forty. But at some point, the various bets make their way back to the dungeon-masters, who collect, coalesce, and start the process again.

Last round, I bid one hundred dollars. Right now, the top bid is five hundred. I'm about to increase it. In the end, whoever bids the most "buys" the right to make the issue their own. Highest bidder has to make the proposition happen, whether it's getting 110 votes on the baseball bill or inserting a tiny land project into Interior Approps. Everyone else who antes in tries to make sure it doesn't happen. If you pull it off, you get the entire pot, including every dollar that's been put in (minus a small percentage to the dungeon-masters, of course). If you fail, the money gets split among everyone who was working against you.

I study the cab number on the five-hundred-dollar receipt: *326*. Doesn't tell me squat. But whoever 326 is, they clearly think they've got the inside track. They're wrong.

Staring down at a blank receipt, I've got my pen poised. Next to *Cab Number,* I write the number *727*. Next to *Fare,* I put *$60.00*. Six hundred now, plus the $125.00 I put in before. If the bet gets too high, I can always drop out by leaving the dollar amount blank. But this isn't the time to fold. It's time to win. Stuffing all the receipts into a new envelope, I seal it up, address it to Harris, and walk it out front. Interoffice mail won't take long.

*   *   *

It's not until one-thirty that the next envelope hits my desk. The receipt I'm looking for has the same chicken scratch as before. Cab number 326. The fare is *$100.00*. One thousand even. That's what happens when the entire bet is centered on an issue that can be decided with a single well-placed phone call. Everyone in this place thinks they've got the jags to get it done. And they may. But for once, we've got more.

I close my eyes and work the math in my head. If I go too fast, I'll scare 326 off. Better to go slow and drag him along. With a flourish, I fill in a fare of *$150.00*. Fifteen hundred. And still counting.

By a quarter after three, my stomach's rumbling and I'm starting to get cranky—but I still don't go to lunch. Instead, I gnaw through the last handfuls of Grape-Nuts that Roy keeps hidden in his desk. The cereal doesn't last long. I still don't move. We're too close to gift-wrapping this up. According to Harris, no bet's ever gone for more than nineteen hundred bucks—and that was only because they got to mess with Teddy Kennedy.

"Matthew Mercer?" a page with cropped blond hair asks from the door. I wave the kid inside.

"You're popular today," Dinah says as she hangs up her phone.

"Blame the Senate," I tell her. "We're battling over language, and Trish not only doesn't trust faxes, but she won't put it on E-mail because she's worried it's too easy to forward to the lobbyists."

"She's right," Dinah says. "Smart girl."

Turning my chair just enough so Dinah can't see, I open the envelope and peer inside. I swear, I feel my testicles tighten. I don't believe it. It's not the amount, which is now up to three thousand dollars. It's the brand-new cab number: 189. The handwriting is squat and blocky. There's another player in the game. And he's clearly not afraid to spend some cash.

My phone screams, and I practically leap from my chair. Caller ID says it's Harris.

"How we doing?" he asks as soon as I pick up.

"Not bad, though the language still isn't there yet."

"You got someone in the room?" he asks.

"Absolutely," I say, keeping my back to Dinah. "And a new section I've never seen before."

"Another player? What's the number?"

"One-eighty-nine."

"That's the guy who won yesterday—with the baseball bill."

"You sure?"

It's a dumb question. Harris lives and breathes this stuff. He doesn't get it wrong.

"Think we should worry?" I ask.

"Not if you can deliver."

"Oh, I'll deliver," I insist.

"Then don't stress. If anything, I'm happy," Harris adds. "With two bidders out there, the pot's that much bigger. And if he won yesterday, he's cocky and careless. That's the perfect time to swipe his pants."

Nodding to myself, I hang up the phone and stare down at the cab receipt with the block writing.

"Everything okay?" Dinah asks from her desk.

Scribbling as fast as I can, I up the bet to four thousand dollars and slide the receipt into the envelope. "Yeah," I say as I head for the metal Out box up front. "Just perfect."

*   *   *

The envelope comes back within an hour, and I ask the page to wait so he can take it directly to Harris. Roxanne's done enough interoffice delivery service. Better to mix it up so she doesn't get suspicious. Clawing my way into the envelope, I search for the signal that we've got the top bid. Instead, I find another receipt. Cab number 189. Fare of five hundred dollars. *Five grand— plus everything else we already put in.*

For one picosecond, I hesitate, wondering if it's time to fold. Then I remind myself we're holding all the aces. And the jokers. And the wild cards. 189 may have the cash, but we've got the whole damn deck. He's not scaring us off.

I grab a blank receipt from the envelope and write in my cab number. In the blank next to *Fare,* I jot *$600.00.* That's a pretty rich cab ride.

Exactly twelve minutes after the page leaves my office, my phone rings. Harris just got his delivery.

"You sure this is smart?" he asks the instant I pick up. From the echo, I'm back on speakerphone.

"Don't worry, we're fine."

"I'm serious, Matthew. This isn't Monopoly money we're playing with. If you add up the separate bets, we're already in for over six thousand. And now you wanna add another six grand on top of that?"

When we were talking about limits last night, I told Harris I had a little over eight thousand dollars in the bank, including all my down-payment money. He said he had four grand at the most. Maybe less. Unlike me, Harris sends part of his paycheck to an uncle in Pennsylvania. His parents died a few years back, but . . . family's still family.

"We can still cover it," I tell him.

"That doesn't mean we should put it all on black."

"What're you saying?"

"I'm not saying anything," Harris insists. "I just . . . maybe it's time to catch our breath and walk away. No reason to risk all our money. We can just bet the other side, and you'll make sure the project never gets in the bill."

That's how it works—if you don't have the high bid, you and the rest of the low bidders shift to the other side and try to stop it from taking place. It's a great way to even the odds: The person with the best chance of making it happen faces off against a group that, once combined, has an amazing amount of muscle. There's only one problem. "You really want to split the winnings with everyone else?"

He knows I'm right. Why give everyone a free ride?

"If you want to ease the stakes, maybe we can invite someone else in," I suggest.

Right there, Harris stops. "What're you saying?"

He thinks I'm trying to find out who's above him on the list.

"You think it's Barry, don't you?" he asks.

"Actually, I think it's Pasternak."

Harris doesn't reply, and I grin to myself. Pasternak may be the closest thing he has to a mentor, but Harris and I go back to my freshman year. You can't lie to old friends.

"I'm not saying you're right," he begins. "But either way, my guy's not gonna go for it. Especially this late. I mean, even assuming 189 is teaming up with his own mentor, that's still a tractorful of cash."

"And it'll be two tractorfuls when we win. There's

gotta be over twenty-five grand in the pot. Think about the check you'll send home after that."

Even Harris can't argue with that one.

There's a crackle on the line. He takes me off speaker-phone. "Just tell me one thing, Matthew—can you really make this happen?"

I'm silent, working every possibility. He's just as quiet, counting every consequence. It's the opposite of our standard dance. For once, I'm confidence; he's concern.

"So can you pull this off?" Harris repeats.

"I think so," I tell him.

"No, no, no, no, no . . . Forget 'think so.' I can't afford 'think so.' I'm asking you as a friend—honestly, no bull-shit. *Can you pull this off?*"

It's the first time I hear the tinge of panic in Harris's voice. He's not afraid to leap off the edge of the cliff, but like any smart politician, he needs to know what's in the river below. The good thing is, in this one case, I've got the life preserver.

"This baby's mine," I tell him. "The only one closer is Cordell himself."

The silence tells me he's unconvinced.

"You're right," I add sarcastically. "It's too risky—we should walk away now."

The silence is even longer.

"I swear to you, Harris. Cordell doesn't care about table scraps. This is what I'm hired to do. We won't lose."

"You promise?"

As he asks the question, I stare out the window at the dome of the Capitol. "On my life."

"Don't get melodramatic on me."

"Fine, then here's pragmatic. Know what the golden

rule of Appropriations is? He who has the gold makes the rule."

"And we got the gold?"

"We got the gold."

"You sure about that?"

"We'll know soon enough," I say with a laugh. "Now, you in?"

"You already filled out the slip, didn't you?"

"But you're the one who has to send it on."

There's another crackle. I'm back on speakerphone. "Cheese, I need you to deliver a package," he calls out to his assistant.

There we go. Back in business.

The clock hits 7:30 and there's a light knock on my office door. "All clear?" Harris asks, sticking his head inside.

"C'mon in," I say, motioning him toward my desk. With everyone gone, we might as well speed things along.

As he enters the office, he lowers his chin and flashes a thin grin. It's a look I don't recognize. Newfound trust? Respect?

"You wrote on your face," he says.

"What're you . . . ?"

He smiles and taps his finger against his cheek. "Blue cheek. Very Duke."

Licking my fingers, I scrub the remaining ink from my face and ignore the joke.

"By the way, I saw Cordell in the elevator," he says, referring to my boss.

"He say anything?"

"Nothing much," Harris teases. "He feels bad that all

those years ago, you signed up for his campaign and drove him around to all those events without knowing he'd eventually turn into an asshole. Then he said he was sorry for dropping every environmental issue for whatever gets him on TV."

"That's nice. I'm glad he's big enough to admit it." My face has a smile, but Harris can always see deeper. When we came here, Harris believed in the issues; I believed in a person. It's the latter that's more dangerous.

Harris sits on the corner of my desk, and I follow his gaze to the TV, which, as always, is locked on C-SPAN. As long as the House is in session, the pages are still on call. And from the looks of it—with Wyoming Congresswoman Thelma Lewis gripping the podium and blathering away—we've got some time. Mountain standard time, to be precise. Right now, it's 5:30 in Casper, Wyoming—prime news hour—which is why Lewis waited until late in the day to make her big speech, and why Members from New Mexico, North Dakota, and Utah are all in line behind her. Why fall in the woods if no one's there to hear?

"Democracy demographics," I mutter.

"If they were smart, they'd wait another half hour," Harris points out. "That's when the local news numbers really kick in and—"

Before he can finish, there's a knock on my door.

"Matthew Mercer?" a female page with brown bangs asks as she approaches with an envelope.

Harris and I share a fast glance. This is it.

She hands me the envelope, and I struggle to play it cool.

"Wait . . . aren't you Harris?" she blurts.

He doesn't flinch. "I'm sorry. Have we met?"

"At orientation . . . you gave that speech."

I roll my eyes, not surprised. Every year, Harris is one of four staffers asked to speak at the orientation for the pages. To most, it's a suck job. Not to Harris. The other three speakers drone on about the value of government. Harris gives them the locker room speech from *Hoosiers* and tells them they'll be writing the future. Every year, the fan club grows.

"That was really amazing what you said," she adds.

"I meant every word," Harris tells her. And he did.

I can't take my eyes off the envelope. "Harris, we should really . . ."

"I'm sorry," the page says. She can't take her eyes off him. And not because of the speech. Harris's square shoulders . . . his dimpled chin . . . even his strong black eyebrows—he's always had a classic look—like someone you see in an old black-and-white photograph from the 1930s, but who somehow still looks good today. All you have to add are the deep green eyes . . . He's never had to work it.

"Listen, you . . . you have a great one," the page adds, still staring as she leaves.

"You, too," Harris says.

"Can you shut the door behind you?" I call out.

The door slams with a bang, and Harris yanks the envelope from my hands. If we were in college, I'd tackle him and grab it back. Not anymore. Today, the games are bigger.

Harris slides his finger along the flap and casually flips it open. I don't know how he keeps his composure. My blond hair is already damp with sweat; his black locks are dry as hay.

Searching for calm, I turn toward the Grand Canyon

photo on the wall. The first time my parents took me there, I was fifteen years old—and already six feet tall. Staring down from the south rim of the canyon was the first time in my life I felt small. I feel the same way next to Harris.

"What's it say?" I demand.

He peeks inside and stays totally silent. If the bet's been raised, there'll be a new receipt inside. If we're top dog, our old slip of paper is the only thing we'll find. I try to read his face. I don't have a prayer. He's been in politics too long. The crease in his forehead doesn't twitch. His eyes barely blink.

"I don't believe it," he finally says. He pulls out the taxi receipt and cups it in the palm of his hand.

"What?" I ask. "Did he raise it? He raised it, didn't he? We're dead . . ."

"Actually," Harris begins, looking up to face me and slowly raising an excited eyebrow, "I'd say we're very much alive." In his hand he flashes the taxi receipt like a police badge. It's my handwriting. Our old bet. For six thousand dollars.

I laugh out loud the moment I see it.

"It's payday, Matthew. Now, you ready to name that tune . . . ?"

5

"MORNING, ROXANNE," I call out as I enter the office the following day. "We all set?"

"Just like you asked," she replies without looking up.

Crossing into the back room, I find Dinah, Connor, and Roy in their usual positions at their desks, already lost in paperwork and Conference notes. This time of year, that's all we do—build the twenty-one-billion-dollar *Rosemary's Baby.*

"They're waiting for you in the hearing room," Dinah points out.

"Thanks," I say as I snatch my notebooks from my desk and head for the oversized beige door that leads next door.

It's one thing to bet on the fact that I can sneak this item past the Senate folks and into the bill. It's entirely another to make it happen.

"Nice to be on time," Trish scolds as I enter the room.

I'm the last of the four horsemen to arrive. It's intentional. Let 'em think I'm not anxious about the agenda. As usual, Ezra's on my side of the oval table; Trish and Georgia, our Senate counterparts, are on the other. On the right-hand wall, there's a black-and-white Ansel Adams photograph of Yosemite National Park. The photo shows the clear glass surface of the Merced River dominated by the snow-covered mountain peak of Half Dome over-head. Some people need coffee; I need the outdoors. Like the Grand Canyon picture in my office, the image brings instant calm.

"So, anything new?" Trish asks, wondering what I've got up my sleeve.

"Nope," I reply, wondering the same about her. We both know the pre-Conference tango. Every day, there's a new project that one of our bosses "forgot" to put in the bill. Last week, I gave her three hundred thousand dollars for manatee protection in Florida; she returned the favor by giving me four hundred thousand to fund a University of Michigan study of toxic mold. As a result, the Senator from Florida and the Congressman from Michigan now have something to brag about during the elections. Around here, the projects are known as "immaculate con-ceptions." Political favors that—poof—appear right out of thin air.

I've got a mental list of every project—including the gold mine—that I need to squeeze in by the time pre-Conference is done. Trish has the same. Neither of us wants to show our hand first. So for two hours, we stick to the script.

"FDR's presidential library," Trish begins. "Senate gave it six million. You gave it four million."

"Compromise at five mil?" I ask.

"Done."

"Over to Philadelphia," I say. "What about the new walkways for Independence Hall? We gave it nine hundred thousand; the Senate, for some reason, zeroed it out."

"That was just to teach Senator Didio to keep his mouth shut. He took a crack at my boss in *Newsweek*. We're not gonna stand for that."

"Do you have any idea how vindictive and childish that is?"

"Not half as vindictive as what they do in Transpo. When one of the Senators from North Carolina pissed off that subcommittee Chairman, they cut Amtrak's funding so the trains wouldn't stop in Greensboro."

I shake my head. Gotta love appropriators. "So you'll give full funding to the Liberty Bell?"

"Of course," Trish says. "Let freedom ring."

By noon, Trish is looking at her watch, ready for lunch. If she's got a project in her pants, she's playing it extra cool—which is why, for the first time today, I start wondering if I should put mine out there first.

"Meet back here at one?" she asks. I nod and slam my three-ring binder shut. "By the way," she adds as I head back to my office, "there's one other thing I almost forgot . . ."

I stop right there and spin around. It takes every muscle in my face to hide my grin.

"It's this sewer project in Marblehead, Mass," Trish begins. "Senator Schreck's hometown."

"Oh, crap," I shoot back. "That reminds me—I almost forgot about this land sale I was supposed to ask you about for Grayson."

Trish cocks her head like she believes me. I do the same for her. Professional courtesy.

"How much is the sewer?" I ask, trying hard not to push.

"Hundred and twenty thousand. What about the land sale?"

"Doesn't cost a thing—they're trying to buy it from us. But the request is coming from Grayson."

She barely moves as I say Grayson's name. If memory serves, she had a run-in with him a few years back. It wasn't pretty. Rumors said he made a pass. But if she wants revenge, she's not showing it.

"What's on the land now?" she asks.

"Dust . . . rabbit turds . . . all the good stuff. What they want is the gold mine underneath."

"They taking cleanup responsibility?"

"Absolutely. And since they're buying the land, we'll actually be *getting* money on this one. I'm telling you, it's a good deal."

She knows I'm right. Under current mining law, if a company wants to dig for gold or silver on public land, all they have to do is stake a claim and fill out some paperwork. After that, the company can take whatever they want for free. Thanks to the mining lobby—who've managed to keep the same law on the books since 1872—even if a company pulls millions in gold from government property, they don't have to give Uncle Sam a single nugget in royalties. And if they buy the land at old mining rates, they get to keep the land when they're done. Like Trish said, let freedom ring.

"And what's BLM say?" she asks, referring to the Bureau of Land Management.

"They already approved it. The sale's just caught up in red tape—that's why they want the language to give it a push."

Standing behind the oval table, Trish shifts her jaw off center, trying to put a dollar value on my ask. Feeling like spectators, Ezra and Georgia do the same.

"Let me call my office," Trish finally says.

"There's a telephone in the meeting room," I say, pointing her and Georgia next door.

As the side door slams behind them, Ezra packs up his own notebooks. "Think they'll go for it?" he asks.

"Depends how bad she wants her sewer, right?"

Ezra nods, and I turn back to the black-and-white Yosemite photo on the wall. Following my eyes, Ezra does the same. We stare silently at it for at least thirty seconds.

"I don't get it," Ezra finally blurts.

"Get what?"

"Ansel Adams—the whole *über*-photographer thing. I mean, all the guy did was take some black-and-white photos of the outdoors. Why the big fuss?"

"It's not just the photo," I explain. "It's the idea." With my open palm facing the photo, I circle the entire snow-capped peak. "Just the mere image of a completely wide-open space . . . There's only one place that could've been taken. It's America. And the idea of protecting huge swaths of land from development just so people could stare and enjoy it—that's an American ideal. We invented it. France, England . . . all of Europe—they took their open spaces and built castles and cities on them. Over here, although we certainly do our share of development, we also set aside huge chunks and called them national parks. I mean, Europeans say the only American art form is jazz. They're wrong. That purple mountain's majesty—that's the John Coltrane of the outdoors."

Ezra cocks his head slightly to take a better look. "I still don't see it."

Turning my head, I wait for the side door to open. It stays shut. I already feel the drips of sweat trickling from my armpits down my rib cage. Trish has been gone too long.

"You doing okay?" Ezra asks, reading my complexion.

"Yeah . . . just hot," I say, unbuttoning the top of my shirt. If Trish is playing the game, we're in severe . . .

Before I can finish, the doorknob clicks and the side door swings open. As Trish reenters the room, I try to read the look on her face. I might as well be trying to read Harris. Cradling her three-ring binder like a girl in junior high, she shifts her weight from one leg to another. I bite the inside of my cheek, trying to ignore the numbers floating through my brain. Twelve thousand dollars. Every nickel I've saved for the past few years. And the twenty-five-grand reward. It all comes down to this.

"I'll trade you the sewer for the gold mine," Trish blurts.

"Done," I shoot back.

We both nod to consummate the deal. Trish marches off to lunch. I march back to my office.

And just like that, we're standing in the winner's circle.

"That's it?" Harris asks, his voice squawking through my receiver.

"That's it," I repeat from my almost empty office. Everyone's at lunch but Dinah, who, like the phone beast she is, is on a call with someone else. I still watch what I say. "When the Members vote for the bill—which they always do since it's filled with goodies for themselves—we're all done."

"And you're sure you don't have any uptight Members who'll read through the bill and take the gold mine out?" Harris asks.

"Are you kidding? These people don't read. Last year,

the omnibus bill was over eleven hundred pages long. I barely read it, and that's my job. More important, once it comes out of Conference, it's a big stack of paper covered in Post-it notes. They put a few copies on the House side and some more on the Senate. That's their only chance to examine it—an hour or so before the vote. Trust me, even the Citizens Against Government Waste—y'know, that group that finds the fifty-thousand-dollar study on Aborigine sweat the government funded—even they only find about a quarter of the fat we hide in there."

"You really gave fifty grand to study Aborigine sweat?" Harris asks.

"Don't laugh. Last month, when scientists announced a huge leap in the cure for meningitis, guess where the breakthrough came from?"

"Aborigine sweat."

"That's right—Aborigine sweat. Think about that next time you read about pork in the paper."

"Great—I'm on the lookout," Harris says. "Now you have everything else?"

Reaching into the jacket pocket of my suit, I pull out a white letter-sized envelope. Checking it for the seventh time today, I open the flap and stare at the two cashier's checks inside. One's for $4,000.00. The other's for $8,225.00. One from Harris, the other from me. Both are made out to cash. Completely untraceable.

"Right here in front of me," I say as I seal the letter-sized envelope and slide it into a bigger manila mailer.

"They still haven't picked it up?" Harris asks. "It's usually promptly at noon."

"Don't stress yourself—they'll be here . . . ."

There's a soft, polite cough as the door to our office

peeks open. "I'm looking for Matt . . . ?" an African-American page says as he clears his throat and steps inside.

". . . any second," I tell Harris. "Gotta run—business calls."

I hang up the phone and wave the page inside. "I'm Matthew. C'mon in."

As the page approaches my desk, it's the first time I notice he's wearing a blue suit instead of the standard blazer and gray slacks. This guy isn't a House page; he's from the Senate. Even the pages dress nicer over there.

"How's everything going?" I ask.

"Pretty good. Just tired of all the walking."

"It's a real haul from the Senate, huh?"

"They tell me where to go—I got no choice," he laughs. "Now, you got a package for me?"

"Right here." I seal the oversized envelope, jot the word *Private* across the back, and reach across the desk to put it in his hands. Unlike the other page visits, this isn't a drop-off. It's a pickup. The day after the bidding, the dungeon-masters expect you to cover your bet.

"So you know where this one's going?" I ask, always searching for extra info.

"Back to the cloakroom," he says with a shrug. "They take it from there."

As he grabs the envelope, I notice a silver ring on his thumb. And another on his pointer finger. I didn't think they let pages wear jewelry.

"So what's with the stuffed fox?" he adds, motioning with his chin toward the bookcase.

"It's a ferret. Courtesy of the NRA."

"The *what?*"

"The NRA—y'know, National Rifle—"

"Yeah, yeah . . . no, I thought you said something else," he interrupts, rubbing his hand over his closely buzzed hair. The ring on his pointer finger catches the light perfectly. He smiles with a big, toothy grin.

I smile right back. But it's not until that moment that I realize I'm about to hand twelve thousand dollars to a complete stranger.

"Be safe now," he sings as he grabs the package and pivots toward reception.

He disappears through the door. The bet's officially on. And I'm left staring at the back of someone's head. It's not a good feeling, and not just because he's carrying every dollar I own and all the savings of my best friend. It's more primal than that—something I feel in the last vertebra of my spine. It's like closing one eye when you're looking at a 3-D image in a View-Master viewer—nothing's necessarily wrong, but it's also not quite right.

I glance at Dinah, who's still haggling on the phone. I've got another half hour before I have to resume the battle with Trish. Plenty of time for a quick run to the Senate cloakroom to check things out. I hop from my seat and race around my desk. Curiosity was good enough for the cat. Why shouldn't it be good enough for me?

"Where you going?" Dinah calls out as I rush for the door.

"Lunch. If Trish starts bitching, tell her I won't be long . . ."

She gives me the okay sign, and I dart through reception. The page can't have more than a thirty-second head start.

Darting into the hallway, I turn a quick corner and make a right at the elevators. I spot him about a hundred feet ahead. His arms are swinging at his side. Not a worry in the world. As his shoes tap against the terrazzo floor, I assume he's headed for the underground tram that'll take him back to the Capitol. To my surprise, he makes a sharp right and disappears down a short flight of stairs. Keeping my distance, I make the same right and follow the stairs down past a pair of Capitol police officers. On my left, the officers herd arriving staff and visitors through the X-ray and metal detector. Straight ahead, the glass door that leads out to Independence Avenue swings shut. Underground is faster. Why's he going outside?

But as I shove my way through the door and hop down the outdoor steps, it makes a bit more sense. The sidewalk's packed with fellow employees who are just now coming back from lunch. The September day is overcast, but the weather's still warm. If he's walking the halls all day, maybe he's just after some fresh air. Besides, there's more than one way to cut across to the Capitol.

I keep telling myself that as he heads up the block. Five steps later, he reaches into his pants pocket and pulls out a cell phone. Maybe that's it—reception's better outside—but as he presses the phone to his ear, he does the oddest thing of all. At the corner of Independence and South Capitol, all he has to do is make a left and cut across the street. Instead, he pauses a moment—and makes a right. *Away* from the Capitol.

My Adam's apple swells in my throat. What the hell is going on?

6

On the corner of Independence and South Capitol, the page turns back to see if anyone's behind him. I duck behind a group of staffers, once again cursing my height. The page doesn't even notice. I'm too far back to be seen. By the time I peek up again, he's long gone. Around the corner.

Racing full speed, I fly up toward the corner, my shoes pounding against the concrete. From here, Independence Avenue rises at a slight incline. It doesn't even slow me down.

I inch my head around the corner, and the page is halfway down South Capitol. He's fast. Even though he's on the phone, he knows where he's going.

Unsure what to do, I go with my first instinct. Whipping out my own phone, I dial Harris's number. Nothing but voice mail, which means he's either on the line or out to lunch. I call back again, hoping his assistant will pick up. He doesn't.

I try to tell myself it still makes sense. Maybe this is how the dungeon-masters play it—the last transfer gets dropped off campus. There's gotta be someplace that's the actual home base. The more I think about it, the more it makes sense. But that doesn't make the reality pill any easier to swallow. He's got our money. I want to know where it's going.

At the end of the block, the page makes a left on C Street and disappears around another corner. I take off after him, carefully angling behind every staffer I can find. Anything to keep myself out of his direct line of sight.

As he turns right on New Jersey Avenue, I'm at least 150 feet behind him. He's still moving fast, yakking away on his phone. By now, fellow staffers and the congressional office buildings are long gone. We're in the residential section of Capitol Hill—brick townhouse squeezed next to brick townhouse. I walk on the other side of the pothole-filled street, pretending I'm looking for my parked car. It's a lame excuse, but if he spins around, at least he won't see me. The only problem is, the further we go, the more the neighborhood shape-shifts around us.

Within two minutes, the brick townhouses and tree-lined streets give way to chain-link fences and broken bottles scattered across the concrete. An illegally parked car has a yellow metal boot on its front tire. A Jeep across the street has its back window smashed, creating an oval black hole at the center of the shattered glass. It's the great irony of Capitol Hill—we're supposed to run the country, but we can't even keep up the neighborhood.

Diagonally up the street, the page still has his cell pressed against his ear. He's too far. I can't hear a word. But I can see it in his stride. There's a new glide in his walk. His whole body bounces to the right with each step. I try to imagine the polished kid who quietly coughed his way into my office barely five blocks ago. He's long gone.

Instead, the page bounces along, tapping the envelope—filled with our money—against his thigh. He moves without a hint of hesitation. To me, this is a rough neighborhood. To the page, this is home.

Up ahead, the street rises slightly, then levels off just below the overpass for I-395 that runs perpendicular overhead. As the page nears the overpass, he once again glances back to see if anyone's following. I duck behind a black Acura, slamming my shoulder into the side mirror. There's a loud chirp. *Oh, no.* I shut my eyes tight. And the Acura's alarm explodes, howling like a police siren.

Hitting the sidewalk chest-first, I scramble on my elbows to the front of the car and pray he doesn't stop. In this neighborhood, alarms go off all the time. Lying on my stomach, I rest my weight on my elbows, which already feel damp. A single sniff tells me I'm lying in a puddle of grease. My suit's ruined. But right now, that's the least of my problems. I count to ten and slowly crawl back to the sidewalk. The alarm's still screaming. I'm on the passenger side, my head still ducked down. Last I saw him, he was diagonally up the street. I slowly pick my head up and take a quick peek. There's no one there. I crane my neck in every direction. The page is gone. And so's our money.

In full panic, I'm tempted to run toward the overpass, but I've seen enough movies to know that the moment you rush in blindly, there's always someone lying in wait. Instead, I stay crouched down, slowly chicken-walking up the block. There're enough parked cars along the street to keep me hidden all the way up to the overpass, but it doesn't calm me down a bit. My heart's punching against my chest. My throat's so dry, I can barely swallow. Car by car, I carefully inch toward the overpass. The closer I get, the more I hear the droning hum of traffic along 395—and the less I hear what's right in front of me.

There's a metal clink to my left, and an empty beer can comes tumbling down the concrete incline underneath the overpass. I go to run, but then I spot the sharp flap of wings on the pigeon that set it in motion. The bird flies out from the overpass and disappears in the gray sky. Even with the clouds hovering above, it's still bright as noon outside, but under the overpass, the shadows at the top of the incline are dark as a forest.

I step out from behind a maroon Cutlass, and the *No Parking* sign takes away the last of my hiding spots. As I enter the underpass, I look up toward the shadows and tell myself no one's there. The buzz of traffic whizzes by overhead. As each car hits the overpass, it's a swarm of bees buzzing above. But I'm still all alone underneath. I look back down the block, retracing my steps. No one's there. No one but me. In a sketchy neighborhood. Without anyone knowing where I am.

What am I, insane? I spin around and walk away. He can keep the money, for all I care; it's not worth my li—

There's a muffled clacking in the distance. Like dice on a gameboard. I twist back to follow the sound. Further down. On the other side of the overpass. I don't see it at first. Then I hear it again. I dart behind one of the enormous concrete pillars that hold the highway overpass in place. Above my head, the bees continue to buzz. But down here, I focus on the sound of the dice, downhill from where I'm standing. From my angle, it's still obscured. Heading deeper into the overpass, I rush from my pillar to one directly ahead. Another die moves across the board. Angling my head around the concrete column, I take my first full look. Outside the overpass, cars once again line the street. But what I'm looking for isn't directly in front of me. It's off to the left.

Up the block, a dip in the sidewalk leads to a gravel driveway. In the driveway, there's a rusted old industrial Dumpster. And right next to the Dumpster is the source of the noise. Dice against a gameboard. Or tiny stones being kicked by someone's feet.

Dead ahead, the page makes his way up the gravel driveway—and in one quick movement, takes off his suit jacket, yanks off his tie, and skyhooks both items up and into the open Dumpster. Without even a pause, he heads back to the sidewalk, looking happy to be free of the monkey suit. It doesn't make sense.

My Adam's apple now feels like a softball in my throat. The page steps out of the driveway, once again kicking the stones at his feet. As he fades up the block, he's still tapping the envelope against his thigh. And for the first time, I wonder if I'm even looking at a page.

How could I be so stupid? I didn't even get his name . . .

. . . tag. His nametag. On his jacket.

My eyes zip toward the Dumpster, then back to the page. At the end of the block, he makes a hard left and vanishes from sight. I give him a solid few seconds to double back. He doesn't. That's my cue. Even with his head start, there's still time to catch up with him, but before I do . . .

I spring out from behind the pillar, dash down the sidewalk, and leave the overpass behind. Rushing across the gravel driveway, I go straight for the Dumpster. It's too tall to see inside. Even for me. On the side, there's a groove that's just deep enough to get a toehold. My suit's already ruined. Up and over . . .

With a sharp yank, I tug myself up to the top of the Dumpster. Scootching around, I let my feet dangle inside. It's like the edge of a swimming pool. But scummier. And with a nauseating acidic stench. Taking one last look around, I spot a pink building with a neon sign that reads, *Platinum Gentleman's Club*. No one else is in sight. In this neighborhood, all the action's at night.

I stare back down at the pool of Hefty bags and push off with a soft nudge.

My feet pound through the plastic. I expect a crunch. Instead, I get a squish. My dress shoes fill with liquid. My socks suck it up like a sponge. Waist-deep in garbage, I tell myself it's just beer.

Wading toward the back corner of the Dumpster, I keep my arms above my shoulders, careful not to touch anything. Lunging forward, I snag the navy suit jacket, hold it above the trash, and go straight for the blue nametag.

Senate Page
Viv Parker

What's a girl's name doing on a guy's jacket?

Unhooking the nametag from the lapel, I check to see if there're any other markings on it. Nothing. Just a standard plastic—

A car door slams in the distance. I turn at the noise. But I can't see anything except the moldy interior walls of the trash bin. Time to get out. Holding the nametag in one hand and tossing the jacket over my shoulder, I grip the top ledge of the Dumpster with my long, spindly fingers. A slight jump gives me enough momentum to boost myself up. My feet scratch and slide against the wall, fighting for traction.

With one final thrust, I press my stomach against the top ledge and seesaw into place. Tires screech in the distance, but I'm in no position to look up. Like an army recruit fighting to get over the obstacle course wall, I twist myself over the top and plummet feetfirst toward the ground, still facing the Dumpster. As my shoes collide with the cement, I hear an engine revving behind me. Dozens of stones clink across the concrete. It's right there. Back toward the driveway. Tires once again screech, and I spin at the sound. Out of the corner of my eye, I see the car's grille coming my way. Straight at me.

The black Toyota plows into my legs and smashes me into the Dumpster. My face flies forward, slamming into the hood of the car. There's an unearthly crackle like a dry log in a fireplace. My legs shatter. Oh, God. I scream out in pain. Bone turns to dust, and as the car shoves the Dumpster backwards, metal grinds against metal, with me in between. My legs . . . m-my pelvis is on fire. I think it's snapped in two. The pain is scorching . . . I take that back. The pain fades. It all goes numb. Time freezes in a warped slow motion. My body's in shock.

"What's wrong wit you?!" a male voice shouts from within the car.

The blood pours from my mouth, raining across the hood of the Toyota. *Please, God. Don't let me pass out . . .* In my left eye, I see nothing but bright red. It takes everything I have to pick my head up and look through the windshield. There's only one person inside . . . holding on to the steering wheel. The page who took our money.

"All you hadda do was sit there!" he screams, pounding the wheel with his fist. He yells something else, but it's muffled . . . all garbled . . . like someone shouting when you're underwater.

I try to wipe the blood from my mouth, but my arm's limp at my side. I stare through the windshield at the page, unsure how long he's been yelling. Around me, everything goes silent. All I hear is my own broken panting—a wet wheeze crawling on its knees through my throat. I try to tell myself that as long as I'm breathing, I'll be okay, right? But like my dad told me on our first camping trip, every animal knows when it's about to die.

Through the windshield, the page throws the car into reverse. The Toyota shifts below my chest. My long fingers scratch wildly for the windshield wipers . . . the grate on the hood . . . anything to grab on to. I don't have a chance. He floors it, and the car flies backwards, sending me sliding off the hood. As my back crashes against the Dumpster, the car's wheels spin, kicking a tornado of rocks and dust in my eyes and mouth. I try to stand but can't feel anything. My legs collapse beneath me and my whole body crumples in the dirt.

Straight ahead, the car bucks to a stop. But he doesn't leave. I don't understand. With my one good eye, I stare through the windshield as the page shakes his head angrily. There's a soft mechanical clunk. He shifts it back into drive. Oh, God. He punches the gas, and the engine howls. Tires gnaw through the gravel. And the rusted grille of the black Toyota comes galloping straight at me. I beg for him to stop, but nothing comes out. My body shakes, convulsing against the base of the Dumpster. The car thunders forward. S-Sorry I got you into this, Harris . . . Mouthing a silent prayer, I shut my eyes tight and try to picture the Merced River in Yosemite.

7

"WHATTYA MEAN, DEAD? How can he be dead?"

"That's what happens when you stop breathing."

"I know what it means, asshole!"

"Then don't ask a stupid question."

Sinking down in his seat, the smartly dressed man felt a sharp contraction around his lungs. "You said no one would get hurt," he stuttered, anxiously unbending a paperclip as he cradled the phone to his chin. "Those were your words . . ."

"Don't blame me," Martin Janos insisted on the other line. "He followed our guy outside the Capitol. At that point, the kid panicked."

"That didn't mean he had to kill him!"

"Really?" Janos asked. "So you'd rather Matthew made his way to *your* office?"

Twisting the paperclip around his finger, the man didn't answer.

"Exactly," Janos said.

"Does Harris know?" the man asked.

"I just got the call myself—I'm on my way down there right now."

"What about the bet?"

"Matthew already slipped it in the bill—last smart thing the guy ever did."

"Don't make fun of him, Janos."

"Oh, now you're having regrets?"

Once again the man was silent. But deep within his chest, he knew he'd be regretting this one for the rest of his life.

8

STANDING IN THE gravel driveway, Janos stared down at Matthew Mercer's broken body, which sagged lifelessly against the Dumpster. More than anything else, Janos couldn't help but notice the awkward bend in Matthew's thighs. And the way his right hand was still stretching upward, reaching for something it would never grasp. Janos shook his head at the mess. So stupid and violent. There were better ways than this.

As the afternoon sun beat down on the bald spot in his short-cropped salt-and-pepper hair, Janos stuffed his hands in the pockets of his blue and yellow FBI windbreaker. A few years back, the Justice Department announced that nearly 450 of the FBI's own pistols, revolvers, and assault rifles were officially missing. Whoever stole the guns clearly thought they were valuable, Janos thought. But in his mind, not nearly as valuable as a single windbreaker, nabbed as the crowd celebrated a homerun during an Orioles game. Even the Capitol Police won't stop a friendly neighborhood FBI agent.

"Where you been?" a voice shouted behind him.

Slowly glancing over his shoulder, Janos had no problem spotting the rusty black Toyota. With the incredibly dented grille. As the car pulled up to the curb, Janos crossed around to the driver's side and leaned into the window, which was missing its side mirror. Flicking his tongue against his top teeth, he didn't say a word.

"Don't look at me like that," the young black man said, shifting awkwardly in his seat. The confidence he'd worn as a page was gone.

"Let me ask you a question, Toolie—do you consider yourself a smart person?"

Travonn "Toolie" Williams nodded hesitantly. "Y-Yeah . . . I guess so."

"That's why we hired you, isn't it? To be smart? To look the part?"

"Uh-huh."

"I mean, why else hire a nineteen-year-old?"

Toolie shrugged his shoulders, unsure how to answer. He didn't like Janos. Especially when he had that look.

Janos stared through the inside of the car and out the passenger-side window at Matthew. Then he looked back at Toolie.

"Y-You didn't tell me he'd follow . . ." Toolie began. "I didn't know what the hell to—!"

"Did you get the money?" Janos interrupted.

Toolie quickly reached over to the passenger seat and grabbed the envelope with the two cashier's checks. His arm was shaking as he handed it over.

"It's all there, just like you wanted. I even avoided the office in case someone followed."

"That sure worked out great," Janos said. "Now where's your jacket?"

Toolie reached into the backseat and handed over the navy suit jacket. Janos noticed it was soaked with blood, but decided not to ask. The damage was done.

"Anything else I should know about?" Janos asked.

Toolie shook his head.

Janos nodded slightly, then patted Toolie on the shoulder. Things were looking up. Reading the positive reaction, Toolie sat up in his seat and finally took a breath. Janos reached into his suit pocket and pulled out a small black box that looked like a thick calculator. "Ever seen one of these?" Janos asked.

"Naw, whut is it?"

On the side of the box, Janos flipped a switch, and a slight electrical hum punctured the air, like a radio being turned on. Next to the switch, he turned a dial, and two half-inch needles clicked into place on the base of the device. They looked like tiny antennas. Just enough to pierce through clothing, Janos thought.

Gripping the black box like a walkie-talkie, Janos cocked his arm backward—and in one sharp movement, pounded the device against the center of Toolie's chest.

"Ow!" Toolie yelled as the tips of the two needles bit into his skin. With a hard shove, he pushed Janos and the device away from his chest. "What the hell're you doin', asshole?"

Janos looked down at the black box and turned the On switch to Off. "You'll see . . ."

To his own surprise, Toolie let out a loud, involuntary grunt.

Seeing the smile on Janos's face, Toolie looked down at his own chest. Ignoring the buttons, he ripped his shirt open, then stretched the collar of his undershirt down until he could see his own bare chest. There were no marks. Not even a pinprick.

That's why Janos liked it. Completely untraceable.

Outside the car, Janos glanced down at his watch. Thirteen seconds was the minimum. But fifteen was average.

"What's going on?!" Toolie screamed.

"Your heart's trying to beat 3,600 times a minute," Janos explained.

As Toolie grabbed at the left side of his chest, Janos cocked his head sideways. They always grabbed the left side, even though the heart's not there. Everyone gets that wrong, he thought. That's just where we feel it beating. Indeed, as Janos knew all too well, the heart was actually in the direct center.

"I'll kill you!" Toolie exploded. "I'll kill you, muthaf—"

Toolie's mouth drooped open, and his entire body ragdolled against the steering wheel like a puppet when you remove the hand.

Fifteen seconds on the nose, Janos thought, admiring his homemade device. Just amazing. Once you know it takes AC power to fibrillate the heart, all you need are eight double-A batteries and a cheap converter from Radio Shack. With the flip of a switch, you convert 12 volts DC to 120 volts AC. Add two needles that are spread far enough to be on either side of the heart, and . . . sizzle . . . instant electrocution. The last thing any coroner will check for. And even if they do, as long as you're in and out fast enough to avoid electrical burns, there's nothing there to find.

Janos pulled two rubber gloves from his pants pocket, slid them on, and carefully scanned the area. Fences . . .

other cars . . . Dumpster . . . strip club. All clear. At least Toolie picked the right neighborhood. Still, it was always better to disappear as fast as possible. Opening the driver's-side door, Janos grabbed the back of Toolie's head in a tight fist and, with a hard shove, smashed Toolie's face against the steering wheel. Then he pulled back and did it again. And again—until Toolie's nose split open and the blood started flowing.

Letting Toolie's head slump back against the seat, Janos reached for the steering wheel and cranked it slightly to the right. He leaned into the car, resting an elbow on Toolie's shoulder and staring out the windshield—just to make sure he was perfectly lined up.

Back by the Dumpster, he found a broken cinder block, which he lugged back to the car. More than enough weight. Shifting the Toyota into neutral, he reached below the dash and pressed the cinder block against the gas. The engine growled to life, revving out of control. Janos let it build for a few seconds. Without the speed, it wouldn't look right. Almost there, he told himself . . . The car was shaking, practically knocking Toolie over. Perfect, Janos thought. With a fast slap, he threw the car into drive, jumped backwards, and let his aim do the rest. The tires spun against the pavement, and the car took off like a slingshot. Up the curb . . . off the road . . . and right into a telephone pole.

Barely pausing to watch the result, Janos headed back to the Dumpster and knelt next to Matthew's already pale body. From his own wallet, Janos took five hundred dollars, rolled it into a small wad, then stuffed it in Matthew's front pocket. That'll explain what he's doing in the neighborhood. White boys in suits only come down here for drugs. As long as the money's on him, the cops'll know it wasn't a jump-and-run. And with the car bow-tied around the telephone pole, the rest of the picture blooms into place. Kid gets hit on the sidewalk. Driver panics and, as he flees, does just as bad a job on himself. No one to hunt for. No one to investigate. Just another hit-and-run.

Flipping open his cell phone, Janos dialed a number and waited for his boss to pick up. No question, that was the worst part of the job. Reporting in. But that's what happens when you work for someone else.

"All clean," Janos said as he bent down to pull the cinder block out of the car.

"So where you off to now?"

Wiping his hands, Janos looked down at the room number next to Harris's name. "Russell Building. Room 427."

9

Harris

"ALL SET?"

"Harris, you sure this is right?" Senator Stevens asks me.

"Positive," I reply, checking the call sheet myself. "Edward—not Ed—Gursten . . . wife is Catherine. From River Hills. Son is named Dondi."

"Dondi?"

"Dondi," I repeat. "You met Edward flying first class last year."

"And is he a Proud American?"

Proud American is the Senator's code word for a donor who raises over ten grand.

"Extremely proud," I say. "You ready?"

Stevens nods.

I dial the final number and grab the receiver. If I were a novice, I'd say, *Hi, Mr. Gursten, I'm Harris Sandler . . . Senator Stevens's chief of staff. I have the Senator here for you . . .* Instead, I hand the phone to the Senator just as Gursten picks up. It's perfectly timed and a beautiful touch. The donor thinks the Senator himself called, instantly making them feel like old buddies.

As Stevens introduces himself, I toss a piece of hamachi in my mouth. Sushi and solicitations—typical Stevens lunch.

"So, Ed . . ." Stevens sings as I shake my head. "Where've you been my last dozen flights? You back in the cheap seats?" His pitch is off, but it still works like a dream. Personal calls from a Senator always hit home. And by *home,* I mean *in the wallet.*

"You were here? In D.C.?" Stevens asks. "Next time you're around, you should give me a call and we can try to grab lunch . . ."

Translation: *We don't have a chance of grabbing lunch. If you're lucky, we'll get five minutes together. But if you don't raise your donation this year, you may only get a senior staffer and some gallery passes.*

". . . we'll get you into the Capitol—make sure you don't have to wait on any of those lines . . ."

My staff will give you an intern who'll take you on exactly the same tour of the Capitol that you'd get on the public tour, but you'll feel far more important this way . . .

"I mean, we have to take care of our friends, don't we?"

I mean, how's about helping us out with some coin, fat man?

Stevens hangs up the phone with a verbal pledge that "Ed" will raise fifteen grand. I pass the Senator some yellowtail and dial the next number.

Years ago, political money came from powerful WASPs you met at a dinner party in a tastefully decorated second home. Today, it comes from a well-vetted call sheet in a fluorescent-lit room that sits directly atop a sushi restaurant on Massachusetts Avenue. The office has three desks, two computers, and ten phone lines. Old money versus new marketing. It's not even close. There's not a Congressman on the Hill who doesn't make these calls. Some do three hours a day; others do three a week. Stevens is the former. He likes his job. And the perks. And he's not about to lose them. It's the first rule of politics: You can do anything you want, but if you don't raise the cash, you won't be doing it for long.

"Who's next?" Stevens asks.

"Virginia Rae Morrison. You know her from Green Bay."

"We went to school together?"

"She was a neighbor. When you were nine," I explain, reading from the sheet. When it comes to fundraising, federal law says you can't make calls from your government office or a government phone—which is why every day, this close to elections, half of Congress leaves the Capitol to make calls from somewhere else. The average Member goes three blocks away to the phone rooms in Republican and Democratic campaign headquarters. Smarter Members hire a fundraising consultant to help build a personal database of reliable supporters and potential donors. And a dozen or so mad-genius Members kiss the ring and hire Len Logan, a fundraising expert so organized, the "Comments" sections of his call sheets have details like: "She just finished treatment for breast cancer."

"Yup, yup—I got her," Stevens says as the phone rings in my ear.

"Hello . . ." a female voice answers.

The Senator slides me the yellowtail; I slide him the receiver. We've got it running smoother than a ballet.

"Hey, there, Virginia, how's my favorite fighter?"

I nod, impressed. Don't reintroduce yourself if you're supposed to be old friends. As Stevens takes a two-minute gallop down memory lane, one of my two cell phones vibrates in my pocket. The one in my right pocket is paid for by the Senator's office. The one in my left is paid by me. Public and private. According to Matthew, in my life, there's no distinction. What he doesn't understand is, if you love your job like I do, there shouldn't be.

Checking to see that Stevens is still busy, I reach for my left pocket and check the tiny screen on my phone. *Caller ID blocked.* That's everyone I know.

"Harris," I answer.

"Harris, it's Cheese," my assistant says, his voice shaking. I already don't like the tone. "I-I don't know how to . . . It's Matthew . . . he . . ."

"Matthew what?"

"He got hit by a car," Cheese says. "He's dead. Matthew's dead."

Every muscle in my body goes limp, and it feels as if my head's floating away from my shoulders. *"What?"*

"I'm just telling you what I heard."

"From who? Who said it?" I ask, going for the source.

"Joel Westman, who got it from his cousin in the Capitol Police. Apparently, someone in Carlin's office forgot their parking pass and had to park out by stripper-land. On their way back, they saw the bodies . . ."

"There was more than one?"

"Apparently, the scumbag who hit him took off in a panic. Smacked into a pole and died instantly."

Shooting to my feet, I run my hand through my hair. "Why didn't . . . I can't believe this . . . When'd it happen?"

"No idea," Cheese stutters. "I just . . . I just got the call. Harris, they said Matthew might've been trying to buy drugs."

"Drugs? Not a chance . . ."

The Senator looks my way, wondering what's wrong. Pretending not to notice, I do the one thing you never do to a Senator. I turn my back to him. I don't care. This is Matthew . . . my friend . . .

"Everything alright?" the Senator calls out as I stumble for the doorknob.

Without answering, I throw the door open and rush from the room. Straight into the stairwell.

"The weird part is, some guy from the FBI was here looking for you," Cheese adds.

The walls of the stairway close in from every side. I tear at my tie, unable to breathe.

"Excuse me?"

"Said he had a few questions," Cheese explains. "Wanted to talk to you as soon as possible."

My sweat-soaked palm slides against the handrail, and my footing gives way. I slide down the top few stairs. A well-placed grasp prevents the fall.

"Harris, you there?" Cheese asks.

Jumping down the last three steps, I shove my way outside, gasping for fresh air. It doesn't help. Not when my friend's dead. My eyes well up with tears, and the words ricochet through my skull. My friend's dead. I can't believe he's—

"Harris, talk to me . . ." Cheese adds.

I tighten my jaw and try to bury the tears in my throat. It doesn't work. Checking the street, I scout for a cab. Nothing's in sight. Without even thinking, I start jogging

up the block. Better to get information. Back by Union
Station, the cab line's too long. No time to waste.

"Harris . . ." Cheese asks for the third time.

"Just tell me where it happened."

"Listen, don't do anything rash—"

"Where'd the damn accident happen?!"

"D-Down on New Jersey. By the strip club."

"Cheese, listen to me. Don't tell anyone what happened.
This isn't office gossip—it's a friend. Understand?"

Before he can answer, I shut my phone, turn the corner, and pick up the pace. My jog accelerates into a run,
which accelerates into a full-on sprint. My tie flaps over
my shoulder, waving in the wind. A noose around my
neck. I should be so lucky.

Rushing toward the overpass on New Jersey Avenue, I
see flashing lights spinning in the distance. But the moment I realize they're yellow instead of red, I know I'm
too late. Up by the gravel driveway, the driver's-side door
of a flatbed tow truck slams shut, and the engine coughs
itself awake. On the back of the flatbed is a black Toyota
with a smashed-in front end. The driver hits the gas, and
the tow truck rumbles deeper into southeast D.C.

"Wait!" I shout, chasing it up the block. *"Please,
wait!"* I don't have a chance. Even I'm not that fast. But
on the back of the truck, the front of the Toyota's still facing me. I keep running full-speed, staring hard at the
grille, which taunts me with its jack-o'-lantern grin. It's a
twisted smile, with a deep indentation on the driver's
side. Like it hit something. Then I catch the dark smudge
toward the bottom of the grille. Not just something.
Someone.

Matthew . . .

"Wait . . . waaaait!" I scream until my throat begins to burn. It still doesn't bury the pain. Nothing does. It's like a corkscrew in my chest, tightening with every second that passes. I'm still running as fast as I can, looking around at the world, searching for something . . . anything that'll make sense. It never does. My toes curl. My feet sting. And the corkscrew continues to tighten.

The tow truck kicks back a black cloud of exhaust and fades up the block. I run out of gas just beyond the gravel driveway—where the truck picked up the Toyota.

Two weeks ago, a seventeen-year-old Asian delivery boy was the victim of a hit-and-run a few blocks from my house. The cops kept police tape around the scene for almost six hours so they could get paint samples from the other vehicles the car collided with. Bent over and covered in sweat, I scan up and down the block. There's not a strand of police tape in sight. Whoever worked this scene . . . whoever cleaned it up . . . they found all the answers they needed right here. No suspects. No loose ends. Nothing to worry about.

Lost in a haze, I kick a loose pebble from the street. It skips across the pavement and clinks against the sidewalk. Just shy of the telephone pole. There's some glass from the headlights scattered at the base and some torn-up grass patches from where they dragged the car out. Otherwise, the pole's untouched. I crane my neck up. Maybe off by ten degrees.

Tracing it backward, it's not hard to follow. Tire tracks in the gravel show me where the Toyota's wheels started to spin. From there, the trail goes straight up the driveway. Dead-ending at the Dumpster.

I kick another pebble through the gravel, but as it hits

the Dumpster, the metal sound is different from before. Hollow. Completely empty.

There's a dent in the base of the Dumpster, and a dark puddle right below it. I tell myself not to look, but . . . I have to. Lowering my chin, I squint with a hesitant peek. I expect it to be red, like some bad slasher sequel. It's not. It's black. Just a shallow black stain. All that remains.

My stomach cartwheels, and a snakebite of acid slithers up my throat. I clench my teeth to fight the vomit. My head again floats from my shoulders, and I stagger backwards, grasping for balance. It doesn't come. Crashing on my ass, I slam against the gravel driveway, my hands slicing across the rocks. I swear, I can't move. I roll on my side, but all it does is bring me back to the dent in the Dumpster. And the black stain. And the crush of rocks surrounding it. I'm not sure why I came. I thought it'd make me feel better. It doesn't. With my cheek against the ground, I've got an ant's-eye view of the thin crawl space below the Dumpster. If I were small enough, I'd hide underneath, tucked behind the gum wrappers, empty beer bottles, and . . . and the one thing that's clearly out of place . . . It's really buried back there—I only see it when the sun hits it just right . . .

Cocking my head sideways, I slide my arm under the Dumpster and pull out the bright blue plastic nametag with the white writing:

Senate Page
Viv Parker

My mouth sags open. My fingers go numb. There's some dirt on the lettering, but it brushes right off. The nametag shines—it hasn't been out here long. I look back at the dent and the dark stain. Maybe just a few hours.

Oh, damn.

There was only one reason for Matthew to interact with a Senate page. Today was the day. Our stupid fucking bet . . . If they were both out here, maybe someone—

My phone rings in my pocket, and I jerk backwards from the vibration against my leg.

"Harris," I answer, flipping the phone open.

"Harris, it's Barry—where are you?"

I look around the empty lot, wondering the same thing myself. Barry may be blind, but he's not stupid. If he's calling me here, he . . .

"Just heard about Matthew," Barry says. "I can't believe it. I'm . . . I'm so sorry."

"Who told you?"

"Cheese. Why?"

I shut my eyes and curse my assistant.

"Harris, where are you?" Barry adds.

It's the second time he's asked that question. For that reason alone, he's not getting an answer.

Climbing to my feet, I brush the dust from my pants. My head's still spinning. I can't do this now . . . but . . . I have to. I need to find out who else knows. "Barry, have you told anyone else about this?"

"No one. Almost no one. Why?"

He knows me too well. "Nothing," I tell him. "What about Matthew's office mates—they heard yet?"

"Actually, that's who I just hung up with. I called to

pass the word, but Dinah . . . Trish from the Senate . . .
they already knew. Somehow, they got the news first."

I look down at the page's nametag in the palm of my
hand. In all the time we were playing the game, it was
never important who we were betting against. That was
the fun of it. But right now, I've got a bad feeling it's the
only thing that matters.

"Barry, I gotta go."

I press the End button and dial a new number. But before I can finish, there's a soft crunch of gravel behind the
Dumpster. I race around to the back of it, but no one's
there.

Keep it together, I tell myself.

I take a deep breath and let it wash down to my ab-
domen. Just like my dad used to do when the bills came.
My finger once again dives for the keypad. Time to go to
the source. And when it comes to the game, the only
source I know is the person who brought me in.

"Bud Pasternak's office—how can I help you?" a female voice answers. Barry's boss. My mentor.

"Melinda, it's me. Is he in?"

"Sorry, Harris. Conference call."

"Can you get him out?"

"Not this one."

"C'mon, Melinda . . ."

"Don't even try with the charm, pumpkin. He's pitch-
ing a big client."

"How big?"

"Rhymes with *Bicrosoft*."

Behind me, there's another crunch of gravel. I spin
around to follow the sound. Farther up the driveway, behind a scrubby bunch of bushes.

That's it. I'm gone.

"Wanna leave a message?" Melinda asks.

Not about this. Matthew . . . the FBI . . . It's like a tidal wave, arched above my head, ready to crash down. "Tell him I'm coming by."

"Harris, you're not interrupting this meeting . . ."

"Wouldn't even think it," I say as I shut the phone. I'm already jogging back toward the overpass. It's only a few blocks to First Street. Home of Pasternak & Associates.

10

"NICE TO SEE YOU," Janos said, blowing through the lobby of Pasternak & Associates and throwing a quick wave to the female security guard.

"Can I have you sign in for me?" the guard asked, tapping her finger on the three-ring binder that was open on her desk.

Janos stopped midstep and slowly turned back to the guard. This wasn't the time to make a scene. Better to play it quiet.

"Absolutely," he replied as he approached the desk. With a flick of his pen, he scribbled the name *Matthew Mercer* onto the sign-in sheet.

The guard stared up at the letters *FBI* on Janos's blue and yellow windbreaker. To seal the deal, Janos quickly flashed a shined-up sheriff's badge he got in an old Army-Navy store. When Janos made eye contact, the guard looked away.

"Nice day outside, huh?" the guard asked, staring out through the lobby's enormous plate-glass window.

"Absolutely," Janos repeated as he headed for the elevators. "Pretty as a peach."

11

"NICE TO SEE YOU, BARB," I say, plowing through the lobby of Pasternak & Associates and throwing an air kiss to the security guard.

She grabs the kiss and tosses it aside. Always the same joke. "How's Stevens?" she asks.

"Old and rich. How's . . . how's your hubby?"

"You forgot his name, didn't you?"

"Sorry," I stutter. "Just one of those afternoons."

"Everybody has 'em, sweets." It doesn't make me feel any better. "You here to see Barry?"

I nod as the elevator dings. Barry's on the third floor. Pasternak's on the fourth. Stepping inside, I hit the button marked *4*. The moment the doors close, I slump against the back wall. My smile's gone; my shoulders sag. In my pocket, I fiddle with the page's nametag. The elevator rattles upward. All the way to the top.

With a ping, the doors slide open on the fourth floor, and I squeeze outside into the modern hallway with its recessed lighting. There's a receptionist on my right. I go left. Pasternak's assistant'll never buzz me through. There's no choice but to go around. The hallway ends at a frosted-glass door with a numeric keypad. I've seen Barry enter it a hundred times. I punch in the code, the lock clicks, and I shove my way inside. Just another lobbyist making the rounds.

Decorated like a law firm but with a bit more attitude, the halls of Pasternak & Associates are covered with stylish black-and-white photos of the American flag waving over the Capitol, the White House, and every other monument in the city—anything to show patriotism. The message to potential clients is clear: Pasternak lobbyists embrace the system—and work within it. The ultimate inside job.

Wasting no time, I avoid all offices and make a sharp right toward the back, past the kitchenette. If I'm lucky, Pasternak will still be in the conference room, away from his—

"Harris?" a voice calls out behind me.

I spin back and paint on a fake grin. To my surprise, I don't recognize the face.

"Harris Sandler, right?" he asks again, clearly surprised. His voice creaks like a loose floorboard, and his green hangdog eyes have a silent darkness to them. They lock on to me like a bear trap. Still, the only thing I'm concerned with is the blue and yellow FBI windbreaker he's wearing.

"Can I talk to you a moment?" the man asks as he points me back toward the conference room. "I promise . . . it'll only take a second."

12

Do I know you?" I ask, searching for info.

The man in the FBI windbreaker puts on his own fake smile and rubs his hand along his buzzed salt-and-pepper hair. I know that move. Stevens does it when he meets constituents. A poor attempt to warm things up. "Harris, maybe we should find a place to talk."

"I-I'm supposed to see Pasternak."

"I know. Sounds like he's been a good friend to you." His body language switches in the most imperceptible way. He's smiling, but his chin pitches toward me. I make my living in politics. Most people wouldn't see it. I do.

"Now, do you want to have this discussion in the conference room, or would you rather discuss it in front of the whole firm?" he asks. Ramming his point home, he nods a quick hello to a middle-aged redhead who steps into the kitchenette for some coffee. Talking without saying. Whoever this guy is, he'd be a great Congressman.

"If this is about Matthew . . ."

"It's about more than Matthew," the man interrupts. "What surprises me is Pasternak trying to keep your name out of it."

"I don't know what you're talking about."

"Please, Harris—even a nongambling man would bet against that."

The reference is as subtle as lighting my chest on fire. He doesn't just know about Matthew. He knows about the game. And he wants me to know it.

I stare at him coldly. "Pasternak's in the conference room?"

"Right this way," he says, motioning up the hallway like a fine maître d'. "After you . . ."

I lead the way. He falls in right behind me.

"Sounds like you two have known each other a long time," he says.

"Me and Pasternak, or me and Matthew?"

"Both," he says as he straightens a black-and-white photo of the Supreme Court that's hanging in the hall. He's asking questions, but he doesn't care about the answers.

I glance over my shoulder and give him a quick once-over. Windbreaker . . . gray slacks . . . and chocolate brown calfskin shoes. The pewter logo says they're Ferragamo. I turn back toward the hallway. Nice shoes for government pay.

"Right in here," he says, pointing to the door on my right. Like the one by the elevators, it's frosted glass, which only shows me the blurry outline of Pasternak as he sits in his favorite black leather chair at the center of the long conference table. It's one of Pasternak's first lessons: better to be at the center than the head of the table—if you want something done, you need to be close to all the players.

I grab the doorknob and give it a twist. I'm not surprised Pasternak picked this conference room—it's the biggest one in the firm—but as the door swings open, I am surprised to find that the lights are off. I didn't notice it at first. Except for the fading sunlight from the large bay windows, Pasternak's sitting in the dark.

The door slams behind me, followed by a slight electrical hum. Like a transistor radio being turned on. I spin around just in time to see the man with the hangdog eyes lunging at me. In his hand is a small box that looks like a black brick. I lean back at the last second and raise my arm as a shield. The box slams into my forearm and burns with a sharp bite. Son of a bitch. Did he just stab me?

He expects me to pull away. Instead, I keep the box in my arm and tug him even closer. As he tumbles toward me off balance, I pivot off my back leg and punch him square in the eye. His head snaps back, and he stumbles, crashing into the closed frosted-glass door. The black box flies from his hand and shatters on the floor, scattering batteries along the carpet. The man doesn't go down as easy. Patting his eye with his fingertips, he looks up at me with an admiring grin, almost like he's enjoying himself. You don't get a face like that without taking a few punches, and he's clearly taken better ones than mine. He licks the corner of his mouth and sends me the message. If I plan on doing any damage, I have to do better than that.

"Who taught you how to punch?" his voice creaks as he scoops up the pieces of the black box and slides them in his pocket. "Your dad or your uncle?"

He's trying to show off some knowledge . . . get me emotional. He doesn't have a chance. I've spent over a dozen years on Capitol Hill. When it comes to mental boxing, I've taken on a Congressful of Muhammad Alis. But that doesn't mean I'm gonna risk it all in a fistfight.

He climbs to his feet, and I look around for help. "Buddy!" I call out to Pasternak. He doesn't move. Back by the conference table . . . he's leaning back in his chair. One arm dangles over the armrest. His eyes are wide open. The world blurs as the tears swell in my eyes. I race toward him, then quickly stop short, raising my hands in the air. Don't touch the body.

"Always thinking, aren't you?" Hangdog calls out.

Behind me, I hear the hiss of his blue and yellow windbreaker as he slowly moves toward me. FBI, my ass. I turn to face him, and he tosses out another cocky grin, convinced he's blocking my only way out. I spin back toward the bay window and the patio behind it. The patio. And the door that leads to it.

I dart like a jackrabbit for the glass door at the back of the room. Like before, there's a numeric keypad. Now Hangdog's moving. My hands are shaking as they tap out Barry's code. *"C'mon . . ."* I beg, waiting for the magnetic click. The man races around the conference table, ten steps behind me. The lock pops. I shove the door open, then spin around, trying to slam it shut. If I lock him in—

He jams his hand into the doorway just as it's about to close. There's a sharp crunch. He grits his teeth at the pain but doesn't let go. I slam the door tighter. He glares at me through the glass, his green eyes darker than ever. He still doesn't let go. His knuckles turn purple, he's squeezing the doorframe so tight. He wedges his shoe in the door and starts to push it open. This isn't a stalemate I can win.

I search over my shoulder at the rest of the patio, which is filled with teak Adirondack chairs and matching footrests. During the spring, the patio's used mainly for high-end congressional fund-raisers. Why rent out a room when you can keep it in-house? On my right and left, wood lattices overrun with ivy create false walls for the rooftop. Straight ahead is a stunning view of the Capitol dome—and more important, the other four-story building that sits directly next door. The only thing between the buildings is the seven-foot alley that separates them.

The man winds up for a final burst. As his shoulder pounds into the door, I step away and let it swing wide. He falls to the floor, and I run straight for the edge of the roof.

"You'll never make it!" he calls out.

Again with the mental game. I don't listen. I don't think. I just run. Straight for the edge. I tell myself not to look at the gap, but as I barrel toward it, I don't see anything else. Four stories up. Seven feet wide . . . maybe six if I'm lucky . . . Please let it be six.

Staring dead ahead and sprinting across the terra-cotta pavers, I clench my teeth, step up on the concrete parapet, and launch myself into the air. When I first met Matthew in college, he told me he was tall enough to hurdle the hood of a Volkswagen Beetle. Let's hope the same is true for me.

As I clear the six-foot canyon, I hit the roof of the adjacent building on the heels of my feet and skid forward until I fall back on my ass-bone. A hot lightning bolt of electricity shoots up my spine. Unlike the patio, the roof over here is tar—it burns as I hit. The impact alone kicks a miniwhirlwind of rooftop dust into my lungs, but there's no time to stop. I look back across to the other building. Hangdog is racing at me, about to match my jump.

Scrambling to my feet, I look around for a doorway or stairwell. Nothing in sight. On the opposite ledge, the metal tendrils of a fire escape creep over the parapet like the legs of a spider. Making a mad dash for it, I hop over the ledge, slide down the rusted ladder, and collide with a clang as I hit the top landing of the fire escape. Holding the railing and circling downward, I leap down the stairs half a flight at a time. By the time I'm on the second floor, I hear a loud scratch and feel the whole fire escape vibrate. Up above, the man hits the top landing. He glares down through the grating. I've got a three-floor head start.

With a kick, I unhinge the metal ladder, sending it sliding down toward the sidewalk in the alley. Following right behind it, I shuffle down, my shoes smacking against the concrete. On my left is a dead end. On my right, across the street, is Bullfeathers, one of Capitol Hill's oldest bars. They should be in the heart of happy hour—the perfect time to get lost in a crowd.

As I race into the street, a horn screams, and a silver Lexus screeches to a stop, almost plowing into me. At Bullfeathers, I spot Dan Dutko—easily the town's nicest lobbyist—holding open the door for his entire party.

"Hey, Harris, saw your boss on TV—you're cleaning him up real nice," he calls out with a laugh.

I force a strained grin and elbow my way in front of the group, almost knocking over a woman with dark hair.

"Can I help you?" the hostess asks as I stumble inside.

"Where're the bathrooms?" I blurt. "It's an emergency."

"B-Back and to the right," she says. I'm clearly creeping her out.

Without slowing down, I rush past the bar, toward the back. But I never make a right toward the bathrooms.

Instead, I run straight through the swinging doors of the kitchen, squeeze past the chef at the fryer, duck past a waiter balancing a serving tray full of hamburgers, and leap up the few steps in the very back. With a shove, I ram into the back door and burst outside into the restaurant's back alley. I've eaten here once a week for over a decade. I know where the bathrooms are. But if I'm lucky, when the man bursts into the restaurant and asks the hostess where I went, she'll send him back and to the right. Stuck in the rest rooms.

I jog backward up the alley, my gaze locked on Bullfeathers's back door. Dead silent. Even he's not good enough t—

The door swings open, and the man bounds outside.

We both freeze. Shaking his head at my predictability, he readjusts his windbreaker. Listening carefully, I notice the jingling of keys on my left. Diagonally behind me, a twenty-year-old kid with a pair of headphones is opening the back door to his apartment building.

Hangdog leaps toward me. I leap toward Headphones.

"'Scuse me, kid—sorry," I say, cutting in front of him. As I slide into the building, I grab his keys from the lock and take them inside with me.

"Jackass!" the kid calls out.

Nodding another apology, I slam the thick metal door shut. He's outside with Hangdog. I'm alone in the building. I already hear him pounding his shoulder against the door. Like before, this isn't gonna last.

Behind me, the gray industrial stairwell can take me up or down. From the view at the banister, up leads to the main lobby and the rest of the building. Down goes down one flight and dead-ends at a bike rack. Logic says to go up. It's the clear way out. More important, every instinct

in my gut tells me to go up. Which is exactly why I go
down. Screw logic. Whoever this psychopath is, he's
been in my head long enough.

Descending toward the dead end, I find two empty
mop buckets and seven bikes, one with training wheels
and rainbow streamers on the handlebars. I'm not
MacGyver. Nothing I can use as a weapon. Hopping over
the metal grating of the bike rack, I curl down into a tight
ball and glance up toward the banister. From this angle,
I'm as hidden as I get.

Up above, the door crashes into the concrete wall, and
he enters the stairwell.

He's at the foot of the stairs, making his decision. No
time to check both—for both of us, every second counts.

I hold my breath and shut my eyes. His suede shoes
tickle the concrete as he takes a slight step forward.
There's a swish from his windbreaker. His fingernail taps
quietly against the banister. He's peering over the edge.

Two seconds later, he races for the stairs . . . but with
each step, the sound gets fainter. In the distance, another
metal door slams into a wall. Then silence. He's gone.

But as I finally raise my head and take a breath, I
quickly realize my problems are just beginning.

I try to stand up, but vertigo hits fast. I can barely keep
my balance—adrenaline has long since disappeared. As
I sink back into the corner, my arms sag like rubber bands
at my side. Like Pasternak. And Matthew.

God . . .

Again I shut my eyes. Again they both stare back at
me. They're all I see. Matthew's soft smile and gawky
stride . . . the way Pasternak always cracked his middle
knuckle . . .

Curled into a ball, I can't even look up. I'm right

where I deserve to be. Matthew always put me up on a pedestal. So did Pasternak. But I was never that different. Or any less afraid. I was just more skilled at hiding it.

I turn away toward the training-wheel bike, but all it does is remind me of Pasternak's two-year-old son . . . his wife, Carol . . . Matthew's parents . . . his brothers . . . their lives . . . all ruined . . .

I lick my upper lip, and the taste of salt stings my tongue. It's the first time I notice the tears running down my face.

It was a game. Just a stupid game. But like any other game, all it took was a single dumb move to stop play and remind everyone how easy it is for people to get hurt. Whatever Matthew saw . . . whatever he did . . . the man chasing me is clearly trying to keep it quiet. At any cost. He's not a novice, either. I think back to how he left Matthew. And Pasternak . . . That's why he scooped up the pieces of the black box. When they find his body, there's no reason for anyone to cock an eyebrow. People die at their desks every day.

I shake my head at my new reality. That creepy nut . . . the way he set it all up . . . and that black box, whatever the hell it was. He may not be FBI, but the guy's clearly a professional. And while I'm not sure if he's shutting down the entire game or just our branch, it doesn't take a genius to spot the trend. Pasternak brought me in, and I brought in Matthew. Two down, one to go. And I'm wearing the bull's-eye in the middle.

I curl my knees to my chest and pray it's all a dream. It's not. My friends are dead. And I'm next.

How the hell did this happen? I look around and catch my reflection in the chrome handlebars of the kid's bicycle. It's like staring into a spoon. The whole world's

warped. I can't get out of this myself—not without some
help.

Racing up the stairs and out the back door, I run five
blocks without stopping. Still not sure it's far enough, I
flip open my phone and dial the number for information.

"What city?" the female recorded voice asks.

"Washington, D.C."

"What listing?"

"The U.S. Department of Justice."

I press the phone to my ear as they give me the number. Seven digits later, I have to go through three secre-
taries before I get through.

They pulled their big gun. Time for me to pull mine.

As always, he picks up on the first ring. "I'm here," he
answers.

"It's Harris," I tell him. "I need some help."

"Just tell me where and when. I'm already on my
way . . ."

13

"YOU LOST HIM?"

"Just for the moment," Janos said into his cell phone as he rounded the block outside Bullfeathers. "But he won't—"

"That's not what I asked. What I asked was: Did. You. Lose. Harris?"

Janos stopped midstep, standing in the middle of the street. A man in a maroon Oldsmobile punched his horn, screaming for him to move. Janos didn't budge. Turning his back toward the Oldsmobile, he gripped the phone and took a deep breath. "Yes," he said into his cell. "Yes, Mr. Sauls. I lost him."

Sauls let the silence sink in.

Asshole, Janos thought to himself. He'd seen this last time he worked with Sauls. Big people always felt the need to make big points.

"Are we done?" Janos asked.

"Yes. We're done for now," Sauls replied.

"Good—then stop worrying. I had a long talk with your inside man. I know where Harris lives."

"You really think he's dumb enough to go home?"

"I'm not talking about his *house*," Janos said into the phone. "I've studied him for six months. I know where he *lives*."

As Janos finally stepped toward the sidewalk, the man in the Oldsmobile let go of his horn and slammed the gas. The car lurched forward, then skidded to a stop right next to Janos. The man inside lowered the passenger-side window about halfway. "Learn some manners, dickface!" he yelled from inside.

Craning down toward the car, Janos calmly leaned his arm against the half-open window, which gave slightly from the pressure. His jacket slid open just enough for the man to see Janos's leather shoulder holster and, more important, the nine-millimeter Sig pistol held within it. Janos raised the right corner of his mouth. The man in the Oldsmobile hit the gas as fast as he could. As the wheels spun and the car took off, Janos kept his arm pressed tightly in place, letting his ring scrape against the Oldsmobile as it zipped away.

14

"CAN I GET YOU anything?" the waitress asks.

"Yeah . . . yeah," I say, looking up from the menu, which she thinks I've been reading for far too long. She's only partially right. I *have* been sitting here for fifteen minutes, but the only reason the menu's up is to hide my face.

"I'll take a Stan's Famous," I tell her.

"Howdaya like it?"

"Rare. No cheese . . . and some grilled onions . . ."

The quote on the menu says, "the best damn drink in town," but the only reason I picked Stan's Restaurant is because of its clientele. Located down the block from the offices of the *Washington Post,* Stan's always has a few reporters and editors lurking around. And since most of the deadlines have already passed, the bar's practically packed. I learned my lesson. If something goes wrong, I want witnesses with access to lots of ink.

"Can I take that from you?" the waitress asks, reaching for the menu.

"Actually, I'd rather hold on to it . . . if that's okay."

She smiles and cocks her head at me. "God, your eyes are so green."

"Th-Thank you."

"I'm sorry," she says, catching herself. "I didn't mean . . ."

"It's okay," I tell her. "My wife says the same thing."

She looks down at my hand but doesn't spot a ring. Annoyed, she walks away. This trip isn't about making new friends—it's about seeing old ones . . .

I glance at my wrist and study the front door. I asked him to meet me at nine. Knowing his schedule, I figured he'd be here at nine-fifteen. It's almost nine-thirty. I pick up my phone just to—

The door swings open, and he strolls inside with the limp he got from an old skiing injury. He keeps his head down, hoping to keep a low profile, but at least four people turn and pretend to look away. Now I know who the reporters are.

When I first met Lowell Nash, I was a second-year staffer in charge of the pen-signing machine; he was the chief of staff who wrote my recommendation for Georgetown Law's night division. Three years later, when he went into private practice, I returned the favor by steering a few big donors his way as clients. Two years back, he returned the favor by having his law firm raise fifty thousand dollars for the Senator's reelection campaign. Last year, when the President nominated him as Deputy Attorney General, I returned the favor again by making sure the Senator—a longtime member of the Judiciary Committee—made the confirmation process as smooth as possible. That's how Washington works. Favors returning favors.

Lowell's now the number two person at Justice—one of the highest law enforcement positions in the country. I've known him for over a decade. The favor was last in his court. I need it returned.

"Congressman," he says with a nod.

"Mr. President," I nod back. It's not entirely impossible. At forty-two years old, Lowell's the youngest black man ever to hold his position. That alone gives him a national profile. Like the headline in *Legal Times* read: THE NEXT COLIN POWELL? Playing to the article, he keeps his hair cut short and always sits at perfect attention. He's never been in the military, but he knows the value of looking the part. Like I said, Lowell's on his way—that is, barring some personal disaster.

"You look like crap," he says, folding his black overcoat across the back of the chair and tossing his keys next to my matching phones.

I don't respond.

"Just tell me what happened . . ."

Again, no response.

"C'mon, Harris—talk to me," he pleads.

It's hard to argue. That is what I came for. Eventually, I look up. "Lowell, I need your help."

"Personal or professional help?"

"Law enforcement help."

He folds his hands on the table with his pointer fingers extended up, church-steeple-style.

"How bad is it?" he asks.

"Pasternak's dead."

He nods. News travels fast in this town. Especially when it's your old boss. "I heard it was a heart attack," he adds.

"That's what they're saying?"

This time, he's the one to stay quiet. He turns back toward the reporters, taking a quick scan of the restaurant, then twists back to me. "Tell me about Matthew," he eventually says.

I start to explain but cut myself off. It doesn't make sense. He doesn't know Matthew.

Lowell and I lock eyes. He quickly looks away.

"Lowell, what's going on?"

"Burger—rare," the waitress interrupts, plopping my plate down in front of me with a clang. "Anything for you?" she asks Lowell.

"I'm great . . . thanks."

She gives me one last chance to make good and offer her a smile. When I don't, she drills me with a silent sneer and heads off to another table.

"Lowell, this isn't—" I stop and fight myself to bring it to a whisper. "Lowell, enough with the anxious silent-guy act—this is my life . . ."

He still won't face me. He's staring at the tabletop, fidgeting with the keys on his key ring.

"Lowell, if you know something—"

"They marked you."

"What?"

"You're marked, Harris. If they find you, you're dead."

"What're you talking about? Who's *they?* How do you know them?"

Lowell looks over his shoulder. I thought he was studying the reporters. He's not. He's studying the door.

"You should get out of here," he says.

"I . . . I don't understand. Aren't you gonna help me?"

"Don't you get it, Harris? The game is—"

"You know about the game?"

"Listen to me, Harris. These people are animals."

"But you're my friend," I insist.

His eyes drop back to his key ring, which has a small plastic picture frame on it. He rubs his thumb against the frame, and I give it a closer look. The photo inside the frame is of his wife and four-year-old daughter. They're at the beach with the surf crashing behind them. "We're not all perfect, Harris," he eventually says. "Sometimes, our mistakes hurt more than just ourselves."

My eyes stay glued to the key ring. Whatever they have on Lowell . . . I don't even want to know.

"You should leave," he says for the second time.

The hamburger in front of me goes completely uneaten. Whatever appetite I had is gone. "Do you know the guy who killed Matthew and Pasternak?"

"Janos," he says as his voice cracks. "The man should be in a cage."

"Who does he work for? Are they law enforcement?"

His hands begin to shake. He's starting to unravel. "I'm sorry about your friends . . ."

"Please, Lowell . . ."

"Don't ask me anymore," he begs. Over his shoulder, the same four reporters turn around.

I close my eyes and rest my palms flat against the table. When I open them up, Lowell's staring at his watch. "Go now," he insists. *"Now."*

I give him one last chance. He doesn't take it.

"I'm sorry, Harris."

Standing from my seat, I ignore the trembling in my legs and take a step toward the front door. Lowell grabs me by the wrist. "Not out the front," he whispers, motioning toward the back.

I pause, unsure whether to trust him. It's not like I have a choice. For the second time today, I dart for the kitchen and push my way through the swinging door.

"You can't go back there," the waitress snips at me.

I ignore her. Sure enough, beyond the sinks, there's an open door in the back. I sprint outside, hurtle up the

concrete steps and keep running, making two sharp rights
down the poorly lit alley. A black rat scrambles in front of
me, but it's the least of my worries. Whoever these people are—how the hell could they move so fast? A biting
pain pinches me at the base of my neck, and the world
swirls for the slightest of seconds. I need to sit down . . .
gather my thoughts . . . find a place to hide. My brain
flips through the short list of people I can count on. But
after watching Lowell's reaction, it's clear that whoever
Janos is working for, they're drilling through my life.
And if they can get to someone as big as Lowell . . .

Straight ahead, a passing ambulance whips up
Vermont Avenue. The sirens are deafening as they rever-
berate through the canyon of the brick alleyway.
Instinctively I reach for one of my phones. I pat all my
pockets. Damn . . . don't tell me I left them in the—

I stop and turn around. The table of the restaurant. No.
I can't go back.

Double-checking to be sure, I stuff my hand inside the
breast pocket of my jacket. There's actually something
there, but it's not a phone.

I open my palm and reread the name off the blue plastic nametag:

Senate Page
Viv Parker

The white letters practically glow in front of me. In the
distance, the siren of the ambulance fades. It's gonna be
a long night ahead, but as I turn the corner and run up
Vermont Avenue, I know exactly where I'm going.

15

OUTSIDE STAN'S RESTAURANT, Lowell Nash slowly scanned the sidewalks up and down Vermont Avenue. He stared at the shadows in the doorways of every storefront. He even studied the homeless man sleeping on the bus-stop bench across the street. But as he turned the corner onto L Street, he couldn't spot a twitch of movement. Even the air hung flat in the night. Picking up speed, he rushed toward his car, which was parked halfway up the block.

Again Lowell checked the sidewalks, the doorways, and the bus-stop benches. If his recent notoriety taught him anything, it was never to take chances. Approaching the silver Audi, he scrambled for his car key, pressed a button, and heard the doors unlock. He gave one last glance to his surroundings, then slipped inside and slammed the door shut.

"Where the hell is he?" Janos asked from the passenger seat.

Lowell yelled out loud, jumping so fast, he banged his funny bone against the car door.

"Where's Harris?" Janos demanded.

"I was . . ." He grabbed his funny bone, holding it in pain. "Aaah . . . I was wondering the same about you."

"What're you talking about?"

"I've been waiting for almost an hour. He finally got up and left."

"He was already here?"

"And gone," Lowell replied. "Where were you?"

Janos's forehead wrinkled in anger. "You said ten o'clock," he insisted.

"I said nine."

"Don't bullshit me."

"I swear, I said nine."

"I heard you say—" Janos cut himself off. He studied Lowell carefully. The sting from the funny bone was long past, but Lowell was still crouched over, cradling his elbow and refusing to make eye contact. If Janos could see Lowell's expression, he'd also see the panic on Lowell's face. Lowell may be weak, but he wasn't an asshole. Harris was still a friend.

"Don't fuck with me," Janos warned.

Lowell quickly looked up, his eyes wide with fear. "Never . . . I'd never do that . . ."

Janos narrowed his glance, studying him carefully.

"I swear to you," Lowell added.

Janos continued to stare. A second passed. Then two.

Janos's arm sprang out like a wildcat, palming Lowell by the face and slamming his head back into the driver's-side window. Refusing to let go, Janos pulled back and smashed him against the glass again. Lowell grabbed Janos's wrist, fighting to break his grip. Janos didn't stop. With a final shove, he put all his weight behind it. The window finally cracked from the impact, leaving a jagged vein zigzagging across the glass.

Slumped down in his seat, Lowell held his head from the pain. He felt a trickle of blood skating down the back of his neck. "A-Are you nuts?"

Without saying a word, Janos opened the door and stepped into the warm night air.

It took Lowell twenty minutes to get his bearings. When he got home, he told his wife some kid on Sixteenth Street threw a rock at the car.

16

"THERE—HE'S DOING it again," Viv Parker said Monday afternoon, pointing to the elderly Senator from Illinois.

"Where?"

"Right *there* . . ."

Across the Floor of the Senate, in the third row of antique desks, the senior Senator from Illinois looked down, away from Viv.

"Sorry, still don't see it," Devin whispered as the gavel banged behind them.

As pages for the United States Senate, Viv and Devin sat on the small carpeted steps on the side of the rostrum, literally waiting for the phone to blink. It never took long. Within a minute, a low buzz erupted from the phone, and a small orange light hiccuped to life. But neither Viv nor Devin picked it up.

"Floor, this is Thomas," a blond-headed page with a Virginia twang answered as he shot to his feet. Viv wasn't sure why he stood up for every call. When she asked Thomas, he said it was part for decorum, part to be prepared in case he had to spot a passing Senator. Personally, Viv thought there was only one "part" that really mattered: to show off the fact that he was head page. Even at the bottom of the totem pole, hierarchy was king.

"Yep—I'm on it," the head page said into the receiver. As he hung up the phone, he looked over to Viv and Devin. "They need one," he explained.

Nodding, Devin stood from his seat at the rostrum and dashed off toward the cloakroom.

Still on the rostrum, Viv glanced over at the Senator from Illinois, who again raised his head and leveled a leering glare directly at her. Viv tried to look away, but she couldn't ignore it. It was as if he were squinting straight through her chest. Fidgeting with the Senate ID around her neck, she wondered if that's what he was staring at. It wouldn't surprise her. The ID was her ticket in. From day one, she was worried someone would step in and snatch it back. Or maybe he was staring at her cheap navy suit . . . or the fact that she was black . . . or that she was taller than most pages, including the boys. Five feet ten and a half inches—and that was without her beat-up shoes and the close-cropped Afro that she wore just like her mom's.

The phone buzzed quietly behind her. "Floor, this is Thomas," the head page said as he shot to his feet. "Yep—I'm on it." He turned to Viv as he hung up the phone. "They need one . . ."

Nodding, Viv stood from her seat but carefully stared down at the blue-carpeted floor in a final attempt to avoid the glance of the Senator from Illinois. Her skin color, she could handle. Same with her height—like her mom taught, don't apologize for what God gave you. But if it was her suit, as stupid as it sounded, well . . . some things hit home. Since the day they started, all twenty-nine of her fellow pages loved to complain about the uniform requirement. Every Senate page bitched about it. Everyone but Viv. As she knew from her school back in Michigan, the only people who moan about required uniforms are the ones who can compete in the fashion show.

"Move it, Viv—they need someone now," the head page called out from the rostrum.

Viv didn't bother to look back. In fact, as she rushed toward the cloakroom in the back of the chamber, she didn't look anywhere but straight down. Still feeling the Senator's stare burning through her, and refusing to risk eye contact, she speed-marched up the center aisle—but as she blew past row after row of antique desks, she couldn't ignore the haunting voice in the back of her head. It was the same voice she had heard when she was eleven and Darlene Bresloff stole her RollerBlades . . . and when she was thirteen and Neil Grubin purposely squirted maple syrup all over her church clothes. It was a strong, unflinching voice. It was her mom's voice. The same mom who made Viv march up to Darlene and demand her RollerBlades back *now* . . . and who, as Viv begged and pleaded to the contrary, personally carried the maple-syrup-covered suit back to Neil's house, up the three flights of stairs, and into the living room, so Neil's mother—whom they'd never met before—could see it for herself. That's whose voice was echoing in the back of her head. And that's the voice she heard halfway up the aisle . . . with the Senator dead ahead.

Maybe I should just say something, Viv decided. Nothing rude, like *What're you looking at?* No, this was still a United States Senator. No reason to be stupid. Better to go with simple: *Hi there, Senator* . . . or *Nice to see you, Senator* . . . or something like . . . like . . . *Can I help you?* There we go. *Can I help you?* Simple but straightforward. Just like Momma.

With less than twenty feet to go, Viv raised her chin just enough to make sure the Senator was still there. He hadn't moved from behind the hundred-year-old desk. His eyes were still on her. Within two steps, Viv's pace slowed imperceptibly, and she again gripped the ID as it dangled from her neck. Her thumbnail flicked at the back of the ID badge, scratching at the piece of Scotch tape that held the cutout picture of her mom in place. Viv's photo on front, Momma on back. It was only fair, Viv had thought the day she Scotch-taped it there. Viv didn't get to the Senate alone; she shouldn't be there alone. And with Mom resting on her chest . . . well . . . everyone hides their strength in a different place.

Ten feet ahead of her, at the end of the aisle, the Senator stood his ground. *Vivian, don't you dare back down,* she could hear her mom warn. *Stay positive.* Viv tightened her jaw and got her first glimpse of the Senator's shoes. All she had to do was look up and say the words. *Can I help you? . . . Can I help you? . . .* She replayed them in her head. Her thumbnail continued to scratch at the back of her ID. *Stay positive.* She was close enough to see the cuff on the Senator's slacks. *Just look up,* she told herself. *Stay positive.* And with one final deep breath, Viv did just that. Steeling herself, she lifted her head, locked on to the Senator's deep-gray eyes . . . and quickly looked back down at the dark blue carpet.

"Excuse me," Viv whispered as she ducked slightly and sidestepped around him. The Senator didn't even look down as she passed. Leaving the aisle and heading across the back of the chamber, Viv finally let go of her ID . . . and felt it slap against her chest.

"Got one for you, Viv," Blutter announced as she pulled open the glass-paned door and smelled the familiar stale air of the cloakroom. Originally designed to store Senators' coats when they had business on the Floor, the cloakroom was still a cramped, tiny space. She didn't have to go far to reach Blutter.

"Is it close?" Viv asked, already exhausted.

"S-414-D," Blutter said from his seat behind the main cloakroom desk. Of the four full-time staffers who answered phones in the cloakroom, Ron Blutter was the youngest at twenty-two, which was also why he was the designated cloakroom boss in charge of the page program. Blutter knew it was a crap job—keeping track of his party's puberty-ridden sixteen- and seventeen-year-olds—but at least it was better than being a page.

"They asked for you personally," Blutter added. "Something to do with your sponsor's office."

Viv nodded. The only way to get a job as a page was to be sponsored by a Senator, but as the only black page in the entire page program, she was well accustomed to the fact that there were other requirements of the job besides delivering packages. "Another photo op?" she asked.

"I'm guessing." Blutter shrugged as Viv signed herself out on the locator sheet. "Though from the room number . . . maybe it's just a reception."

"Yeah, I'm sure." Behind her, the door to the cloakroom opened, and the Senator from Illinois lumbered inside, heading straight for the old wooden phone booths that lined the narrow L-shaped room. As always, Senators were tucked into the booths, returning calls and gabbing away. The Senator stepped into the first booth on the right and slid the door shut.

"By the way, Viv," Blutter added as his phone started to ring, "don't let Senator Spooky creep you out. It's not you—it's him. Whenever he prepares for a Floor speech, he stares through everyone like they're a ghost."

"No, I know . . . I just—"

"It's not you. It's him," Blutter reiterated. "You hear me? It's him."

Lifting her chin, Viv pushed her shoulders back and buttoned her blue suit jacket. Her ID dangled from around her neck. She headed for the door as quickly as she could. Blutter went back to the phones. There was no way she'd let him see the smile on her face.

S-414-B . . . S-414-C . . . S-414-D . . . Viv counted to herself as she followed the room numbers on the fourth floor of the Capitol. She hadn't realized that Senator Kalo had offices up here, but that was typical Capitol—everyone scattered all over the place. Remembering the story about the female staffer giving new meaning to the term *briefing the Senator,* she stopped at the heavy oak door and gave it a sharp knock. Truth be told, she knew the story was bullshit—just something Blutter told them so they'd watch their manners. Indeed, a few staffers may've had some fun, but from the looks of the rest . . . the stiffness she saw in the halls . . . none of these people were having sex.

Waiting for a response, she was surprised not to find one.

She knocked again. Just to be safe.

Again, no answer.

With a twist, she opened the door a tiny crack. "Senate page," she announced. "Anyone here . . . ?"

Still no response. Viv didn't think twice. If a staffer was

tracking down the Senator for a photo op, they'd want her just to take a seat by the desk. But as Viv entered the dark office, there wasn't an open seat. In fact, there wasn't even a desk. Instead, at the center of the room were two large mahogany tables, pushed together so they could hold the dozen or so outdated computer monitors piled on top. On her left, three red leather rolling chairs were stacked one on top of the other, while on her right, empty file cabinets, storage boxes, a few spare computer keyboards, and even an upside-down refrigerator were shoved together in a makeshift pile. The walls were bare. No pictures . . . no diplomas . . . nothing personal. This wasn't an office. More like storage. From the layer of dust that covered the half-lowered blinds, the place was clearly deserted. In fact, the only evidence that anyone had even been in there was the handwritten note on the edge of the conference table:

Please pick up the phone

At the bottom of the note was an arrow pointing to the right, where a telephone sat atop one of the open file cabinets.

Confused, Viv raised an eyebrow, unsure why someone would—

The phone rang, and Viv jumped back, bumping into the closed door. She searched around the room. No one there. The phone rang again.

Viv reread the note and cautiously stepped forward. "H-Hello," she answered, picking up the receiver.

"Hello, who's this?" a warm voice countered.

"Who's this?" Viv countered.

"Andy," the man answered. "Andy Defresne. Now, who's this?"

"Viv."

"Viv who?"

"Viv Parker," she replied. "Is this . . . Is this some kinda joke? Thomas, is that you?"

There was a click. The phone went dead.

Viv hung up the receiver and looked up to check the corners of the ceiling. She saw something like this on *Bloopers and Practical Jokes* once. But there wasn't a camera anywhere. And the longer Viv stood there, the more she knew she'd already been there too long.

Spinning around, she rushed to the door and clutched the doorknob in her sweat-covered hand. She fought to turn it, but it wouldn't budge—like someone was holding it from the outside. She gave it one last twist, and it finally gave. But as the door swung open, she stopped in her tracks. A tall man with messy black hair was blocking her way.

"Viv, huh?" the man asked.

"I swear, you touch me, and I'll scream so loud, it'll make your nuts shatter like crystal . . . uh . . . like crystal balls."

"Relax," Harris said as he stepped inside. "All I want to do is talk to you."

17

I SEARCH FOR A NAMETAG on the girl's lapel. It's not there. Reading my reaction, she's obviously scared. I don't blame her. After what happened with Matthew, she should be.

"Stay back," she threatens. Stepping backward into the room, she takes a deep breath, winding up to scream. I raise my hand to cut her off; then, out of nowhere, she tilts her head to the side.

"What a minute . . ." she says, raising an eyebrow. "I *know* you."

I match her raised eyebrow with one of my own. "Excuse me?"

"From that . . . from the speech you gave. With the pages . . ." She bumps back into the edge of the conference table and looks up at me. "You were . . . you were really good. That bit about making the right enemies . . . I thought about that for a week."

She's trying to sweet-talk. My guard's already up.

"And then when you . . ." She cuts herself off, staring at her feet.

"What?" I ask.

"That thing you did with the Lorax . . ."

"I don't know what you're talking about."

"Nu-uh . . . c'mon—you put that pin on Congressman Enemark. That was . . . that was the coolest thing ever."

Like I said, my guard's up. But as I spot the wide-eyed smile on her face, I'm already starting to second-guess. At first glance, she's slightly imposing, and it's not just from the dark navy suit that adds another year or two to her age. Her height alone . . . almost five feet eleven . . . she's taller than me. But the longer she stands there, the more I see the rest of the picture. Back against the table, she slumps her shoulders and lowers her neck. It's the same trick Matthew used to use to make himself look shorter.

"He never found out, did he?" she asks, suddenly hesitant. "About the Lorax, I mean?"

She's trying not to push, but excitement's getting the best of her. At first, I assumed it was all an act. Now I'm not so sure. I narrow my eyes, studying even closer. The frayed stitching on her suit . . . the worn creases in her white shirt . . . She's definitely not from money, and the way she's fidgeting and trying to hide a loose button, it's still an issue for her. It's hard enough to fit in when you're seventeen; it's even worse when everyone around you is at least a decade or two older. Still, her mocha brown eyes have a real age to them. I'm guessing early independence from the lack of cash—either that or she's getting the Oscar for best actress. Only way to find out which is to get her talking. "Who told you about the Lorax?" I ask.

She shyly turns away at the question. "You can't tell him I told you, okay? Please promise . . ." She's truly embarrassed.

"You have my word," I add, pretending to play along.

"It was LaRue . . . from the bathroom."

"The shoeshine guy?"

"You promised you wouldn't say anything. It's just . . . we saw him in the elevator . . . He was laughing, and Nikki and I asked what's so funny and he said it, but no one's supposed to know. He swore us to secrecy . . ." The words tumble from her mouth like she's confessing a junior high school crush. There's a hint of panic behind each syllable, though. She takes trust seriously.

"You're not mad, are you?" she asks.

"Why would I be mad?" I reply, hoping to keep her talking.

"No . . . no reason . . ." She cuts herself off, and her wide-eyed smile returns. "But can I just say . . . putting that Lorax on him . . . that's easily, without exaggeration, *the greatest prank of all time!* And Enemark's the perfect Member to do it to—not just for the prank part, but just the principle of it," she adds, her voice picking up steam. She's all gush and idealism. There's no slowing her down. "My granddad . . . he was one of the last Pullman Porters, and he used to tell us if we didn't pick the right fights—"

"Do you have any idea how much trouble you're in?" I blurt.

She finally hits the brakes. "Wha?"

I forgot what it was like to be seventeen. Zero to sixty, and sixty to zero, all in one breath.

"You know what I'm talking about," I say.

Her mouth gapes open. "Wait," she stutters as she starts fingering the ID around her neck. "Is this about the Senate pens Chloe stole? I told her not to touch 'em, but she kept saying if they were in the cup—"

"Lose anything lately?" I ask, pulling her blue nametag from my pocket and holding it out between us.

She's definitely surprised. "How'd you get that?"

"How'd you lose it?"

"I have . . . I have no idea . . . it disappeared last week—they just ordered me a new one." Whether she's lying or serious, she's not stupid. If she's really in trouble, she wants to know how much. "Why? Where'd you find it?"

I bluff hard. "Toolie Williams gave it to me," I say, referring to the young black kid who drove his car into Matthew.

"Who?"

I have to clench my jaw to keep myself calm. I reach once more into my pocket and pull out a folded-up picture of Toolie from this morning's Metro section. He's got big ears and a surprisingly kind grin. I almost tear the picture in half as I struggle to unfold it.

"Ever seen him before?" I ask, handing her the photo. She shakes her head. "I don't think so . . ."

"You sure about that? He's not a boyfriend? Or some kid you know from—"

"Why? Who is he?"

There're forty-three muscular movements that the human face is capable of making. I have friends, Senators, and Congressmen lie directly to me every day. Pull the bottom lip in, raise the upper eyelids, lower the chin. By now, I know all the tricks. But for the life of me, as I stare up at this tall black girl with the tight-cropped Afro, I can't find a single muscle twitch that shows me anything but seventeen-year-old innocence.

"Wait a minute," she interrupts, now laughing. "Is this another prank? Did Nikki put you up to this?" She flips her blue nametag over as if she's searching for the Lorax. "What'd you do, rig it with ink so it'll spray all over the next Senator I talk to?"

Leaning forward, she takes a cautious look at the nametag. Around her neck, her ID badge begins to twirl. I spot a photo of a black woman Scotch-taped to the back. I'm guessing Mom or an aunt. Someone who keeps her strong—or at least is trying to.

I once again study Viv. No makeup . . . no trendy jewelry . . . no fancy haircut—none of the totems of popularity. Even those slumped shoulders . . . There's a girl like her in every school—the outsider looking in. In five years, she'll kick off her shell, and her classmates will wonder why they never noticed her. Right now, she sits in the back of the class, watching in silence. Just like Matthew. Just like me. I shake my head to myself. No way this girl's a killer.

"Listen, Viv . . ."

"The only thing I don't understand is who this Toolie guy is," she says, still giggling. "Or did Nikki put you up to that, too?"

"Don't worry about Toolie. He just . . . he's just someone who knew a friend of mine."

Now she's confused. "So what's it have to do with my nametag?"

"Actually, I'm trying to figure that out myself."

"Well, what's the name of your friend?"

I decide to give it one last shot. "Matthew Mercer."

"Matthew Mercer? Matthew Mercer," she says again. "How do I know that name?"

"You don't; you just—"

"Waitaminute," she interrupts. "Isn't that the guy who got hit by the car?"

I reach out and snatch the newspaper photo from her hands.

Now she's the one studying me. "Is he the one who had my nametag?"

I don't answer.

"Why would he . . . ?" She stops herself, noticing my stare. "If it makes you feel better, I don't know how he got it. I mean, I understand you're upset about your friend's accident . . ."

I look up as she says the word *accident*. She locks right on me. Her mouth hangs open, revealing her age— but her eyes show something different. She's got depth in her gaze.

"What?" she asks.

I turn away, pretending to follow an imaginary sound.

"It was an accident, wasn't it?"

"Okay, everybody calm down," I say, forcing a laugh. "Listen, you should really get going, Viv. That's your name, right? Viv? Viv, I'm Harris." I extend a soft handshake and put my other hand on her shoulder. That one I got from the Senator. People don't talk when they're being touched. She doesn't budge. But she still stares at me with those mocha eyes.

"Was it an accident or not?" she asks.

"Of course it was an accident. I'm sure it was an accident. Positive. I just . . . when Matthew was hit by the car, your nametag happened to be in one of the Dumpsters near the scene. That's it. No big deal—nothing to panic about. I just figured if you saw anything . . . I promised his family I'd ask around. Now we at least know it was just something in the nearby trash."

It's a pretty good speech and would work on ninety-nine percent of the populace. The problem is, I still can't tell if this girl is in the top one percent. Eventually, though, I get lucky. She nods, looking relieved. "So you're okay? You got everything you need?"

In the ten minutes since I've met her, it's the hardest question she's asked. When I woke up this morning, I thought Viv would have all the answers. Instead, I'm back to another blank slate—and right now, the only way to fill the chalkboard is to figure out who else is playing the game. Matthew's got files in his office . . . I've got notes in my desk . . . time to dig through the rest of the mess. The thing is, Janos isn't stupid. The moment I try to step back into my life, he'll stab his little shock box straight into my chest. I already tried calling in friends . . . Only a fool would risk that again. I glance around the tiny room, but there's no way to avoid it—I don't have a chance. Not unless I figure out how to make myself invisible . . . or get some help in that department.

"Thanks again for finding the nametag," Viv interrupts. "Let me know if I can ever return the favor."

I jerk my head toward her and replay the words in my head.

It's not the safest bet I've ever made, but right now, with my life on the line, I don't think I've got much of a choice. "Listen, Viv, I hate to be a pain, but . . . were you really serious about that favor?"

"S-Sure . . . but does it have to do with Matthew, because . . ."

"No, no—not at all," I insist. "It's just a quick errand—for an upcoming hearing we're working on. You'll be in and out in two minutes. Sound okay?"

Without a word, Viv scans the room around us, from the multiple keyboards to the stack of discarded office chairs. It's the one flaw in my story. If everything were truly kosher, why're we talking in a storage room?

"Harris, I don't know . . ."

"It's just a pickup—no one'll even know you're there. All you have to do is grab one file and—"

"We're not supposed to do pickups unless they come through the cloakroom . . ."

"Please, Viv—it's just one file."

"I'm sorry about your friend."

"I told you, it has nothing to do with Matthew."

She looks down, noticing the stitching in the knee of my suit. I had a local dry cleaner sew up the hole from yesterday's leap off the building. But the scar's still there. Her hand goes back to fidgeting with her ID. "I'm sorry," she says, her voice breaking slightly. "I can't."

Knowing better than to beg, I wave it off and force a smile. "No, I understand. No big deal."

When I was seventeen years old, the moment a thought came into my head, it came out of my mouth. To Viv's credit, she stays perfectly silent. She opens the door, her body still halfway in the room. "Listen, I should . . ."

"You should go," I agree.

"But if you—"

"Viv, don't sweat it. I'll just call the cloakroom—it'll be done in no time."

She nods, staring right through me. "I really am sorry about your friend."

I nod a thank-you.

"So I guess I'll see you around the Capitol?" she asks.

I force another smile. "Absolutely," I say. "And if you ever need anything, just call my office."

She likes that one. "And don't forget," she adds,

lowering her voice in her best impression of me, "the best thing you can do in life is make the right enemies . . ."

"No doubt about that," I call out as the door closes. She's gone, and my voice tumbles to a whisper. "No doubt about it."

18

Heading up the fourth-floor hallway as the door slammed behind her, Viv told herself not to look back. However her nametag had gotten there, all she needed was to see the desperate look on Harris's face to know where this was headed. When she first saw him speak to the pages, he'd glided through the room so smoothly, she was tempted to look at his feet to see if they touched the ground. Even today, she still wasn't sure of the answer. And it wasn't just because of his charm. At her church in Michigan, she'd seen plenty of charm. But Harris had something more.

Of the four speakers who welcomed the pages during orientation, two gave warnings, one gave advice . . . and Harris . . . Harris gave them a challenge. Not just as pages, but as people. As he'd said, it was the first rule of politics: Don't count even the smallest person out. When the words left his lips, the entire room sat up straight. Yet today, what she just saw in that room—today, the man who had the balls to give that speech—that man was long gone. Today, Harris was shaken . . . on edge . . . Without a doubt, his confidence was broken. Whatever had hit him, it'd clearly cracked him in the sternum.

Picking up her pace, Viv rushed toward the elevator. It didn't take a lifetime in politics to see the hurricane coming, and right now, the last thing she needed was to step inside the whirlwind. *Not your problem,* she told herself. *Just keep going.* But as she pressed the call button for the elevator, she couldn't help it. With a sharp pivot, she took a fast glance at Harris's door. Still shut. No surprise. From the ashen look on his face, he wouldn't be coming out for a bit.

A hushed rumble broke the silence, and the door to the elevator slid open, revealing the elevator operator—a dark-skinned black woman with cobwebs of gray hair at her temples. From her wooden stool in the elevator, she looked up at Viv and lifted an eyebrow at her height.

"Momma fed you the good stuff, huh?" the operator asked.

"Yeah . . . I guess . . ."

Without another word, the operator raised her newspaper in front of her face. Viv was used to it by now. From high school to here, it was never easy fitting in.

"Home base?" the operator asked from behind the paper.

"Sure," Viv answered with a shrug.

The operator turned away from her paper, studying Viv's reaction. "Crappy day, huh?"

"More like a weird one."

"Look at the good side: Today we got taco salad bar at lunch," the operator said, turning back to her paper as the elevator lurched downward.

Viv nodded a thank-you, but it went unnoticed.

Without looking back, the operator added, "Don't sulk, sweetie—your face'll stick and all that."

"I'm not . . . I—" Viv cut herself off. If she'd learned

anything in the past few weeks, it was the benefit of staying quiet. It was the one thing her family always tried to teach—from her dad's work in the military to her mom's job in the dental practice, she knew the value of keeping her mouth shut and ears open. Indeed, it was one of the reasons Viv got the job in the first place. A year ago, as her mom was hunched over the dental chair, a patient in a pinstriped suit was having his wisdom teeth taken out ASAP. If she hadn't been listening to the mumbled small talk, she'd never have heard that the patient was Senator Kalo from Michigan—one of the oldest proponents of the page program. Four impacted teeth later, the Senator walked out with Viv's name in his suit pocket. That was all it took to change her life: one kind favor from a stranger.

Leaning against the back railing of the elevator, Viv read the newspaper over the elevator operator's shoulder. Another Supreme Court Justice was stepping down. The President's daughter was once again in trouble. But none of it seemed important. On the floor, the rest of the newspaper was tucked below the wooden stool. The Metro section was on top. Viv's eyes went right to the headline: *Hit-and-Run Driver's Identity Released.* Below the headline was the photo Harris just showed her. The young black man with the soft smile. Toolie Williams. Viv couldn't take her eyes off him. For some reason, her nametag was found near a dead man. Even the very best reason couldn't be good.

"Can I borrow this a sec?" she asked as she bent down and grabbed the paper from under the stool. Her eyes narrowed as she pulled it close. The photo blurred into a forest of gray dots. With a blink, it snapped back—and Toolie Williams was once again staring straight at her.

Her thoughts rolled back to the Senator. That was all it took to change her life. One kind favor from a stranger.

"Here you go," the elevator operator announced as the elevator bucked to a halt and the door creaked open. "Second floor . . ."

From the moment Viv lowered her head to duck past the Senator from Illinois and his leering glare, she could hear her mother's insistent scolding in the back of her brain. *Stand up for yourself. Always stand up for yourself.* That was part of the reason Momma had wanted her to come to Capitol Hill. But right now, as Viv looked down at the grainy photo in the newspaper, she realized Mom only had part of the picture. It's not just about standing up for yourself—it's also about standing up for those who need it.

"This your stop or not?" the operator asked.

"Actually, I forgot something upstairs," Viv replied.

"You're the boss lady. Fourth floor it is—up, up, and away . . ."

Squeezing outside the elevator the moment the door opened, Viv rushed up the hallway, hoping she wasn't too late. Her oversized suit jacket fanned out behind her as she ran. If she missed him now . . . No. She didn't want to think it. Stay positive. Stay positive.

"Sorry . . . coming through . . ." she called out, cutting between two male staffers, each carrying a redwell accordion file.

"Slow down," the taller of them warned.

Typical, Viv thought. Everyone likes to boss around the pages. Instinctively she slowed her pace to a calm walk—but within two steps, she looked back at the two men. They were just staffers. Sure, she was a page, but . . . they were just staffers. Picking up speed, she started to run. It felt even better than she thought.

At the end of the hall, she stopped short, made sure the hallway was empty, and knocked on the door.

"It's me!" she called out.

No answer.

"Harris, it's Viv. You in there?"

Again, no reply. She tried the doorknob. It didn't budge. Locked.

"Harris, it's an emergency . . . !"

There was a click. The doorknob turned, and the heavy door flew open. Harris stuck his head out, cautiously checking the hallway.

"You okay?" he finally asked.

Wiping her palm against her pant leg, Viv reasked herself the question. If she wanted to walk away, this was her chance. She could feel her ID dangling from her neck. She never reached for it. Not once. Instead, she stared Harris straight in the eye.

"I . . . uh . . . I just . . . you still need help with that pickup?"

Harris tried to hide his grin, but even he wasn't good enough to pull it off. "It's not gonna be as easy as you think. Are you sure you can—?"

"Harris, I'm one of two black girls in an all-white school, and I'm the dark-skinned one. One year, they broke into my locker and wrote *nigger* across the back of my gym shirt. How much harder can it get? Now tell me where to go before I get all skeezed out and change my mind."

19

STARING AT THE sheet of paper taped to the side of the cloakroom's stainless steel refrigerator, Viv followed her pointer finger up the alphabetical list of Senators. Ross . . . Reissman . . . Reed. Behind her, out on the Senate Floor, Senator Reed from Florida was delivering yet another speech on the importance of the rent-to-own industry. For Reed, it was the perfect way to get his pro-business ratings up. For Viv, it was the perfect moment to bring the long-winded speaker some water. Whether he wanted it or not.

Scanning the water chart one last time, she read through the three columns: *Ice, No Ice,* and *Saratoga Seltzer.* Viv still saw it as one of the Senate's best perks of power. They didn't just know how you liked your coffee. They knew how you liked your water. According to the chart, Reed was a no-ice guy. *Figures,* Viv thought.

Anxious to get moving, she pulled a bottle of water from the fridge, poured it into a chilled glass, and made her way out to the Senate Floor. Senator Reed hadn't asked for any water, nor did he raise his hand to summon a page. But Viv was all too aware of how security in the page program worked. Indeed, with so many seventeen-year-olds working alongside grown staffers, the program made sure that every page was always accounted for. If Viv wanted to disappear for an hour or so, the best way was to pretend it was work-related.

As Viv placed the water next to the Senator's lectern, the Senator, as usual, ignored her. Smiling to herself, she still leaned in close—just long enough to make it look real—as if she were getting directions. Spinning around with newfound purpose, Viv marched back to the cloakroom and headed straight for the head of the page program's desk.

"Reed just asked me to run an errand," she announced to Blutter, who was, as usual, dealing with another call. Flipping through the locator sheet on the desk, Viv signed herself out. Under *Destination,* she wrote *Rayburn*—the farthest building in the Capitol complex where Senate page deliveries were still allowed. That alone bought her at least an hour. And an hour was all it would take.

Within five minutes, Viv pushed open the burled-walnut door of the House cloakroom. "Here for a pickup," she had told the security guard. He buzzed her right in. As she stepped into the cloakroom, she was smacked in the face with the steamy smell of hot dogs. Further up on her left, she followed the smell to the small crush of Members and staff crowded in front of a tiny lunch counter, the source of the hot dog smell. Forget cigars and other backroom clichés—on the House side of the Capitol, this was the real cloakroom whiff. And in that one sniff, Viv saw the subtle but inescapable difference: Senators got catered ice preferences; House Members fought for their own hot dogs. The Millionaire Club versus the House of the People. One nation, under God.

"Can I help you?" a female voice asked as she made her way out to the House Floor.

Turning around, she saw a petite young woman with frizzy blond hair sitting behind a dark wood desk.

"I'm looking for the page supervisor," Viv explained.

"I prefer the term *sovereign*," the woman quipped just seriously enough to leave Viv wondering if it was a joke. Before she could comment, the phone on the woman's desk rang, and she pounced for the receiver. "Cloakroom," she announced. "Yep . . . room number? . . . I'll send one right now . . ." Waving a single finger in the air, she signaled the pages who sat on the mahogany benches near her desk. A second later, a seventeen-year-old Hispanic boy in gray slacks and a navy sport coat hopped out of his seat.

"Ready to run, A.J.?" the woman asked as the boy gave Viv the once-over. Seeing her suit, he added an almost unnoticeable sneer. Suit instead of sport coat. Even at the page level, it was House versus Senate. "Pickup in Rayburn B-351-C," the woman added.

"Again?" the page moaned. "Haven't these people ever heard of E-mail?"

Ignoring the complaint, the woman turned back to Viv. "Now what can I help you with?" she asked.

"I work over in the Senate—"

"Clearly," the woman said.

"Yeah, well . . . we . . . uh . . . we were wondering if you guys keep track of your page deliveries. We have a Senator who got a package last week and swears he gave the page another envelope on the way out—but naturally, since he's a Senator, he has no idea if the page was House or Senate. We all look alike, y'know."

The woman smiled at the joke, and Viv breathed a sigh of relief. She was finally in.

"All we keep is the current stuff," the woman said, motioning to the sign-out sheet. "Everything else goes in the trash."

"So you don't have anything before . . ."

"Today. That's it. I trash it every night. To be honest, it's only there to keep track of you guys. If one of you disappears—well, you know what happens when you let seventeen-year-olds run around with a room-full of Congressmen . . ." Tilting her head back, the woman snorted loudly through her nose.

Viv was dead silent.

"Relax, honey—just some page humor."

"Yeah," Viv said, forcing a strained grin. "Listen, uh . . . can I make some copies of these? At least that way we show him something."

"Help yourself," the woman with the frizzy hair said. "Whatever makes your life easy . . ."

20

Stuck in the storage room and waiting for Viv, I hold the receiver to my ear as I dial the number.

"Congressman Grayson's office," a young man with a flat South Dakota accent eventually answers. Gotta give Grayson points for that. Whenever a constituent calls, the receptionist is the first voice they hear. For that reason alone, smart Congressmen make sure their front office people always have the right accent.

Looking past the stack of chairs in the storage room, I grip the receiver and give the receptionist just enough of a pause to make him think I'm busy. "Hi, I'm looking for your Appropriations person," I finally say. "Somehow, I think I misplaced his info."

"And who should I say is calling?"

I'm tempted to use Matthew's name, but the news probably already traveled. Still, I stick to the fear factor. "I'm calling from Interior Approps. I need to—"

Cutting me off, he puts me on hold. A few seconds later, he's back.

"I'm sorry," he says. "His assistant says he just stepped out for a moment."

It's an obvious lie. At this level, House staffers don't have assistants. Regardless, I shouldn't be surprised. If I'm calling through the main line, it's not a call worth taking.

"Tell him I'm from the Chairman's office and that this is about Congressman Grayson's request . . ."

Again I'm on hold. Again he's back in seconds.

"Hold on one moment, sir. I'm transferring you to Perry . . ."

First rule of politics: Everyone's afraid.

"This is Perry," a scratchy but gruff voice answers.

"Hey, Perry, I'm calling from Interior Approps—filling in on Matthew's issues after what—"

"Yeah, no . . . I heard. Really sorry about that. Matthew was a sweetheart."

He says the word *was*, and I close my eyes. It still hits like a sock full of quarters.

"So what can I do for you?" Perry asks.

I think back to the original bet. Whatever Matthew saw that day . . . the reason he and Pasternak were killed . . . it started with this. A gold mine sale in South Dakota that needed to be slipped into the bill. Grayson's office made the initial request. I don't have much information beyond that. This guy can give me more. "Actually, we're just re-examining all the different requests," I explain. "When Matthew—with Matthew gone, we want to make sure we know everyone's priorities."

"Of course, of course . . . happy to help." He's a staffer for a low-level Member and thinks I can throw him a few projects. Right there, the gruffness in his voice evaporates.

"Okay," I begin, staring down at my blank sheet of paper. "I'm looking at your original request list, and obviously, I know you're not shocked to hear you can't have everything on it . . ."

"Of course, of course . . ." he says for the second time, chuckling. I can practically hear him slapping his knee. I don't know how Matthew dealt with it.

"So which projects are your must-gets?" I ask.

"The sewer system," he shoots back, barely taking a breath. "If you can do that . . . if we improve drainage . . . that's the one that wins us the district."

He's smarter than I thought. He knows how low his Congressman is on the ladder. If he asks for every toy on the Christmas list, he'll be lucky if he gets a single one. Better just to focus on the Barbie Dream House.

"Those sewers . . . It really will change the election," he adds, already pleading.

"So everything else on this list . . ."

"Is all second-tier."

"What about this gold mine thing?" I ask, teeing up my bluff. "I thought Grayson was really hot for it."

"Hot for it? He's never even heard of it. We threw that out for a donor as a pure try-our-best."

When Matthew told me about the bet, he said exactly the same: Grayson's office supposedly didn't care about the mine—which means this guy Perry is either genuinely agreeing or is single-handedly setting the new world record for bullshit.

"Weird . . ." I say, still trying to dig. "I thought Matthew got some calls on it."

"If he did, it's only because Wendell Mining lobbied up."

I write the words *Wendell Mining* on the sheet of paper. When it comes to the game, I've always thought the various votes and different asks were inconsequential—but not if they tell me who else was playing.

"What about the rest of your delegation?" I ask, referring to the South Dakota Senators. "Anyone gonna scream if we kill the mining request?"

He thinks I'm covering my ass before I cut the gold mine loose, but what I really want to know is, who else in Congress has any interest in the project?

"No one," he says.

"Anyone against it?"

"It's a dumpy gold mine in a town that's so small, it doesn't even have a stoplight. To be honest, I don't think anyone even knows about it but us." He tosses me another knee-slapping laugh that curdles in my ear. Three nights ago, someone bid $1,000 for the right to put this gold mine in the bill. Someone else bid five grand. That means there're at least two people out there who were watching what was going on. But right now, I can't find a single one of them.

"So how we looking on our sewer system?" Perry asks on the other line.

"I'll do my best," I tell him, looking down at my nearly blank sheet of paper. The words *Wendell Mining* float weightlessly toward the top. But as I grab the paper and reread it for the sixth time, I slowly feel the chessboard expand. Of course. I didn't even think about it . . .

"You still there?" Perry asks.

"Actually, I gotta run," I say, already feeling the sharp bite of adrenaline. "I just remembered a call I have to make."

21

"HI, I'M HERE FOR a pickup," Viv announced as she stepped into room 2406 of the Rayburn Building, home office of Matthew's former boss, Congressman Nelson Cordell from Arizona.

"Excuse me?" the young man behind the front desk asked with a Native American accent. He wore a denim shirt with a bolo tie that had a silver clasp with the Arizona state seal on it. Viv hadn't seen it in the offices of the other Arizona Members. Good for Cordell, Viv thought. It was nice to see someone remembering where they were from.

"We got a call for a package pickup," Viv explained. "This is 2406, right?"

"Yeah," the young receptionist said, searching his desk for outgoing mail. "But I didn't call for a page."

"Well, someone did," Viv said. "There was a package for the Floor."

The young man stood up straight, and his bolo tie bounced against his chest. Everyone's terrified of the boss—just like Harris said.

"You have a phone I can use?" Viv asked.

He pointed to the handset on the wrought-iron southwestern-style end table. "I'll check in back and see if anyone else called it in."

"Great . . . thanks," Viv said as the young man disappeared through a door on the right. The instant he was gone, she picked up the phone and dialed the five-digit extension Harris had given her.

"This is Dinah," a female voice answered. As Matthew's office mate and head clerk for the House Appropriations Interior subcommittee, Dinah had incredible access and a staggering amount of power. More important, she had caller ID, which was why Harris said the call had to be made from here. Right now, the words *Hon. Cordell* appeared on Dinah's digital phone screen.

"Hey, Dinah," Viv began, careful to keep her voice low and smooth, "this is Sandy over in the personal office. I'm sorry to bother you, but the Congressman wanted to take a look at some of Matthew's project books, just to make sure he's up to speed for Conference . . ."

"I don't think that's such a good idea," Dinah blurted. "Pardon?"

"It's just . . . the information in there . . . It's not smart to let that wander outside the office."

Harris had warned her this might happen. That was why he gave her the ultimate comeback.

"The Congressman wants them," Viv insisted.

There was a short pause on the other line. "I'll get them ready," Dinah eventually said.

Over Viv's shoulder, the door on her right opened, and the young receptionist reentered the room.

"Great," Viv stuttered. "I-I'll send someone down to pick 'em up."

Hanging up the phone, Viv turned back to the main

reception desk. "Oops on me—wrong room," Viv said to the receptionist as she headed for the door.

"Don't worry," he replied. "No harm done."

Refusing to wait for the elevator, Viv ran down the four flights of stairs, eventually jumping down the last two steps and landing with a smack against the polished floor in the basement of the Rayburn Building. On average, a Senate page walked seven miles of hallway each day, picking up and delivering packages. On a typical day, those seven miles could take them from the hearing room where Nixon was impeached during Watergate, past the old Supreme Court chamber, where the Court first decided the *Dred Scott* case, to the west front of the Capitol, where every new President takes the oath of office, to the center of the enormous rotunda—underneath the vaulted majesty of the Capitol dome—where the bodies of both Abraham Lincoln and John F. Kennedy once lay in state. Viv saw it every single day. But she hadn't been this excited since her first day on the job.

Still unsure if it was thrill or fear, she didn't let it slow her down. As her heart jabbed against her chest and she whipped around the corner of the ghostly white hallway, Viv Parker was done shuffling mail and finally doing what the page program had originally promised—making an actual difference in someone's life.

Sliding to a stop in front of room B-308, she felt more than just her momentum come to a halt. This was still Matthew's office—and if she wasn't careful, she'd never be able to pull it off. As she reached out to grab the door-knob, she checked the hall, just as Harris had instructed. On her left, the door to a utility closet peeked open, but as far as she could tell, no one was inside. On her right, the hallway was empty.

Holding her breath, she twisted the brass knob, surprised by how cold it was. As she shoved her weight against the door, the first thing she heard was the ringing phone—on her left, past the Sioux quilt. Again, just like Harris said.

Following the ring, beyond the overflowing In and Out boxes on the edge of the desk, Viv turned the corner and was hit with a sudden sense of relief when she realized that the receptionist was black. Without a word, Roxanne glanced up at Viv, studied her ID, and gave her a slight, unmistakable nod. Viv had been on the receiving end of that one at least a dozen times before. From the cafeteria ladies . . . from one of the elevator operators . . . even from Congresswoman Peters.

"Whatcha need, doll?" Roxanne asked with a warm smile.

"Just here to pick up some briefing books." When Harris first told Viv about this, she was worried that someone would wonder why a Senate page was making a pickup in the House. Roxanne didn't even take a second glance. Forget what it says on the nametag—even to receptionists, a page is a page.

"Is Dinah . . . ?"

"Right through the door," Roxanne said, pointing Viv toward the back.

Viv headed for the door, and Roxanne turned back to the current vote on C-SPAN. Viv couldn't help but grin. On Capitol Hill, even the support staff were political junkies.

Picking up speed, Viv rushed forward and pushed her way inside.

". . . so where are we now?" a male voice asked.

"I told you, we're working on it," Dinah replied. "He's only been gone for two—"

The door swung into the wall, and Dinah cut herself off, abruptly turning toward Viv.

"Sorry," Viv offered.

"Can I help you?" Dinah barked.

Before Viv could answer, the man in front of Dinah's desk turned around, following the sound. Viv looked him straight in the eye, but something was off. He stared too high, like he was . . .

Viv spotted the white cane as the man rubbed his thumb against the handle. That's why he seemed so familiar . . . She'd seen him tapping in the hallway, outside the Senate Chamber during votes.

"I said, can I help you?" Dinah repeated.

"Yeah," Viv stuttered, pretending to study the stuffed ferret in the bookcase. "I was just . . . that ferret . . ."

"You here for the briefing books?" Dinah interrupted.

"I'm here for the briefing books."

"On the chair," Dinah said, pointing a finger toward the desk across from her own.

As quickly as she could, Viv wove across the carpet and slipped behind the desk, where she saw two enormous three-ring notebooks sitting in the chair. The spine of one was marked *A–L;* the other was *M–Z.* Pulling the chair out to lift the books, Viv noticed a pile of three picture frames stacked faceup on the center of the desk. Like someone was packing up . . . or someone was *being* packed up. The computer on the desk was off, even though it was the middle of the day. The diplomas that were once on the back wall were now leaning against the floor. Time froze as she bent toward the chair and her ID smacked against the edge of the desk.

She took another glance at the top photo, where a man with sandy-blond hair was standing in front of a sapphire blue lake. He was tall, with a thin neck that made him extra gawky. More noticeably, he stood so far to the left, he was almost out of the frame. As his open hand motioned to the lake, Matthew Mercer made it perfectly clear who he thought was the real star of the show. The smile on his face was pure pride. Viv had never met this man, but once she saw his photo, she couldn't take her eyes off him.

Behind her, she felt a strong hand on her shoulder. "You okay?" Barry asked. "Need any help?"

Jerking away, Viv yanked the notebooks from the chair and stumbled around the other side of the desk, acting like the weight of the books was keeping her off balance. Within seconds, she steadied herself and took a last look at Matthew's desk.

"Sorry about your friend," she said.

"Thanks," Dinah and Barry said simultaneously.

Forcing an awkward grin, Viv speed-walked to the door. Barry didn't move, but his cloudy blue eyes followed her movements the entire way.

"Just make sure we get them back," Dinah called out, readjusting her fanny pack. As Matthew's office mate, she'd sat next to him for almost two years, but she was still head clerk for the committee. Those books were vital business.

"Will do," Viv said. "Soon as the Congressman's done, they're all yours."

22

"WHAT ABOUT HIS HOUSE?" Sauls's voice squawked through the cell phone.

"He's got a loft on the outskirts of Adams Morgan," Janos said, keeping his voice down as he turned the corner of the long, pristine marble hallway in the Russell Senate Office Building. He wasn't running, but his pace was fast. Determined. Just like everyone around him. That was always the best way to disappear. "He doesn't own the place, though—or much of anything else. No car, no stocks, nothing left in his bank account. I'm guessing he's still paying off loans. Otherwise, he's got nothing permanent."

"Have you been to his place yet?"

"What do you think?" Janos shot back.

"So I take it he wasn't there?"

Janos didn't answer. He hated stupid questions. "Anything else you want to know?" he asked.

"Family and friends?"

"The boy's smart."

"That we know."

"I don't think you do. He's been in Congress ten years. Know how ruthless that makes you? The boy's a razor—

he's thought it through. Even though he's well connected, the game alone keeps him from reaching out to coworkers . . . and after we tagged his buddy at the U.S. Attorney's . . . I don't think Harris gets fooled twice."

"Bullshit. Everyone gets fooled twice. That's why they keep reelecting their Presidents."

Following the room numbers on the wall, Janos was again silent.

"You think I'm wrong?" Sauls asked.

"No," Janos replied. "No one survives alone. There's someone out there he trusts."

"So you can find him?"

Stopping in front of room 427, Janos gripped the doorknob on the twelve-foot mahogany door and gave it a hard twist. "That's my job," he said as he clicked the End button on his phone and stuffed it into the pocket of his FBI windbreaker.

Inside, the office was exactly the same as last time he was here. Harris's desk was untouched behind the glass divider, and Harris's assistant still sat at the desk out front.

"Agent Graves," Cheese called out as Janos stepped into Harris's office. "What can I help you with today?"

23

DURING MY VERY first job interview on the Hill, a burned-out staff director with the worst case of Brillo hair I'd ever seen leaned across his desk and told me that at its core, Congress operated like a small town. Some days it was grumpy; others, it was riled up and ready to pick a fistfight with the world. As someone who grew up in a small town, the analogy hit home. Indeed, that's the very reason I'm pacing back and forth across the storage room, waiting for someone to pick up on the other end of the line. As any small-town resident knows, if you want to get at the real secrets of a town, you have to visit the hall of records.

"Legislative Resource Center," a woman with a matronly voice answers.

"Hi, I'm hoping you can help me out. I'm searching for some information on a lobbyist."

"Let me transfer you to Gary."

In small-town talk, the Legislative Resource Center is like sitting on the porch with the grumpy old lady whose house is across from the only motel. It's not a sexy place to hang out, but when all is done and said, she knows exactly who's screwing who.

"Gary Naftalis," a man answers. His voice is dry, showing almost no emotion. "How can I assist?"

"Hey, Gary—I'm calling from Senator Stevens's office. We've got a company that's been calling us on this bill, and we're trying to figure out which lobbyists they're working with. You guys still do that?"

"Only if we want to keep the lobbyists honest, sir," he laughs to himself.

It's a bad joke, but a valid point. Every year, over seventeen thousand lobbyists descend on Capitol Hill, each one armed with a tommy gun of asks and special requests. Combine that with the boatloads of bills that're submitted and voted on every day, and it's overwhelming. As anyone on the Hill knows, there's too much work for a staffer to be an expert on it all. So if you need some research? Call the lobbyists. Want some talking points? Call the lobbyists. Confused by what a specific amendment does? Call the lobbyists. It's like buying drugs. If what they give you is good, you'll keep coming back. And that's how influence is peddled. Quietly, quickly, and without leaving fingerprints.

The thing is, right now I need those fingerprints.

If Pasternak was playing the game, other lobbyists played as well. Fortunately, all lobbyists are required to register with the Legislative Resource Center and list the names of their clients, which gives me the chance to see who's working for Wendell Mining.

"Is it possible to just put in a particular company?" I ask.

"Sure, sir . . . all you have to do is come in and—"

"Can I ask you a huge favor?" I interrupt. "My Senator's about to rip my head off and vomit down my windpipe . . . So if I gave you the name right now, would you mind looking it up for us? It's just one company, Gary . . ."

I say his name for the final sell. He pauses, leaving me in silence.

"It'd really save my ass," I add.

Again he gives me the pause. That's what I hate about being on the phone . . .

"What's the name of the company, sir?"

"Great . . . that's great. Wendell Mining," I tell him. "Wendell Mining."

I hear the clicking of his keyboard, and I stop my pacing. Staring out below the dust-covered vertical blinds, I have a clear view of the narrow pathway and marble railing that run along the west front of the building. The morning sun's beating down on the copper roof, but it pales to the heat I'm feeling right now. I wipe a puddle of sweat from the back of my neck and unbutton the top of my shirt. The suit and tie were enough to get me back in the building without a second glance, but if I don't get some answers soon . . .

"Sorry," Gary says. "They're not coming up."

"Whattya mean, they're not coming up? I thought every lobbyist had to disclose their clients . . ."

"They do. But this time of year . . . we're barely halfway through the pile."

"What pile?"

"The disclosure forms—that the lobbyists fill out. We get over seventeen thousand forms each registration period. Know how long that takes to scan in and update our database?"

"Weeks?"

"Months. The deadline was just a few weeks ago in August, so we've still got a ton that aren't in."

"So it's possible there's a lobbyist working on their issue . . ."

"This is Congress, sir. Anything's possible."

I roll my tongue inside my cheek. I hate government humor.

"They add about seven hundred names to the database each day," Gary continues. "Best bet is to just give us a call back later in the week, and we can check if it's in there."

I remember that this is the second year Wendell Mining made the request. "What about last year?" I ask.

"Like I said, nothing came up—which means they either didn't have someone, or that person didn't register."

That part actually makes sense. When it comes to getting earmarks, the smaller companies try to do it by themselves. Then, when they fail, they get smart and cough up the beans for a pro. If Wendell had someone pulling for them, the name'll eventually show up in this database. "Listen, I appreciate th—"

There's a loud knock on the door. I go silent.

"Sir, are you there?" Gary asks through the receiver.

The person knocks again. This time to the tune of *shave-and-a-haircut.*

"It's me, you shut-in!" Viv calls out. "Open up!"

I leap for the door and undo the lock. The phone cord is pulled so far, it knocks over the stack of keyboards, which go crashing to the floor as the door swings open.

"Mission accomplished, Mr. Bond. What's next?" Viv sings, cradling the two notebooks as if she were still in high school. That's when it hits me. She *is* still in high school. Sliding inside, she whips past me with a frenetic new bounce in her step. I've seen the same thing on staffers the first day they get on the Senate Floor. Power rush.

Gary's voice crackles through the receiver. "Sir, are you—?"

"I'm here . . . sorry," I say, turning back to the phone. "Thanks for the help—I'll give you a call next week."

As I hang up, Viv dumps the notebooks across the desk. I was wrong before. I thought she was the girl who sits silently in the back of the class—and while that part's true, I'm quickly starting to realize that she's also the girl who, when she gets around people she knows, never shuts up.

"I guess you didn't have any problems," I say.

"You should've seen it! I was unstoppable—I'm telling you, it was like being in the *Matrix*. They're all standing there dumbfounded, then I weave around in super-slow-mo . . . dodging their bullets . . . working my voodoo . . . Oh, they didn't know what hit 'em!"

The jokes are coming too fast. I know a defense mechanism when I see one. She's afraid. Even if she doesn't know it.

"Viv . . ."

"You woulda been proud of me, Harris . . ."

"Did Dinah say anything?"

"You kidding? She was blinder than the blind guy . . ."

"The blind guy?"

"All I need now is a code name . . ."

"Barry was there?"

". . . something cool, too—like Senate Grrl . . ."

"Viv . . ."

". . . or Black Cat . . ."

"Viv!"

". . . or . . . or Sweet Mocha. Howbout that? Sweet Mocha. Ooh, yeah, let's get down to Viv-ness!"

"Dammit, Viv, shut up already!"

She stops midsyllable.

"You sure it was Barry?" I ask.

"I don't know his name. He's a blind guy with a cane and cloudy eyes . . ."

"What'd he say?"

"Nothing—though he kept following me as I walked. I can't . . . he was slightly off . . . but it's like he was trying to prove—not that it matters—but trying to prove he wasn't that blind, y'know?"

I lunge for the phone and dial his cell. No. I hang up and start again. Go through the operator. Especially now.

Five digits later, the Capitol operator transfers me to Matthew's old office.

"Interior," Roxanne answers.

"Hey, Roxanne, it's Harris."

"Harris . . . how are you?"

"Fine. Can you—"

"Y'know you're in my prayers, sweetie. Everything with Matthew . . ."

"No . . . of course. Listen, I'm sorry to bother you, but it's kind of an emergency. Is Barry still floating around back there?"

Viv waves for my attention, slowly moving toward the door. "I'll be right back," she whispers. "Just one more stop . . ."

"Wait," I call out.

She doesn't listen. She's having too much fun to sit around for a scolding.

"Viv!"

The door slams, and she's gone.

"Harris?" a voice asks in my ear. I'd know it anywhere. Barry.

24

H OW ARE YOU? You okay?" Barry asks.

"Why wouldn't I be?" I shoot back.

"With Matthew . . . I just figured . . . Where're you calling from anyway?"

It's the third question out of his mouth. I'm surprised it wasn't the first.

"I'm home," I tell him. "I just needed some time to— I just wanted to take some time."

"I left you four messages."

"I know . . . and I appreciate it—I just needed the time."

"No, I completely understand."

He doesn't buy it for a second. But not because of what I said.

A few years back, some coworkers threw a surprise birthday party for Ilana Berger, press secretary for Senator Conroy. As old friends of Ilana from college, Matthew, Barry, and I were all invited, along with everyone in the Senator's office, and seemingly everyone else on the Hill. Ilana's friends wanted an *event*. Somehow, though, Barry's invitation went to the wrong address.

Forever worried about being left out, Barry was crushed. When we told him it must've been a mistake, he wouldn't believe it. When we told him to call the party's hosts, he refused. And when we called the hosts, who felt terrible that the invitation didn't get there and immediately sent out a new one, Barry saw it as a pity fix. It's always been Barry's greatest flaw—he can walk down a crowded street completely unaided, but when it comes to personal interactions, the only thing he ever sees is himself sitting alone in the dark.

Of course, when it comes to Hill gossip, his radar's still better than most.

"So I assume you heard about Pasternak?" he asks.

I stay quiet. He's not the only one with radar. There's a slight rise in his pitch. He's got something to tell.

"Doctors said it was a heart attack. Can you believe it? Guy runs five miles every morning and wham—it stops pumping in a . . . in a heartbeat. Carol is heartbroken . . . his whole family . . . it's like a bomb went off. If you gave them a call . . . they could really use it, Harris."

I wait for him to get every last word out. "Can I ask you a question?" I finally say. "Do you have a dog in this race?"

"What?"

"Wendell Mining . . . the request Matthew was working on . . . Are you lobbying it?"

"Of course not. You know I don't do that . . ."

"I don't know anything, Barry."

He offers a playful laugh. I don't laugh back.

"Let me say it again for you, Harris—I've never once worked on Matthew's issues."

"Then what're you doing in his office?!"

"Harris . . ."

"Don't *Harris* me!"

"I know you've had two huge losses this week—"

"What the hell is wrong with you, Barry? Stop with the mental massage and answer the fucking question!"

There's a long pause on the other line. He's either panicking or in shock. I need to know which.

"Harris," he eventually begins, his voice teetering on the first syllable. "I-I've been here ten years . . . these are my friends . . . this is my family, Harris . . ." As he says the words, I close my eyes and fight the swell of tears. "We lost Matthew. C'mon, Harris. This is Matthew . . ."

If he's yanking on my heartstrings, I'll kill him for this.

"Listen to me," he pleads. "This isn't the time to zip yourself in a cocoon."

"Barry . . ."

"I want to come see you," he insists. "Just tell me where you really are."

My eyes pop open, staring down at the phone. When Pasternak first hired me all those years ago, he told me a good lobbyist is one who, if you're sitting next to him on an airplane and his knee touches yours, it's not uncomfortable. Asking where I am, Barry's officially uncomfortable.

"I gotta run," I tell him. "I'll talk to you later."

"Harris, don't . . ."

"Good-bye, Barry."

Slamming the phone in its cradle, I once again turn toward the window and study the sunlight as it ricochets off the roofline. Matthew always warned me about competitive friendships. I can't argue with him anymore.

25

Towering over Cheese's desk, Janos carefully took a slight step back and painted on a semifriendly grin. From the anxious look on Harris's assistant's face, the FBI windbreaker was already more than enough. As Janos well knew, if you squeeze the egg too hard, it shatters.

"You think he's okay?" Janos asked in his best concerned tone.

"He sounded okay in his message," Cheese replied. "More tired than anything else. He's had a rough week, y'know, which is obviously why he's taking the week off."

"So he called this morning?"

"Actually, I think it was late last night. Now tell me again why you need to speak to him."

"We're just following up on Matthew Mercer's death. The accident happened on federal land, so they wanted us to talk to a few of his friends." Reading the look on Cheese's face, Janos added, "Don't worry . . . it's just standard follow-up . . ."

The front door to the office opened, and a young black girl in a navy suit stuck her head inside. "Senate page,"

Viv announced, balancing three small red, white, and blue boxes. "Flag delivery?" she said.

"The who what?" Cheese asked.

"Flags," she repeated, checking out both Cheese and Janos. "American flags . . . y'know, the ones they fly over the Capitol, then sell to people just because it went up a flagpole on the roof . . . Anyway, I've got three here for a . . ." She read the words from the top box, ". . . for someone named Harris Sandler."

"You can just leave 'em here," Cheese said, pointing to his own desk.

"And mess up your stuff?" Viv asked. She motioned through the glass partition at Harris's messy work space. "That your boss's pigpen?" Before Cheese could answer, Viv headed through the door in the partition. "He wants the flags . . . let him deal with them."

"See, now that's what we gotta see more of," Cheese called out, slapping his own chest. "Respect for *the Kid!*"

Eyeing the girl carefully, Janos watched as Viv approached Harris's desk. She had her back to him, and her body blocked most of what she was doing, but from what Janos could tell, it was just a routine drop-off. Without a word, she cleared a space for the flag boxes, set them on Harris's desk, and in one smooth motion, spun back toward the rest of the office. Viv jumped when she saw Janos staring right at her. There it was. Contact.

"H-Hey," she said with a smile as their eyes locked. "Everything okay?"

"Of course," Janos replied dryly. "Everything's perfect."

"So can you fly *anything* over the Capitol?" Cheese asked. "Socks? Underwear? I've got this vintage *Barney Miller* T-shirt that would love to go for a whirl."

"Who's Barney Miller?" Viv asked.

Cheese grabbed his chest in mock pain. "Do you have any idea how much that physically hurt? I'm slayed. Seriously. I'm bleeding inside."

"Sorry," Viv laughed, moving toward the door.

Janos looked back at Harris's desk, where the flag boxes were neatly stacked in place. Even then, he didn't think much of it. But as he turned back to Viv—as he listened to her giggle and as he watched her bounce toward the door—he saw the last passing glance that she aimed his way. Then he realized it wasn't at him. It was at his windbreaker. *FBI.*

The door slammed, and Viv was gone.

"So what were we singing about again?" Cheese asked.

Still locked on the door, Janos didn't answer. It wasn't that unusual for someone to check out an FBI jacket . . . but add that to the way she walked in . . . going straight for Harris's office . . .

"I know that look," Cheese teased. "You're rethinking that underwear-over-the-Capitol thing, aren't you?"

"Have you ever seen her before?" Janos blurted.

"The page? No, not that I—"

"I have to go," Janos said as he calmly turned toward the door.

"Just let me know if you need more help," Cheese called out, but Janos was already on his way—out the door and up the hallway. She couldn't have gotten . . .

There, Janos thought, smiling to himself.

Reaching into the pocket of his windbreaker, Janos felt his way along the small black box and flipped the switch. The electrical hum rumbled quietly in his hand.

26

FLIPPING OPEN THE first of the two notebooks, I thumb to the *G*s and continue to turn the pages until I finally reach the tab marked *Grayson*. Alphabetically organized by Member name, the subsections of the book have an in-depth analysis of every project that a Congressman asks for—including the transfer of a gold mine to a company called Wendell Mining.

Skimming past the original request that Grayson's office submitted, I lick my finger and flip straight to the analysis. But as I speed-read the next three pages, I hear a familiar voice in my head. Oh, jeez. It's unmistakable . . . the rambling at the beginning of a new thought . . . his overuse of the word *specifically* . . . even the way he rants a bit at the end. Without a doubt, these three pages were written by Matthew. It's like he's sitting right here next to me.

To his credit, the analysis is the same as what he originally said. The Homestead gold mine is one of the old-est in South Dakota, and both the town and state would benefit if Wendell Mining got the land and took over the mine. To drive the point home, there are three photocopied letters clipped into the notebook: one from the Bureau of Land Management, one from the Wendell Mining CEO, and a final gushing recommendation from the mayor of Leed, South Dakota, the town where the mine is located. Three letters. Three letterheads. Three new phone numbers to call.

The first call to BLM gets me voice mail. Same with the call to the CEO. That leaves only the mayor. Fine by me. I'm better with politicians any day.

Dialing the number, I let the phone ring in my ear and glance down at my watch. Viv should be back any . . .

"L-and-L Luncheonette," a man with a cigarette-burned voice and Hollywood-cowboy drawl answers. "What c'n I do?"

"I'm sorry," I stutter, glancing down at the bottom of the letter. "I was looking for Mayor Regan's office."

"And who should I say is calling?" the man asks.

"Andy Defresne," I say. "From the House of Representatives. In Washington, D.C."

"Well, why didn't you say?" the man adds with a throaty laugh. "This is Mayor Regan."

I pause, suddenly thinking of my dad's barbershop.

"Not used to small towns, are ya?" the mayor laughs.

"Actually, I am."

"From one?"

"Born and raised."

"Well, we're smaller," he teases. "Guaranteed or your money back."

God, he reminds me of home.

"Now, what c'n I do?" he asks.

"To be honest—"

"Wouldn't expect anything but," he interrupts, laughing wildly.

He also reminds me why I left.

"I just had a quick question about the gold mine that's—"

"The Homestead."

"Exactly. The Homestead," I say, nervously tapping a finger against one of the spare keyboards in the room. "So, getting back . . . I'm working on Congressman Grayson's request for the land sale . . ."

"Oh, don't everybody love a fight."

"Some do," I play along. "Personally, I'm just trying to make sure we do the right thing and put local interests first." He's silent at that, enjoying the sudden attention. "Anyway, as we push for the request, we're trying to think who else we should go to for support, so would you mind walking me through how the town might benefit from the sale of the mine taking place? Or better yet, is there anyone in particular who's excited by the deal going through?"

As he's done twice before, the mayor laughs out loud. "Son, to be honest, you got as much chance sucking bricks through a hose as you do finding someone who'll benefit from this one."

"I'm not sure I understand."

"And maybe I don't, either," the mayor admits. "But if I were putting up my money for a gold mine, I'd at least want one that had some gold."

My finger stops tapping against the keyboard. "Excuse me?"

"The Homestead mine. Place is empty."

"You sure about that?"

"Son, the Homestead may've broke ground in 1876, but the last ounce of gold was mined almost twenty years ago. Since then, seven different companies have tried to prove everyone wrong, and the last one went bust so ugly, they took most of the town with 'em. That's why the land's been sitting with the government. There used to be nine thousand of us here in town. Now we're a hundred and fifty-seven. You don't need an abacus to do that math."

As he says the words, the storage room is dead silent, but I can barely hear myself think. "So you're telling me there's no gold in that mine?"

"Not for twenty years," he repeats.

I nod even though he can't see me. It doesn't make any sense. "I'm sorry, Mr. Mayor—maybe I'm just dense, but if there's no chance of finding gold, then why'd you write that letter?"

"What letter?"

My eyes drop to the desk, where Matthew's old notebook holds a letter endorsing the land transfer to Wendell Mining. It's signed by the mayor of Leed, South Dakota.

"You are Mayor Tom Regan, right?"

"Yep. Only one."

I study the signature at the bottom of the letter. Then I reread it again. There's a slight smudge on the *R* in *Regan* that makes it look just messy enough that it'd never get a second glance. And right there, for the first time since this all started, I start to see the ripple in the mirror.

"You still there, son?" the mayor asks.

"Yeah . . . no . . . I'm here," I say. "I just . . . Wendell Mining . . ."

"Let me tell you about Wendell Mining. When they first came sniffing here, I personally called MSHA to—"

"Em-sha?"

"Mine Safety and Health Administration—the safety boys. When you're mayor, you gotta know who's coming to your town. So when I talked to my buddy there, he said these guys at Wendell may've bought the original mining claims to the land, and filed all the right paperwork, and even put enough money in someone's pocket to get a favorable mineral report—but so help me, when we looked up their track record, these boys've never operated a single mine in their lives."

A sharp pain in my stomach burns, and the fire quickly spreads. "You sure about that?"

"Son, did Elvis love bacon? I've seen this one a hundred and nineteen times before. A company like Wendell has a little bit of money, and a lotta bit of greed. If anyone would bother to ask me my opinion, I'd tell 'em that the last thing we need around here is to get everyone's hopes up and then see 'em squashed once again. You know how it is in a small town . . . when those trucks showed up—"

"Trucks?" I interrupt.

"The ones that showed up last month. Isn't that what you're calling about?"

"Y-Yeah. Of course." Matthew transferred the gold mine barely three days ago. Why were trucks there a month ago? "So they're already mining?" I ask, completely confused.

"God knows what they're doing . . . I went up there myself—y'know, just to make sure they're doing things right with the union . . . Let me tell you right now, they don't have a single piece of mining equipment up there. Not even a pelican pick. And when I asked them about it . . . let me just say . . . *crickets* aren't as jumpy. I mean, those boys shooed me away like a fly on the wrong end of a horse."

My hand holds tight to the receiver. "You think they're doing something other than mining?"

"I don't know what they're doing, but if it were up to me—" He cuts himself off. "Son, can you hold on one second?" Before I can answer, I hear him in the background. "Aunt *Mollie,*" he calls out, suddenly excited. "What can I get you, dear?"

"Just the regular," a woman with the sweetest hometown twang replies. "No jelly on the toast."

Behind me, someone pounds *shave-and-a-haircut* against the door. "It's me," Viv calls out. I stretch the phone cord and undo the lock.

Viv steps inside, but the tap dance in her step is gone.

"What's wrong?" I ask. "Did you get the—"

She pulls my electronic organizer from the waist of her pants and tosses it straight at me. "There—you happy?" she asks.

"What happened? Was it not where I said it was?"

"I saw an FBI agent in your office," she blurts.

"What?"

"He was there—talking to your assistant."

I slam down the phone on the mayor. "What'd he look like?"

"I don't know . . ."

"No—forget *I don't know.* What'd he look like?" I insist.

She reads my panic easily but, unlike last time, doesn't brush it off. "I didn't see him that long . . . buzzed salt-and-pepper hair . . . I guess a creepy smile . . . and eyes that kinda, well . . . kinda look like a hound dog if that makes any sense . . ."

My throat locks up, and my eyes flash over to the door. More specifically, the doorknob. It's unlocked.

I dart full speed at the door, ready to twist the lock shut. But just as I'm about to grab it, the door bursts toward me, slamming into my shoulder. Viv screams, and a thick hand slides through the crack.

27

THE DOOR'S BARELY open an inch, but Janos already has his hand inside. Viv's still screaming, and I'm still moving. Lucky for me, momentum's on my side.

My full weight collides with the door, pinching Janos's fingers in the doorjamb. I expect him to yell as he yanks his hand free. He barely grunts. Viv also goes dead silent, and I look over to make sure she's okay. She's standing there, eyes closed and hands clasped around her ID. Praying.

As the door slams shut, I dive for the lock and click it into place. The door thunders as Janos rams himself against it. The hinges shudder. We're not gonna last long.

"Window!" I say, turning back toward Viv, who finally looks up. She's frozen in shock. Her eyes look like they're about to explode. I grab her hand and twirl her toward the small window that's high up on the wall. It's got two panes that swing outward like shutters.

There's another thunderclap against the door.

Viv turns and panics. "He's—"

"*Just go!*" I shout, pulling one of the spare chairs toward the windowsill.

Hopping up on the chair, Viv can't stop her hands from shaking as she tries to unhook the window latch.

"Hurry!" I beg as the door once again rumbles.

She pounds the windows, but they don't move.

"Harder!" I tell her.

She hits them again. She's not a small girl—the impact's tremendous.

"I think they're painted shut!"

"Here, let me—"

With the base of her palm, Viv gives it one final shove, and the left window pops open, swinging out toward the rooftop. Her hands lock on the windowsill, and I give her a boost up. There's a loud bang against the front door. The lock buckles. Two screws look like they're about to come loose.

Viv turns toward the sound.

"Don't look!" I tell her.

She's already halfway out the window. I grab her ankles and give her one final push.

Another screw flies from the lock and clinks against the floor. We're out of time. I hop on the chair just as Viv crashes against the balcony outside. Behind me, I spot Matthew's notebooks sitting on the nearby table. Janos is one good kick away. I'll never make it . . .

I don't care. I need that info. Leaping off the chair, I scramble back toward the desk, grab the Grayson section, and tear the pages from the three-ring binder.

The door flies open and crashes to the ground. I don't even bother to look back. In one mad dash, I leap on the chair and dive toward the open window. My pelvis crashes against the windowsill, but it's enough to get me through. Teetering forward, I tumble outside, blinded by the sun as I hit the floor of the balcony.

"Which way?" Viv asks, slamming the window shut as I climb to my feet.

Rolling up the stack of papers and shoving them in my front pocket, I grab Viv's wrist and tug her to the left, along the three-foot-wide pathway just outside the window.

Overlooking the Washington Monument, we're on the long balcony outside the Senate wing. Unlike the enormous Capitol dome, which rises up in front of us, the path on this side of the building is flat.

I glance over my shoulder just as the window bursts open behind us. The glass shatters as it swings into the white wall of the building. As Janos sticks his head out, it only makes us run harder. We're moving so fast, the intricate marble railing on my right starts to blur. To my surprise, Viv's already a few steps ahead of me.

The sun beats down, reflecting off the white railing so brightly, I have to squint to see. Good thing I know where I'm going. Up ahead, the pathway forks as we approach the base of the Capitol dome. We can go straight and follow the pathway, or make a sharp left into a nook around the corner. Last time we did this, Janos caught me off guard. This time, we're on my turf.

"Left," I say, yanking the shoulder of Viv's suit. As I tug her around the corner, there's a rusted metal staircase dead ahead. It leads up to a catwalk that'll take us up to the roof, directly on top of the room we were just in. "Keep going," I say, pointing her toward the stairs.

Viv keeps running. I stay where I am. By my feet, a trio of thin steel wires runs along the floor of the balcony, just outside the windows. During the winter, the maintenance division sends a small electric current through the wiring to melt the snow and prevent the ice from piling up. During the rest of the year, the wires just sit there, useless. Until now. Squatting down, I press my knuckles against the floor and grab the wires. As Janos runs, I hear his shoes pounding against the roof.

"He's right around the corner!" Viv yells from her perch on the catwalk.

That's what I'm counting on. Tugging up like I'm curling a barbell, I pull the wires as hard as I can. The staples that hold them in place pop through the air. The metal wiring goes taut, rising a few inches from the ground. Perfect ankle height.

Just as Janos turns the corner, his legs slam into the wiring. At his speed, the thin metal slices into his shins. For the first time, he yells out in pain. It's not much more than a muted roar, but I'll take it. Tumbling forward, he skids face first against the ground. The sound alone is worth it.

Before he can get up, I leap toward him, gripping him by the back of his head and pressing his face against the burning-hot green copper floor. As his cheek hits, he finally screams—a guttural rumble that vibrates against my chest. It's like trying to pin a bull. Even as I grab the back of his neck, he's already on his knees, climbing to his feet. Like a trapped panther, he lashes out, swiping a meaty paw at my face. I duck back, and his knuckles barely connect with a spot below my shoulder, just under my armpit. It doesn't hurt—but as my entire right arm tingles and goes numb, I realize that's where he was aiming all along.

"*Harris, run!*" Viv shouts from the catwalk.

She's right about that. I can't beat him one-on-one. I spin back toward Viv and sprint as fast as I can. My arm's dead, flapping lifelessly at my side. Behind me, Janos is still on the ground, clawing at the wires. As I race toward the metal staircase that leads up to the roof, a half-dozen more staples pop through the air. He'll be loose in seconds.

"C'mon!" Viv yells, standing on the edge of the top step and waving me up.

Using my good arm to hold the railing, I scutter up the stairs to the catwalk that zigzags across the roof. From here, with the dome at my back, the flat roof of the Senate wing is spread out in front of me. Most of it's covered with air ducts, vents, a web of electrical wiring, and a handful of scattered rounded domes that rise like waist-high bubbles from the rooftop. Weaving through all of it, I follow the catwalk as it curves around the edge of the small dome that's right in front of us.

"You sure you know where you're—?"

"Here," I say, cutting to the left, down an offshoot of metal stairs that takes us off the catwalk and back down to a different section of the balcony. Thank God neoclassical architecture is symmetrical. Along the wall on my left, there's a corresponding window that'll take us back into the building.

I kick the window frame as hard as I can. The glass shatters, but the frame holds. Pulling some glass out to get a good handhold, I yank as hard as I can. I can hear the pounding of Janos's feet up on the catwalk.

"Pull harder!" Viv yells.

The wood splinters in my hands, and the window flies open, swinging toward me. The pounding's getting closer.

"Go . . ." I say, helping Viv slide inside. I'm right behind her, landing hard as I hit the gray-carpeted floor. I'm in someone's office.

A stocky coworker comes rushing to the door. "You can't be in here—"

Viv shoves him aside, and I fall in right behind her. As a page, Viv knows the inside of this place as well as anyone. And the way she's running—sharp turns without a pause—she's not trailing anymore. She's leading.

We cut through the main welcoming area of the Senate curator's office and fly down a curving narrow staircase that echoes as we run. Trying to stay out of sight, we jump down the last three steps and duck out on the third floor of the Capitol. The closed door in front of us is marked *Senate Chaplain*. Not a bad place to hide. Viv tries the doorknob.

"It's locked," she says.

"So much for your prayers."

"Don't say that," she scolds.

There's a loud thud from above. We both look up just in time to see Janos at the top of the staircase. The left side of his face is bright red, but he never says a word.

Viv jackrabbits to her left, up the hallway and toward another flight of stairs. I head for the elevator, which is a bit further, just around the corner.

"Elevator's faster . . ." I tell her.

"Only if it's—"

I hit the call button and hear a high-pitched ping. Viv quickly catches up. As the doors slide open, we hear Janos lumbering down the stairs. Shoving Viv in the elevator, I follow her inside, frantically trying to pull the door shut.

Viv jabs wildly at the *Door Close* button. "C'mon, c'mon, c'mon . . ."

I wedge my fingers in the door's metal molding and pull as hard as I can, trying to tug the door shut. Viv ducks under me and does the same. Janos is a few feet away. I see the tips of his outstretched fingers.

"Get ready to pull the alarm!" I shout at Viv.

Janos lunges forward, and our eyes lock. He jabs his hand toward us just as the door clicks, thunks, and slides shut.

The elevator rumbles downward, and I can barely catch my breath.

"My . . . my hand . . ." Viv whispers, picking something from her palm, which is bright red with blood. She pulls out a piece of glass from one of the broken windows.

"You okay?" I ask, reaching out.

Focused on her palm, she doesn't answer. I'm not even sure she hears the question. Her hand shakes uncontrollably as she stares down at the blood. She's in shock. But she's still sharp enough to know she's got far more important things to worry about. She grips her wrist to stop the shaking. "Why's the FBI chasing you?" she asks, her voice cracking.

"He's not FBI."

"Then who the hell is he?"

This isn't the time for an answer. "Just get ready to run," I tell her.

"What're you talking about?"

"You think he's not sprinting down the stairs right now?"

She shakes her head, trying to look confident, but I can hear the panic in her voice. "It's not a continuous staircase—he'll have to stop and cross the hallway at two of the landings."

"Only at one," I correct her.

"Yeah, but . . . he still has to stop at each floor to make sure we didn't get out." She's trying hard to convince herself, but even she's not buying it. "There's no way he'll beat us down . . . right?"

The elevator bobs to a stop in the basement, and the door slowly slides open. Sprinting out, I barely get two steps before I hear a loud click-clack on the metal treads of the staircase that rises directly in front of us. I crane my neck up just in time to see Janos whipping around the corner of the top step. He's still silent, but the smallest of grins spreads across his lips.

Son of a bitch.

Viv takes off to the left, and I'm again right behind her. Janos storms down the stairs. We've got nothing more than a thirty-step head start. Viv makes a sharp left so we're not in his direct line of sight, then a quick right. Down here, the basement's got low ceilings and narrow halls. We're like rats in a maze, twisting and turning as the cat licks his chops behind us.

Dead ahead, the long hallway widens. At the end, a bright shot of sunlight glows through the glass in the double doors. There's our way out. The west exit—the door the President uses as he steps out for his inauguration. From here, it's a straight shot.

Viv looks back for a half second. "You know what's . . ."

I nod. She understands.

Pouring on the speed, Viv clenches her fists and heads for the light. A few drops of blood drip to the floor.

Behind us, Janos is galloping like a racehorse, slowly closing the gap. I can hear him breathing—the closer he gets, the louder it grows. We all dig in hard, and the pounding of our shoes echoes through the hallway. I'm neck and neck with Viv, who's slowly losing steam. She's now a half step behind. *C'mon, Viv . . .* Only a few feet to go. I study her face. Wide eyes. Mouth open. I've seen that look on people at mile twenty-five in the marathon. She's not gonna make it. Sensing her pain, Janos shifts a bit to the left. Right behind Viv. He's so close, I can almost smell him. "Viv . . . !" I shout.

Janos reaches out, raising his hand for the final grab. He lunges forward. The door's straight ahead. But just as he swipes down, I grip Viv's shoulder and make a sharp right, whipping us both around the corner, away from the door.

Janos skids across the polished floor, struggling to follow us through the turn. It's too late. By the time he's back in pursuit, Viv and I shove our way through a set of black vinyl double doors that look like they lead to a restaurant kitchen.

But as the doors swing shut, we find fourteen armed policemen milling around the hallway. The office on our right is the internal headquarters of the Capitol Police.

Viv's already got her mouth open. "There's a guy back there who's trying to—"

I shoot her a look, shaking my head. If she blows the whistle on Janos, he'll blow the whistle on me—and right now, I can't afford to be taken in. From the confused look on her face, Viv doesn't understand, but it's still enough to let me take the lead.

"There's a guy back there who's muttering to himself," I say to the three nearest officers. "He started following us for no reason, saying we were the enemy."

"I think he snuck off his tour," Viv adds, knowing just how to rile these guys. Pointing to the ID badge around her neck, she says, "He doesn't have an ID."

Janos shoves open the black vinyl doors. Three Capitol policemen move in.

"Can I help you with something?" one of them asks. He's unimpressed with the FBI windbreaker, which he knows can be bought in the gift shop.

Before Janos can even make up a lame excuse, Viv

and I continue further up the hallway that's spread out in front of us.

"Stop them!" Janos shouts, taking off after us.

The first officer grabs him by the windbreaker, pulling him back.

"What're you doing?" Janos roars.

"My job," the officer says. "Now let's see some ID."

Twisting and turning back through the maze of the basement, we eventually push our way outside on the east front of the Capitol. The sun's already passed to the other side of the building, but darkness is still an hour or so away. Hurtling past the groups of tourists taking pictures in front of the dome, we race toward First Street, hoping the Capitol Police give us enough of a head start. The white marble pillars of the Supreme Court are directly across the street, but I'm too busy looking for a cab.

"Taxi!" Viv and I shout simultaneously as one slows down.

We both slide inside, locking our respective doors. Back by the Capitol, Janos is nowhere in sight. For now. "I think we're okay," I say, ducking down in my seat and searching the crowds.

Next to me, Viv doesn't bother to look outside. She's too busy glaring directly at me. Her brown eyes burn— part of it's fear, but now . . . part of it's anger.

"You lied . . ." she finally says.

"Viv, before you—"

"I'm not a moron, y'know," she adds, still catching her breath. "Now what the hell is going on?"

28

RIDING THE ESCALATOR down to the lower floors of the Smithsonian's Museum of American History, I keep my eyes on the crowds and my hands on Viv's shoulders. It's still the best way to keep her calm. She's one step down but twice as nervous. After what happened in the Capitol, she doesn't trust anyone—including me—which is why she jerks her shoulder and shoos me away.

Without a doubt, the museum's not the ideal place to change her mind, but it is enough of a public place to make it an unlikely spot for Janos to start hunting. As we continue our descent, Viv's gaze flits around the room, searching the face of every person she can find. I'm guessing it's nothing new. She said she was one of two black girls in an otherwise white school. In the Senate, she's the only black page they've got. No doubt, she's an outsider on a daily basis. But never like this. Unfolding the museum map I got from the info desk, I block us from the crowd. If we want to blend in as tourists, we have to play the part.

"Want some ice cream?" I ask as we step off the escalator and spot the old-fashioned ice-cream parlor along the wall.

Viv hammers me with a look I usually see only on the press corps. "Do I look thirteen to you?"

She's got every right to be pissed. She signed up to do a simple favor. Instead, she spent the past half hour running for her life. For that reason alone, she needs to know what's really going on.

"I never meant for it to happen like this," I begin.

"Really?" she asks. She presses her lips together and pierces me with a scowl.

"Viv, when you said you would help . . ."

"You shouldn't have let me! I had no idea what I was getting into!"

There's no arguing with that. "I'm sorry," I tell her. "I never thought they'd—"

"I don't want your apologies, Harris. Just tell me why Matthew was killed."

I wasn't sure she knew what it was about. It's not the first time I underestimated her.

As we walk through an exhibit labeled *A Material World,* we're surrounded by glass cases that track America's manufacturing process. The first case is filled with timber, bricks, slate, and cowhide; the last case features the bright colored plastic of a Rubik's Cube and a PacMan machine. "This is progress," a nearby tour guide announces. I look at Viv. Time to make some progress here, too.

It takes me almost fifteen minutes to tell her the truth. About Matthew . . . and Pasternak . . . and even about my attempt to go to the Deputy Attorney General. Amazingly, she doesn't show a hint of reaction—that is, until I tell her what set all the dominos tumbling. The game . . . and the bet.

Her mouth drops open, and she puts both hands on her head. She's primed to explode.

"You were betting?" she asks.

"I know it sounds nuts . . ."

"That's what you were doing? Gambling on Congress?"

"I swear, it was just a stupid game."

"*Candyland*'s a stupid game! *Mad Libs* is a stupid game! This was real!"

"It was just on the small issues—nothing that ever mattered . . ."

"*It all matters!*"

"Viv, please . . ." I beg, looking around as a few tourists stop and stare.

She lowers her voice, but the anger's still there. "How could you do that? You told us we should—" She cuts herself off as her voice cracks. "That entire speech you gave . . . Everything you said was crap."

Right there, I realize I've been reading her wrong. It's not anger in her voice. It's disappointment—and as her shoulders sag even lower than usual, it's already bleeding into sadness. I've been on the Hill for a decade, but Viv's barely been here a month. It took me three years of getting backstabbed to get the look she's wearing right now. Her eyes sag with a brand new weight. No matter when it happens, idealism always dies hard.

"That's it—I'm out," she announces, shoving me aside and rushing past me.

"Where're you going?"

"To deliver some Senator's mail . . . and gossip with friends . . . and check on our running tally of Senators with bad hair and no rear end—there're more than you think."

"Viv, wait," I call out, chasing after her. I put a hand on her shoulder, and she tries to yank herself free. I hold tight, but unlike before, it doesn't calm her down.

"Get. *Off!*" she shouts. With one final shove, she slaps me away. She's not a small girl. I forget how strong she is.

"Viv, don't be stupid . . ." I call out as she storms through the exhibit.

"I've already been stupid—you're my quota for the month!"

"Just wait . . ."

She doesn't slow down. Marching through the main section of the exhibit hall, she cuts in front of a couple trying to get their photo taken with Archie Bunker's chair.

"Viv, please . . ." I beg, quickly racing after her. "You can't do this."

She stops at the ultimatum. "What'd you say?"

"You're not listening—"

"Don't you *ever* tell me what to do."

"But I—"

"Didn't you hear what I said?!"

"Viv, they'll kill you."

Her finger's frozen in midair. "What?"

"They'll kill you. They'll snap your neck and make it look like you tripped down some stairs. Just like they did with Matthew." She's silent as I say the words. "You know I'm right. Now that Janos knows who you are—you saw what he's like; he doesn't care if you're seventeen or seventy. You think he's just gonna let you go back to refilling Senators' water glasses?"

She tries to respond, but nothing comes out. Her brow unfurrows, and her hands start to shake. Like before, she starts to pick anxiously at the back of her ID. "I-I need to make a call," she insists, rushing for the pay phone in the ice cream parlor. I'm a step behind her. She won't say it, but I see the way she's clutching her ID. She wants Mom.

"Viv, don't call her . . ."

"This isn't about you, Harris."

She thinks I'm only looking out for myself. She's wrong. The guilt's been swirling through my gut since the moment I first asked her for that one little favor. I was terrified it'd come to this.

"I wish I could take it back . . . I really do," I tell her. "But if you're not careful—"

"I *was* careful! Remember, I'm not the one who caused this!"

"Please, just stop for a minute," I beg as she once again takes off. "Janos is probably drilling through your life right now."

"Maybe he's not. Ever think of that?"

She's getting too riled. It breaks my heart to do this, but it's the only way to keep her safe. As she's about the enter the ice-cream store, I cut in front of her. "Viv, you make that call and you're putting your whole family at risk."

"You don't know that!"

"I don't? Out of thirty pages, you're the only five-foot-ten black girl. He'll find your name in two seconds. That's what he does. Now, I know you hate me right now—and you should—but please . . . just listen . . . If you go in there and call your parents, that's two more people Janos has to clean up to make this mess go away."

That's all it takes. Her shoulders rise, revealing her full height, while the tears in her eyes give away her age. It's so easy to forget how young she is.

On my left, I catch our reflection in a nearby exhibit case: me in a black suit, Viv in her navy one. So professional and put together. Behind the glass are Mr. Rogers's red sweater and an Oscar the Grouch puppet. Oscar's frozen in his garbage can with his mouth wide open.

Following my gaze, Viv stares at the Grouch, whose empty black and white eyes stare hauntingly back.

"I'm sorry, Viv." It's the second time I've said those words. But this time, she needs them.

"I-I was just doing you a favor," she stutters, her voice breaking.

"I shouldn't have asked you, Viv—I never thought . . ."

"My mom . . . if she—" She cuts herself off, trying not to think about it. "What about my aunt in Philly? Maybe she can—"

"Don't put your family at risk."

"*I* shouldn't put them at risk? How could . . . how could you do this to me?!" She stumbles backwards, once again scanning each passing tourist. I thought it was because she was scared, nervous—forever the outsider trying to fit in—but the longer I watch her, the more I realize that's only part of the picture. People who look for help tend to be the type of people who're used to getting it. Her hand continues to clutch her ID. Her mom. . . her dad . . . her aunt—they've been there her whole life, pushing, aiding, cheering. Now they're gone. And Viv's feeling it.

She's not the only one. As she nervously searches the crowd, a sharp, nauseous pain continues to slice through my belly. No matter what else happens, I'll never forgive myself for hurting her like this.

"Whatta I do now?" she asks.

"It's okay," I promise, hoping to soothe. "I have plenty of cash—maybe we can . . . I can hide you in a hotel."

"By myself?"

The way she asks the question, I can already tell it's a bad idea. Especially if she panics and doesn't stay put. I made her a sitting duck once. I'm not abandoning her and doing it again. "Okay . . . forget the hotel. What if we—?"

"You wrecked my life," she blurts.

"Viv . . ."

"Don't *Viv*. You wrecked it, Harris, and then you—oh, God . . . do you have any idea what you've done?"

"It was supposed to be one little favor—I swear, if I thought this would happen . . ."

"Please don't say that. Don't say you didn't know . . ."

She's absolutely right. I *should've* known—I spend every day calculating political permutations—but when it came to this, the only thing I was worried about was myself.

"Viv, I swear, if I could undo it . . ."

"But you can't!"

In the last three minutes, she's hit all the stages of emotional response: from anger to denial, to despair, to acceptance, and now back to anger. It's all in reaction to one unchangeable fact: Now that I've gotten her involved, Janos isn't giving up until we're both dead.

"Viv, I need you to focus—we have to get out of here."

". . . and I made it worse," she mumbles. "I did this to myself."

"That's not true," I insist. "This has nothing to do with you. *I* did this. To both of us."

She's still in shock, struggling to process everything that's happened. She looks at me, then down at herself. It's not just *me* anymore. *We*. From here on in, we're chained at the wrist.

"We should call the police . . ." she stutters.

"After what happened with Lowell?"

She's quick enough to see the big picture instantly. If Janos got to the number two person at Justice, all paths to law enforcement take us straight back to him.

"What about going to someone else . . . ? Don't you have any friends?"

The question backhands me across the face. The two people I'm closest to are already dead, Lowell's turned, and there's no way to tell who else Janos has gotten to. All the politicians and staffers I've worked with over the years—sure they're friends, but in this town, well . . . that doesn't mean I trust them. "Besides," I explain, "anyone we talk to—we're painting a target on their chest. Should we do to someone else what I did to you?"

She stares me down, knowing I'm right. But it doesn't stop her from searching for a way out.

"What about any of the other pages?" she asks. "Maybe they can tell us who they made drop-offs to . . . y'know, who else was playing the game."

"That's why I wanted the delivery records from the cloakroom. But there's nothing there from any of the game days."

"So all of us—all the pages—we were being used without even knowing it?"

"Maybe for the other bets, but not for the gold mine."

"What're you talking about?"

"That kid who hit Matthew—Toolie Williams—he's the one who had your nametag. He was dressed up to look like a page."

"Why would someone want to look like a page?"

"I'm guessing Janos paid him to do it . . . and that Janos is acting on behalf of someone else who had a vested interest in the outcome."

"You think it goes back to the gold mine?"

"Hard to say, but they're the only ones who benefit."

"I still don't understand," Viv says. "How does Wendell Mining benefit if there's supposedly no gold in the mine?"

"Or more specifically," I add, "why does a company that has no mining experience spend two years trying to buy a gold mine with no gold in it?"

We both stare at each other, but Viv quickly looks away. We may be stuck together, but she's not forgiving me that quickly. More important, I don't think she wants to know the answer. Too bad for her, that only makes one of us.

I pull the rolled-up pages from Matthew's briefing book out of my pocket. I can still hear the mayor's voice in my head. Wendell was already getting to work, but there wasn't a piece of mining equipment in sight. "So what're they doing down there?"

"You mean other than mining?"

I shake my head. "The way the mayor said it . . . I don't think they're mining."

"Then what else do you need a gold mine for?"

"That's the question, isn't it?"

She knows what I'm thinking. "Why don't you just call the mayor back and—"

"And what? Ask him to take a little snoop around and then put his life in danger? Besides, even if he did, would you trust the answer?"

Viv again goes silent. "So what do we do?" she finally asks.

All this time, I've been looking for a lead. I reread the name of the town from the sheet of paper in my hands. *Leed.* Leed, indeed. The only place that has the answer.

Checking the exhibit hall one last time, I take off for the escalator. "Let's go," I call out to Viv.

She's right behind me. She may be mad, but she understands the danger of being by herself. The fear alone sends her from anger back to acceptance, reluctant though it may be. As she falls in next to me, she takes one last look at Oscar the Grouch. "You really think it's smart to go all the way to South Dakota?"

"You think it's any safer here?"

She doesn't answer.

Sure, it's a gamble—but not nearly as risky as a company betting on a gold mine that has no gold in it, then keeping all the locals away so no one sees what they're really up to. Even a seventeen-year-old knows something here stinks—and the only way to find out *what* is by going directly to the source.

29

TWO HOURS LATER, WE'RE in the back of a taxi in Dulles, Virginia. The sign out front is easy to miss, but I've been here before. Piedmont-Hawthorne's Corporate Aviation Terminal.

"Just give me five back," I say to the cab driver, who's taken far too many glances at us in his rearview mirror. Maybe it's our silence . . . maybe it's the fact Viv won't even look at me. Or maybe it's the fact I just gave him a crappy tip.

"Actually, keep the change," I tell the cabbie as I paint on a warm grin and force a laugh at the *Elliot in the Morning* promo that screams from the radio. The cabbie smiles back and counts his money. People are far less likely to remember you when you haven't pissed them off. "Have a great day," I add as Viv and I climb outside. He gives us a wave without looking back.

"You sure this is legal?" Viv asks, forever the good girl as she follows me toward the squatty modern building.

"I didn't say anything about legal—all I'm looking for is smart."

"And this is smart?"

"You'd rather fly commercial?"

Viv goes back to her silence. We went through this on the ride over here. This way, they won't even ask for ID.

There aren't many places you can get a private plane in less than two hours. Thankfully, Congress is one of them. And all it took was a single phone call. Two years ago, during a key vote on a controversial aviation bill, the head of FedEx's government relations office called and asked to speak to Senator Stevens. Personally. Knowing they never cried wolf, I took a chance and put the call through. It was a gorgeous chess move by them. With Stevens on board, it set the tone for the rest of the Midwest Senators, who quickly followed with support for the bill.

Exactly two hours ago, I called FedEx's government relations office and asked them to return the favor. The Senator, I explained, didn't want to miss a last-minute fundraising opportunity in South Dakota, so he asked me to call. Personally.

That's what brings us here. According to the ethics rules, a Senator can use a private corporate jet as long as he reimburses the company for the price of a first-class commercial ticket, which we can repay later. It's a genius loophole— and Viv and I just jumped headfirst right through it.

As we're about to enter the building, an automatic door slides open, revealing a room that reminds me of a fancy hotel lobby. Upholstered head chairs. Victorian bronze lamps. Burgundy and gray carpet.

"Can I help you find your aircraft?" a woman in a business suit asks as she leans over the reception desk on our right.

Viv smiles but then makes a face when she realizes that the sudden helpfulness is directed toward me.

"Senator Stevens," I say.

"Here you go," a deep voice calls out just past the reception desk. I look over as a pilot with brushed-back blond hair nods our way.

"Tom Heidenberger," he says, introducing himself with a pilot's grip. From the handshake alone, I know he's former military. He reaches over and shakes Viv's hand as well. She stands straight up, enjoying the attention.

"Senator on his way?" the pilot asks.

"Actually, he's not gonna make it. I'm speaking in his place."

"Lucky you," he says with a grin.

"And this is Catherine, our new legislative assistant," I say, introducing Viv. Thanks to her navy suit and above-average height, she doesn't even get a second glance. Congressional staffs are full of kids.

"So you ready to go, Senator?" the pilot asks.

"Absolutely," I reply. "Though I'd love if I could use one of your phones before we take off."

"No problem at all," the pilot says. "Is it a regular call, or private?"

"Private," Viv and I say simultaneously.

The pilot laughs. "Calling the Senator himself, huh?" We laugh along with him as he points us around the corner and down the hallway. "First door on your right."

Inside, it's a miniature conference room no bigger than a kitchenette. There's a desk, a single leather chair, and on the wall, an inspirational poster of a man climbing a mountain. At the center of the desk is a shiny black telephone. Viv picks up the receiver; I hit the button for the speakerphone.

"What're you doing?" she asks as the dial tone hums through the room.

"Just in case you need help . . ."

"I'll be okay," she shoots back, annoyed that I'm checking up on her. As she hits the button marked *Speaker,* the dial tone disappears.

I can't say I blame her. Even forgetting that I got her into this (which she doesn't), this is her show—and these two phone calls are ones only she can make.

Her fingers tap at the Touch-Tones, and I hear the ringing through the receiver. A female voice picks up on the other end.

"Hey, Adrienne, it's Viv," she says, pumping excitement into her voice. The show's already on. "No . . . yeah . . . nuh-uh, really? And she said that?" There's a short pause as Viv plays along. "That's why I'm calling," Viv explains. "No . . . just listen . . ."

The female voice on the other line belongs to Adrienne Kaye, one of Viv's two roommates in the Senate page dorm. As Viv told me on the ride over, every night, when the pages get back from work, they're supposed to sign the official check-in sheet to make sure everyone's accounted for. For the thirty pages, it's a simple system that works just fine—that is, until last week, when Adrienne decided to ditch curfew and stay out late with a group of interns from Indiana. The only reason Adrienne got away with it was because Viv signed Adrienne's name at the check-in desk and told the proctors she was in the bathroom. Now, Viv's trying to get the favor returned.

Within thirty seconds, the job's done. "Great—yeah, no—just tell them it's that time of the month; that'll keep them away," Viv says, giving me the thumbs-up. Adrienne's in. "Nuh-uh . . . no one you know," Viv adds as she glances my way. There's no smile on her face.

"Jason? *Never,*" Viv laughs. "Are you a nutbag? I don't care if he's cute—he can pick his nose with his tongue . . ."

She keeps the conversation going just long enough to keep it believable. "Cool, thanks again, Adrienne," she says, finally hanging up.

"Well done," I tell her as she stands in front of the desk and dials the next number.

She nods to herself, showing the tiniest hint of pride. The chase with Janos pulled her down a few pegs. She's still trying to climb her way back up. Too bad for Viv, the next call will only make it harder.

As the phone rings on the other line, I already see the change in her posture. She lowers her chin, ducking down just slightly. Her toes turn inward, one shoe picking at the tip of the other. As her hand grips the receiver, she again glances at me and turns away. I know a call for help when I see one.

I hit the button for the speakerphone just as a female voice picks up on the other line. Viv looks down at the red light marked *Speaker*. This time, she doesn't shut it off.

"Doctor's office," a female voice answers.

"Hey, Momma, it's me," Viv says, forcing the same amount of bubbliness through the phone. Her tone is pitch perfect—even better than the last call.

"What's wrong?" her mom asks.

"Nothing . . . I'm great," Viv says as she leans her left hand against the desk. She's already having trouble standing up. Two minutes ago, she was seventeen, going on twenty-seven. Now she's barely thirteen.

"Why'm I on speakerphone?" Mom asks.

"You're not, Momma; it's a cell phone that's—"

"Take me off speaker—y'know I hate it."

Viv looks my way, and I instinctively step back. She hits the button marked *Speaker*, and the call leaves the room. The good news is, thanks to the volume of Mom's voice, I can still hear her through the receiver.

Earlier, I said we shouldn't make this call. Now we have to. If Mom pulls the fire alarm, we're not going anywhere.

"Better," Mom says. "Now, whatsa matter?"

There's real concern in her voice. Sure, Mom's loud . . . but not from anger . . . or bossiness. Senator Stevens has the same tone. That sense of immediacy. The sound of strength.

"Tell me what happened," Mom insists. "Someone make another comment?"

"No one made a comment."

"What about that boy from Utah?"

I can't place Mom's accent—part southern Ohio drawl, part broad vowels of Chicago—but whatever it is, when I close my eyes . . . the intonations . . . the speed of each syllable . . . it's like hearing Viv twenty years in the future. Then I open my eyes and see Viv hunched over from the stress. She's got a long way to go.

"What about the Utah boy?" Mom persists.

"That boy's an ass—"

"Vivian . . ."

"Momma, please—it isn't a cuss. They say *ass* on every dumb sitcom on TV."

"So now you live in a sitcom, huh? Then I guess your *sitcom* mom will be the one paying your bills and taking care of all your problems."

"I don't have problems. It was one comment from one boy . . . The proctors took care of it . . . It's fine."

"Don't let them do that to you, Vivian. God says—"

"I said *I'm fine*."

"Don't let them—"

"Mom!"

Mom pauses—a triple-length pause only a mother can

give. All the love she has for her daughter—you can tell she's dying to scream it through the phone . . . but she also knows that strength isn't easily transferred. It has to be found. From within.

"Tell me something about the Senators," Mom finally says. "They ask you to write any legislation yet?"

"No, Mom, I haven't written any legislation yet."

"You *will*."

It's hard to explain, but the way she says it, even I believe her.

"Listen, Momma . . . the only reason I'm calling . . . they're taking us on an overnight to Monticello . . . Thomas Jefferson's home . . ."

"I know what Monticello is."

"Yeah, well . . . anyway, I didn't want you fretting when you called and we weren't here." Viv stops, waiting to see if Mom buys it. We both hold our breath.

"I told you they'd take you up there, Viv—I saw pictures in the old brochure," Mom says, clearly excited. And just like that, it's done.

"Yeah . . . they do it every year," Viv adds. There's a sudden sadness in her voice. Almost as if she wished it weren't that easy. She glances up at the poster on the wall. We all have our mountains to climb.

"So when you coming back?"

"I think tomorrow night," Viv says, checking with me. I shrug and nod at the same time. "Yeah . . . tomorrow night," she adds.

"Don't forget to ask about Sally Hemings . . ."

"Don't worry, Momma—I'm sure it's part of the tour."

"It better be—what'd they think, we're just gonna forget about all that? *Please*. It's bad enough they're trying to sell it now as some tender love affair . . ." She stops a moment. "You got enough money and all that?"

"Yeah."

"Good. Right answer."

Viv lets out a soft smile at the joke.

"You okay, Boo?" Mom asks.

"I'm great," Viv insists. "Just getting excited for the trip."

"You should be. Treasure every experience, Vivian. They all matter."

"I know, Momma . . ."

Like before, there's a maternal pause. "You sure you're okay?"

Viv shifts her weight, leaning even harder on the desk. The way she's hunched over, it's almost as if she needs the desk to hold her up. "I told you, Momma. I'm great."

"Yes. You are. True greatness." Mom's voice practically beams through the phone. "Make us proud, Vivian. God gave you to us for a reason. Love, love, love you."

"Love you, too, Momma."

As Viv hangs up the phone, she's still hunched on the desk. Sure, both phone calls can get her grounded and maybe even expelled—but it's still far better than being dead.

"Viv, just so you know—"

"Please, Harris . . ."

"But I—"

"Harris . . . please, for once . . . stop talking."

"Ready to fly?" the pilot asks as we return to the main reception area.

"All set," I say as he leads us toward the back of the

building. Over my shoulder, Viv stays silent, purposely walking a few steps behind. I'm not sure if she doesn't want to see me or doesn't want me seeing her. Either way, I've already pushed enough.

Up the hallway, there are two locked security doors straight ahead. Behind me, I take one last look at the reception area and notice a thin man in a pinstriped suit sitting in one of the upholstered chairs. He wasn't there when we walked in. It's like he appeared out of nowhere. We weren't gone that long. I try to get a better look at him, but he quickly averts his eyes, flipping open his cell phone.

"Everything okay?" the pilot asks.

"Yeah . . . of course," I insist as we reach the doors.

The woman at the reception desk hits a button, and there's a loud magnetic thunk. The doors unlock, and the pilot shoves them open, ushering us outside. No metal detector . . . no wanding . . . no screening . . . no luggage . . . no hassle. Fifty feet in front of us, sitting on the runway, is a brand-new Gulfstream G400. Along the side of the jet, a thin blue and orange stripe shines in the late afternoon sunlight. There's even a tiny red carpet at the base of the stairs.

"Beats the heck outta flying coach, huh?" the pilot asks. Viv nods. I try to act unimpressed. Our chariot awaits.

As we climb the stairs to the plane, I look back at the plate-glass window of the hangar, trying to get another look at the thin man inside. He's nowhere in sight.

Ducking down and stepping into the cabin, we find nine leather club chairs, a buttery tan leather sofa, and a flight attendant who's waiting just for us.

"Let me know if there's anything you need," she offers. "Champagne . . . orange juice . . . anything at all."

A second pilot's already in the cockpit. When they're

both on board, the flight attendant shuts the door, and we're on our way. I take the first chair in front. Viv takes the one all the way in back.

The flight attendant doesn't make us put on our seat belts or read a list of rules. "The seats recline all the way," she offers. "You can sleep the whole flight if you want."

The sweetness in her voice is at fairy godmother levels, but it doesn't make me feel any better. Over the past six months, Matthew and I spent countless hours trying to figure out which of our friends and coworkers were potentially playing the game. We narrowed it down to everyone—which is why the only person I trust anymore is a seventeen-year-old who's terrified and hates me. So even though I'm sitting on a thirty-eight-million-dollar private airplane, it doesn't change the fact that two of my closest friends in the world are gone forever, while some killer for hire is chasing after us, ready to make sure we join them. No question, there's nothing to celebrate.

The plane rumbles forward, and I sink down in my seat. Outside the window, a man in blue cargo pants and a blue-and-white-striped button-down shirt rolls up the red carpet, stands at attention, and salutes us as we leave. Even when he's finished, he just stands there, frozen in place—which is why I notice the sudden movement over his shoulder. Back in the hangar. The thin man on the cell phone presses his open palms against the plate-glass window and watches us leave.

"Any idea who that is?" I ask the flight attendant, noticing that she's staring at him, too.

"No idea," she says. "I figured he was with you."

30

"THEY'RE ON A PLANE," Janos said into his phone as he stormed out of the Hotel George, signaling the doorman for a cab.

"How do you know?" Sauls asked on the other line.

"Believe me—I know."

"Who told you?"

"Does it matter?"

"Actually, it does."

Janos paused, refusing to answer. "Just be content with the fact that I know."

"Don't treat me like a schmuck," Sauls warned. "Suddenly, the magician can't reveal his tricks?"

"Not when the assholes backstage are always opening their mouths."

"What're you talking about?"

"Sell any good Renoirs lately?" Janos asked.

Sauls stopped. "That was a year and a half ago. And it was a Morisot."

"I'm well aware what it was—especially when it almost got me killed," Janos pointed out. This wasn't the first time he and Sauls had worked together. But as Janos knew, if they couldn't get back in control soon, it easily could be their last.

"Just tell me how you—"

"Redial on Harris's phone said he was talking to the mayor."

"Aw, piss," Sauls moaned. "You think he's going to Dakota?"

As a cab stopped in front of him and the doorman opened the door, Janos didn't answer.

"I don't believe it," Sauls added. "I got an embassy dinner tonight, and they're fuckin'—" He cut himself off. "Where're you now?"

"In transit," Janos said as he tossed his leather duffel into the backseat.

"Well, you better get your ass to South Dakota before they—"

Janos hit the End button and slapped his phone shut. After his run-in with the Capitol Police, he already had one headache. He didn't need another. Sliding inside the cab and slamming the door, he pulled a copy of *MG World* magazine from his duffel, flipped to a feature story on a restored 1964 MGB roadster, and lost himself in the details of adding a smaller steering wheel to complement the car's diminutive size. It was the one thing that brought calm to Janos's day. Unlike people, machines could be controlled.

"Where to?" the cabbie asked.

Janos glanced up from the magazine for barely a moment. "National Airport," he replied. "And do me a favor—try to avoid the potholes . . ."

31

THE SOUTH DAKOTA sky is pitch black by the time our Chevy Suburban turns west onto Interstate 90, and the windshield is already covered with the rat-a-tat-tat of dead bugs kamikaze-ing toward the headlights. Thanks to FedEx, the Suburban was waiting for us when we landed, and since it's their rental, we didn't have to put down a license or credit card. In fact, when I told them that the Senator was trying to be more conscious of cultivating his farm-boy image, they were more than happy to cancel the private driver and just give us the car instead. Anything to keep the Senator happy. "Yessiree," I say to Viv, who's sitting in the passenger seat next to me. "Senator Stevens would much prefer to drive himself."

Refusing to say a word, Viv stares straight out the front window and keeps her arms crossed in front of her chest. After four hours of similar treatment on the plane, I'm used to the silence, but the further we get from the lights of Rapid City, the more disconcerting it gets. And not just because of Viv's mood. Once we passed the exit for Mount Rushmore, the bright lamps on the highway started appearing less and less frequently. First they were every hundred or so feet . . . then every few hundred . . . and now—I haven't seen one for miles. Same with other cars. It's barely nine o'clock local time, but as our headlights joust through the darkness, there's not another soul in sight.

"You sure this is right?" Viv asks as we follow a sign for Highway 85.

"I'm doing my best," I tell her. But as the road narrows to two lanes, I glance over and notice that her arms are no longer crossed in front of her chest. Instead, her hands grip the strap of her seat belt where it runs diagonally across her chest. Holding on for dear life.

"Is this right?" she repeats anxiously, turning toward me for the first time in five hours. She sits higher in the seat than I do, and as she says the words, her saucer-cup eyes practically glow in the darkness. Right there, the adolescent who's mad I got her into this snaps back into the little girl who's just plain scared.

It's been a long time since I was seventeen, but if there's one thing I remember, it was the need for simple reassurance.

"We're doing fine," I reply, forcing confidence into my voice. "No lie."

She smiles faintly and looks back out the front window. I'm not sure if she believes it, but at this point—after traveling this long—she'll take anything she can get.

Up ahead, the two-lane road swerves to the right, then back to the left. It's not until my headlights bounce off the enormous cliff sides on either side of us that I realize we're weaving our way through a canyon. Viv leans forward in her seat, craning her neck and looking up through the windshield. Her eye catches something, and she leans forward a bit further.

"What's wrong?" I ask.

She doesn't answer. The way her head's turned, I can't see her expression, but she's no longer holding on to the seat belt. Instead, both hands are on the dashboard as she stares skyward.

"Oh . . ." she finally whispers.

I lean up against the steering wheel and crane my neck toward the sky. I don't see a thing.

"What?" I ask. "What is it?"

Still staring upward, she says, "Are those the Black Hills?"

I take a second look for myself. In the distance, the walls of the cliff rise dramatically—at least four hundred feet straight toward the clouds. If it weren't for the moonlight—where the outlined edges of the cliff are black against the dark gray sky—I wouldn't even be able to see where they end.

I glance back at Viv, who's still glued to the sky. The way her mouth hangs open and her eyebrows rise . . . At first, I thought it was fear. It's not. It's pure amazement.

"I take it they don't have mountains like these where you're from?" I ask.

She shakes her head, still dumbfounded. Her jaw is practically in her lap. Watching the sheer wonder in her reaction—there's only one other person who looked at mountains like that. Matthew always said it—they were one of the only things that ever made him feel small.

"You okay there?" Viv asks.

Snapped back to reality, I'm surprised to find her staring straight at me. "O-Of course," I say, turning back to the curving yellow lines at the center of the road.

She raises an eyebrow—too sharp to believe it. "You're really not as great a liar as you think."

"I'm fine," I insist. "It's just . . . being out here . . .

Matthew would've liked it. He really . . . he would've liked it."

Viv watches me carefully, measuring every syllable. I stay focused on the blur of yellow lines snaking along the road. I've been in this awkward silence before. It's like the thirty-second period right after I brief the Senator on a tough issue. Perfect quiet. Where decisions get made.

"Y'know, I . . . uh . . . I saw his picture in his office," she eventually says.

"What're you talking about?"

"Matthew. I saw his photo."

I stare at the road, picturing it myself. "The one with him and the blue lake?"

"Yeah . . . that's the one," she nods. "He looked . . . he looked nice."

"He was."

She eventually turns back toward the dark skyline. I stay with the swerving yellow lines. It's no different from the conversation with her mom. This time, the silence is even longer than before.

"Michigan," she quietly whispers.

"Excuse me?"

"You said, *they don't have mountains where you're from.* Well, that's where I'm from."

"Michigan?"

"Michigan."

"Detroit?"

"Birmingham."

I tap my thumbs against the steering wheel as another bug splats against the windshield.

"That still doesn't mean I forgive you," Viv adds.

"I wouldn't expect you to." Up ahead, the walls of the cliff disappear as we leave the canyon behind. I hit the gas, and the engine grumbles toward the straightaway. Like before, there's nothing on our right or left—not even a guardrail. Out here, you have to know where you're going. Though it still always starts with that crucial first step.

"So do you like Birmingham?" I ask.

"It's high school," she replies, making me feel every year of my age.

"We used to go up for basketball games in Ann Arbor," I tell her.

"Really? So you know Birmingham . . . you've been there?" There's a slight hesitation at the back of her voice. Like she's looking for an answer.

"Just once," I say. "A guy in our fraternity let us crash at his parents'."

She looks out her window at the side mirror. The canyon's long gone—lost in the black horizon.

"Y'know, I lied," she says, her tone flat and lifeless.

"Pardon?"

"I lied . . ." she repeats, her eyes still on the side mirror. "What I said up in the storage room—about being one of only two black girls in the school . . . ?"

"What're you taking about?"

"I know I shouldn't have . . . it's stupid . . ."

"What—"

"I said there were two, but there're actually fourteen of us. Fourteen black kids. Swear to God. I guess . . . yeah . . . fourteen."

"Fourteen?"

"I'm sorry, Harris . . . I just wanted to convince you I could handle myself . . . Don't be mad . . ."

"Viv . . ."

"I thought you'd think I was strong and tough and—"

"It doesn't matter," I interrupt.

She finally turns toward me. "Wha?"

"It doesn't matter," I reiterate. "I mean, fourteen . . . out of how many? Four hundred? Five hundred?"

"Six hundred and fifty. Maybe six-sixty."

"Exactly," I say. "Two . . . twelve . . . fourteen . . . You're still pretty outnumbered."

The smallest of smiles creeps up her cheeks. She likes that one. But the way her hands once again grip the seat belt across her chest, it's clearly still an issue for her.

"It's okay to smile," I tell her.

She shakes her head. "That's what my mom always says. Right after *rinse and spit.*"

"Your Mom's a dentist?"

"No, she's a . . ." Viv pauses and offers a slight shrug. ". . . she's a dental hygienist."

And right there I spot it. That's where her hesitation comes from. It's not that she's not proud of her mom . . . but she knows what it feels like to be the one kid who's different.

Again, I don't remember much from when I was seventeen, but I do know what it's like to have Career Day at school when you secretly hope your dad's not invited. And in the world of Ivy League Washington, I also know what it's like to feel second-class.

"Y'know, my dad was a barber," I offer.

She shyly glances my way, rechecking me up and down. "You serious? Really?"

"Really," I say. "Cut all my friends' hair for seven bucks apiece. Even the bad bowl cuts."

Turning toward me, she gives me an even bigger grin.

"Just so you know, I'm not embarrassed of my parents," she insists.

"I never thought you were."

"The thing is . . . they wanted so bad to get me in the school district, but the only way to afford it was by buying this tiny little house that's literally the last one on the district line. Right on the line. Y'know what that's like? I mean, when that's your starting point . . ."

". . . you can't help but feel like the last man in the race," I say, nodding in agreement. "Believe me, Viv, I still remember why I first came to the Hill. I spent my first few years trying to right every wrong that was done to my parents. But sometimes you have to realize that some fights are unwinnable."

"That doesn't mean you don't fight them," she challenges.

"You're right—and that's a great quote for all the Winston Churchill fans out there—but when the sun sets at the end of the day, you can't win 'em . . ."

"*You can't win 'em all?* Nuh-uh, you really think that?" she asks with complete sincerity. "I figured that was just in bad movies and . . . I don't know . . . people say the government is faceless and, y'know, broken, but even if you're here a long time . . . like when I saw you . . . that speech . . . You really think that?"

I grip the steering wheel as if it were a shield, but it doesn't stop her question from stabbing through my chest. Next to me, Viv waits for her answer—and single-handedly reminds me what I'd forgotten long ago. Sometimes you need a slap in the face to realize what's coming out of your mouth.

"No . . ." I finally say. "That's not what I'm saying at all . . ."

Viv nods, content that everything's right in at least that part of her world.

"But let me tell you something," I quickly add. "There's something else that goes along with feeling like you're last in the race—and it's not a bad thing. Being last means you've got a hunger in your gut no one else'll ever be able to comprehend. They couldn't buy it with all their money. And know what that hunger gives you?"

"Besides my big butt?"

"Success, Viv. No matter where you go, or what you do. Hunger feeds success."

We sit in silence for a full minute as my words fade beneath the hum of the engine. She lets the quiet sink in—and this time, I think she's doing it on purpose.

Staring out the front window, Viv studies the long, angled road in front of us and, to her credit, never lets me know what she's thinking. She's gonna be a ruthless negotiator one day.

"How much further till we get there?" she finally asks.

"Fifteen miles until we hit Deadwood . . . then this town called Pluma . . . then it's at least a good hour or so after that. Why?"

"No reason," she says, pulling her legs up so she's sitting Indian-style in the passenger seat. With her pointer and middle fingers, she opens and closes an imaginary pair of finger-scissors. "I just wanna know how much time we have for you to tell me about your barber shop."

"If you want, I bet we can grab a bite to eat in Deadwood. Even out here, they can't mess up grilled cheese."

"See, now we got something," Viv says. "Grilled cheese in Deadwood sounds great."

32

Janos's trip took two different planes, one stopover, and a three-hour leg with a petite Asian woman whose lifelong dream was to open a soul food restaurant that served fried shrimp. Yet he still hadn't reached his final destination.

"Minneapolis?" Sauls asked through the cell phone. "What're you doing in Minneapolis?"

"I heard they have a great Foot Locker at the Mall of America," Janos growled, pulling his bag from the conveyor belt. "Getting stuck in the airport just wasn't enough fun for one night."

"What about the jet?"

"They couldn't turn it around fast enough. I called every place on the list. Any other wonderful suggestions?"

"And now they canceled your flight?"

"Never was one—I figured I'd find another connection to Rapid City, but let's just say South Dakota isn't the top priority on the airlines' flight plans."

"So when's the next—?"

"First thing tomorrow," Janos said as he shoved his way outside and noticed a sky blue 1965 Mustang convertible passing by. The grille emblem was from a '67, but the tonneau cover looked original. Nice work.

"Janos . . ."

"Don't worry," he said, his eyes still on the red tail-lights of the convertible as they faded into the night. "As soon as they wake up, I'll be standing on their chests."

33

THERE ARE FEW THINGS more instantly depressing than the stale, mildewed smell of an old motel room. The sour, mossy whiff is still in the air as I wake up. *Enjoy your stay at the Gold House*, a plastic placard on the night-stand reads. There's a dot-matrix cartoon drawing of a pot of gold at the bottom corner of the sign, which looks like it was made the same year they last changed these sheets.

Last night, we didn't get in until after midnight. Right now, the digital lights on the alarm clock tell me it's five in the morning. I'm still on East Coast time. Seven A.M. it is. Kicking the thin, fuzzy blanket aside (I might as well've covered myself with a gauze pad), I look back at the pancake pillow and count seventeen black hairs. Already I know it's gonna be a bad day.

Next to me, the other bed is still made. When we checked in last night, I made Viv wait in the car as I told the woman at the front desk that I needed one room for myself and one for my kids. I don't care how tall and ma-ture Viv looks. A white guy in his thirties checking into a motel with a younger black girl—and no luggage. Even in a *big* town, that'll get people chatting.

On my left, the seventies-era flower-patterned curtains are closed, but I can still see a sliver of the dark sky outside. On my right, the sink is right next to the bed, and as I grab the toothbrush and toiletries we bought in the gas station, I plug in the iron I borrowed from the front desk. With all the running around, our suits look like we played baseball in them. If we plan on pulling this off, we're gonna have to look the part and get the sharp corners back.

As the iron heats up, I turn to the phone on the nightstand and dial Viv's room. It rings over and over. No answer. I'm actually not surprised. After what we went through yesterday, she has to be exhausted. I hang up and dial again. Still nothing. I was the same way in high school. The clock radio could scream for an hour, but nothing got me up until Mom banged on the door.

Putting on my slacks, I again check my watch. Even the earliest flight won't get Janos in for another ten minutes, not including the two hour drive to get here. We're okay. Just go knock and get her up.

Undoing the chain lock, I tug the door open. A puff of fresh air shoves back at the mustiness—but as I step out and head to my right, I immediately feel something smack into my ankles. I plummet face first toward the concrete breezeway. It's impossible. He can't be here yet . . .

My cheek scrapes against the ground, even as my hands try to break my fall. I turn over as fast as I can. I can already picture Janos's face . . . Then I hear the voice behind me.

"Sorry . . . sorry," Viv says, sitting on the floor of the concrete breezeway, tucking her long legs out of the way. "You alright?"

"I thought you were sleeping."

"I don't sleep . . . at least not that well," she says, looking up from a small brochure. "I don't mind, though . . . My mom says some things just *are*. I'm a bad sleeper. That's the way I was built."

"What're you doing out here?"

"My room stinks. Literally. Like a geriatric barn. Think about it: old people mixed with animals—it's a good description."

Climbing to my feet, I roll my tongue inside my cheek. "So you're always up this early?"

"Page school starts at six-fifteen. The woman at the front desk . . . she's all talky, but in a cool way, y'know? I've been chatting with her for the past half hour. Can you believe she had two people in her graduating class? This town's in trouble."

"What're you—? I told you not to speak to anyone."

Viv shrinks down, but not by much. "Don't worry—I told her I'm the au pair . . . taking care of the kids."

"In a blue business suit?" I ask, pointing to her outfit.

"I didn't wear the jacket. Don't worry—she believed it. Besides, I was hungry. She gave me an orange," she explains, pulling it from her pocket. "One for you, too."

She hands me a plastic Baggie with an already peeled orange inside.

"She peeled it for you?"

"Don't ask. She insisted. I didn't want to upset her. We're the first guests they've had since . . . since the actual gold rush."

"So she's the one who gave you the brochures?"

She looks back down at a faded pamphlet entitled *The Homestead Mine—Staking a Claim in Our Future*. "I just thought I should read up on it. That's okay, right . . . ?"

There's a faint noise by the stairwell door. Like a crash.

"What was . . ."

"Shh," I say.

We both check the breezeway, following the sound up the walkway. The stairwell's at the far end. No one's there. There's another crashing sound. That's when we see the source of the noise. An ice machine dumping ice. Just ice, I tell myself. It doesn't make me feel any calmer.

"We should . . ."

". . . get out of here," Viv agrees.

We head for our respective doors. Four minutes of ironing later, I'm dressed to go. Viv's already waiting outside, her head once again buried in one of the old tourist pamphlets.

"All set?" I ask.

"Harris, you really gotta look at this place—you've never seen anything like it."

I don't need to read the pamphlet to realize she's right. We have no idea what we're getting into, but as I run up the walkway—as Viv chases right behind me—there's no slowing us down. Whatever Wendell's digging for, we need to know what's going on.

From the stairwell, Viv and I rush out into the Gold House's main lobby. Even considering the time, it's emptier than I expected. The front desk is vacant, the soda machines have black tape over the coin slots, and the *USA Today* vending machine has a handwritten sign in it that says, *Buy newspapers at Tommy's (across street).* Looking out onto Main Street, we see the signs in every window. *Out of Business*, it says at the gas station; *Lost*

Lease, it says at Fin's Hardware. Naturally, my eyes go straight to the barber shop: *Gone to Montana—God Bless*.

Across the lobby, I spot a metal display rack filled with the tourist brochures Viv picked up. *See How a Real Gold Bar Is Made! Visit the Leed Theater! Explore the Mining Museum!* But from the faded, yellowed paper, we already know the museum's closed, the theater's shut down, and the gold bars haven't been seen in years. It was the same way when I had to clean out the house after my dad passed. Sometimes you can't bring yourself to throw stuff away.

When we were heading here, I thought I'd be in my element. I'm not even close. This isn't a small town. It's a dead one.

"Pretty sad, huh?" a female voice asks.

I spin around, and a young woman with short black hair enters the lobby from the back room and steps behind the front desk. She can't be more than twenty-five, and while her complexion identifies her as Native American, even without it, her high cheekbones would be a clear giveaway.

"Hiya, Viv," she calls out, wiping some sleep from her eyes.

I shoot Viv a look. *You gave her your name?*

Viv shrugs and steps forward. I shake my head, and she steps back. "I'll go check on the kids," she says, moving for the front door.

"They're fine," I say, refusing to let her out of my sight. She's already said enough. The only reason we should be talking to anyone is because we need information, or help, or in this particular case, some last-minute directions.

"Can you tell us how to get to the Homestead mine?" I say as I head for the front desk.

"So they're reopening it again?" she asks.

"I have no idea," I counter, leaning an elbow on the front desk and fishing for info. "Everyone seems to have a different answer."

"Well, that's what I hear—though Dad says they still haven't talked to the union."

"Have they at least been throwing some business your way?" I ask, wondering if she's seen anybody in the motel.

"You'd think they would . . . but they got it all in trailers up there. Kitchens . . . sleeping quarters . . . everything. I'm telling you, they get an F in making friends."

"They're probably just mad they couldn't find a Holiday Inn," I say.

She smiles at the jab. In any small town, everyone hates the chains.

Studying me carefully, she cocks her head to the side. "Have I seen you before?" she asks.

"I don't think so . . ."

"You sure? Not at Kiwanis?"

"Pretty sure. I'm not really from the neighborhood."

"Really? And here I thought all the locals wore slacks and button-downs."

I pull back the slightest bit. She's starting to warm up, but that's not my goal. "Listen, about those directions . . ."

"Of course. Directions. All you gotta do is follow the road."

"Which one?"

"We only got but one," she says, tossing me another grin. "Left outta the driveway, then a sharp right up the hill."

I smile instinctively.

With a quick hop, she boosts herself over the front counter, grabs my arm, and leads me to the door.

"See that building . . . looks like a giant metal teepee?" she asks, pointing up the mountain to the only structure on top. "That's the headframe."

She immediately reads the confused look on my face.

"It covers the mine shaft," she adds. My look stays the same. ". . . also known in some circles as the *big hole in the ground*," she explains with a laugh. "It protects it from bad weather. That's where you'll find the cage."

"The cage?"

"The elevator," she says. "I mean, assuming you wanna go down . . ."

Viv and I share a glance, but neither of us says a word. Up until this point, I didn't even think that was an option.

"Just follow signs for *The Homestead*," the woman adds. "Won't take you five minutes. You got business up there?"

"Not until later. That's why we figured we'd check out Mount Rushmore first," I explain. "How do we get there?"

It's a pathetic bluff, but if Janos is as close as I think, we at least need to attempt to hide the trail. As she gives us directions, I pretend to write them down.

When she's done, I wave good-bye and head for our Suburban. Viv's right next to me, shaking her head. "Is that on purpose or is it just natural?" she finally asks as we pull out of the parking lot.

"I don't understand."

"The charm thing: leaning into the counter . . . her swooning at the small-town flair . . ." She stops a moment. "Y'know, who we are now is who we always were and who we'll always be. Is that how you've always been?" she asks.

The Suburban swings wide around a sharp right turn, pinning me against my door, and Viv against the armrest. As we weave our way up the hill, we're focused on the two-story triangular building that sits on top. Turning the final corner, the trees disappear, the paved road ends, and the ground levels off and turns rocky. Up ahead, a space the size of a football field spreads out in front of us. The ground's dirt, flanked by some jagged rock outcroppings that circle the entire field and rise about twenty feet in the air. It's as if they shaved off the top of the mountain and built the flat encampment that's directly ahead of us.

"So you have any idea what we're even looking for?" Viv asks, studying the terrain. It's a fair question—and one I've been asking myself since the moment we stepped off the plane.

"I think we'll know it when we see it," I tell her.

"But with Matthew . . . you really think Wendell Mining were the ones who had him killed?"

I continue watching the road in front of me. "All I know is, for the past two years, Wendell has been trying to buy this old middle-of-nowhere gold mine. Last year, they failed. This year, they tried to cut through the red tape by sliding it into the Appropriations bill, which according to Matthew, would've never gotten anywhere— that is, until it showed up as the newest item up for bid in our little Showcase Showdown."

"That doesn't mean Wendell Mining had him killed."

"You're right. But once I started digging around, I find out Wendell not only completely forged at least one of the letters endorsing the transfer, but that this wonderful gold mine they supposedly want doesn't have enough gold in it to make an anklet for a Barbie doll. Think about that a second. These guys at Wendell have spent the last two years killing themselves for a giant empty hole in the ground, and they're so anxious to get inside, they've already started moving in. Add that to the fact that two of my friends were killed for it and, well . . . with all the insanity going on, you better believe I want to see this thing for myself."

As we pull toward the edge of the gravel-covered makeshift parking lot, Viv turns to me and nods. "If you wanna know what the fuss is, you gotta go see the fuss yourself."

"Who said that, your mom?"

"Fortune cookie," Viv whispers.

At the center of the field is the teepee-shaped building with the word *Homestead* painted across the side. Closer to us, the parking lot is filled with at least a dozen other cars, and off to the left, three double-wide construction trailers are busy with guys in overalls going in and out, while two separate dump trucks back up toward the building. According to Matthew's report, the place is supposed to be abandoned and empty. Instead, we're staring at a beehive.

Viv motions to the side of the building, where another man in overalls is using a mud-covered forklift to unload a huge piece of computer equipment from the back of an eighteen-wheeler. Compared to the muddy forklift, the brand-new computer stands out like a Mack truck on a golf course.

"Why do you need a computer system to dig a giant hole in the ground?" Viv asks.

I nod in agreement, studying the front entrance to the triangular building. "That's the hundred-thousand-dollar question, isn't—"

There's a sharp tap as a knuckle raps against my

driver's-side window. I turn and spot a man with the filth-
iest construction hat I've ever seen. He puts on a smile; I
hesitantly roll down the window.

"Hiya," he says, waving with his clipboard. "You guys
here from Wendell?"

34

SO WE'RE DONE?" Trish asked, sitting back in her chair in the House Interior Committee's hearing room.

"As long as you have nothing else," Dinah said, shuffling the thick stack of loose pages together and drumming them into a neat pile on the long oval conference table. She wasn't thrilled to be stepping in for Matthew, but as she told her other office mates, the job still had to be done.

"No, I think that's—" Cutting herself off, Trish quickly flipped open her three-ring binder and shuffled through the pages. "Aw, crap," she added. "I just remembered . . . I got one last project . . ."

"Actually, me, too," Dinah said dryly, thumbing through her own notebook but never taking her eyes off her Senate counterpart.

Trish sat up straight and stared back at Dinah. For almost twenty seconds, the two women sat there, on opposite sides of the conference table, without saying a word. Next to them, Ezra and Georgia watched them like the spectators they usually were. *Samurai standoff*, Matthew used to call it. Happened every time they tried to close the bill. The final grab at the goody bag.

Dinah tapped the point of her pencil against the table, readying her sword. Even with Matthew gone, the battle had to go on. That is, until someone gave up.

"My mistake . . ." Trish finally offered. "I was reading it wrong . . . That project can wait till next year."

Ezra smiled. Dinah barely grinned. She was never one to gloat. Especially with the Senate. As she well knew, if you gloated with the Senate, they'd always bite you back.

"Glad to hear it," Dinah replied, zipping her fanny pack and standing up from the table.

Enjoying the victory, Ezra hummed *Someone's in the kitchen with Dinah* under his breath. Matthew used to do the same thing when his office mate would come in and throw around her weight. *Someone's in the kitchen I knooooow* . . .

"So that's it?" Georgia asked. "We're finally finished?"

"Actually, Matthew said you should've been finished a week ago," Dinah clarified. "Now we're in a mad scramble with a vote at the end of the week."

"The bill's on the Floor at the end of the week?" Trish asked. "Since when?"

"Since this morning, when Leadership made the announcement without asking anyone." All three of her colleagues shook their heads, but it really wasn't much of a surprise. During election years, the biggest race in Congress was always the one to get home. That's how campaigns were won. That and the individual projects Members brought home for their districts: a water project in Florida, a new sewer system in Massachusetts . . . and even that tiny gold mine in South Dakota, Dinah thought.

"You really think we can finish Conference in a week?" Trish called out.

"I don't see why not," Dinah replied, lugging the rest

of the paperwork to the door that connected to her office. "All you have to do now is sell it to your boss."

Trish nodded, watching Dinah leave. "By the way," she called out, "thanks for taking over for Matthew. I know it's been hard with everything that's—"

"It had to get done," Dinah interrupted. "It's as simple as that."

With a slam, the door shut behind her, and Dinah crossed back into her office. She was never one for the falsities of small talk, but more important, if she'd waited any longer, she might've missed the person who, as she looked across the room, was waiting so patiently for her.

"All set?" Barry asked, leaning against the short filing cabinet between Matthew's and Dinah's desks.

"All set," Dinah replied. "Now where do you want to go to celebrate?"

35

Y EAH . . . ABSOLUTELY . . . WE'RE from Wendell," I say, nodding to the big guy in overalls standing outside our car window. "How'd you know?"

He motions to my button-down shirt. Under his overalls, he's sporting a *Spring Break '94* T-shirt with neon orange letters. Doesn't take a genius to know who's the outsider.

"Shelley, right?" I ask, reading the name that's written in black magic marker across the front of his banged-up construction helmet. "Janos told me to say hi."

"Who's Janos?" he asks, confused.

That tells me the first part. Whatever's going on down there, these guys are just hired hands. "Sorry . . ." I say. "He's another Wendell guy. I thought you two might've—"

"Shelley, you there?" a voice squawks through the two-way radio on his belt.

" 'Scuse me," he says, grabbing the radio. "Mileaway?" he asks.

"Where you at?" the voice shoots back.

"They got me up top the whole day," Shelley says.

"Surface rat."

"Mole."

"Better than deep-level trash," the voice shoots back.

"Amen to that," Shelley says, shooting me a grin and inviting me in on the joke. I nod as if it's the best mining barb I've heard all week, then quickly point to one of the few open parking spaces. "Listen, should we . . . ?"

"Uh—ya . . . right there's perfect," Shelley says as the guy on his two-way continues talking. "There's gear in the dry," Shelley adds, motioning to the large brick building just behind the metal teepee. "And here . . ." He pulls a key ring of round metal tags from his pocket and undoes the latch, dropping four of the tags in my hand. Two are imprinted with the number *27;* the other two have the number *15.* "Don't forget to tag in," he explains. "One in your pocket, one on the wall."

With a quick thanks, we're headed for our parking spot, and he's back on his radio.

"You sure you know what you're doing?" Viv asks. She's sitting up slightly taller in the seat than yesterday, but there's no mistaking the way she stares anxiously in her rearview mirror. When I was listening to Viv's conversation with her mother, I said that strength had to be found from within. The way Viv continues to eye the rearview, she's still searching for it.

"Viv, this place doesn't have a single drop of gold in it, but they're setting up shop like that scene from *E.T.* when the government shows up."

"But if we . . ."

"Listen, I'm not saying I want to go down in the mine, but you have any better ideas for figuring out what's going on around here?"

She looks down at her lap, which is covered with the

brochures from the motel. On the front page, it reads, *From the Bible to Plato's* Republic, *the underground has been associated with Knowledge*.

That's what we're counting on.

"All my friends' dads used to mine," I add. "Believe me, even if we do go in, it's like a cave—we're talking a few hundred feet down, max . . ."

"Try eight thousand," she blurts.

"What?"

She freezes, surprised by the sudden attention. "Th-That's what it says. In here . . ." she adds, passing me the brochure. "Before it was closed down, this place was the oldest operating mine in all of North America. It beat every gold, coal, silver, and other mine in the country."

I snatch the brochure from her hands. *Since 1876*, it says on the cover.

"They've been shoveling for over a hundred and twenty-five years. That'll get you pretty deep," she continues. "Those miners who were trapped in Pennsylvania a few years back—what were they at, two hundred feet?"

"Two hundred and forty," I say.

"Well, this is eight thousand. Can you imagine? *Eight thousand*. That's six Empire State Buildings straight into the ground . . ."

I flip the brochure to the back and confirm the facts: Six Empire State Buildings . . . fifty-seven levels . . . two and a half miles wide . . . and three hundred and fifty *miles* of underground passageways. At the very bottom, the temperature gets to 133 degrees. I glance out the window at the road beneath us. Forget the beehive. We're standing on an entire ant farm.

"Maybe I should stay up here," Viv says. "Y'know . . . sorta just to keep lookout . . ."

Before I can respond, she glances back to her rearview. Behind us, a silver Ford pickup pulls across the gravel, into the parking lot. Viv anxiously eyes the driver, checking to see if he looks familiar. I know what she's thinking. Even if Janos is just touching down right now, he can't be far behind. That's the choice: the demon aboveground versus the demon below.

"You really think it's safer to be up here by yourself?" I ask.

She doesn't answer. She's still watching the silver pickup.

"Please just promise me we'll be fast," she begs.

"Don't worry," I say, swinging my door open and hopping outside. "We'll be in and out before anyone even knows it."

36

LIGHTLY TAPPING THE side of his thumb against the top of
the Hertz rental car counter in the Rapid City airport,
Janos made no attempt to hide his frustration with the
South Dakota way of life. "What's taking so long?" he
asked the young employee with the skinny Mount
Rushmore tie.

"Sorry . . . just been one of those busy mornings," the
man behind the counter replied, shuffling through a short
pile of paperwork.

Janos looked around the main lounge of the airport.
There were a total of six people, including a Native
American janitor.

"Okay—and when will you be returning the car?" the
man behind the counter asked.

"Hopefully, tonight," Janos shot back.

"Just a quick visit, eh?"

Janos didn't answer. His eyes stared at the key chain in
the man's hand. "Can I just have my key?"

"And will you be needing any insurance on the—"

Janos's hand shot out like a dart, gripping the man's
wrist and swiping the key from his hand.

"We done?" Janos growled.

"I-It's a blue Ford Explorer . . . in spot fifteen," the man said as Janos ripped a map from the pad on the counter and stormed toward the exit. "You have a good day, now, Mr . . ." The man looked down at the photocopy of the New Jersey driver's license Janos had given him. Robert Franklin. "You have a good day, now, Mr. Franklin. And welcome to South Dakota!"

37

WALKING AS FAST AS I can with my briefing book in hand, I keep up my Senator stride as we head for the red brick building. The book is actually the owner's manual from the glove compartment of the Suburban, but at the pace we're moving, no one'll ever get a good look. On my right, Viv completes the picture, trailing behind me like the faithful aide to my Wendell executive. Between her height and her newly pressed navy suit, she looks old enough to play the part. I tell her not to smile, just to be safe. The only way to belong is to act like you belong. But the closer we get to the brick building, the more we realize there's almost no one around to call us out and scream bullshit. Unlike the trailers behind us, the pathways over here are all empty.

"You think they're underground?" Viv asks, noticing the sudden decrease in population.

"Hard to say; I counted sixteen cars in the parking lot—plus all that machinery. Maybe all the work's being done back by the trailers."

"Or maybe whatever's up here is something they don't want tons of people to see."

I pick up my pace; Viv matches my speed. As we turn the corner of the brick building, there's a door in front and a metal grated staircase that heads down and into an entrance on the side of the building. Viv looks my way. I agree. Sticking to the back roads, we both go for the stairs. As we step down, little bits of rock slide from our shoes through the grating and down to a concrete alley twenty feet below. It's not even close to the drop we're about to take. I look over my shoulder. Staring through the steps, Viv starts slowing down.

"Viv . . ."

"I'm fine," she calls out, even though I never asked the question.

Inside the red brick building, we cross through a dark tiled hallway and enter a kitchenette that feels like it's been picked over and left for dead. The vinyl floor is cracked, the refrigerator is open and empty, and a cork bulletin board sits flat on the floor, filled with brittle, yellowed union notices that're dated at least two years ago. Whatever these guys are up to, they've only come back here recently.

Back in the hallway, I stick my head in a room where the door is off its hinges. It takes me a second to weave inside, but when I do, I stop midstep on the tile floor. In front of me are row after row of open industrial showers, but the way they're set up, it's like a gas chamber—the nozzles are just pipes sticking out of the wall. And though I know they're just showers, when I think of the miners washing away another grueling day of work, it's truly one of the most depressing sights I've ever seen.

"Harris, I got it!" Viv says, calling me back to the hallway, where she taps her pointer finger against a sign that says *The Ramp*. Below the words, there's a tiny directional arrow pointing down another set of stairs.

"You sure that's the—?"

She motions to the old metal punch clock that's next to the sign, then looks back at the bulletin board and the refrigerator. No question about it. When miners used to fill this place, here's where they started every day.

Down the stairs, the hallway narrows, and the ceiling is low. From the mustiness alone, I know we're in the basement. There are no more rooms off to the side—and not a single window in sight. Following another sign for *The Ramp*, we dead-end at a rusted blue metal door that's caked in mud and reminds me of the door on an industrial freezer. I give it a sharp push, but the door seems to push back.

"What's wrong?" Viv asks.

I shake my head and try again. This time, the door cracks open slightly, and a sharp, hot gust of air bursts out, licking me in the face. It's a wind tunnel down there. I shove a little harder, and the door swings open, its rusty hinges screaming as the full dry heat of the breeze bounces against our chests.

"Smells like rocks," Viv says, covering her mouth.

Reminding myself that the man in the parking lot told us to come this way, I will myself to take my first step into the narrow concrete hallway.

As the door shuts behind us, the wind dies down, but the dryness is still in the air. I keep licking my lips, but it doesn't help. It's like eating a sand castle.

Up ahead, the hallway curves to the right. There are some full mop buckets along the floor, and a fluorescent light in the ceiling. Finally, a sign of life. Heading deeper into the turn, I'm not sure what we're breathing, but as I taste the bitter air on my tongue, it's dusty, hot, and bad. On the left-hand wall, there's a 1960s-era *Fallout Shelter* sign with an arrow pointing dead ahead. Caked in dirt, you can still make out the black and yellow nuclear logo.

"Fallout shelter?" Viv asks, confused. "Eight thousand feet below ground? A little overkill, no?"

Ignoring the comment, I stay focused on the hallway, and as it straightens out, we get our second sign of life.

"What is it?" Viv says, hesitantly moving forward.

Up ahead, the right and left sides of the hall are covered from floor to ceiling with metal storage racks that look like shallow bookshelves. But instead of books, they're filled with gear: dozens of knee-high rubber boots, thick nylon tool belts, and most important, mine lights and white construction helmets.

"Is this gonna fit?" Viv asks, forcing a laugh as she pulls a helmet onto her short-cropped Afro. She's trying her best to act ready for this, but before she convinces me, she has to convince herself. "What's this?" she adds, nervously tapping the metal clip on the front of her helmet.

"For the light," I say, pulling one of the mine lights off the shelf. But as I attempt to grab the round metal bulb, I notice that it's connected by a black wire to a red plastic case that holds a paperback-sized version of a car battery—and that the battery is connected to some clips on the shelf. This isn't just a bookcase—it's a charging station.

Unlatching the clips, I unhook the battery, pull it from the shelf, and slide it onto one of the nearby tool belts. As Viv fastens it around her waist, I thread the wire over the back of her shoulder and hook the light onto the front of her helmet. Now she's all set. An official miner.

She flips a switch, and the light turns on. Twenty-four hours ago, she would've bobbed her head back and forth, teasing me by shining the light in my face. Now the light shines on her feet as she stares at the floor. The excitement's long gone. It's one thing to say you're going underground; it's entirely another thing to do it.

"Don't say it . . ." she warns as I'm about to open my mouth.

"It's safer than being—"

"I said *don't say it*. I'll be fine," she insists. She clenches her teeth and takes a deep breath of the hot, chalky air.

"How do we know which ones are charged?" she asks. Reading my expression, she points to the bookshelves on our right and left. Both are filled with battery packs. "What if one's a check-in station and one's a checkout?" she adds, knocking on the red casing of her own battery. "For all we know, this came back ten minutes ago."

"You think that's how they—?"

"That's what they do at laser tag," she points out.

I give her a long look. I hate myself for bringing her here.

"You keep yours from the left, I'll take mine from the right," I say. "Either way, we'll at least have one that works."

She nods at the logic as I grab two orange mesh construction vests from a nearby garbage can. "Put this on," I tell her, tossing one of the vests her way.

"Why?"

"The same reason every bad spy movie has someone sneaking in dressed as a janitor. An orange vest'll take you anywhere . . ."

Skeptically examining herself as she tightens the Velcro straps on the side of the vest, she adds, "I look like I should be doing roadwork."

"Really? I was thinking more crossing guard."

She laughs at the joke—and from the smile on her face, it looks like it's exactly what she needed.

"Feeling better?" I ask.

"No," she says, unable to hide her smirk. "But I'll get there."

"I'm sure we will."

She likes the sound of that.

"So you really think we can pull this off?" she asks.

"Don't ask me—I'm the one who said you can't win 'em all."

"You still feel that way?"

I lift one shoulder and move up the dust-filled hallway. Viv's right behind me.

At the far end of the hall, the metal bookshelves are gone, and the basement walls are instead lined with wooden benches that sit end to end for at least a few hundred feet. Based on the photos in the brochure, during the mine's heyday, miners lined up here every morning, waiting for their ride to work. Back in D.C., we do the same thing on the metro—line up underground and take the subway downtown. The only difference out here is, the subway isn't a horizontal ride. It's vertical.

"What's that noise . . . ?" Viv asks, still standing a few steps behind me.

Straight ahead, the mouth of the hallway opens into a room with a thirty-foot ceiling, and we hear a deafening rumble. The wood benches vibrate slightly, and the lights begin to flicker—but our eyes are glued to the elevator shaft that slices from floor to ceiling through the center of the tall room. Like a vertical freight train, the elevator rockets up through the floor and disappears through the ceiling. Unlike a normal elevator shaft, however, this one is only enclosed on three sides. Sure, there's a yellow stainless steel door that prevents us from peeking into the shaft and having our heads chopped off, but above the door—in the twenty-foot space before the ceiling starts—we can see straight into the elevator as it flies by.

"You see anyone?" I ask Viv.

"It was only half a second."

I nod. "I thought it looked empty, though."

"Definitely empty," she agrees.

Stepping further into the room, we simultaneously crane our necks up at the elevator shaft. For some reason, there's water running down the walls. As a result, the wooden walls of the shaft are dark, slick, and slowly corroding. The closer we get, the more we feel the draft of cold air emanating from the open hole. We're still at basement level, but the way the tunnel curved us around, I'm guessing we're in another building.

"Think that's the teepee up there?" Viv asks, pointing with her chin at the sliver of sunlight that creeps through the very top of the shaft.

"I think it has to be—the woman in the motel said that's where the—"

A dull thud echoes down the shaft from the room above. It's followed by another . . . and another. The noise stays steady but never gets louder. Just soft and even—like footsteps. Viv and I both freeze.

"Frannie, it's Garth—cage is at station," a man's voice announces with a flat South Dakota accent. His voice reverberates through the shaft—it's coming from the room above us.

"Stop cage," a female voice replies, crackling through an intercom.

There's a loud shriek of metal that sounds like a store-front's rolltop gate being thrown open—the steel safety gate on the front of the cage. The footsteps clunk as they enter the cage. "Stop cage," the man says as the door slides shut with another shriek. "Going to thirteen-two," he adds. "Lower cage."

"Thirteen-two," the woman repeats through the intercom. "Lowering cage."

A second later, there's a soft rumble, and the benches behind us again start to vibrate. "Oh, shit . . ." Viv mutters.

If we can see them, they can see us. As the elevator plummets downward, we both race to opposite sides of the shaft. Viv goes left; I go right. The elevator screeches past us like a freefall ride in an amusement park, but within seconds, the thundering sound is muffled as it fades down the rabbithole. Ducked around the corner, I still don't move. I just listen—waiting to see how long it takes. It's a seemingly endless drop. Six Empire State Buildings straight down. And then . . . deep below us, the metal of the cage whispers slightly, lets out one final gasp, and finally—poof—disappears in the dark silence. The only thing we hear now is the calming swish of the water as it runs down the walls of the shaft.

Above my head, next to the rusted-out yellow door, there's a short wall with a break-glass-in-emergency fire alarm. Next to the alarm is a phone receiver and a matching rusty keypad. There's our way in.

I glance back at Viv, who's got her hands up on her head and a dumbfounded look on her face as she studies the elevator. "Nuh-uh-uh," she says. "Nuh-uh. No *way* you're gettin' me in that . . ."

"Viv, you knew we were going down . . ."

"Not in that rusty old thing, I didn't. Forget it, Harris—I'm done. Gone. Nn-nnn. Momma don't let me get on buses that run inta *that bad* a neighborhood . . ."

"This isn't funny."

"I agree . . . That's why I'm keeping my black ass right here."

"You can't hide here."

"I can . . . I will . . . I am. You go jump in the well— I'll be the one up here turning the crank so we can at least get the water bucket back at the end of the day."

"Where're you gonna hide up here?"

"Plenty of places. Lots of 'em . . ." She looks around at the wooden benches . . . the narrow hallway . . . even the empty elevator shaft, where there's nothing but a cascade of running water. The rest of the room is just as bare. There're some old tires in the corner and an enormous wooden spool of discarded electrical wire in the back.

I cross my arms and stare her down.

"C'mon, Harris, *stop* . . ."

"We shouldn't separate, Viv. Trust me on this—I can feel it in my gut: we need to stay together."

Now she's the one staring at me. She studies my eyes, then glances over at the intercom. Just behind us, leaning against the wall, is a bright blue sign with white stenciled letters:

Level	Station Code
Top	1-1
Ramp	1-3
200	2-2
300	2-3
800	3-3

The list continues through all fifty-seven levels. Right now, we're on the *Ramp*. At the very bottom, the list ends with:

Level	Station Code
7700	12-5
7850	13-1
8000	13-2

The eight-thousand-foot level. Station code: *thirteen-two*. I remember it from the guy with the flat accent barely two minutes ago. That's the code he yelled into the intercom to take the elevator down, which means that's where the action is. *Thirteen-two*. Our next destination. I turn back to Viv.

She's still glaring at the blue sign and the word *8000*. "Hurry up and call it in," she mutters. "But if we get stuck down there," she threatens, sounding just like her mom, "you're gonna pray God gets you before I do."

Wasting no time, I pick up the receiver and take a quick check of the ceiling for video cameras. Nothing in sight— which means we've still got some wiggle room. I dial the four-digit number that's printed on the base of the rusty keypad: *4881*. The numbers stick as I press each one.

"Hoist . . ." a female voice answers.

"Hey, it's Mike," I announce, playing the odds. "I need a ride down to thirteen-two."

"Mike who?" she shoots back, unimpressed. From her accent, I know she's a local. From my accent, she knows I'm not.

"*Mike*," I insist, pretending to be annoyed. "From Wendell." If the Wendell folks are just moving in, she's been having conversations like this all week. There's a short pause, and I can practically hear the sigh leave her lips.

"Where are you?" she asks.

"The Ramp," I say, reading it again from the sign.

"Wait right there . . ."

As I turn toward Viv, she reaches into her pocket and takes out a metal device that looks like a thin version of a calculator, but without as many buttons.

Reading my look, she holds it up so I can see it. Below the digital screen is a button marked $O_2\%$. "Oxygen detector?" I ask as she nods. "Where'd you get that?"

She motions over her shoulder to the shelves in the hallway. The black digital numbers on the screen read 20.9.

"Is that good or bad?"

"That's what I'm trying to figure out," she says, reading the instructions on the back. "Listen to this: *Warning: Lack of oxygen may be unnoticeable and will quickly cause unconsciousness and/or death. Check detector frequently.* You gotta be friggin'—"

The thought's interrupted by the giant rumble in the distance. It's like a train pulling into a station—the floor starts to vibrate, and I can feel it against my chest. The lights flicker ever so slightly, and Viv and I twist back toward the elevator shaft. There's a sharp screech as the brakes kick in and the cage rattles toward us. But unlike last time, instead of continuing through the ceiling, it stops right in front of us. I glance through the cutout window in the yellow steel door, but there's no light inside the cage. It's gonna be a dark ride down.

"See anything?" the female hoist operator asks sarcastically through the receiver.

"Yeah . . . no . . . it's here," I reply, trying to remember the protocol. "Stop cage."

"Okay, get yerself in and hit the intercom," she says.
"And don't forget to tag in before you go." Before I can
ask, she explains, "The board behind the phone."

Hanging up the receiver, I cross behind the short wall
that holds the phone and fire alarm.

"We okay?" Viv asks.

I don't answer. On the opposite side of the wall, short
nails are hammered into a square plank of wood and
numbered *1* through *52*. Round metal tags hang from
nails *4, 31,* and *32*. Three men are already in the mine,
plus however many entered from the level above. From
my pocket I pull out my own two tags—both numbered
27. *One in your pocket, one on the wall*, the guy out front
said.

"You sure that's smart?" Viv asks as I put one of my
tags on the nail labeled *27*.

"If something happens, it's the only proof we're down
there," I point out.

Tentatively she pulls out her own tag and hooks it on
the nail labeled *15*.

"Harris . . ."

Before she can say it, I cross back to the front of the
cage. "It's just insurance—we'll be up and down in a half
hour," I say, hoping to keep her calm. "Now c'mon, your
Cadillac awaits . . ."

With a sharp yank, I pull the lever on the steel door.
The lock unhooks with a thunk, but the door weighs a
ton. As I dig in my feet and finally tug it open, a mist of
cold water sprays against my face. Up above us, a drumbeat of thick droplets bangs against the top of my construction helmet. It's like standing directly under the edge
of an awning during a rainstorm. The only thing between
us and the cage is the metal safety gate on the cage itself.

"Let's go . . ." I say to Viv, reaching down and twisting the latch at the bottom of the gate. With one last pull and a final metal shriek, the gate rolls open like a garage door, revealing an interior that reminds me of the Dumpster where I found Viv's nametag. Floors . . . walls . . . even the low ceiling—it's all rusted metal, slick with water and covered in dirt and grease.

I motion to Viv, and she just stands there. I motion again, and she hesitantly follows me inside, desperately looking for something to hold on to. There's nothing. No banisters, no handrails, not even a fold-down seat. "It's a steel coffin," she whispers as her voice echoes off the metal. I can't argue with the analogy. Built to carry as many as thirty men standing shoulder to shoulder below the earth and to withstand any random blasting that might be happening on any level, the space is as cold and bare as an abandoned boxcar. The thing is, as thick drops of water continue to drumbeat against my helmet, I realize there's one thing worse than being stuck in a coffin: being stuck in a leaky coffin.

"This *is* just water, right?" Viv asks, squinting up at the mist.

"If it were anything bad, those other guys would never've gotten in," I point out.

Flipping a switch on the front of her helmet, Viv turns on her mine light and stares down at the directions for her oxygen detector. I flip on my own light and approach the intercom, which looks like the buzzer outside my old apartment building. The only difference is, thanks to years of water damage, the entire front panel is covered with a thick mossy film that smells like wet carpet.

"You gonna touch that?" Viv asks.

I don't have a choice. I press the large red button with

just the very tips of my fingers. It's caked in slippery goo. My fingers slide as I hit it.

"Stop cage," I say into the speaker.

"You close the safety gate?" the woman's voice buzzes through the intercom.

"Doing it right now . . ." Reaching up, I grab the wet nylon strap and drag the garage door back into place. It screeches against the rollers and slams with a metal clang. Viv jumps at the sound. No turning back.

"Just one more question," I say into the intercom. "All the water down here . . ."

"That's just for the shaft," the woman explains. "Keeps the walls lubricated. Just don't drink it and you'll be fine," she adds with a laugh. Neither of us laughs back. "Now, you ready or not?" she asks.

"Absolutely," I say, staring through the metal grate at the emptiness of the basement. The way Viv's light shines over my shoulder, I can tell she's giving it one last look herself. Her light points toward the fire alarm and the telephone. On the other side of the wall are our metal tags. The only proof of our descent.

I turn around to say something but decide against it. We don't need another speech. We need answers. And whatever's down here, this is the only way we'll get them.

"Going to thirteen-two," I say into the intercom, using the same code from before. "Lower cage."

"Thirteen-two," the woman repeats. "Lowering cage."

There's a grinding of metal and one of those never-ending pauses you find on a roller coaster. Right before the big drop.

"Don't look," the woman teases through the intercom. "It's a long way down . . ."

38

"YOU THERE YET?" Sauls asked, his voice breaking up as it came through Janos's cell phone.

"Almost," Janos replied as his Ford Explorer blew past yet another thicket of pine, spruce, and birch trees as he made his way toward Leed.

"What's *almost?*" Sauls asked. "You an hour away? Half hour? Ten minutes? What's the story?"

Gripping the steering wheel and studying the road, Janos stayed silent. It was bad enough that he had to drive this piece of dreck—he didn't need to listen to the nagging as well. Flipping on the radio in the truck, Janos turned the dial until he found nothing but static.

"You're breaking up . . ." he said to Sauls. "Can't hear you . . ."

"Janos . . ."

Slapping his phone shut, he tossed it into the empty passenger seat and focused back on the road in front of him. The morning sky was crystal blue, but from the non-stop bending of the two-lane road, and the claustrophobia from the surrounding mountains, this was a tough drive during the day, let alone at night—especially if you'd never done it before. Add that to the late hour of Harris and Viv's arrival, and they may've even turned off for a snack, or even some sleep. Whipping around yet another curve, Janos shook his head. It was a nice thought, but as he realized an hour ago when he blew past that diner in Deadwood, it's one thing to stop for food or toiletries— it's quite another to set up camp before you reach your destination. If Harris was smart enough to get them this far, he was also smart enough to make sure they didn't stop until they got to the very end.

Welcome to Leed—Home of the Homestead Mine, the billboard said along the side of the road.

Janos breezed right by it, recalculating the timeline in his head. Even if their jet got off immediately, they couldn't have arrived before midnight. And if they didn't get in until midnight, they had to sleep somewhere . . .

Making a sharp left into the parking lot of the squat sixties-era building, Janos read the signs in the neighboring storefront windows: *Out of Business . . . Lost Lease . . . Gone to Montana*. Sauls was at least right about that—Leed was definitely on its last legs. But as he parked his car and eyed the neon *Vacancy* sign out front, it was clear at least one place was still open: *the Gold House Motel*.

Janos opened his door and headed straight inside. On his left, he noticed the metal rack of tourist brochures. All of them were faded by the sun, every single one of them—except for the one entitled *The Homestead Mine*. Janos studied the rich red, white, and blue colors of the pamphlet. The sun hadn't faded it a bit—almost as if . . . as if it'd just been exposed in the last hour or so.

"Hiya, there," the woman at the front desk called out with a friendly smile. "So what can I do for you today?"

39

My STOMACH LEAPS into my chest as the cage plummets. For the first few feet, it's no different from an elevator ride, but as we pick up speed and plunge down the shaft, my stomach sails up toward my esophagus. Jerking back and forth, the cage bangs wildly against the walls of the shaft, almost knocking us off our feet. It's like trying to stand on a rocking rowboat as it bottoms out under you.

"Harris, tell her to slow down before—!"

The floor of the cage heaves violently to the left, and Viv loses her chance to finish the thought.

"Lean against the wall—it makes it easier!" I call out.

"What?!" she shouts, though I can barely hear her. Between the pounding of the cage, the speed of our descent, and the rumble of the waterfall, everything's drowned in a never-ending, screeching roar.

"Lean against the wall!" I yell.

Taking my own advice, I lean back and fight to keep my balance as the rowboat rattles beneath me. It's the first time I take a glance outside the cage. The safety gate may be closed, but through the grating, the subterranean world rushes by: a blur of brown dirt . . . then a flash of an underground tunnel . . . another blur of dirt . . . another tunnel. Every eight seconds, a different level whizzes by. The openings to the tunnels whip by so fast, I can barely get a look—and the more I try, the more it blurs, and the dizzier I get. Cave opening after cave opening after cave opening . . . We've gotta be going forty miles an hour.

"You feel that?" Viv calls out, pointing to her ears.

My ears pop, and I nod. I swallow hard, and they pop again, tighter than before.

It's been over three minutes since we left, and we're still headed down what's easily becoming the longest elevator ride of my life. On my right, the entrances to the tunnels continue to whip by at their regular blurred pace . . . and then, to my surprise, they start to slow down.

"We there?" Viv asks, looking my way so her mine light shines in my face.

"I think so," I say as I turn toward her and accidentally blind her right back. It takes a few seconds for us to realize that as long as our lights are on, the only way we can talk is by turning our heads so we're not eye to eye. For some people in the Capitol, that comes naturally. For me, it's like fighting blind. Every emotion starts in our eyes. And right now, Viv won't face me.

"How we doing on air?" I ask as she looks down at her oxygen detector.

"Twenty-one percent is normal—we're at 20.4," she says, flipping to the instructions on the back. Her voice wobbles, but she's doing her best to mask her fear. I check to see if her hands are shaking. She turns slightly so I can't see them. "Says here you need sixteen percent to breathe normally . . . nine percent before you go unconscious . . . and at six percent, you wave bye-bye."

"But we're at 20.4?" I say, trying to reassure her.

"We were 20.9 up top," she shoots back.

The cage bucks to a final halt. "Stop cage?" the woman asks through the intercom.

"Stop cage," I say, pressing the red button and wiping the slime against my tool belt.

As I take my first peek through the metal safety gate, I look up at the ceiling, and my mine light bounces off a bright orange stenciled sign dangling from two wires: *4850 Level.*

"You gotta be kidding me," Viv mumbles. "We're only *halfway* there?"

I press the intercom button and lean toward the speaker. "Hello . . . ?"

"What's wrong?" the hoist operator barks back.

"We wanted to go to the eight thousa—"

"Cross the drift and you'll see the Number Six Winze. The cage is waiting for you there."

"What's wrong with this one?"

"It's fine if you wanna stop at 4850, but if you plan on going deeper, you gotta take the other."

"I don't remember this last time," I say, bluffing to see if it's changed.

"Son, unless you were here in the 1900s, there ain't nothin' that's different. They got cables now that'll hold a cage at ten thousand feet, but back then, the furthest they could go was five thousand at a time. Now, step outside, cross the drift, and tell me when you're in."

I tug on the safety gate, and it rolls up and out of the way. A downpour of water from the shaft forms a wet wall that partially blocks us from seeing out. Darting straight through the waterfall and feeling the freezing water pummel my back, I dash out into the mine, where the floor, walls, and ceiling are all made of tightly packed brown dirt. No different from a cave, I tell myself, stepping ankle-deep in a puddle of mud. On both sides of the tunnel as it stretches out in front of us are another twenty feet of side-by-side benches. They're no different from the ones up top, except for the elongated American flag that someone's spray-painted along the entire backrest. It's the only patch of color in this otherwise muddy-brown underworld, and as we walk past the long stretches of bench, if I close my eyes, I swear I can see the ghostly afterimages of hundreds of miners—heads hung low, elbows resting on their knees—as they wait in the dark, beaten from another day spent huddled underground.

It's the same look my dad had on the fifteenth of every month—when he'd count up how many haircuts he'd need to make the mortgage. Mom used to scold him for refusing tips, but back then, he thought it was bad taste in a small town. When I was twelve, he gave up the shop and moved the business into the basement of our house. But he still had that look. I used to think it was regret for spending his whole day down there. It wasn't. It was dread—the pain you feel from the thought that you have to do it again tomorrow. Entire lives spent underground. To cover it up, Dad put up posters of Ralph Kiner, Roberto Clemente, and the emerald green outfield at Forbes Field; down here, they use the red, white, and blue of the flag—and the bright yellow door of the cage that sits fifty feet dead ahead.

Crossing the drift, we plow through the mud, heading straight for the door marked *Winze No. 6.*

As I enter the new cage and pull the safety gate down,

Viv scans the even tinier metal shoebox. The lower ceiling makes the coffin feel even smaller. As Viv cranes her neck downward, I can practically smell claustrophobia setting in.

"This is Number Six Hoist," the woman announces through the intercom. "All set?"

I glance at Viv. She won't even look up. "All set," I say into the intercom. "Lower cage."

"Lower cage," she repeats as the coffin starts to rumble. We both lean back against our respective walls, prepping ourselves for the freefall. A bead of water swells on the ceiling of the cage, drops to the ground, and plinks into a small puddle. I hold my breath . . . Viv looks up at the noise . . . and the floor once again plummets from beneath us.

Next stop: eight thousand feet below the earth's surface.

40

THE CAGE PLUNGES straight down as my ears once again pop and a sharp pain corkscrews through my forehead. But as I fight for balance and try to steady myself on the vibrating wall, something tells me my instant headache isn't just from the pressure in my ears.

"How's our oxygen?" I call out to Viv, who's cradling the detector in both hands and struggling to read as we're jarred back and forth. The roaring sound is once again deafening.

"What?" she shouts back.

"How's our oxygen?!"

She cocks her head at the question, reading something on my face.

"Why're you suddenly worried?" she asks.

"Just tell me what the percentages are," I insist.

She studies me again, soaking it all in. Over my shoulder, a different level in the mine flashes by every few seconds. Viv's features sink just as fast. Her bottom lip starts to quiver. For the past five thousand–plus feet, Viv's anchored herself to my own emotional state: the confidence that snuck us in here, the desperation that got us on the first cage, even the stubbornness that kept us moving. But the moment she gets her first whiff of my fear—the moment she thinks my own anchor is unmoored—she's floundering and ready to capsize.

"How's our oxygen?" I ask again.

"Harris . . . I wanna go up . . ."

"Just give me the number, Viv."

"But—"

"Give me the number!"

She looks down at the detector, almost lost. Her forehead's covered in sweat. But it's not just her: All around us, the cold breeze that whipped through the top of the shaft is long gone. At these levels, the deeper we go underground, the hotter it gets—and the more Viv starts to lose it.

"Nineteen . . . we're down to nineteen," she stutters, coughing and holding her throat. Nineteen percent is still within normal range, but it doesn't calm her down. Her chest rises and falls in quick succession, and she staggers backwards into the wall. I'm still breathing fine.

Her body starts to tremble, and not just from the movement of the cage. It's her. The color drains from her face. Her mouth gapes open. As her shaking gets faster, she can barely stand up. A loud, empty gasp echoes from deep within her chest. The oxygen detector drops from her hand, smacking into the floor. Oh, no. If she's hyperventilating . . .

The cage rumbles down the shaft at forty miles an hour. Viv looks across at me. Her eyes are wide, begging for help. "Hhhh . . ." Gripping her chest, she lets out a long, protracted gasp and crumples to the floor.

"Viv . . . !"

I leap toward her just as the cage is slammed to the

right. Off balance and knocked to the left, I crash into the wall shoulder first. A jolting pain runs down my arm. Viv's still gasping, and the sudden jolt sends her falling forward. Sliding on my knees, I dive at her, catching her just as she's about to hit face first.

I turn her around and cradle her body in my arms. Her helmet falls to the ground as her eyes dance wildly back and forth. She's in full panic. "I got you, Viv . . . I got you . . ." I tell her, whispering the words over and over. Her head's in my lap, and she's trying to catch her breath, but the deeper we plummet, the more we feel the heat. I lick a puddle of sweat from the dimple of my top lip. It's easily over ninety degrees down here.

"Wh-What's happening?" Viv asks. As she looks up at me, her tears run back toward her temples and are swallowed by her hair.

"The heat's normal . . . It's just the pressure from the rocks above us . . . plus we're getting closer to the earth's core . . ."

"What about oxygen?" she stutters.

I turn to the detector, which is lying beside her. As my light shines across the digital screen, it goes from *19.6%* . . . to *19.4%*

"Holding steady," I tell her.

"You lying to me? Please don't lie . . ."

This is no time to send her spiraling. "We're gonna be fine, Viv . . . Just keep taking deep breaths."

Following my own instructions, I suck in a chest-full of steamy, hot air. It burns my lungs like a deep breath in a sauna. The sweat is pouring from my face, dripping off the tip of my nose.

Kneeling behind Viv, who's still on the ground, I take off her orange vest and jacket and push her forward so her head's between her knees. The back of her neck is drenched, and a long, wet sweat stain runs down her spine, soaking through her shirt. "Deep breaths . . . deep breaths . . ." I tell her.

She whispers something back, but as the cage hurtles downward, the rumbling of the walls is too loud for me to hear. One . . . two . . . three entrances to the tunnels whiz by within thirty seconds. We have to be close to seven thousand feet.

"Almost there . . ." I add, putting both hands on her shoulders and holding her tight. She needs to know I won't let go.

As another tunnel whizzes by, my ears pop once more, and I swear my head's about to explode. But just as I clench my teeth and shut my eyes, my stomach lurches back into place. There's an audible screech and a sudden tug in forward momentum that reminds me of an airplane coming to a sharp stop. We're finally slowing down. And as the cage settles into a slow rumble, Viv's breathing does the same. From frenetic . . . to rushed . . . to the steady in-and-out of calm . . . The slower we go, the more she levels off.

"There you go . . . just like that . . ." I say, again holding the back of her neck. Her huffing and puffing is smooth and steady as the cage jerks to its final stop. For a full minute, we dangle there, not moving. Viv is slumped in the bottom of the cage; the cage is slumped at the bottom of the shaft.

Her breathing settles like a pond after a thrown rock ripples through it. "Hhhh . . . hhhh . . . hh . . ."

I pull away, climbing to my feet. It takes Viv a moment, but she eventually turns around and offers an appreciative grin. She's trying to be strong, but from the manic way she's looking around, I can see she's still freaked.

"Stop cage?" the hoist operator asks through the intercom.

Ignoring the question, I turn to Viv. "How you doing?"

"Yeah," she replies, sitting up straight, trying to convince me she's fine.

"It wasn't a yes-or-no question," I say. "Now, you wanna try again? *How you doing?*"

"O-Okay," she admits, biting her bottom lip.

That's all I need to hear. I head for the intercom. "Hoist, you there?"

"What's the word?" the operator begins. "Everybody happy?"

"Actually, can you bring me back to the—"

"Don't!" Viv calls out.

I let go of the intercom and stare her down.

"We're here," Viv pleads. "All you gotta do is lift the stupid door . . ."

". . . after we get you back to the top."

"Please, Harris—not after we got this far. Besides, you really think it's safer up there than down here? Up top, I'm alone. You said it yourself: *We shouldn't separate.* Those were your words, weren't they? *Stay together?*"

I don't bother to answer.

"Now, c'mon," she continues. "We came all this way—to South Dakota . . . down eight thousand feet— you're gonna turn back now?"

I stand there in silence. She knows what's riding on this.

"You okay down there?" the operator asks through the intercom.

My eyes stay locked on Viv.

"I'm fine," she promises. "Now tell her you're alright before she starts to worry."

"Sorry, Hoist," I say into the intercom. "Just wanted to readjust some gear. All's well. Stop cage."

"Stop cage," the operator repeats.

I raise the safety gate and give the outer door a shove. Like before, a hot wind seeps through the opening—but this time, the heat's almost unbearable. My eyes burn as I squeeze them shut.

"W-What's going on?" Viv asks behind me. From the sound of her voice, she's still on the floor, crawling outside.

I push through the waterfall that drips from above the door and step out onto the dirt floor. Just like that, the vacuum of wind is gone, dissipating up the open shaft.

Blinking the dust from my eyes, I turn back to Viv, who still hasn't stood up. She's sitting on a plank of wood outside the cage and staring up at the ceiling.

Following her glance, I crane my neck up toward the highest part of the cave. The roof rises about thirty feet in the air and has an industrial light hanging from the center. "What're you looking—?"

Oh.

"Is that doing what I think it's doing?" Viv asks, still studying the ceiling.

Straight above us, a long black crevice cuts through the ceiling like a deep scar that's about to split open. Indeed, the only things holding it together—and thereby keeping the ceiling from splitting open—are nine-foot-long strips of rusted steel that're bolted to the roof like metal stitches across the crevice. From this distance, they look like the girders from an old Erector Set—lined with circular holes that the bolts are riveted into.

"I'm sure it's just a precaution," I say. "At this

level . . . with all the pressure from above . . . they just don't want a cave-in. For all we know, it's just a simple crack."

She nods at the explanation but doesn't move from her plank-of-wood seat.

In front of me, the ceiling lowers and the walls narrow like a wormhole. It can't be more than nine feet high, and just wide enough for a tiny car. Along the muddy floor, I follow the ancient metal train tracks. They're more compact than standard tracks, but they're in good enough shape to tell me how the miners are moving all that computer equipment through the mine.

When I was twelve, Nick Chiarmonte's dad took our entire sixth-grade class to Clarion, Pennsylvania, to tour a working coal mine. We got to go a hundred feet below the surface, which back then felt like we were burrowing toward the very center of the earth. When we got to the bottom, Nick's dad said a mine was a living organism no different from the human body—a main central artery with dozens of intersecting branches that move the blood to and from the heart. It's no different here. The train tracks run straight ahead, then branch out like spokes on a wheel—a dozen tunnels in a dozen different directions.

I eye each one, searching to see if any of them are different. The mud on most of the tracks is caked and dried. But in the far left tunnel, it's soaking wet, complete with a Sherlock Holmes boot print from the group that came down right before us. It's not much of a lead, but right now it's all we've got.

"You ready?" I call back to Viv.

She doesn't budge.

"C'mon . . ." I call again.

She's motionless.

"Viv, you coming or not?"

Shaking her head, she refuses to look up. "I'm sorry, Harris. I can't . . ."

"Whattya mean, *you can't?*"

"I can't," she insists, curling her knees toward her chin. "I just . . . I can't . . ."

"You said you were okay."

"No, I said I didn't want to be upstairs all by myself." It's the first time she faces me. Beads of sweat dot her face—even more than before. It's not just from the heat.

Viv looks up at the crack in the roof, then over at an emergency medical stretcher that's leaning against the wall. Bolted above that is a metal utility box with a sign that says: *In case of serious injury, open box and remove blanket.* Right now, as the temperature rises past a hundred, a blanket's the last thing we need—but Viv can't take her eyes off it.

"You should go," she blurts.

"No . . . if we split up—"

"Please, Harris. Just go . . ."

"Viv, I'm not the only one who thinks you can do it—your mom—"

"Please don't bring her up . . . not now . . ."

"But if you—"

"Go," she insists, fighting back tears. "Find what they're doing."

With everything we've been through in the past forty-eight hours, it's the first time I've ever seen Viv Parker completely paralyzed. I'm not sure if it's the claustrophobia, her hyperventilating on the elevator, or just the simple, stark grasp of her own limitations, but as Viv buries her face in her knees, I'm reminded that the worst beatings we take are the ones we give ourselves.

"Viv, if it makes you feel better, no one else would've made it this far. *Nobody.*"

Her head stays buried in her knees.

It wasn't until my senior year of college—when my dad died—that I realized I wasn't invulnerable. Viv's learning it at seventeen. Of all the things I've taken from her, this is the one I'll always hate myself for.

I turn to leave, sloshing through the wet mud.

"Take this," she calls out. In her hand, she holds up the oxygen detector.

"Actually, you should keep it here—just in case th—"

She wings it through the air, directly at me. As I catch it, there's a loud screeching noise behind her. The cage rumbles back to life, rising up the elevator shaft and disappearing through the ceiling. Last plane out.

"If you want to leave," I tell her, "just pick up the receiver and dial the—"

"I'm not going anywhere," she insists. Even now she won't completely give up. "Just find what they're doing," she says for the second time.

I nod her way, and my helmet light draws an imaginary line up and down her face. As I spin back toward the tunnels, it's the last good look I get.

41

So can I get you a room?" the woman behind the motel's front desk asked.

"Actually, I'm just looking for my friends," Janos replied. "Have you seen—"

"Doesn't anyone just want to rent a room anymore?"

Janos cocked his head slightly to the side. "Have you seen my friends—a white guy and a young black girl?"

The woman cocked her head right back. "Those're your friends?"

"Yes. They're my friends."

The woman was suddenly quiet.

"They're my friends from work—we were supposed to fly in together last night, but I got delayed and—" Janos cut himself off. "Listen, I got up at four A.M. for my flight this morning. Now are they upstairs or not? We've got a big day ahead of us."

"Sorry," the woman said. "They already checked out."

Janos nodded. He figured as much, but he had to be sure. "So they're already up there?" he added, pointing at the tall triangular building at the top of the hill.

"Actually, I thought they said they were headed to Mount Rushmore first."

Janos couldn't help but grin. Nice try, Harris.

"They left over an hour ago," the woman added. "But if you hurry, I'm sure you can catch them."

Nodding to himself, Janos stayed locked on the headframe as he headed for the door. "Yeah . . . I'm sure I can."

42

TEN MINUTES LATER, I'm ankle-deep in runny mud that, as my light hits it, shines with a metallic rust color. I assume it's just oil runoff from the engine that runs along the tracks, but to be safe, I stick to the sides of the cave, where the mud flow is lightest. All around me, the walls of the rocky cave are a patchwork of colors—brown, gray, rust, mossy green, and even some veins of white zigzag through them. Straight ahead, my light bounces off the jagged curves of the tunnel, slicing through the darkness like a spotlight through a black forest. It's all I've got. One candle in a sea of silent darkness.

The only thing making it worse is what I can actually see. Up above, along the ceiling of the tunnel, the rustiest pipes I've ever seen in my entire life are slick with water. It's the same on the walls and the rest of the ceiling. At this depth, the air is so hot and humid, the cave itself sweats. And so do I. Every minute or so, a new wave of heat plows through the tunnel, dissipates, and starts again. In . . . and out. In . . . and out. It's like the mine is breathing. At this depth, the air pressure forces its way to the nearest blowhole, and as another huge belch of heat vomits up through the shaft, I can't help but feel that if this is the mouth of the mine, I'm standing right on its tongue.

As I move in deeper, another burning yawn hits, even hotter than before. I feel it against my legs . . . my arms . . . at this point, even my teeth are sweating. I roll up my sleeves, but it doesn't do any good. I was wrong before—this isn't a sauna. With this heat . . . it's an oven.

Feeling my breathing quicken, and hoping it's just from the temperature, I glance down at the oxygen detector: *18.8%*. On the back, it says I need sixteen percent to live. The footprints ahead of me tell me at least two others have made the trek. For now, that's good enough for me.

Wiping the newest layer of sweat from my face, I spend ten minutes following the curve of the railroad tracks back through the tunnel—but unlike the brown and gray dreariness of the other parts, the walls back here are filled with red and white graffiti spray-painted directly on the rock: *Ramp This Way . . . Lift Straight Ahead . . . 7850 Ramp . . . Danger Blasting*. Each sign has an arrow pointing in a specific direction—but it's not until I follow the arrows that I finally realize why. Up ahead, my light doesn't disappear up the never-ending tunnel. Instead, it hits a wall. The straightaway's over. Now there's a fork in the road with five different choices. Shining the light on each one, I reread the signs and examine each new tunnel. Like before, four of them are caked in dried mud, while one's wet and fresh. *Danger Blasting*. Damn.

Retracing my steps, I open my wallet, pull out my bright pink California Tortilla *Burrito Club* card, and wedge it under a rock by the entrance of the tunnel I just left—the mining equivalent of leaving bread crumbs. If I can't find my way out, it doesn't matter how far in I get.

Following the sign that says *Danger Blasting*, I make a sharp right into the tunnel, which I quickly realize is slightly wider than the rest. From there, I stick with the train tracks, following the soupy mud through a fork that goes left, and another that goes right. Spray-painted signs again point to *Lift* and *7850 Ramp*, but the arrows are now pointing in different directions. To be safe, I put down more bread crumbs at each turn. My Triple-A card at the first left, the scrap of paper that holds my list of movies to rent at the next right. The distances aren't far, but even after two minutes, the jagged walls . . . the muddy train tracks—everything in every direction looks alike. Without the wallet bread crumbs, I'd be lost in this labyrinth—and even with them, I'm still half expecting to turn the corner and be back by Viv. But as I make a left and wedge my gym membership card under a rock, my eye catches something I've never seen before.

Dead ahead . . . less than thirty feet . . . the tunnel widens slightly on the right, making space for a narrow turnoff that holds a bright red mining car that looks like an ice-cream pushcart with a sail attached to the roof. Up close, the sail is nothing more than a plastic shower curtain, and on top, the cart is sealed by a circular door that looks like a hatch on a ship, complete with one of those rotating steering wheel twist locks. There's clearly something inside—and whatever it is, if it's important enough to put a lock on it, it's important enough for me to open.

Shoving the sail out of the way, I grip the steering wheel with both hands and give it a hard twist. Red paint cracks off in my hands, but the hatch lets out a metal thunk. With a strong tug, I crack the hatch and pull it open. The smell hits me first. Stronger than the acidic stench of vomit . . . sharper than bad cheese . . . Ugggh . . . Crap. Literally.

Inside the hatch is a mound of juicy brown lumps. The whole cart's filled with shit. Tons of it. Stumbling backwards, I hold my nose and fight to keep myself from throwing up. Too late. My stomach heaves, my throat erupts, and a firehose of last night's grilled cheese sprays across the earth. Bent over and grabbing my gut, I spray the ground two more times. All the blood rushes to my face as I spit out the last few chunks. My body lurches with one final dry heave . . . then another. By the time I open my eyes, my light's shining off the long, extended strand of drool that dangles from my lower lip. I glance back up at the wagon, and it finally makes sense. The shower curtain's for privacy; the hatch is the seat. Even this far underground, these guys still need a bathroom.

Banging into the back wall, I fight for balance, my face still scrunched up from the whiff. I didn't have time to close the hatch, and there's no way I'm getting close enough to do it now. With a sharp shove, I push myself away from the wall and stagger back up the tunnel. On my left, there's a shallow hole dug into the wall. My light shines directly into it, casting deep shadows along the jagged fangs of the hole. The light's almost yellow in color. But as I pass the hole and continue even further into the cave, I'm surprised to see that the yellow tint is still there.

Oh, no—don't tell me it's—

A high-pitched buzz erupts above my forehead. I immediately look up—but it doesn't take long to realize the sound's coming from my helmet. In front of me, the yellow glow from my light takes on an almost gold color.

Before, I could see at least fifty feet in front of me. Now it's down to thirty. I pull the helmet off my head and stare into the mine light. It pulses slightly, its color fading. I don't believe it. My hands start shaking, the light quivers back and forth, and I stare down at the battery pack on my tool belt. Viv was right about the charging station . . . The problem is, as the light on my helmet hums once more and fades to a brown, it's becoming increasingly clear I picked the wrong side.

Spinning around as quickly as I can, I tell myself not to panic—but I can already feel the tightening in my chest. My breathing rises and falls at lightspeed, trying to compensate. I look up . . . down . . . side to side . . . The world's starting to shrink. Along the walls and floor, the shadows creep in closer. I can barely see back to the red wagon in the distance. If I don't get out of here fast . . .

Darting forward, I sprint full speed back the way I came, but the thousands of rocks underfoot make it even harder to run than I thought. My ankles bend and turn with every step, fighting for traction. As the walls of the tunnel blur by, the helmet light jerks wildly in front of me, struggling to slice through the darkness like a dying flashlight through a cloud of black smoke. Worst of all, my breathing's at full gallop. I'm not sure if it's the depth of the mine or just plain fear, but within a minute, I'm completely winded. I've run marathons. This can't be . . .

A sharp burst of air leaves my lips, sending dust twirling through my still-fading light. I breathe in . . . then exhale just as fast. I can't slow it down. I'm already feeling light-headed. *No, don't pass out. Stay calm,* I beg myself. I don't have a chance. I glance down at the oxygen detector, but before I can get a look, my foot clips a rock, and my ankle twists out from under me.

Falling forward, I drop the detector and put out my hands to break my fall. With a crash, I skid across the ground, getting a fresh mouthful of dirt and a sting in my left wrist. I can still move it. Just a sprain. My mine light fades to amber, and I lose another eight feet of visual distance. Scrambling to my feet, I don't even bother to stop for the detector. If I don't get out of here now . . . Don't even think about it.

Picking up speed, I focus on the white gym membership card that's dead ahead. Those bread crumbs are my only way out. My light shrinks to a fading candle. I can barely see twenty feet. At this rate, I don't think I've got another thirty seconds.

Locked on the gym card, I have to squint to see. There's no time to take it slow—I've still got ten feet before I reach the archway it marks. If I can get through there, I can at least get one last look at the other bread crumbs so I know where to turn. The candle flickers, and it takes everything I have to ignore the burning pain in my chest. Almost there . . .

To make it easier, I hold my breath, my eyes glued to the archway. *Don't let it go. Don't lose it.* As the light shrivels, I lean forward. I'm still not there—and as my hand reaches out for the opening in front of me, the entire cave and everything in it goes completely . . . and utterly . . . black.

43

"WELCOME TO TWO QUAIL," the maître d' said as he cupped his hands together. "Do you have a—"

"It should be under *Holcomb*," Barry interrupted with perfect charm. "Party of two . . ."

"Holcomb . . . Holcomb . . ." the maître d' repeated, his glance lingering a second too long on Barry's glass eye. "Of course, sir. The window table. Right this way." Extending his arm to the left, he pointed Barry toward a meticulously set table that sat in a small, private nook at the front of the restaurant. Barry turned his head but didn't take a step.

"Sir, shall I—?"

"We'll be fine," Dinah said, holding Barry's elbow and walking him toward the table. "Thank you for offering."

As Barry tapped his cane, Dinah glanced around the restaurant, which was decorated to evoke the feeling of an eclectic but wealthy family home. Unmatched silverware and antique furniture gave it plenty of charm; its location within walking distance of the Capitol gave it plenty of lobbyist clients.

With a quick pat-down of the table and its two ultra-hip chairs—one wing-back, one art deco—Barry motioned for Dinah to sit, then took the seat opposite her.

"The waiter will be with you shortly," the maître d' added. "And if you need additional privacy . . ." With a sharp pull, he tugged a cord by the wall, and a burgundy velvet curtain slid into place, separating the nook from every other table in the restaurant. "Enjoy your lunch."

"So what do you think?" Barry asked.

Dinah craned her neck, staring through a thin opening in the curtain. She didn't usually eat in places like this. Not on a government salary. "How'd you find this place?" she said.

"I actually read about it in a book."

Dinah was silent.

"Why, you don't like it?" Barry added.

"No . . . it's fine . . . it's great . . . I just . . . after Matthew . . ."

"Dinah . . ."

"*He* should be the one sitting here."

"*Dinah . . .*"

"I can't help it . . . our desks are so close they're almost on top of each other—every time I look over at his stuff, I just keep . . . I keep seeing him. I close my eyes and . . ."

". . . and he's standing right there, hunched over and scratching at that bird's nest of blond hair. You think I don't feel the exact same thing? I spoke to his mom the day it happened. And then Pasternak. That alone . . . I haven't slept in three nights, Dinah. They've been my friends for years—ever since—" Barry's voice cracked, and he stopped himself.

"Barry . . ."

"Maybe we should just get out of here," he said, standing to leave.

"No, don't . . ." She reached for his sleeve and held tight.

"You said it yourself."

"Just sit," she begged. "Please . . . just sit."

Slowly, cautiously, Barry made his way back to his seat.

"It's hard," she said. "We both know that. Let's just take some time and . . . Let's just try to have a nice lunch."

"You sure?"

"Absolutely," she said as she picked up her water glass. "Let's not forget—even with all this, we've still got a big day ahead."

44

As the darkness hits, I keep my arm outstretched in front of me to stop myself from ramming into the wall. I never get there. My foot sinks into a divot, and I lurch off balance. Crashing into the ground, my knees tear across the rocky floor, making me feel every stray, pointy pebble. From the loud rip and the sudden pain across my kneecaps, I feel another fresh hole slice through my pants. I again put my hands out to break my fall, but the momentum's too much. Sliding headfirst into home plate, I face-plant across the gravel as the rocks roll against my chest. By the time I open my eyes, I taste my ever-present mouthful of dust and dirt, but this time, I can't see it. I can't see anything. *Anything.*

Coughing violently and still fighting to catch my breath, I feel a final hunk of yesterday's grilled cheese hurl up my esophagus and slam into the back of my teeth. I spit it out and hear the wet splat against the floor. Lying on the ground until my breathing settles, I keep my eyes shut, trying to take a small victory in the fact that I at least was smart enough to leave bread crumbs. It doesn't do any good. The darkness is already overwhelming. I hold my hand to my face, but nothing's in front of me. I bring it close enough that I'm touching my eyebrows. Still nothing. This isn't like shutting the lights in your bedroom and waiting for your eyes to adjust. I wave my hand back and forth. It's like it doesn't even exist. Still fighting for proof, I close my eyes, then open them. No difference.

The light is gone. But sound is an entirely different story.

"Viv!" I call out, shouting through the tunnels. *"Viv, can you hear me?!"*

My voice echoes through the chamber, eventually dying in the distance. The question goes unanswered.

"Viv! I need help! Are you there?"

Again, my question fades and dies. For all I know, she took the elevator back to the top.

"Is anyone here?!" I scream as loud as I can.

The only sound I hear is my own labored breathing and the grinding of rocks as I shift my weight. I grew up in a rural town of less than five hundred people, yet I've never heard the world as silent as it is right now, eight thousand feet below the earth. If I plan on getting out of here, I'm gonna have to do it myself.

Instinctively I start to stand up, but quickly change my mind and sit back down again. I'm pretty sure the archway that'll lead me back to the earlier part of the tunnel is in front of me, but until I'm positive, I'd better not wander around in the dark. The only thing helping me grab my bearings is the bitter smell of feces coming from the nearby wagon. As I follow the smell and trace it to the left, I'm crawling on all fours and patting the rocky ground like I'm looking for a lost contact lens. The smell is so awful, it's starting to make my eyes water, but right now that pile of reeky shit is the only beacon I've got.

Crawling forward, I hold one hand out, petting the air and searching for the wagon. If I can find it, I'll at least know which way is out. Or at least, that's the plan. My fingertips quickly collide with the jagged edges of a sharp, wet rock. But as I open my hand to get a better feel, I trace it upward, and it just keeps going. It's not a rock. It's the whole wall.

Tapping the floor slightly, I search for the wagon, but it's not there. It was on my right as I was coming in, so to get out, I keep heading left, feeling my way. Over my shoulder, there's a metallic twang as my foot collides with something behind me. Still on all fours, I reach back and pat my way along the ground until I feel the thin spokes of the red wagon's wheels. It doesn't make sense.

I freeze right there, putting both hands flat against the dirt floor. The wagon's supposed to be on my left. I reach out and feel it again. It's on my right. I'm completely turned around. Worst of all, I'm headed the wrong way, deeper into the tunnel and away from the exit. I close my eyes, already dizzy from the darkness. The smell seems like it's coming from everywhere. Ten steps and I'm already lost.

Spinning around and searching for security, I frantically braille my way across the ground and crawl forward. With one extended stretch, I reach out in front of me and feel the rest of the red wagon. The scabby edges of chipped metal. The rounded curves of the wheels. Even though I can't actually see it, my mind mentally puts the puzzle pieces together, showing me a perfect view. To my own surprise, I erupt with an anxious laugh. Copping one feel after another, my fingers soak up every sharp corner and dented curve, caressing the base of the wagon and rubbing the frayed edges of the plastic shower curtain between my thumb and pointer finger. It's an amazing sensation to take it all in by touch—and I can't help but wonder if this is how Barry feels.

Anxious to get out, I palm my way across the wagon until I find the jagged wall. As my left hand stays with the wall, my right hand sweeps back and forth like a human metal detector, brushing the ground and making sure I don't hit another divot. Still crawling, I make a sharp right through the archway at the mouth of the cave. If I wanted, I could stick with the train tracks that run down the center, but right now, the wall somehow feels more stable and secure.

Twenty-five feet later, my knees are aching, the stench is fading, and an opening on my right leads to a parallel tunnel where I can go right or left. There are openings like this in every direction, but I'm pretty sure this is the one that dumped me here. Palming the curved edge of the chunky, muddy threshold, I follow it down to the ground, searching for the scrap of paper I left behind. The list of movies I want to rent is somewhere along the floor. If I can find it, it means I have a chance of following the rest of my bread crumbs back.

Using just my fingertips, I lightly pat the rocky earth, systematically sifting through the pebbles at the base of the threshold. I work from the right-hand side of the opening to the left. I'm bent so close to the ground, blood starts rushing to my head. The pressure builds at the center of my forehead. The list of movies is nowhere to be found. For five minutes, my fingers massage the rocks as I listen for a crinkle. It never comes. Still, I don't need a scrap of paper to tell me I made a right-hand turn into this section of the tunnel. Feeling my way, I palm the wall, find the edge of the archway, and follow it out to the left.

Heading further up the hallway and crawling diagonally across the train tracks, I reach out in the darkness for the right-hand wall. It should be right in front of me . . . I stretch out my arm all the way . . . reaching . . . reaching . . . But for some reason, the wall isn't there. I stop midcrawl and grip the train tracks. If I took a wrong turn . . .

"Viv!" I call out.

No one answers.

Struggling to get my bearings, I close my eyes in the hope that it'll be less dizzying. I keep telling myself it's just a dark tunnel, but in this much darkness, I feel like I'm crawling through my own elongated coffin. My nails dig through the dirt for no other reason than to convince myself there's no coffin and I'm not trapped. But I am.

"Viv!" I shout again, begging for help.

Still nothing.

Refusing to panic, I scootch around on my butt and slowly extend my leg out as far as it goes. The wall's gotta be here somewhere. It has to be. I point my toes outward, sliding further from the tracks. Thousands of pebbles grumble underneath me. For all I know, I'm dangling my entire leg into an open hole. But if the wall's really here—and I'm pretty sure it is—it'll . . . *Thunk.*

There we go.

Keeping my foot pressed against the wall, but still lying on my back, I let go of the train track, lean forward, and hug the wetness of the wall with my hands. I keep patting it and patting it, just to make sure it's there. It's exactly where I thought it was—I just can't believe how much my spatial relations are off. Still huffing and puffing, I let out a deep breath, but my mouth is so close to the wall, I feel a whirlwind of excess dirt and water ricochet back in my face. Coughing uncontrollably, I turn my head, blinking the dirt from my eyes and spitting the rest from my mouth.

Back on my knees, it takes me two minutes to crawl along the rubble, my right hand petting the wall, my left hand tracing the ground for any other surprises. Even when I can feel what's coming—even when I know it's just another pile of loose rock—each movement is like closing your eyes and reaching the bottom step on a staircase. You tentatively put your foot out for the final step, but you never know where it's gonna be. And even when you find it, you still keep tapping against the floor—not just to be safe, but because, for that one unnerving moment, you don't completely trust your senses.

Finally feeling the rounded curve of the archway as the cave tunnel opens up on my right, I pat the floor, searching for my Triple-A card. Like before, I don't have a prayer—but unlike last time, I'm done memorizing lefts and rights. This is the cavern with five different tunnels to choose from. I pick the wrong one, and this place really will be my coffin.

"Viv!" I call out, crawling into the room. The whole world is tar. *"Please, Viv—are you there?!"*

I hold my breath and listen as my plea echoes down each of the tunnels. It rumbles everywhere at once. The original surround sound. Holding my breath and digging my nails into the dirt, I wait for a response. No matter how faint, I don't want to miss it. But as my own voice reverberates and disappears down the labyrinth, I'm once again buried in underground silence. I look around, but the view doesn't change. It only adds to my dizziness. The merry-go-round's started, and I can't make it stop.

"Viv!" I cry again in the opposite direction. *"Anybody! Please!"*

The echo trails off like the wispy tail of a ghost in my old childhood nightmares. Swallowed by the darkness. Just like me.

There's no up, down, left, or right. The world teeters sideways as dizziness flips to vertigo. I'm on all fours but still can't hold my balance. My forehead feels like it's about to explode.

With a crash, I fall on my side. My cheek rolls into the rocks. It's the only thing that tells me where the ground is. There's nothing but ink in every direction— and then, out of the corner of my eye, I spot tiny, tiny flashes of silver light. They only last a second—bursts of sparkles, like when you shut your eyes too tight. But even as I turn my head to follow the glow, I know it's just my imagination. I've heard of this before . . . when your eyes are deprived of light for too long. Miner mirages.

"Harris . . . ?" a voice whispers in the distance.

I assume it's another trick of my imagination. That is, until it starts talking back.

"Harris, I can't hear you!" it shouts. "Say something else!"

"Viv?"

"Say something else!" Her voice echoes through the room. It's hard to pinpoint the direction.

"Viv, is that you?!"

"Keep talking! Where are you?"

"In the dark—my light went out!"

There's a one-second pause, like there's a time delay on her voice. "You okay?"

"I need you to come get me!"

"What?"

"Come get me!" I shout.

The pause is still there. "I can't!" she yells. "Just follow the light!"

"There is no light! I turned too many corners—c'mon, Viv, I can't see!"

"Then follow my voice!"

"Viv!"

"Just follow it!" she pleads.

"Are you listening?! It's bouncing through every tunnel!" I stop and pause, keeping my sentences short, so the echo doesn't interfere. She needs to hear what I'm saying. "It's too dark! If I take the wrong turn, you'll never find me!"

"So I should get lost with you?!" she says.

"You have a light!"

"Harris . . . !"

"You have a light! We're running out of time!"

Her pause is even longer. She knows what I'm getting at. The longer she waits, the less likely we'll be alone down here. We've been lucky so far, but when it comes to Janos, it can't last.

"Don't be afraid, Viv! It's just a tunnel!"

This time, the pause is her longest yet. "If this is a trick . . . !"

"It's not a trick! I need help . . . !"

She knows I'm not playing around. Besides, as the Senator always says when he's talking about our top donors, "Even when they tell you the well is dry, if you dig a little deeper, there's always a little something tucked back in reserve."

"You really need me to come there?" she asks, her voice shaking.

"I can't move," I call back. "Viv . . . Please . . ."

As I lie in the darkness, the cave once again goes silent. Just the thought of heading into the darkness . . . especially by herself . . . I saw the pain in her eyes before. She's terrified.

"Viv, you still there?!"

She doesn't answer. Not a good sign. The silence keeps going, and I can't help but think that even the reserves are long dry. She's probably curled on the ground and—

"Which of these tunnels do I take?!" she shouts, her voice booming through the caves.

I sit up straight, my hands still in the dirt. "You're the greatest, Viv Parker!"

"I'm not joking, Harris! Which way do I go?"

Her voice is far off in the distance, but there's no mistaking her desperate tone. This isn't easy for her.

"The one with the freshest mud! Look for my footprints!" My voice echoes through the chamber, fading into nothing.

"Did you find it?" I ask.

Again my voice fades away. It all comes down to a seventeen-year-old girl with a flashlight on her head.

"You have tiny feet!" she calls back.

I try to smile, but we both know she's got a long way to go. Back by the cage, there's still the big industrial light up by the ceiling. Not for long. That light will be out of her sight any—

"Harris . . . !"

"You can do it, Viv! Pretend you're in a fun-house!"

"I hate fun-houses! They scare the crap outta me!"

"How about the Tilt-A-Whirl? Everyone likes the Tilt-A-Whirl!"

"Harris, it's too dark!"

The pep talk's not working.

"I can barely see . . . !"

"Your eyes'll adjust!"

"The ceiling—!" she screams. Her voice gets cut off.

I give her a second, but nothing comes back.

"Viv, everything okay?"

No response.

"Viv . . . ? Are you there?!"

Dead silence.

"*VIV!*" I shout at the top of my lungs, just to make sure she hears it.

Still nothing.

My jaw tightens, the silence sinks in, and for the first time since I left, I start wondering if we're the only ones down here. If Janos caught a different flight—

"Just keep talking, Harris!" her voice finally rings through the air. She must've entered the main stretch of tunnel. Her voice is clearer . . . less of an echo.

"Are you—?"

"Just keep talking!" she shouts, stuttering slightly. Something's definitely wrong. I tell myself it's just her fear of being trapped underground, but as the silence once again descends, I can't help but think it's something worse. "Tell me about work . . . your parents . . . anything . . ." she begs. Whatever else is going on, she needs something to take her mind off it.

"M-My first day in the Senate," I begin, "I was riding the metro to work, and as I got on board, there was an ad—I forget what it was for—but the ad said, *Reach Beyond Yourself.* I remember staring at it the entire—"

"Don't give me locker room speeches—I saw *Rudy!*" she shouts. "Tell me something real!"

It's a simple request, but I'm surprised how long it takes me to come up with an answer.

"Harris . . . !"

"I make breakfast for Senator Stevens every morning!" I blurt. "When we're in session, I have to pick him up at his house at seven A.M., go inside, and make him Cracklin' Oat Bran with fresh blueberries . . ."

There's a short pause.

"You serious?" Viv asks. She's still wavering, but I hear the laughter in the back of her throat.

I smile to myself. "The man's so insecure, he makes me walk him to every vote on the Floor, just in case he's cornered by another Member. And he's so cheap, he doesn't even go to dinner anymore without bringing a lobbyist. That way, he doesn't have to pick up the bill . . ."

After the pause, I hear a single word from Viv: "More . . ."

"Last month, Stevens turned sixty-three . . . We threw four different birthday parties for him—each one a thousand-dollar-a-plate fundraiser—and at each one, we told the invitees it was the only party he was having. We spent fifty-nine thousand on salmon and some birthday cake—we raked in over two hundred grand . . ." I sit up on my knees, shouting into the darkness. "In his office, there's a homerun baseball from when the Atlanta Braves won the World Series a few years back. It's even signed by Jimmy Carter—but the Senator was never meant to keep it. They asked him to sign it, and he never gave it back."

"You making that up . . . ?"

"Two years ago, at a fundraiser, a lobbyist handed me

a check for the Senator—I handed it back and said, *'Not enough.'* Right to his face."

I hear her laugh. That one she likes.

"When I finished college, I was such an idealist, I started and quickly dropped out of a graduate theological program. Even Matthew didn't know that. I wanted to help people, but the God part kept getting in the way . . ."

From the silence, I know I've got her attention. I just have to bring her in. "I helped redraft the bankruptcy law, but since I'm still paying back my Duke loans, I have five different MasterCards," I tell her. "My most distinctive memory from childhood is catching my dad crying in the boys' department of Kmart because he couldn't afford to buy me a three-pack of white Fruit of the Loom undershirts and had to buy the Kmart label instead . . ." My voice starts to sag. "I spend too much time worrying what other people think of me . . ."

"Everyone does," Viv calls back.

"When I was in college, I worked in an ice-cream store, and when customers would snap their fingers to get my attention, I'd break off the bottom of their cone with a flick of my pinky, so when they were a block or two away, their ice cream would drip all over them . . ."

"Harris . . ."

"My real name is *Harold*, in high school they called me *Harry*, and when I got to college, I changed it to *Harris* because I thought it'd make me sound more like a leader . . . Next month—if I still have a job—even though I'm not supposed to, I'll probably leak the name of the new Supreme Court nominee to the *Washington Post* just to prove I'm part of the loop . . . And for the past week, despite my best efforts to ignore it, I'm really feeling the fact that with Matthew and Pasternak gone, after ten years on Capitol Hill, there's no one . . . I don't have any real friends . . ."

As I say the words, I'm on my knees, cradling my stomach and curling down toward the floor. My head sinks so low, I feel the tips of the rocks press against my forehead. A sharp one digs in just under my hairline, but there's no pain. There's no anything. As the realization hits, I'm completely numb—as hollow as I've been since the day they unveiled my mom's headstone. Right next to my dad's.

"Harris . . ." Viv calls out.

"I'm sorry, Viv—that's all I've got," I reply. "Just follow the sound."

"I'm trying," she insists. But unlike before, her voice doesn't boomerang through the room. It's coming directly from my right. Picking up my head, I trace the noise just as the darkness cracks. Up ahead, the neck of the tunnel blinks into existence with the faint glow of light—like a lighthouse turning on in the midst of an ocean. I have to squint to adjust.

From the depths of the tunnel, the light turns my way, glowing at me.

I look away just long enough to collect my thoughts. By the time I turn back, I've got a smile pressed into place. But the way Viv's light shines directly at me, I know what she sees.

"Harris, I'm really sorry . . ."

"I'm fine," I insist.

"I didn't ask how you were." Her tone is soft and reassuring. There's not an ounce of judgment in it.

I look up at her. The light's glowing from the top of her head.

"What, you ain't never seen a guardian angel with an Afro before? There's like, fourteen of us up in Heaven."

She turns her head so the light no longer blinds me. It's the first time we make eye contact. I can't help but grin. "Sweet Mocha . . ."

". . . to the rescue," she says, completing my thought. Standing over me, she lifts her arms like a bodybuilder, flexing her muscles. It's not just the pose. Her shoulders are square. Her feet are planted deep. I couldn't knock her over with a wrecking ball. Forget reserves—the well's overflowing. "Now who's ready to get down to Viv-ness?" she asks.

Extending a hand, she offers to pull me up. I've never been averse to accepting someone's help, but as she wiggles her fingers and waits for me to take her up on it, I'm done worrying about every possible consequence. *What do I owe her? What does she need? What's this gonna cost me?* After ten years in Washington, I've gotten to the point where I look suspiciously at the supermarket cashier when she offers *paper or plastic.* On the Hill, an offer for help is always about something else. I look up at Viv's open hand. Not anymore.

Without hesitation, I reach upward. Viv grabs my hand in her own and gives me a hard tug to get me back on my feet. It's exactly what I needed.

"I'll never tell anyone, Harris."

"I didn't think you would."

She thinks about it for a moment.

"Did you really do that thing with the ice-cream cones?"

"Only to the real jerk-offs."

"So . . . uh . . . hypothetically, if I was working at some unnamed burger place, and some woman with a bad fake tan and some trendy haircut she saw in *Cosmo* came in and ripped my head off, telling me I'd be working there for the rest of my life—just because her food was taking too long—if I went in the back and theoretically hocked a back-of-the-throat loogie into her Diet Coke, then mixed it in with a bendy straw, would that make me a bad person?"

"Hypothetically? I'd say you get points for the bendy straw, but it's still pretty darn gross."

"Yeah," she says proudly. "It was." Looking at me, she adds, "Nobody's perfect, Harris. Even if everyone else thinks you are."

I nod, continuing to hold her hand. There's only one light between us, but as long as we stay together, it's more than enough. "So you ready to see what they're digging for down here?" I ask.

"Do I have a choice?"

"You always have a choice."

As she shoves her shoulders back, there's a new confidence in her silhouette. Not from what she did for me—what she did for herself. She looks out toward the tunnel on my left, her mine light carving through the dark. "Just hurry up before I change my mind."

I plow forward along the rocks, deeper into the cavern. "Thank you, Viv—I mean it . . . thanks."

"Yeah, yeah, and more yeah."

"I'm serious," I add. "You won't regret it."

45

KICKING THROUGH THE gravel of the Homestead mine's parking lot, Janos counted two motorcycles and a total of seventeen cars, most of them pickup trucks. Chevrolet . . . Ford . . . Chevrolet . . . GMC . . . All of them American-made. Janos shook his head. He understood the allegiance to a car, but not to a country. If the Germans bought the rights to build the Shelby Series One and moved the factory to Munich, the car would still be the car. A work of art.

Stuffing his hands in the pockets of his jean jacket and taking another hard glance at the trucks in the lot, he slowly sifted through the details: mud-covered wheel wells . . . dented rear quarter panels . . . beat-up front clips. Even on the trucks that were in the best shape, stripped wheel nuts betrayed the wear and tear. Out of the whole lot, only two trucks looked like they had ever met a car wash: the Explorer that Janos drove . . . and the jet black Suburban parked in the far corner.

Janos slowly made his way toward the truck. South Dakota plates like everyone else's. But from what he could tell, the locals didn't buy their trucks in black. The beating from the sun was always too much of a paint risk. Executive cars, however, were an entirely different story. The President always rode in black. So did the VP and the Secret Service. And sometimes, if they were big enough names, so did a few Senators. And their staffs.

Janos lightly put his hand on the driver's-side door, caressing the polished finish. His own reflection bounced back at him from the shine in the window, but from what he could tell, no one was inside. Behind him, he heard a crush of loose gravel and, in an eye blink, spun to follow the sound.

"Whoa, sorry—didn't mean to surprise you," the man in the *Spring Break '94* T-shirt said. "Just wanted to know if you needed some help."

"I'm looking for my coworkers," Janos said. "One's about my height . . ."

"With the black girl—yeah, of course—I sent 'em inside," Spring Break said. "So you're from Wendell, too?"

"Inside where?" Janos asked, his voice as calm as ever.

"The dry," the man said, pointing with his chin at the red brick building. "Follow the path—you can't miss it."

Waving good-bye with a salute from his mining helmet, the man headed back toward the construction trailers. And Janos marched straight toward the red brick building.

46

Retracing my steps, I take Viv on the quick tour to catch her up to date.

"They can run a phone line down here, but they can't build an outhouse?" she asks as we pass the red wagon. With each step, she tries to maintain the brave face, but the way her sweaty hand is gripping my own . . . the way she's always at least a half-step or so behind me, it's clear adrenaline fades fast. When she picks up the oxygen detector from the floor and looks down at the readout, I expect her to stop dead in her tracks. She doesn't. But she does slow down.

"18.8?" she asks. "What happened to the 19.6 from the elevator?"

"The cage connects to the surface—it has to be higher up there. Believe me, Viv, I'm not going anywhere that'll put us in danger."

"Really?" she challenges. She's done taking my word for it. "So where we are right now—this is no different than strolling by the Jefferson Memorial, taking photos with the cherry blossoms?"

"If it makes you feel better, the cherry blossoms don't bloom until April."

She looks around at the dark, mossy walls that're splattered with mud. Then she shines the light in my face. I decide not to push back. For five minutes, we continue to weave slowly through the darkness. The ground slants slightly downward. As the never-ending hole takes us even deeper, the temperature keeps getting hotter. Viv's behind me, trying to stay silent, but between the heat and the sticky air, she's once again breathing heavy.

"You sure you're . . . ?"

"Just keep going," she insists.

For the next two hundred or so feet, I don't say a word. It's even hotter than when we started, but Viv doesn't complain. "You okay back there?" I finally ask.

She nods behind me, and her light stretches out in front of us, bouncing up and down with the movements of her head. On the wall is another red spray-painted sign marked *Lift,* with an arrow pointing to a tunnel on our right.

"You sure we're not going in circles?" she asks.

"The ground keeps going down," I tell her. "I think most of these places are required to have a second elevator as a precaution—that way, if something goes wrong with one, no one gets trapped down here."

It's a nice theory, but it doesn't slow Viv's breathing. Before I can say another word, there's a familiar tinkle in the distance.

"Leaky faucet?" Viv whispers.

"No question, it's running water . . ." The sound's too faint to trace. "I think it's coming from up there," I add as she points her light in the distance.

"You sure?" she asks, checking behind us.

"It's definitely up there," I say, rushing forward and trying to follow the sound.

"Harris, wait . . . !"

I start to run. A series of ear-splitting chirps rips through the air. The sound is deafening, like a nuclear assault warning. I freeze and look around. If we tripped an alarm . . .

Deeper down the tunnel, a bright headlight ignites, and an engine rumbles to life. It was down here all along, hidden in the dark. Before we can even react, it barrels toward us like an oncoming freight train.

Viv tries to take off. I tug her back by the wrist. The thing's moving so fast, we'll never outrun it. Better that we not look guilty.

The metal brakes grind to a halt a few feet in front of us. I follow Viv's light as it shines across the side of the banged-up yellow car and the man who's sitting inside it. The car looks like a miniature train engine without the roof. There's a large spotlight attached to the hood. Behind the wheel is a bearded middle-aged man in a ratty old pair of overalls. He shuts the engine, and the chirping finally stops.

"Sorry about the heat—we'll have it fixed up in the next few hours," he offers.

"Fixed?"

"You think we like it like this?" he asks, using his mine light to circle the walls and ceiling. "We're a belch shy of a hundred and thirty degrees . . ." He laughs to himself. "Even for eight thousand, that's hot." I quickly recognize the flat South Dakota accent of the man who came down in the cage before us. Garth, I think. Definitely Garth. But what catches my attention isn't his name—it's the tone in his voice. He's not attacking. He's apologizing. "Don't worry," he adds. "We got this at the top of the list."

"Th-That's great," I reply.

"And now that the air conditioner and exhaust's in place, we'll have you seeing your breath in no time. You won't be sweating like that anymore," he adds, motioning to our soaked shirts.

"Thanks," I laugh back, anxious to change the subject.

"No, *thank you*—if it weren't for you guys, this place woulda still been boarded up. Once the gold was plucked, we didn't think we had a shot."

"Yeah, well . . . happy to help, Garth." I throw in his name to get his attention—and to keep him from staring at Viv. As always, it does the trick. "So how's it look otherwise?" I ask as he turns back to me.

"Right on time. You'll see when you get down there. Everything's in place," he explains. "I should really get back, though . . . We got another shipment coming in. I just wanted to make sure we had the space ready."

With a wave, he gets back in the man-car and starts the engine. The shrill scream of the chirping pierces the entire tunnel. Just a warning system as he drives through the dark—like the beeping sound when a big truck goes in reverse. As he races past us, the chirping fades just as fast.

"Whattya think?" Viv asks as I watch him disappear in the darkness.

"No idea. But from the sound of it, there's no gold left down here."

Nodding, Viv heads deeper into the mine. I stay with the man-car, making sure it's gone.

"By the way, how'd you remember his name?" she adds.

"I don't know—I'm just good with names."

"See, nobody likes people like that."

Behind me, I hear her feet crunching against the rocks. I'm still focused on the man-car. It's almost gone.

"Hey, Harris . . ." she calls out.

"Hold on, I want to make sure he's—"

"Harris, I think you should take a look at this . . ."

"C'mon, Viv—just gimme a second."

Her voice is dry and flat. "Harris, I think you should take a look at this *now* . . ."

I turn around, rolling my eyes. If she's still worried about the—

Oh, jeez.

Up ahead . . . at the very end of the tunnel . . . I have to squint to make sure I'm seeing it right. The man-car was blocking it before, but now that it's gone, we've got a clear view. Down at the lowest part of the tunnel, two brand-new shiny steel doors gleam in the distance. There's a circular glass window cut into each one, and while we're too far to see through them, there's no mistaking the bright white glow that seeps out through the glass. Two pinholes in the darkness—like the fiery white eyes of the Cheshire cat.

"C'mon . . ." Viv calls out, dashing toward the doors.

"Wait!" I call out. It's already too late. Her mine light bounces as she runs, and I chase behind the lightning bug as she weaves deeper into the cave.

The truth is, I don't want to stop her. This is what we came for. The actual light at the end of the tunnel.

47

SLAMMING BOTH HANDS against the polished steel double doors, Viv pushes as hard as she can. They don't budge. Behind her, I stand on my tiptoes to get a look through the windows, but the glass is opaque. We can't see inside. The sign on the doors says, *Warning: Authorized Personnel Only.*

"Let me try," I say as she steps aside. Shoving my shoulder against the center of the doors, I feel the right one give slightly, but it doesn't go anywhere. As I step back for another pass, I see my warped reflection in the rivets. These things are brand-new.

"Hold on a second," Viv calls out. "What about ringing the doorbell?"

On my right, built into the rock, is a metal plate with a thick black button. I was so focused on the door, I didn't even see it. Viv reaches out to push it.

"Don't—" I call out.

Again I'm too late. She rams her palm into the button.

There's a tremendous hiss, and we both jump back. The double doors shudder, the hiss slowly exhales like a yawn, and two pneumatic air cylinders unfold their arms.

The left door opens toward me; the right door goes the other way.

I crane my head to get a better look. "Viv . . ."

"I'm on it," she says, pointing her light inside. But the only thing that's there—about ten feet ahead—is another set of double doors. And another black button. Like the doors behind us, there's a matching set of opaque windows. Whatever's giving off that light is still inside.

I nod to Viv, who once again presses the black button. This time, though, nothing happens.

"Press it again," I say.

"I am . . . It's stuck."

Behind us, there's another loud hiss as the original steel doors begin to close. We'll be locked in. Viv spins around, about to run. I stay where I am.

"It's okay," I say.

"What're you talking about?" she asks, panicking. The doors are about to squeeze shut. This is our last chance to get out.

I scan the cave walls and the exposed rocky ceiling. No video cameras or any other security devices. A tiny sign on the top left-hand corner of the door says, *Vapor-Tight Door.* There we go.

"*What?*" Viv asks.

"It's an air-lock."

There's less than an inch to go.

"A what?"

With a heavy thunk, the outer doors slam shut and the cylinders lock into place. A final, extended hiss whistles through the air, like an old-fashioned train settling into the station.

We're now stuck between the two sets of doors.

Twisting back to the black button, Viv pounds it as hard as she can.

There's an even louder mechanical hiss as the doors in front of us rumble. Viv looks back at me. I expect her to be relieved. But the way her eyes jump around . . . She's hiding it well, but she's definitely scared. I don't blame her.

As the doors churn open, a burst of bright light and a matching gust of cold wind come whipping through the hairline crack. It blows my hair back, and we both shut our eyes. The wind dies fast as the two zones equalize. I can already taste the difference in the air. Sweeter . . . almost sharp on my tongue. Instead of sucking in millions of dust particles, I feel a blast of icy air cooling my lungs. It's like drinking from a dirty puddle, then having a glass of purified water. As I finally open my eyes, it takes me a few seconds to adjust. The light is too bright. I lower my eyes and blink back to normalcy.

The floor is bright white linoleum. Instead of a narrow tunnel, we're in a wide-open, stark white room that's bigger than an ice-skating rink. The ceiling rises to at least twenty feet, and the right-hand wall is covered with brand-new circuit breakers—top-notch electricals. Along the floor, hundreds of red, black, and green wires are bundled together in electronic braids that're as thick as my neck. On my left, there's an open alcove labeled *Changing Station,* complete with cubbies for dirty boots and mine helmets. Right now, though, the alcove's filled with lab tables, a half-dozen bubble-wrapped computer hubs and routers, and two state-of-the-art slick, black computer servers. Whatever Wendell Mining is doing down here, they're still setting up.

I turn to Viv. Her eyes are locked on the stacks of cardboard boxes piled all around the immaculate white room.

On the side of each box, there's one word written in black Magic Marker: *Lab*.

She looks down at the oxygen detector. "21.1 percent."

Even better than what we had up top.

"What the hell's going on?" she asks.

I shake my head, unable to answer. It doesn't make any sense. I look around at the polished chrome and the marble tabletops and replay the question over and over in my head: What's a multimillion-dollar laboratory doing eight thousand feet below the surface of the earth?

48

DOWN IN THE BASEMENT of the red brick building, Janos stopped at the charging station for the battery packs and mine lights. He'd been there once before—right after Sauls hired him. In the six months since, nothing had changed. Same depressing hallway, same low ceiling, same dirt-caked equipment.

Taking a closer look, he counted two openings in the charging station—one on each side. Thinking they were playing the odds, they gambled, he realized. That's how it always is, especially when people are panicking. Everybody gambles.

As he moved further up the hallway, Janos stepped past the wooden benches and entered the large room with the elevator shaft. Avoiding the shaft, he headed for the wall with the phone and fire alarm. No one goes down without first making a call.

"Hoist . . ." the operator answered.

"Hey, there—was hoping you could help me out," Janos said as he pressed the receiver to his ear. "I'm looking for some friends . . . two of them . . . and was just wondering if you sent them down in the cage, or if they're still up top?"

"From Ramp Level, I sent one guy down, but I'm pretty sure he was alone."

"You positive? He should've definitely been with someone . . ."

"Honey, all I do is move 'em up and down. Maybe his friend went in up top."

Janos looked up through the elevator shaft at the level that was directly above. That's where most people came in . . . but Harris and Viv . . . they'd be looking to keep it quiet. That's why they would've followed the tunnel down here . . .

"You sure he didn't just go down by himself?" the operator asked.

But just as Janos was about to answer, he stopped. His first wife called it *intuition*. His second wife called it *lion's instinct*. Neither was right. It'd always been more cerebral that that. Don't just *follow* your prey. *Think* like them. Harris and Viv were trapped. They'd be searching for a safety net . . . and they'd look everywhere to find it . . .

Gripping the edge of the short wall, Janos slid around to the opposite side, where a square piece of wood held fifty-two nails. He focused on the two metal tags labeled *15* and *27*. Two tags. They were still together.

Swiping both tags from the board, he looked down at them in his hand. Everybody gambles, he said to himself—but what's most important to remember is that at some point, everybody also loses.

49

THINK THEY KNOW we're here?" Viv asks, shutting off her mine light.

I look around, checking the corners of the laboratory. The brackets are attached to the wall, and exposed wiring dangles down, but the surveillance cameras aren't up yet. "I think we're clear."

As I said, she's done taking my word for it. "Hello . . . anyone home?" she calls out.

No one answers.

Stepping deeper into the lab, I point to the trail of muddy footprints along the otherwise stark white floor. It weaves back and toward the far left corner of the room, then down another corridor in the rear. Only one way to go . . .

"I thought you said Matthew authorized the land transfer to Wendell a few days ago," Viv points out as we head toward the back corner. "How'd they get all this built so quick?"

"They've been working on the request since last year—my guess is, that was just a formality. In a town like this, I bet they figured no one would mind the sale of a dilapidated mine."

"You sure? I thought when you spoke to the mayor . . . I thought you said he was rumbling."

"Rumbling?"

"Angry," she clarifies. "Raging."

"He wasn't angry—no . . . he was just mad he wasn't consulted—but for everyone else, it still brings life back to the town. And even if they don't know the full extent of it, as far as I can tell, there's nothing illegal about what Wendell's done."

"Maybe," she says. "Though it depends what they're building down here . . ."

As we head further down the hallway, there's a room off to our right. Inside, a large wipe-off board leans against a four-drawer file cabinet and a Formica credenza. There's also a brand-new metal desk. There's something strangely familiar about it.

"What?" Viv asks.

"Ever see one of those desks before?"

She takes a long hard look at it. "I don't know . . . they're kinda standard."

"Very standard."

"What're you talking about?"

"They just redid some of our staff offices. We got the same ones for all our legislative assistants. Those desks . . . they're government issue."

"Harris, those desks are in half the offices in America."

"I'm telling you, they're government issue," I insist.

Viv looks back at the desk. I let the silence drive home the point.

"Time-out . . . time, time, time—so now you think the government built all this?"

"Viv, take a look around. Wendell said they wanted

this place for the gold, and there's no gold. They said they were here to mine, and there's no mining. They said they're a small South Dakota company, and they've got the entire friggin' Batcave down here. It's all right in front of our face—why would you possibly believe that they're really who they say they are?"

"That doesn't mean they're a front for the government."

"I'm not saying that," I reply, heading back into the hallway. "But let's not ignore the fact that all this equipment—the lab tables, the forty-thousand-dollar computer servers, not to mention what it took to build a pristine facility eight thousand feet underground . . . These boys aren't kneeling in the dirt, shaking sand through their sifters. Whoever Wendell really is, they're clearly hunting for something bigger than a few gold nuggets—which in case you missed . . ."

". . . aren't even here anymore. I know." Chasing right behind me, Viv follows me up the hallway. "So what do you think they're after?"

"What makes you think they're after something? Look around—they've got everything they need right here." I point to the stacks of boxes and canisters that line both sides of the hallway. The canisters look like industrial helium tanks—each one comes up to my chin and has red stenciled letters running lengthwise down the side. The first few dozen are marked *Mercury;* the next dozen are labeled *Tetrachloroethylene.*

"You think they're building something?" Viv asks.

"Either that, or they're planning on kicking ass at next year's science fair."

"Got any ideas?"

I go straight for the boxes that are stacked up to the ceiling throughout the hallway. There're at least two hundred of them—each one tagged with a small sticker and bar code. I tear one off to get a closer look. Under the bar code, the word *Photomultiplier* is printed in tiny block letters. But as I open a box to see what a photomultiplier actually is, I'm surprised to find that it's empty. I kick a nearby box just to be sure. All the same—empty.

"Harris, maybe we should get out of here . . ."

"Not yet," I say, plowing forward. Up ahead, the muddy footprints stop, even though the hall keeps going, curving around to the left. I rush through the parted sea of photomultiplier boxes that're piled up on each side and turn the corner. A hundred feet in front of me, the hallway dead-ends at a single steel door. It's heavy, like a bank vault, and latched tightly shut. Next to the door is a biometric handprint scanner. From the loose wires that're everywhere, it's still not hooked up.

Moving quickly for the door, I give the latch a sharp pull. It opens with a pop. The frame of the door is lined with black rubber to keep it airtight. Inside, running perpendicular to us, the room is long and narrow like a two-lane bowling alley that seems to go on forever. At the center of the room, on a lab table, are three hollowed-out red boxes that're covered with wires. Whatever they're building, they're still not finished, but on our far right, there's a ten-foot metal sculpture shaped like a giant O. The sign on the top reads, *Danger—Do Not Approach When Magnet Is On.*

"What do they need a magnet for?" Viv asks behind me.

"What do they need this tunnel for?" I counter, pointing to the metal piping that runs down the length of the room, past the magnet.

Searching for answers, I read the sides of all the boxes that're stacked around us. Again, they're all labeled *Lab.* A huge crate in the corner is labeled *Tungsten*. None of it's helpful—that is, until I spot the door directly across the narrow hallway. It's not just any door, though—this one's tall and oval, like the kind they have on a submarine. There's a second biometric scanner that looks even more complex than the one we just passed. Instead of flat glass for a handprint, it's got a rectangular box that looks as if it's full of gelatin. I've heard of these—put your hand in the gelatin, and they measure the contour of your palm. Security's getting tighter. But again, wires are everywhere.

As I fly toward the door, Viv's right behind me—but for the first time since we've been together, she grabs my sleeve and tugs me back. Her grip is strong.

"What?" I ask.

"I thought you're supposed to be the adult. Think first. What if it's not safe in there?"

"Viv, we're a mile and a half below the surface—how much more unsafe can it get?"

She studies me like a tenth-grader measuring a substitute teacher. When I came to D.C., I had that look every day. But seeing it on her . . . I haven't had it in years. "Look at the door," she says. "It could be radioactive or something."

"Without a warning sign out front? I don't care if they're still setting up shop—even these guys aren't that stupid."

"So what do you think they're building?"

It's the second time she's asked the question. I again ignore her. I'm not sure she wants to know my answer.

"You think it's bad, don't you?" Viv says.

Yanking free of her grip, I head for the door.

"It could be anything, right? I mean, it didn't look like a reactor in there, did it?" Viv asks.

Still marching, I don't slow down.

"You think they're building a weapon, don't you?" Viv calls out.

I stop right there. "Viv, they could be doing anything from nanotech to bringing dinosaurs back to life. But whatever's in there, Matthew and Pasternak were both killed for it, and it's now our necks they're sizing the nooses for. Now you can either wait out here or come inside—I won't think less of you either way—but unless you plan on living in a car for the rest of your life, we need to get our rear ends inside that room and figure out what the hell is behind curtain number three."

Spinning back toward the submarine door, I grab the lock and give it a sharp turn. It spins easily, like it's been newly greased. There's a loud *tunk* as the wheel stops. The door unlatches from the inside and pops open slightly.

Over my shoulder, Viv steps in right behind me. As I glance back, she doesn't make a joke or a cute remark. She just stands there.

I have to push the door with both hands to get it open. Here we go. As the door swings into the wall, we're once again hit with a new smell—sharp and sour. It cuts right to my sinuses.

"Oh, man," Viv says. "What is that? Smells like a . . ."

". . . dry cleaner's," I say as she nods. "Is that what was in those canisters out there? Dry-cleaning fluid?"

Stepping up and over the oval threshold, we scan around for the answer. The room is even more spotless than the one we came from. I can't find a speck of dirt. But it's not the cleanliness that catches our eyes. Straight in front of us, an enormous fifty-yard-wide crater is dug into the floor. Inside the crater is a huge, round metal bowl that's the size of a hot-air balloon cut in half. It's like a giant empty swimming pool—but instead of being filled with liquid, the walls of the sphere are lined with at least five thousand camera lenses, one right next to the other, each lens peering inward toward the center of the sphere. The ultimate effect is that the five thousand perfectly aligned telescopes form their own glass layer within the sphere. Hanging from the ceiling by a dozen steel wires is the other half of the sphere. Like the lower half, it's filled with thousands of lenses. When the two halves are put together, it'll be a perfect spherical chamber, but for now, the top is still suspended in the air, waiting to be loaded into place.

"What in the hell?" Viv asks.

"No idea, but I'm guessing those things are the photo-multiplier—"

"What do you think you're doing?" someone yells from the left side of the room. The voice is grainy, like it's being broadcast through an intercom.

I turn to follow the sound, but I almost fall over when I see what's coming.

"Oh, Lord . . ." Viv whispers.

Rushing straight at us is a man in a bright orange haz-ardous-materials suit, complete with its own Plexiglas face plate and built-in gas mask. If he's wearing that . . .

"We're in trouble . . ." Viv mutters.

50

"Y OU HAVE ANY IDEA what you've done?" the man yells, racing toward us in the orange containment suit.

I want to run, but my legs won't move. I can't believe I led us into this—even the smallest amount of radiation could . . .

The man reaches toward the back of his neck, then yanks the radiation hood off his head, tossing it to the ground. "These are supposed to be clean-room conditions—you know how much time and money you just cost us?!" he shouts, raging forward. If I had to guess his accent, I'd go with eastern European, but something's off. He's got sunken dark eyes, a black mustache, and silver wire-rimmed glasses. He's also much thinner than he looked when the hood was on.

"There's no radiation?" Viv asks.

"How'd you get down here?!" the man shoots back. Ignoring our orange vests, he takes one look at our clothes. Slacks and button-downs. "You're not even mining people, are you?" Along the wall is an intercom with a telephone receiver. Right next to that is a red button. The man goes right for it. I know an alarm when I see one.

"Harris . . ."

I'm already on it. The man with the mustache dives for the alarm. I grab him by the wrist and shove him back. He's stronger than I expected. Using my own weight against me, he whips me around, slamming me into the white concrete wall. My head jerks backward, and my helmet hits the wall so hard, I actually see stars. He adds a rabbit punch to my gut, hoping it'll take the fight out of me. He doesn't know me at all.

His head's exposed; *I'm* wearing an unbreakable mine light. Grabbing him by the shoulders, I ram my head forward, put all my weight behind it, and head-butt him with my helmet. The brim slices him across the bridge of his nose. As he staggers backwards, I look over at Viv.

She stares at me blankly, unclear what to do.

"Get out of here!" I tell her.

"They'll kill you for this!" the man with the mustache yells.

Holding him tight, I grip his shoulder with one hand and wind up to hit him again. Thrashing wildly, he digs his fingers into my wrist. As I let go, he tries to make a run for it. He's heading straight toward Viv—but before he gets there, I grab him by the back of his containment suit and yank him as hard as I can. He may not have been the one to kill Matthew and Pasternak, but right now he's the only punching bag I've got. As he stumbles off balance, I give him one last shove—straight for the edge of the crater.

"No . . . !" he screams. "It'll all—!"

There's a loud, shattering crash as he clears the ledge and lands on half a dozen of the photomultiplier tubes. Sliding headfirst down the inside of the sphere, he smashes through every tube he hits like a human sled, clearing a path all the way to the bottom. The tubes crack easily, barely slowing him down . . . that is, until he smacks into the thick metal pylon at the base of the sphere. He looks up just in time to hit it face first. He tries to turn, but the pylon collides with his collarbone. There's a sharp, muted crunch. Bone against metal. As his shoulder hits, his body spins awkwardly around the pylon— but the man doesn't move. Facedown and unconscious, he's sprawled across the base of the sphere.

"Time to go!" Viv says, tugging me back toward the entrance.

I look around the rest of the room. Across the sphere, there're two more submarine doors. They're both shut.

"Harris, c'mon!" Viv begs, pointing down at the scientist. "The moment he gets up, he's gonna howl at the moon! We gotta get out of here now!"

Knowing she's right, I turn around and leap out through the submarine door. Jackrabbiting out of there, we run back through the lab, retracing our steps past the mercury, past the tetrachloroethylene, and past the lab tables and computer servers. Just behind the servers, I notice a small bookshelf filled with black three-ring binders and empty clipboards. From the angle we originally came in, it was easy to miss.

"Harris . . ."

"Just a sec . . ."

I shove the server out of the way and scan the binders as fast as I can. Like the clipboards, they're all empty. All but one. On the top shelf is a black binder with a printed label that reads: *The Midas Project*. Pulling it off the shelf, I flip to the first page. It's filled with numbers and dates. All meaningless. But in the top right-hand corner of the page are the words *Arrivals/Neutrino*. As I continue to flip, it's the same on every page. *Neutrino*.

Neutrino. Neutrino. I have no idea what a neutrino is, but I don't need a Ph.D. to see the trend.

"Harris, we gotta get out of here . . . !"

I slap the book shut, tuck it under my arm, and follow Viv through the room.

As we reach the first door of the air-lock, I toss the notebook to Viv and grab a fire extinguisher that's leaning against the wall. If anyone's waiting for us in the tunnel, we should at least have a weapon.

Viv punches the black button that's just beside the door, and we wait for the hydraulic hiss. As the doors swing open, we step into the air-lock, facing the next set of doors. Viv again pounds the black button.

"Put your mine light on," I tell her.

She flips a switch, and the light blinks on. Behind us, the doors to the lab slam shut—but unlike before, the door in front of us doesn't open. We're trapped. We give it another second.

"Why aren't they—?"

There's another screaming hiss. The doors in front of us slowly wheeze open.

"You think anyone's out there?" she asks.

I pull the safety pin on the fire extinguisher. "We'll know in a second."

But as the doors finally open, there's nothing there but the long darkness of the black tunnel. It's not gonna last long. The moment someone finds the guy with the mustache, alarms'll start ringing. The best thing we can do now is get moving.

"Let's go . . ." I call out, darting into the tunnel.

"You know where you're going?"

"To find the cage. Once we get to the top, we're as good as gone."

51

STANDING IN FRONT of the empty elevator shaft, Janos narrowed his eyes at the steel cable, waiting for it to start churning. "Did you try to reach your guy down there?" he said into his cell phone.

"I've been trying since early this morning—no answer," Sauls replied.

"Well, then don't blame me when you don't get what you want," Janos said. "You should've called in security the moment I said they were headed this way."

"I told you sixteen times: Those locals down there . . . they may be thrilled to be working again, but they don't know the extent of all this—we start calling in armed guards, and we might as well shove the microscope straight up our own ass. Believe me, the longer they think it's a research lab, the better off we'll all be."

"I hate to break it to you, but it is a research lab."

"You know what I mean," Sauls shot back.

"That still doesn't mean you should just risk it all for—"

"Listen, don't tell me how to run my own operation. I hired you because—"

"You hired me because two years ago, a scaly little Taiwanese silk dealer with an Andy Warhol dye job had a surprisingly finer eye for art than you anticipated. Remarkably, just as he rang the inspector to call you out on that poorly forged Pissarro—which you must admit had none of the lushness of the original—that tiny bug of a man suddenly disappeared. Quite a coincidence, don't you think?" Janos asked.

"Truly," Sauls replied, surprisingly calm. "And to be clear, the Pissarro was the *original*—it's the museum that has the fake—not that you or Mr. Lin were ever sharp enough to consider that, am I right?"

Janos didn't answer.

"Do your job," Sauls demanded. "Understand? We clear on the mine now? Once the system's in place and we can clean out all the local trash, this place'll be locked down tighter than a flea's dickhole. But in terms of calling in security, y'know what? I already did—and you're it. Now fix the problem and stop with the damn lecturing. You found their car; you found their tags—it's just a matter of waiting at the mine."

Hearing the click in his ear, Janos turned back to the elevator shaft. He was tempted to call the cage and go down into the tunnels himself, but he also knew that if he did, and Harris and Viv got off on a different level, he'd just as easily miss them. For now, Sauls had it right. What goes down must come up. All he had to do was wait.

52

THE RUSTED STEEL SAFETY gate lets out a high-pitched howl as I tug it from the ceiling of the cage and send it pounding to the floor. The metal rollers spin as it crashes into place. We're on the 4,850 level of the mine, finally settling into the cage that'll take us the rest of the way to the top. Like before, I ignore the leaky water that drips from above and go straight for the intercom.

"Stop cage," I announce as I press the goo-covered button. "We're all clear—going to one-three."

"One-three," the operator repeats. The same level we started at.

"Hoist cage," I say.

"Hoist cage," she repeats.

There's a sharp tug from above. The steel cable goes taut, the cage rockets upward, and as we fly toward the surface, my testicles sink down to my ankles.

Across from me, Viv's eyes and jaw are clamped shut. Not in fear—in pure obstinacy. She lost it once; she's not letting it happen again. The cage is banging back and forth against the wood shaft, raining even more water against the top of our helmets. Fighting to keep her balance, she leans back against the greasy walls, but the ride feels like we're surfing the top of a moving elevator. Aside from a quick glance at the oxygen detector—"20.4," she says—she stays completely silent.

I'm still breathing heavy, but some things can't wait. Wasting no time, I open the *Midas Project* notebook.

"Wanna shine that candle over here?" I ask, hoping to take her mind off the ride.

Between the two of us, she's still got the only light—but right now, it's staying aimed down at the metal floor. For Viv, until we're actually out of here, this box isn't just a moving leaky coffin. It's a mountain. A mountain to be conquered.

The only good news is, as we rocket up toward the surface, we don't have far to go. The oxygen numbers continue to rise: *20.5 . . . 20.7 . . .* Fresh air and freedom are only a minute away.

53

THE INSTANT THE STEEL cable started moving, Janos pounced for the nearby phone on the wall.

"Hoist . . ." the female operator answered.

"This cage that's coming up right now—can you make sure its next stop is at the Ramp?" Janos asked, reading the location from the sign.

"Sure, but why do you—?"

"Listen, we got an emergency up here—just bring the cage as fast as you can."

"Everyone alright?"

"Did you hear what I—?"

"I got it . . . the Ramp."

Buttoning his jacket, Janos watched as the water rained down and a cold wind blew from the mouth of the open hole. Shoving his hands in the side pocket of his jean jacket, he felt for the black box and flicked the switch. Thanks to the rumble of the approaching cage, he couldn't even hear the electrical hum.

Over his shoulder, the wood benches started to rattle. Farther up the tunnel, the fluorescent lights began to flicker. The bullet train was on its way, and from the deafening roar, it wouldn't be long.

With a final wheeze, the metal vault popped up from the abyss.

Janos dove at the latch on the corroded yellow door. Don't give them a chance to catch their breath. Grab them and keep them boxed in.

Yanking on the lock, he whipped the door open. A slap of shaft water flicked him in the face. As the door crashed into the wall, Janos's jaw shifted to the right. He clenched his teeth even tighter.

"Sons of bitches . . ."

Inside the cage, drips of water rained down from the ceiling and slithered down the greasy metal walls. Other than that, the cage was empty.

54

"Hurry . . . run . . . !" I yell at Viv as I shove open the door to the cage and sprint through the wide room that stretches out in front of us. According to the sign on the wall, we're at level 1-3—the same level we came in on. The only difference is, we used a different shaft to get out. Wasn't hard to find—all we had to do was follow the spray-painted *Lift* signs. Eight thousand feet later, we're back on top.

"I still don't see why we had to take the other shaft," Viv says, trailing behind me as I dart forward.

"You've met Janos once—you really want to go on a second date?"

"But to say he's waiting for us . . ."

"Look at your watch, Viv. It's almost noon—that's plenty of time to catch up to us. And if he's already within spitting distance, the last thing we need to do is make it easy."

Like the tunnels down below, the room up here has metal rail tracks running all along the floor. There are at least half a dozen empty man-cars, two mud-soaked Bobcat diggers, a small swarm of three-wheel ATVs, and even a few red toilet wagons. The whole place stinks of gasoline. This is clearly the vehicle entrance, but right now, all I care about is the exit.

Sidestepping between two man-cars, I continue running toward the enormous sliding garage door on the far wall—but as I get there, I spot the chain and the padlock that's holding it shut. "Locked!" I call back to Viv.

Searching around, I still don't see a way out. Not even a window.

"There!" Viv yells, pointing to her right, just past all the red wagons.

As I follow behind her, she runs toward a narrow wooden door that looks like a closet. "You sure that's it?" I call out.

She doesn't bother to answer.

Moving in closer, I finally see what's got her so excited—not just the small door, but the sliver of bright light that's peeking through underneath. After all that time underground, I know daylight when I see it.

I'm two steps behind Viv as she throws the door open. It's like coming out of a dark movie theater and stepping straight into the sun. The blast of sunlight burns my eyes in the best way possible. The whole world lights up with fall colors—orange and red leaves . . . the baby blue sky—that seem neon when compared with the mud below. Even the air—forget that recycled stuff downstairs; as I head up the dirt road in front of us, the sweet smell of plum bushes fills my nose.

"And on the tenth day, God created candy," Viv sings, sniffing the air for herself. She stares around to take it all in, but I grab her by the wrist.

"Don't stop now," I say, tugging her up the dirt road. "Not until we're out of here."

Two hundred yards to our left, above the trees, the triangular outline of the main Homestead building slices toward the sky. It takes me a second to get my bearings, but from what I can tell, we're on the opposite side of the parking lot from where we first started.

A loud siren bursts through the air. I follow it to a bullhorn up on the metal teepee building. There goes the alarm.

"Don't run," Viv says, slowing us down even more.

She's right about that. On the steps of one of the construction trailers, a stocky man with overalls and a buzz cut glances our way. I slow to a casual walk and nod my mining helmet at him. He nods right back. We may not have the overalls, but with the helmets and orange vests, we've at least got part of the costume.

A half-dozen men run toward the main mining entrance. Following the road past the trailers, we head in the opposite direction, letting it lead us back to the parking lot. A quick scan around tells me everything's just as we left it. Tons of cruddy old pickup trucks, two classic Harleys, and— Wait . . . something's new . . .

One shiny Ford Explorer.

"Hold on a sec," I say to Viv, who's already climbing into our Suburban.

"What're you doing?"

Without answering, I peek through the side window. There's a map with a Hertz logo on the passenger seat.

"Harris, let's go! The alarm . . . !"

"In a minute," I call back. "I just want to check one thing . . ."

55

"Hoist . . ." THE FEMALE operator answered.

"You were supposed to bring the cage straight here!" Janos shouted into the receiver.

"I-I did."

"You sure about that? It didn't make any other stops?"

"No . . . not one," she replied. "There was no one in it—why would I make it stop anywhere?"

"If there was no one in it, why was it even *moving?!*" Janos roared, looking around at the empty room of the basement.

"Th-That's what he asked me to do. He said it was important."

"What're you talking about?"

"He said I should bring both cages to the top . . ."

Janos clamped his eyes shut as the woman said the words. How could he possibly miss it? "There're *two* cages?" he asked.

"Sure, one for each shaft. You have to have two—for safety. He said he had stuff to move from one to the other . . ."

Janos gripped the receiver even tighter. "Who's he?"

"Mike . . . he said his name was Mike," the woman explained. "From Wendell."

Locking his jaw, Janos turned slightly, peering over his shoulder at the tunnel that led outside. His cagey eyes barely blinked.

"Sorry," the operator pleaded. "I figured if he was from Wendell, I should—"

With a loud slam, Janos rammed the receiver back in its cradle and took off for the basement stairs. A shrill alarm screamed through the room, echoing up and down the open shaft. In a flash, Janos was gone.

Rushing up the stairs two at a time, Janos burst outside the red brick building and tore back toward the gravel parking lot. On the concrete path in front of him, the man in the *Spring Break* T-shirt was the only thing blocking his way. With the alarm wailing from above, the man took a long look at Janos.

"Can I help you with something?" the man asked, motioning with his clipboard.

Janos ignored him.

The man stepped closer, trying to cut him off. "Sir, I asked you a question. Did you hear what I—?"

Janos whipped the clipboard from the man's hands and jammed it as hard as he could against his windpipe. As Spring Break doubled over, clutching his throat, Janos stayed focused on the parking lot, where the black Suburban was just pulling out of its spot.

"Shelley . . . !" a fellow miner shouted, rushing to Spring Break's aid.

Locked on the gleaming black truck, Janos raced for the lot—but just as he got there, the Suburban peeled out, kicking a spray of gravel through the air. Undeterred, Janos went straight to his own Explorer. Harris and Viv barely had a ten-second head start. On a two-lane road. It'd be over in no time. But as he reached the Explorer, he almost bumped his head getting inside. Something was wrong. Stepping back, he took another look at the side of the truck. Then the tires. They were all flat.

"Damn!" Janos screamed, punching the side mirror and shattering it with his fist.

Behind him, there was a loud crunch in the gravel.

"That's him," someone said.

Spinning around, Janos turned just in time to see four pissed-off miners who now had him cornered between the two cars. Behind them, the man with the *Spring Break '94* T-shirt was just catching his breath.

Moving in toward Janos, the miners grinned darkly.

Janos grinned right back.

56

WITH MY EYES ON THE rearview mirror, I veer to the right, pull off the highway, and follow the signs for the Rapid City airport. There's a maroon Toyota in front of us that's moving unusually slow, but I'm still watching our rear. It's barely been two hours since we blew out of the mine parking lot, but until we're on that plane and the wheels are off the ground, Janos still has a shot—a shot he's aiming straight at our heads. Slamming my fist against the steering wheel, I honk at the maroon car. "C'mon, *drive!*" I shout.

When it doesn't budge, I weave onto the shoulder of the road, punch the gas, and leave the Toyota behind us. Next to me, Viv doesn't even look up. Since the moment we left, she's been reading every single word in the *Midas Project* notebook.

"And . . . ?"

"Nothing," she says, flipping the notebook shut and checking her side mirror for herself. "Two hundred pages of nothing but dates and ten-digit numbers. Every once in a while, they threw in someone's initials—*JM . . . VS . . .* there's a few *SC*s—but otherwise, I'm guessing it's just a delivery schedule."

Viv holds the book up to show me; I look away from the road to check the schedule for myself.

"What's the earliest date in there?" I ask.

Resting it back on her lap, Viv flips to the first page. "Almost six months ago. April fourth, 7:36 A.M.—item number 1015321410," she reads from the schedule. "You're right about one thing—they've definitely been working on this for a bit. I guess they figured getting the authorization in the bill was just a formality."

"Yeah, well . . . thanks to me and Matthew, it almost was."

"But it wasn't."

"But it almost was."

"Harris . . ."

I'm in no mood for a debate. Pointing back to the notebook, I add, "So there's no master list to help decipher the codes?"

"That's why they call 'em codes. 1015321410 . . . 1116225727 . . . 1525161210 . . ."

"Those are the photomultiplier tubes," I interrupt.

She looks up from the book. "Wha?"

"The bar codes. In the lab. That last one was the bar code on all the photomultiplier boxes."

"And you remember that?"

From my pocket, I pull out the sticker I ripped off earlier and slap it against the center of the dashboard. It sticks in place. "Am I right?" I ask as Viv rechecks the numbers.

She nods, then looks down, falling silent. Her hand snakes into her slacks, where I spot the rectangular outline of her Senate ID badge. She pulls it out for a split second and steals a glance at her mom. I look away, pretending not to see.

Avoiding the main entrance for the airport, I head for the private air terminal and turn into the parking lot outside an enormous blue hangar. We're the only car there. I take it as a good sign.

"So what do you think the tubes and the mercury and the dry-cleaning smell is for?" Viv asks as we get out of the car.

I stay silent as we head under a bright red canopy and follow the sign marked *Lobby*. Inside, there's an executive lounge with oak furniture, a big flat-screen TV, and a Native American rug. Just like the one Matthew used to have in his office.

"Senator Stevens's party?" a short-haired blond asks from behind the reception desk.

"That's us," I reply. Pointing over my shoulder, I add, "I didn't know where to return the car . . ."

"There is fine. We'll have it picked up for you, sir."

It's one less thing to worry about, but it doesn't even come close to lightening my load. "So the plane is all set to go?"

"I'll let the pilot know you're here," she says, picking up the phone. "Shouldn't be more than a few minutes."

I look over at Viv, then down at the notebook in her hands. We need to figure out what's going on—and the way I left things in D.C., there's still one place I need to follow up on. "Do you have a phone I can use?" I ask the woman at the reception desk. "Preferably somewhere private?"

"Of course, sir—upstairs and to the right is our conference room. Please help yourself."

I give Viv a look.

"Right behind you," Viv says as we head up the stairs.

The conference room has an octagonal table and a matching credenza that holds a saltwater aquarium. Viv goes for the aquarium; I go for the window, which over-looks the front of the hangar. All's clear. For now.

"So you never answered the question," Viv says. "Whattya think that sphere in the lab is for?"

"No idea. But it's clearly got something to do with neutrinos."

She nods, remembering the words from the corner of each page. "And a neutrino . . ."

"I think it's some type of subatomic particle."

"Like a proton or electron?"

"I guess," I say, staring back out the window. "Beyond that, you're already out of my league."

"So that's it? That's all we've got?"

"We can do more research when we get back."

"But for all we know it could be good, though, right? It might be good."

I finally look away from the window. "I don't think it's gonna be good."

She doesn't like that answer. "How can you be so sure?"

"You really think it's something good?"

"I don't know . . . maybe it's just research—like a government lab or something. Or maybe they're just try-ing to turn stuff into gold. That can't hurt anyone, can it?"

"Turn stuff into gold?"

"The project is called *Midas*."

"You really think it's possible to turn things to gold?"

"You're asking me? How should I know? Anything's possible, right?"

I don't respond. In the past two days, she's relearned the answer to that one. But the way she bounces on her heels, she still hasn't completely given up on it. "Maybe it's something else with the Midas story," she adds. "I mean, he turned his daughter into a statue, right? He do anything else beside giving her the ultimate set of gold teeth?"

"Forget mythology—we should talk to someone who knows their science," I point out. "Or who can at least tell us why people would bury a neutrino lab in a giant hole below the earth."

"There we go—now we're moving . . ."

"We can call the National Science Foundation. They helped us with some of the high-tech issues when we did hearings on the cloning bill last year."

"Yeah—good. Perfect. Call 'em now."

"I will," I say as I pick up the phone on the octagonal table. "But not until I make one other call first."

As the phone rings in my ear, I look back out the window for Janos's car. We're still alone.

"Legislative Resource Center," a woman answers.

"Hi, I'm looking for Gary."

"Which one? We've got two Garys."

Only in Congress.

"I'm not sure." I try to remember his last name, but even I'm not that good. "The one who keeps track of all the lobbying disclosure forms."

Viv nods. She's been waiting for this. If we plan on figuring out what's going on with Wendell, we should at least find out who was lobbying for them. When I spoke to Gary last week, he said to check back in a few days. I'm not sure if we even have a few hours.

"Gary Naftalis," a man's voice answers.

"Hey, Gary, this is Harris from Senator Stevens's office. You said to give you a call about the lobbying forms for—"

"Wendell Mining," he interrupts. "I remember. You were the one in the big rush. Let me take a look."

He puts me on hold, and my eyes float over to the salt-water aquarium. There are a few tiny black fish and one big purple and orange one.

"I'll give you one guess which ones we are," Viv says.

Before I can reply, the door to the conference room flies open. Viv and I spin toward the sound. I almost swallow my tongue.

"Sorry . . . didn't mean to scare you," a man wearing a white shirt and a pilot's hat says. "Just wanted to let you know we're ready whenever you are."

I once again start to breathe. Just our pilot.

"We'll only be a sec," Viv says.

"Take your time," the pilot replies.

It's a nice gesture, but time's the one thing we're running out of. I again glance out the window. We've already been here too long. But just as I'm about to hang up, I hear a familiar monotone voice. "Today's your birthday," Gary says through the receiver.

"You found it?"

Viv stops and turns my way.

"Right here," Gary says. "Must've just got scanned in."

"What's it say?"

"Wendell Mining Corporation . . ."

"What's the name of the lobbyist?" I interrupt.

"I'm checking," he offers. "Okay . . . according to the records we have here, starting in February of this past year, Wendell Mining has been working with a firm called Pasternak and Associates."

"Excuse me?"

"And based on what it says here, the lobbyist on record—man, his name's everywhere these days . . ." My stomach burns as the words burn through the telephone. "Ever hear of a guy named Barry Holcomb?"

57

EVERYBODY SMILE," Congressman Cordell said as he stretched his own practiced grin into place and put his arms around the eighth-graders who flanked him on both sides of his desk. It took Cordell the first six months of his career to get the perfect smile down, and anyone who said it wasn't an art form clearly knew nothing about making an impression when cameras were clicking. Smile too wide and you're a goon; too thin and you're cocky. Sure, going no-teeth was perfect for policy discussions and sophisticated amusement, but if that's all you had, you'd never win the carpool moms. For that, you needed to show enamel. In the end, it was always a range: more enthusiastic than a smirk, but if you flashed all the Chiclets, you went too far. As his first chief of staff once told him, no President was ever a toothy grinner.

"On three, say, 'President Cordell' . . ." the Congressman joked.

"President Cordell . . ." all thirty-five eighth-graders laughed. As the flashbulb popped, every student in the room raised his chest just a tiny bit. But no one raised his higher than Cordell himself. Another perfect grin.

"Thank you so much for doing this—it means more than you know," Ms. Spicer said, shaking the Congressman's hand with both of her own. Like any other eighth-grade social studies teacher in America, she knew this was the highlight of her entire school year—a private meeting with a Congressman. What better way to make the government come alive?

"They got a place we can get T-shirts?" one of the students called out as they made their way to the door.

"You're leaving so soon?" Cordell asked. "You should stay longer . . ."

"We don't want to be a bother," Ms. Spicer said.

"A bother? Who do you think I'm working for?" Cordell teased. Turning to Dinah, who was just making her way into the office, he asked, "Can we push our meeting back?"

Dinah shook her head, knowing full well that Cordell didn't mean it. Or at least, she didn't think he meant it. "Sorry, Congressman . . ." she began. "We have to—"

"You've already been incredible," Ms. Spicer interrupted. "Thank you again. For everything. The kids . . . It's just been amazing," she added, locked on Cordell.

"If you need tickets to the House Gallery, ask my assistant out front. She'll get you right in," Cordell added, doing the math in his head. According to a study he read about the pass-along rate of information and gossip, if you impress one person, you impress forty-five people— which meant he had just impressed 1,620 people. With a single three-minute photo op.

Giving the top-teeth-but-no-gum-line grin, Cordell waved as the group filed out of his office. Even when the door slammed shut, the smile lingered. At this point, it was pure instinct.

"So how do we look?" Cordell asked Dinah as he collapsed in his seat.

"Actually, not too bad," Dinah replied, standing in front of his desk and noticing his use of the word *we*. He trotted that out whenever the issue at hand was potentially ugly. If it were pretty—like a school photo op—it was always *I*.

"Just tell me what they're gonna bust our nuts on," he added.

"I'm telling you, not much," Dinah began, handing him the final memo for the Conference on the Interior Appropriations bill. Now that pre-Conference and the hagglings with Trish were over, the Final Four—a Senator and a House Member from each party—would spend the next two days hammering out the last loose ends so the bill could go to the Floor, thereby funding all the earmarks and pork projects tucked within.

"We've got about a dozen Member issues, but everything else played out pretty much as usual," Dinah explained.

"So all our stuff's in there?" Cordell asked.

Dinah nodded, knowing that he always covered his projects first. Typical Cardinal.

"And we got the things for Watkins and Lorenson?"

Again, Dinah nodded. As Members of Congress, Watkins and Lorenson weren't just the recipients of brand-new visitor centers for their districts, they were also the Cardinals of, respectively, the Transportation and the Energy and Water subcommittees. By funding their requests in the Interior bill, Cordell was guaranteed to get eight million dollars in highway funds for a Hoover Dam bypass, and a two-million-dollar earmark for ethanol research at Arizona State University, which just happened to be in his district.

"The only speed bump will be the White House structural improvements," Dinah explained. "Apelbaum zeroed them out, which truthfully doesn't matter—but if the White House gets pissed . . ."

". . . they'll shine the spotlight on all our projects as well. I'll take care of it." Looking down at the memo, Cordell asked, "How much did you offer him?"

"Three and a half million. Apelbaum's staff says he'll take it—he just wants a big enough fuss to get his name in *USA Today*."

"Any others?"

"Nothing big. You should probably give in on O'Donnell's Oklahoma stuff—we gutted most of his other requests, so it'll make him feel like he got something. By the way, we also got that South Dakota land transfer—the old gold mine—I think it was the last thing Matthew grabbed from the goody bag."

Cordell gave a silent nod, telling Dinah he had no idea what she was talking about. But by bringing the gold mine up here—and pairing it with Matthew's name—she knew that Cordell would never give it away during Conference.

"Meanwhile," Cordell began, "about Matthew . . ."

"Yes?"

"His parents asked me to speak at his funeral."

Dinah paused, but that was all her boss would say. As usual, though, she knew what he meant. Staff always did.

"I'll write up a eulogy, sir."

"Great. That'd be great. As office mates, I thought you'd want to take the first draft." Turning back to the memo, he added, "Now, about this thing Kutz wants for the Iditarod Trail . . ."

"I marked it up how you like it," Dinah said as she

readjusted her fanny pack and headed for the door. "If it's got a *K* next to it, it means *keep it;* if it's got a *G,* it means we can *give it away.* Truthfully, though, it's been a pretty easy year."

"So we got what we wanted?"

Just as she was about to leave the office, Dinah turned around and smiled. All teeth. "We got everything and more, sir."

Cutting back through the welcome area of her boss's personal office, Dinah said a quick hello to the young receptionist in the denim shirt and bolo tie, then grabbed the last cherry Starburst from the candy bowl on his desk.

"Bastard eighth-graders cleaned me out," the receptionist explained.

"You should see what happens when the AARP people come visit . . ." Never slowing down, she zigzagged through reception, bounding out through the front door and into the hallway. But as she glanced right and left up the white marble hall, she didn't see the person she was looking for—not until he stepped out from behind the tall Arizona state flag that stood outside Cordell's office.

"Dinah?" Barry called out, putting his hand on her shoulder.

"Whah—" she said, spinning around. "Don't scare me like that!"

"Sorry," he offered as he held her elbow and followed her up the hallway. "So we done?"

"All done."

"Really done?"

"Trust me—we just solved the puzzle without even buying a vowel."

Neither of them said another word until they turned the corner and stepped into an empty elevator.

"Thanks **again** for helping me out with this," Barry began.

"If it's important to you . . ."

"It was actually important to Matthew. That's the only reason I'm involved."

"Either way—if it's important to you, it's important to me," Dinah insisted as the elevator doors slid shut.

With a single sweep of his cane, Barry looked around, listening. "We're alone, aren't we?"

"That we are," she said, stepping closer.

Barry once again reached out for her shoulder, this time lightly brushing his fingers against the edge of her bra strap. "Then let me say a proper thank-you," he added as the elevator bucked slightly, descending toward the basement. Sliding his hand up the back of her neck and through her short blond hair, he leaned forward and gave her a long, deep kiss.

58

"FINAL BOARDING CALL for Northwest Airlines flight 1168 to Minneapolis–St. Paul," a female voice announced through the Rapid City airport terminal. "All ticketed passengers should now be on board."

Shutting the switch for the PA system, the gate attendant turned to Janos, checking his boarding pass and driver's license. *Robert Franklin.* "You have a good day now, Mr. Franklin."

Janos looked up, but only because his cell phone started vibrating in his jacket pocket. As he pulled the phone out, the gate attendant smiled and said, "Hope it's a quick call—we're about to push back . . ."

Shooting the attendant a dark glare, he headed up the jetway. As he turned his attention to the phone, he didn't need to check caller ID to know who it was.

"Do you have any conception how much money your sloppiness just cost me?" Sauls asked through the phone. His voice was as calm as Janos had ever heard it, which meant it was even worse than Janos thought.

"Not now," Janos warned.

"He threw our technician into the sphere. Sixty-four

photomultiplier tubes completely shattered. You know how much each of those costs? The components alone came from England, France, and Japan—then had to be assembled, tested, shipped, and reassembled under clean-room conditions. Now we have to redo it sixty-four damn times."

"You done yet?"

"I don't think you heard me. You blew it, Janos."

"I'll take care of it."

Sauls went silent. "That's the third time you've said that," he finally growled. "But let me promise you right now, Janos—if you don't take care of it soon, we'll be hiring someone to take care of you."

With a soft click, the phone went dead.

"Nice to see you tonight," a flight attendant said as Janos boarded the plane.

Ignoring the attendant, he went straight for his seat in first class and stared out the oval window at the concrete runway. Sauls was still right about one thing: He had been getting sloppy lately. From getting stranded on the first flight, to the second elevator—he should've seen those coming. It was the most basic rule of tracking: cover every exit. Sure, he'd underestimated Harris—even with Viv slowing him down, and despite the panic that had to be swirling through his brain, he still somehow managed to plot a few moves ahead. No doubt, all those years in the Senate served him well. But as Janos knew, this was far more serious than politics. Leaning back against the headrest and losing himself in the roar of the jet engines, Janos closed his eyes and took another mental look at the pieces on the board. Time to get back to basics. No question, Harris was playing great chess—but even the best grandmasters know there's no such thing as a perfect game.

59

D ADDY'S GOING TO WORK NOW," Lowell Nash called out to his four-year-old daughter early the following morning.

Staring at the TV, she didn't respond.

As Deputy Attorney General, Lowell wasn't used to being ignored, but when it came to family . . . family was a whole different story. He couldn't help but laugh.

"Say good-bye to Daddy," Lowell's wife added from the living room of their Bethesda, Maryland, home.

Never taking her eyes off the videotaped glow of *Sesame Street,* Cassie Nash sucked the tip of one of her braided pigtails and waved her hand through the air at her dad. "Bye, Elmo . . ."

Lowell smiled and waved good-bye to his wife. At formal events, his colleagues at the Justice Department called him *Deputy General Nash*—he worked twenty-five years to earn that title—but ever since his daughter learned that the voice of Elmo was done by a tall black man who resembled her dad (*Elmo's best friend,* according to Cassie), Lowell's name was changed. *Elmo* beat *Deputy General* any day.

Leaving his house at a few minutes past seven A.M.,

Lowell locked the door behind himself, then twisted the doorknob and checked it three times. Directly above, the sky was gray, the sun tucked behind the clouds. No question, rain would be here soon. By the time he reached the driveway on the side of the old stucco colonial, his smile was gone—but the ritual was still the same. As he'd done every day for the past week, he checked every bush, tree, and shrub in sight. He checked the cars that were parked on the street. And most important, as he pushed a button and unlocked the doors on his silver Audi, he checked his own front seat as well. The lightning-shaped fracture was still fresh in the side window, but Janos was gone. For now.

Starting the car and pulling out onto Underwood Street, Lowell scanned the rest of the block, including the rooftop of every nearby house. Since the day he graduated from Columbia Law School, he had always been careful with his professional life. He paid his cleaning woman over the table, told his accountant not to be greedy on his taxes, and in a town of freebies, reported every gift he ever got from a lobbyist. No drugs . . . no outrageous drinking . . . nothing stupid at any of the social events he'd attended over the years. Too bad the same couldn't be said of his wife. It was just one dumb night—even for the college kid she was back then. A few too many drinks . . . a cab would take too long . . . If she got behind the wheel, she'd be home in minutes instead of an hour.

By the time she was done, a boy was paralyzed. The car hit him so hard, it shattered his pelvis. Through some quick thinking and expensive legal maneuvers, the lawyers expunged her record. But somehow, Janos found it. THE NEXT COLIN POWELL? the *Legal Times* headline read. *Not if this gets out,* Janos warned the first night he showed up.

Lowell didn't care. And he wasn't afraid to tell Janos. He didn't get to be number two at Justice by running and hiding at every political threat. Sooner or later, the news about his wife would come out—so if it was sooner, well . . . there's no way he'd hurt Harris for that.

That's when Janos started showing up at Lowell's daughter's preschool. And at the playground where they took her on weekends. Lowell saw him immediately. Not doing anything illegal, just standing there. With those dark, haunting eyes. For Lowell, that was it. He knew it all too well—family was a different story.

Janos didn't ask for much: Keep him informed when Harris called—and stay the hell out of it.

Lowell had thought it'd be easy. It was harder than he ever imagined. Every night, the tossing and turning increased. Last night he was up so late, he heard the paper hit his doorstep at five A.M. Turning onto Connecticut Avenue and heading downtown, he could barely keep the car straight on the road. A droplet of water splattered against his windshield. Then another. It was starting to pour. Lowell didn't even notice.

No doubt, Lowell had been careful. Careful with his money . . . with his career . . . and with his future. But right now, as the shrapnel of rain sprayed across his windshield, he slowly realized there was a fine line between *careful* and *cowardly.* On his left, a navy Acura blew past him. Lowell turned his head slightly to follow it, but the only thing he saw was the crack in his side window. He looked back at the road, but it wouldn't go away.

Elmo beat *Deputy General,* he reminded himself—but the more he thought about it, that was precisely why he couldn't just sit there any longer. Picking up his cell phone, he dialed the number for his office.

"Deputy Attorney General's office. This is William Joseph Williams," a male voice answered. During his interview for the job, William said his mother picked his name because it sounded like a President. Right now, he was still Lowell's assistant.

"William, it's me. I need a favor."

"Sure thing. Name it."

"In my top left-hand drawer, there's a set of fingerprints I got off my car door last week."

"The kids that cracked your window, right? I thought you already ran those."

"I decided not to," Lowell said.

"And now?"

"I changed my mind. Put 'em in the system; do a full scan—every database we've got, including foreign," Lowell said as he flicked on his windshield wipers. "And tell Pilchick I'm gonna need some detail to watch my family."

"What's going on, Lowell?"

"Don't know," he said, staring dead ahead at the slick road in front of him. "Depends what we find."

60

HARRIS, SLOW DOWN," Viv begs, chasing behind me as I cross First Street and wipe the rain from my face.

"Harris, I'm talking to you . . . !"

I'm barely listening as I plow through a puddle toward the four-story brick building halfway up the block.

"What was it you said when we landed last night? Be calm, right? Wasn't that the plan?" Viv calls out.

"This *is* calm."

"It's not calm!" she calls out, hoping to keep me from doing something stupid. Even if I'm not listening, I'm glad she's using her brain.

I whip open the glass doors and charge into the building. It's just a hair past seven. Morning security shift hasn't started yet. Barb's not in.

"Can I help you?" a guard with some acne scars asks.

"I work here," I insist just forcefully enough that he doesn't ask twice.

He looks to Viv.

"Nice to see you again," she adds, not slowing down. She's never seen him before in her life. He waves back. I'm impressed. She's getting better every day.

By the time we reach the elevator, Viv's ready to tear my head off. The good news is, she's smart enough to wait at least until the doors close.

"We shouldn't even be here," she says as they finally slam shut and the elevator lurches upward.

"Viv, I don't want to hear it." Early this morning, I picked up a new suit from the locker at my gym. Last night, after throwing our shirts in the plane's washer-dryer and clocking a half hour each in the onboard shower, we spent the entire flight back using the plane's satellite phones to track people down at the National Science Foundation. Because of the time zones, we couldn't get any of their scientists directly, but thanks to a jittery assistant and the promise that we'd be bringing the Congressman himself, we were able to wrangle a meeting.

"First thing this morning," she reminds me for the fifth time.

The NSF can wait. Right now, this is more important.

As the doors open on the third floor, I rush past the modern paintings in the hallway and head for the frosted-glass door with the numeric keypad. As quickly as I can, I punch in the four-digit code, shove open the door, and weave my way through the inner hallway's maze of cubicles and offices.

It's still too early for support staff to be in, so the whole place is silent. A phone rings in the distance. One or two offices have people sipping coffee. Other than that, the only sounds we hear are our own feet thumping against the carpet. The drumbeat quickens the faster we run.

"You sure you even know where you're—?"

Two steps past the black-and-white photo of the White House, I make a sharp right into an open office. On the black lacquered desk, there's a keyboard with a braille display, and no mouse. You don't need one if you're blind. There's also a high-definition scanner, which converts his mail to text, then gets read aloud by his computer. If there were any doubt, the Duke diploma on the wall tells me I've got it right: Barrett W. Holcomb. Where the hell are you, Barry?

He wasn't home when we went by last night—during the day, he's trolling the Capitol. We spent the last few hours hiding in a motel a few blocks away, but I figured if we came here early enough . . .

"Why don't you just beep him and ask him to meet you?" Viv asks.

"And let him know where I am?"

"But by coming here . . . Harris, this is just dumb! If he's working with Janos, they can—"

"Janos isn't here."

"How can you be so sure?"

"For the exact reason you said: It *is* dumb for us to be here."

From her look, she's confused. "What're you talking about?"

There's a tapping sound behind us. I turn just as he steps through the door.

"Harris?" Barry asks. "Is that you?"

61

YOU SCHEMING PIECE of shit . . . !" I yell, lunging forward.

Barry hears me coming and instinctively tries to side-step. He's too late. I'm already on him, shoving him in the shoulder and forcing him backwards.

"A-Are you nuts?" Barry asks.

"They were our friends! You've known Matthew since college!" I shout. "And Pasternak . . . he took you in when no one else would hire you!"

"What're you talking about?"

"Was that why it happened? Some business deal that went wrong with Pasternak? Or did he just pass you up for partner, and this was your easy shot at revenge?!" I shove him again, and he stumbles off balance. He's struggling to get to his desk. His shin smashes into the waste-basket, sending it wobbling to the floor.

"Harris!" Viv shouts.

She's worried because he's blind. I don't care.

"How much did they pay you?!" I yell, staying right behind him.

"Harris, please . . ." he begs, still searching for balance.

"Was it worth it? Did you get everything you wanted?!"

"Harris, I'd never do anything to hurt them."

"Then why was your name in there?" I ask.

"What?"

"Your name, Barry! Why was it in there?!"

"In where?"

"In the damn lobbying disclosure form for Wendell Mining!" I explode with one final shove.

Staggering sideways, Barry slams into the wall. His diploma crashes to the floor as the glass shatters.

Locking onto the wall, he presses his back against it, then palms the surface, searching for stability. Slowly, he picks his chin up to face me.

"You think that was me?" he asks.

"Your name's on it, Barry!"

"My name's on all of them—every single client in the entire office. It's part of being the last guppy in the food chain."

"What're you talking about?"

"Those forms—filling them out—it's grunt work, Harris. All the forms are done by support staff. But ever since we got fined ten grand because a partner didn't fill his out a few years back, they decided to put someone in charge. Some people are on the recruitment committee . . . others do associate benefits and staff policy. I collect all the disclosure forms and put an authorizing signature at the bottom. Lucky me."

I stop right there, searching his eyes. One of them's made of glass; the other's all cloudy, but locked right on me. "So you're telling me Wendell Mining isn't your client?"

"Not a chance."

"But all those times I called—you were always there with Dinah . . ."

"Why shouldn't I be? She's my girlfriend."

"Your what?"

"Girlfriend. You still remember what a girlfriend is, don't you?" He turns to Viv. "Who else is here with you?"

"A friend . . . just a friend," I say. "You're dating Dinah?"

"Just starting—it's been less than two weeks. But you can't say anything—"

"Why didn't you tell us?"

"You kidding? A lobbyist dating the head clerk in Appropriations? She's supposed to judge every project on its merits . . . If this got out, Harris, they'd string us up just for the fun of it. Her reputation . . . It'd be over."

"How could you not tell me? Or Matthew?"

"I didn't want to say anything—especially to Matthew. You know how much crap he'd give me . . . Dinah busts— Dinah busted his balls every day."

"I-I can't believe you're dating her."

"What? Now I can't be happy?"

Even now, that's all he sees. Perceived slights. "So the help you've been giving to Wendell . . ."

"Dinah said it was one of the last things Matthew was pushing for—I just . . . I just thought it'd be nice if he got his last wish."

I stare at Barry. His cloudy eye hasn't moved, but I see it all in the pained crease between his eyebrows. The sadness is all over his face.

"I swear to you, Harris—they're not my client."

"Then whose are they?" Viv asks.

"Why're you so crazed for—?"

"Just answer the question," I demand.

"Wendell Mining?" Barry asks. "They've only been with us a year, but as far as I know, they only worked with one person: Pasternak."

62

. . . WENDELL MINING was working with *Pasternak?*"
I ask.

The words hit like a cannonball in my gut. If Pasternak
was in on it from the start . . . "He knew all along," I
whisper.

"Knew what?" Barry asks.

"Hold on," Viv says. "You think he set you up?"

"M-Maybe . . . I don't know . . ."

"What're you talking about?" Barry insists.

I turn toward Viv. Barry can't see us. I shake my head
at her. *Don't say a word.*

"Harris, what's going on?" Barry asks. "Set you up for
what?"

Still reeling, I look out through Barry's door, into the
rest of the office. It's still empty—but it won't be for
long. Viv shoots me another look. She's ready to get out
of here. I can't say I disagree. Still, I've been on the Hill
long enough to know that you don't start flinging accusa-
tions unless you can prove they're true.

"We should leave," Viv says. "Now."

I shake my head. Not until we get some proof.

"Barry, where does the firm keep its billing records?" I ask.

Viv's about to say something. She cuts herself off. She sees what I'm getting at.

"Our what?" Barry asks.

"Billing records . . . time sheets . . . anything that shows Pasternak was working with Wendell."

"Why would you—?"

"Barry, listen to me—I don't think Matthew was hit by that car accidentally. Now please . . . we're running out of time . . . where are the billing records?"

Barry's frozen. He turns his head slightly, listening to the fear in my voice. "Th-They're on-line," he mumbles.

"Can you get them for us?"

"Harris, we should call the—"

"Just get them, Barry. Please."

He pats the air, feeling for his desk chair. As he slides into place, his hands leap for his keyboard, which looks like a regular keyboard except for the thin two-inch plastic strip that's just below the space bar and runs along the bottom. Thanks to the hundred or so pin-sized dots that pop up from the strip, Barry can run his fingers across it and read what's on-screen. Of course, he can also use the screen reader.

"*JAWS for Windows is ready,*" a computerized female voice says through Barry's computer speakers. I remember the screen-reading software from college. The computer reads whatever comes on screen. The best part is, you can choose the voice. *Paul* is the male; *Shelley's* the female. When Barry first got it, we used to play with the pitch and speed to make her sound more slutty. We all grew up. Now the voice is no different from a robotic female secretary.

"Log-in user name? Edit," the computer asks.

Barry types in his password and hits *Enter.*

"Desktop," the computer announces. If Barry's monitor were on, we'd see his computer's desktop. The monitor's off. He doesn't need it.

A few quick keystrokes activate prewritten computer scripts that take him directly where he's going. *"File menu bar. Menu active."* Finally, he hits the letter *B.*

"Billing Records," the computer says. *"Use F4 to maximize all windows."*

I stand behind Barry, watching over his shoulder. Viv's by the door, staring up the hallway.

"Leaving menu bar. Search by—" Barry hits the *Tab* key. *"Company name? Edit,"* the computer asks.

He types the words *Wendell Mining.* When he hits the space bar, the computer announces whatever word he types, but his fingers are moving so fast, it comes out *Wen— Mining.*

The computer beeps, like something's wrong.

"Client not found," the computer says. *"New search? Edit."*

"What's going on?" Viv asks.

"Try just *Wendell,*" I add.

"Wendell," the computer repeats as Barry types the word and hits *Enter.* There's another beep. *"Client not found. New search? Edit."*

"This doesn't make sense," Barry says. His hands are a blur of movement.

The female voice can't keep up. *"Ne— Sys— Wen— Min— Searching database . . ."*

He's widening the search. I stare intensely at the computer screen even though it's all black. It's better than watching Viv panic by the door.

"Harris, you still there?" Barry asks.

"Right here," I reply as the computer whirs.

"Client not found in system," the mechanized voice replies.

Barry respells it.

"Client not found in system."

"What's the problem?" I ask.

"Hold on a second."

Barry hits the *W*, then the downward arrow key. *"Waryn Enterprises,"* the computer says. *"Washington Mutual* . . . Washington Post . . . *Weiner & Robinson* . . ." It's searching alphabetically. *"Wong Pharmaceuticals* . . . *Wilmington Trust* . . . *Xerox* . . . *Zuckerman International* . . . *End of record,"* the computer finally says.

"You kidding me?" Barry says, still searching.

"Where are they?" I ask.

"End of record," the computer repeats.

Barry hits the keyboard once more.

"End of record."

"I don't understand," Barry says. His hands move faster than ever. *"Full— Sys— Searching . . ."*

"Barry, what the hell is going on?"

"Search error," the female mechanized voice interrupts. *"Client name not in system."*

I stare at the blank screen; Barry stares down at his keyboard.

"They're gone," Barry says. "Wendell Mining's gone."

"What're you talking about? How can it be gone?"

"It's not there."

"Maybe someone forgot to enter it."

"It already *was* entered. I checked it myself when I did the lobbying forms."

"But if it's not there now . . ."

"Someone took it out . . . or deleted the file," Barry says. "I checked every spelling of Wendell . . . I went through the entire database. It's like they were never clients."

"Morning . . ." a short man in an expensive pinstriped suit says to Viv as he walks past the door to Barry's office.

She turns my way. People are starting to arrive. "Harris, the longer we're here . . ."

"I got it," I say to Viv. My eyes stay on Barry. "What about hard copies? Is there anything else that might show that Pasternak worked with Wendell?"

Barry's been blind for as long as I've known him. He knows panic when he hears it. "I-I guess there's Pasternak's client files . . ."

A loud chirp screeches through the air. All three of us wince at the sharpness of the sound.

"What in the hell—?"

"Fire alarm!" Viv calls out.

We give it a few seconds to shut itself off. No such luck.

Viv and I once again exchange glances. The alarm continues to scream. If Janos is here, it's a perfect way to empty the building.

"Harris, please . . ." she begs.

I shake my head. Not yet.

"Does Pasternak still keep his files in his office?" I shout to Barry over the noise.

"Yeah . . . why?"

That's all I need. "Let's go," I call to Viv, motioning her out into the hallway.

"Wait . . . !" Barry says, shooting out of his seat and following right behind us.

"Keep going," I say to Viv, who's a few steps in front

of me. If Barry's not involved, the last thing I want to do is suck him in.

As Barry steps into the hallway, I look back to make sure he's okay. The short man in the pinstriped suit comes by to help him make his way outside. Barry brushes him off, rushing after us. "Harris, wait!"

He's faster than I thought.

"Oh, crap," Viv calls out as we turn the corner. Forcing our way out to the bank of elevators, we see this isn't just a drill.

All three elevator doors are closed, but now there's a chorus of three elevator alarms competing with the main fire alarm. A middle-aged man shoves open the metal emergency door to the stairs, and a wisp of dark gray smoke swims into the hall. The smell tells us the rest. Something's definitely burning.

Viv looks at me over her shoulder. "You don't think Janos—"

"C'mon," I insist, rushing past her.

I dart for the open door of the stairs—but instead of heading down, I go straight up, toward the source of the smoke.

"What're you doing?" Viv calls out.

She knows the answer. I'm not leaving without Pasternak's records.

"Harris, I'm not doing this anymore . . ."

An older woman with jet black dyed hair and reading glasses around her neck comes down the stairs from the fourth floor. She's not running. Whatever's burning up there is more smoke than threat.

I feel a sharp tug on the back of my shirt.

"How do you know it's not a trap?" Viv asks.

Again I stay silent, pulling away from Viv and continuing up the stairs. The thought of Pasternak working against us . . . Is that why they killed him? He was already involved? Whatever the answer, I need to know.

Leaping up the stairs two at a time, I quickly reach the top, where I squeeze between two more lobbyists just as they enter the stairwell.

"Hey there, Harris," one calls out with a friendly laugh. "Wanna grab some breakfast?"

Unreal. Even in a fire, lobbyists can't help but politic.

Twisting and turning through the hallway, I head toward Pasternak's office and follow the smoke, which is now a thick dark cloud that fills the narrow hallway. I'm blinking as fast as I can, but it's burning my eyes. Still, I've been coming this way for years. I could make it here in pitch dark.

As I make a sharp right around the last corner, there's a crackle in the air. A wave of heat punches me hard in the face—but not nearly as hard as the hand that reaches out and clutches my arm. I can barely see him through the smoke.

"Wrong way," a deep voice insists.

I jerk my arm to the side, quickly freeing myself. My fist is clenched, ready to take the first swing.

"Sir, this area's closed. I need you to make your way to the stairs," he says over the screaming alarm. On his chest is a gold-and-blue *Security* badge. He's just a guard.

"Sir, did you hear what I said?"

I nod, barely paying attention. I'm too busy staring over his shoulder at the source of the fire. Up the hallway . . . through the thick oak door . . . I knew it . . . I knew it the moment the alarm went off. A tiny burst of flame belches through the air, licking the ceiling tiles in Pasternak's office. His desk . . . the leather chair . . . the presidential photos on the wall—they're all on fire. I don't stop. If the file cabinet's fireproof, I can still . . .

"Sir, I need you to exit the building," the guard insists.

"I need to get in there!" I call out, trying to rush past him.

"Sir!" the man shouts. He extends his arm, blocking my way and ramming me in the chest. He's got four inches and over a hundred pounds on me. I don't let up. And neither does he. As I shove him aside, he pinches the skin on the side of my neck and gives it a ruthless twist. The pain's so intense, I almost fall to my knees.

"Sir, are you listening to me?!"

"Th-The files . . ."

"You can't go in there, sir. Can't you see what's happening?"

There's a loud crash. Up the hallway, the oak door to Pasternak's office collapses off its hinges, revealing the file cabinets that run along the wall just behind it. There are three tall cabinets side by side. From the looks of it, all of them are fireproof. The problem is, all of them have their drawers pulled wide open.

The papers inside crackle and burn, charred beyond recognition. Every few seconds, a sharp pop kicks a few singed black scraps somersaulting through the air. I can barely breathe through all the smoke. The world blurs through the flames. All that's left are the ashes.

"They're gone, sir," the guard says. "Now, please . . . head down the stairs."

I still don't move. In the distance, I can hear the orchestra of approaching sirens. Ambulances and fire engines are on their way. Police won't be far behind.

The guard reaches out to turn me around. That's when I feel the soft hand on the small of my back.

"Ma'am . . ." the guard starts.

Behind me, Viv studies the burning file cabinets in Pasternak's office. The sirens slowly grow louder.

"C'mon," she tells me. My body's still in shock, and as I turn to face her, she reads it in an instant. Pasternak was my mentor; I've known him since my first days on the Hill.

"Maybe it's not what you think," she says, tugging me back up the hallway and toward the stairs.

The tears run down my face, and I tell myself it's from the smoke. Sirens continue to howl in the distance. From the sound of it, they're right outside the building. With a sharp tug, Viv drags me into the dark gray fog. I try to run, but it's already too hard. I can't see. My legs feel like they're filled with Jell-O. I can't do it anymore. My run slows to a lumbering walk.

"What're you doing?" Viv asks.

I can barely look her in the eye. "I'm sorry, Viv . . ."

"What? Now you're just giving up?"

"I said, I'm sorry."

"That's not good enough! You think that takes the guilt off your plate? You got me into this, Harris—you and your dumb frat-boy, I-own-the-world-so-let's-play-with-it egoism! *You're* the reason I'm running for my life, and wearing the same underwear for three days, and crying myself to sleep every night wondering if this psychopath is gonna be standing over me when I open my eyes in the morning! I'm sorry your mentor tricked you, and that your Capitol Hill existence is all you have, but I've got an entire life in front of me, and I want it back! Now! So get your rear end moving, and let's get out of here. We need to figure out what the hell we saw in that underground lab, and right now we've got an appointment with a scientist that you're making me late for!"

Stunned by the outburst, I can barely move.

"You've really been crying yourself to sleep?" I finally ask.

Viv pummels me with a dark stare that gives me the answer. Her brown eyes glow through the smoke. "No."

"Viv, you know I'd never—"

"I don't want to hear it."

"But I—"

"You did it, Harris. You did it, and it's done. Now, you gonna make it right or not?"

Outside the building, someone barks safety instructions through a bullhorn. The police are here. If I want to give up, this is the place to do it.

Viv heads up the hallway. I stay put.

"Good-bye, Harris," she calls out. The words sting as she says them. When I first asked her for help, I promised her she wouldn't get hurt. Just like I promised Matthew that the game was harmless fun. And promised Pasternak, when I first met him, that I'd be the most honest person he'd ever hire. All those words . . . when I originally said them . . . I meant every syllable—but no question, those words were always for me. Myself. I, I, I. It's the easiest place to get lost on Capitol Hill—right inside your own self-worth. But as I watch Viv disappear in the smoke, it's time to look away from the mirror and finally refocus.

"Hold on," I call out, chasing after her and diving into the smoke. "That's not the best way."

Stopping midstep, she doesn't smile or make it easy. And she shouldn't.

It takes a seventeen-year-old girl to treat me like an adult.

63

"How's it look?" Lowell asked as his assistant stepped into his fourth-floor office in the main Justice building on Pennsylvania Avenue.

"Let me put it like this," William began, brushing his messy brown hair from his chubby, boyish face. "There's no Santa Claus, no Easter bunny, no cheerleader who liked you in high school, your 401K is toilet paper, you didn't marry the prom queen, your daughter just got knocked up by a real scumbag, and y'know that beautiful view you've got of the Washington Monument?" William asked, pointing over Lowell's shoulder at the nearby window. "We're gonna paint it black and replace it with some modern art."

"Did you say modern art?"

"No joke," William said. "And that's the good news."

"It's really that bad?" Lowell asked, motioning to the red file folder in his assistant's hands. Outside Lowell's office and across the adjacent conference room, two receptionists answered the phones and put together his schedule. William, on the other hand, sat right outside Lowell's door. By title, he was Lowell's "confidential assistant," which meant he had security clearance to deal with the most important professional issues—and, after three years with Lowell, the personal ones as well.

"On a scale of one to ten, it's Watergate," William said.

Lowell forced a laugh. He was trying to keep it light, but the red folder already told him this was only getting worse. Red meant FBI.

"The fingerprints belong to Robert Franklin of Hoboken, New Jersey," William began, reading from the folder.

Lowell made a face, wondering if the name Janos was fake. "So he's got a record?" he asked.

"Nosiree."

"Then how'd they have his fingerprints?"

"They got 'em internally."

"I don't get it."

"Their staffing unit. Personnel," William explained. "Apparently, this guy applied for a job a few years back."

"You're kidding, right?"

"Nosiree. He applied."

"At the FBI?"

"At the FBI," William confirmed.

"So why didn't they hire him?"

"They're not saying. That one's too high up for me. But when I begged for a hint, my buddy over there said they thought the application was sour."

"They thought he was trying to infiltrate? On his own, or as a hired gun?"

"Does it matter?"

"We should run him outside the system—see if he—"

"Whattya think I've been doing for the last hour?"

Lowell forced another grin, gripping the armrests of

his leather chair and fighting to keep himself from standing. They'd worked together long enough that William knew what the grip meant. "Just tell me what you found," Lowell insisted.

"I ran it through a few of our foreign connections . . . and according to their system, the prints belong to someone named Martin Janos, a.k.a. Janos Szasz, a.k.a. . . ."

"Robert Franklin," Lowell said.

"And Bingo was his name-o. One and the same."

"So why'd they have his prints over there?"

"Oh, boss-man, that's the cherry on top. He used to work at Six."

"What're you talking about?"

"Martin Janos—or whatever his real name is—he used to be MI-6. Britain's Secret Intelligence Service."

Lowell closed his eyes, trying to remember Janos's voice. If he was British, the accent was long gone. Or well hidden.

"When he joined, he was barely a kid—just out of college," William added. "Apparently, he had a sister who was killed in a car bomb. That got him sufficiently riled up. They brought him in as a straight recruit."

"So no military background?"

"If there is, they're not saying."

"He couldn't have been too high on the totem pole."

"Just an analyst in the Forward Planning Directorate. Sounds to me like he was staring at a computer, stapling lots of papers together. Whatever it was, he spent two years there, then was fired."

"Any reason why?"

"Insubordination, surprise surprise. They put him on a job; he refused to do it. When one of his superiors got in his face about it, the argument got a little heated, at which point young Janos picked up a nearby stapler and started beating him with it."

"Wound a little tight, isn't he?"

"The smartest ones always are," William said. "Though it sounds to me like he was a powder keg to begin with. Once he leaves, he goes out on his own, finds some work for the highest bidder . . ."

"Now he's back in business," Lowell agrees.

"Certainly a possibility," William said as his voice trailed off.

"What?" Lowell asked.

"Nothing—it's just . . . after Her Majesty's Service, Janos is gone for almost five years, reappears one day over here, applies to the FBI under a new ID, gets rejected for trying to infiltrate, then steps back into the abyss, never to be heard from again—that is, until a few days ago, when he apparently uses all his hard-trained skills to . . . uh . . . to smash the side window on your car."

Letting the silence take hold, William stared hard at his boss. Lowell stared right back. The phone on his desk started to ring. Lowell didn't pick it up. And the longer he studied his assistant, the more he realized this wasn't an argument. It was an offer.

"Sir, if there's anything you need me to—"

"I appreciate it, William. I truly do. But before I get you knee-deep in this, let's just see what else we can find."

"But I can—"

"Believe me, you're invaluable to the case, William— I won't forget it. Now let's just keep hunting."

"Absolutely, sir," William said with a grin. "That's what I'm working on right now."

"Any leads worth talking about?"

"Just one," William said, pointing down to the folder, where a fax from the Financial Crimes Enforcement Network poked out from the top. "I ran all of Janos's identities through the guys at FinCEN. They came up with an offshore account that bounces back through Antigua."

"I thought we couldn't get to those . . ."

"Yeah, well, since 9-11, some countries have been a little more cooperative than others—especially when you say you're calling from the Attorney General's office."

Now Lowell was the one who was grinning.

"According to them, the account has four million dollars' worth of transfers from something called the Wendell Group. So far, all we know is, it's a shelf company with a fake board of directors."

"Think you can trace ownership?"

"That's the goal," William said. "It'll take some peeking in the right places, but I've seen these guys work before . . . If I gave them your last name, they'd find the twelve-dollar savings account your mom opened for you when you were six."

"Then we're in good hands?"

"Let me put it like this, sir—you can go get coffee and some McDonaldland Cookies. By the time you come back, we'll have Wendell—or whoever they are—sitting in your lap."

"I still appreciate what you're doing," Lowell said, holding his glance tight on his assistant. "I owe you for this."

"You don't owe me a Canadian penny," William said. "It all goes back to what you taught me on day one: Don't fuck with the Justice Department."

64

"THIS IS IT?" Viv asks, craning her neck skyward and stepping out of the cab in downtown Arlington, Virginia. "I was expecting a huge science compound."

Dead ahead, a twelve-story modern office building towers over us as hundreds of commuters pour out of the nearby Ballston Metro Station and scurry past the surrounding coffee shops and trendy eateries that are about as edgy as suburbia gets. The building is no bigger than the others around it, but the three words carved into the salmon-colored stone facade immediately make it stand out from everything else: *National Science Foundation*.

Approaching the front entrance, I pull open one of the heavy glass doors and check the street one last time. If Janos were here, he wouldn't let us get inside—but that doesn't mean he's not close.

"Morning, dear—how can I help you today?" a woman wearing a lime green sweater set asks from behind a round reception desk. On our right, there's a squatty black security guard whose eyes linger on us a few seconds too long.

"Yeah . . . we're here to see Doctor Minsky," I say, trying to stay focused on the receptionist. "We have an appointment. Congressman Cordell . . ." I add, using the name of Matthew's boss.

"Good," the woman says as if she's actually happy for us. "Photo IDs, please?"

Viv shoots me a look. We've been trying to avoid using our real names.

"No worries, Teri, they're with me," a peppy female voice interrupts.

Back by the elevators, a tall woman in a designer suit waves at us like we're old friends.

"Marilyn Freitas—from the director's office," she announces, pumping my hand and smiling with a game show grin. The ID badge around her neck tells me why: *Director of Legislative and Public Affairs*. This isn't a secretary. They're already pulling out the big guns—and while I've never seen this woman in my life, I know this tap dance. The National Science Foundation gets over five billion dollars annually from the Appropriations Committee. If I'm bringing one of their appropriators here, they're gonna roll out the brightest red carpet they can find. That's why I used Matthew's boss's name instead of my own.

"So is the Congressman here?" she asks, smile still in place.

I look back through the glass door. She thinks I'm searching for my boss. I'm actually checking for Janos. "He should be joining us shortly—though he said we should start without him," I explain. "Just in case."

Her smile sinks a bit, but not by much. Even if she'd rather see the Congressman, she's smart enough to know the importance of staff. "Whenever he gets here is good

by us," she says as she leads us back to the elevators.
"Oh, and by the way," she adds, "welcome to the NSF."

As the elevator rises to the tenth floor, my mind bounces
back to yesterday's elevator ride: the cage pounding
against the walls as the water rained down on our mud-
coated helmets. Leaning back against the polished brass
railing, I toss a thin smile at Viv. She ignores it, keeping
her eyes on the red digital numbers that mark our ascent.
She's done being friends. She wants out.

"So I understand you're here to talk to Dr. Minsky
about neutrinos," Marilyn says, hoping to keep the conversation going.

I nod. Viv nibbles. "Everyone said he's the expert,"
she says, trying not to make it sound like a question.

"Oh, he is," Marilyn replies. "That's where he got his
start—subatomic. Even his early work on leptons . . .
sure, it may seem basic now, but back then, it set the
standard."

We both nod as if she's talking about the *TV Guide*
crossword puzzle.

"So he does his research right here?" Viv adds.

The woman lets out the kind of laugh that usually
comes with a pat on the head. "I'm sure Dr. Minsky
would love to get back in the lab," she explains. "But
that's no longer part of the job description. Up here,
we're primarily concerned with the funding side."

It's a fair description but a complete understatement.
They're not just *concerned* with the funding side; they
control it. Last year, the National Science Foundation
funded over two thousand studies and research facilities
across the globe. As a result, they have a hand in just

about every major science experiment in the world—from a radio telescope that can see the evolution of the universe, to a climate theory that'll help us control the weather. If you can dream it up, the NSF will consider giving it financial support.

"And here we are," Marilyn announces as the elevator doors glide open.

On our left, silver letters emblazoned on the wall read: *Directorate for Mathematical and Physical Sciences*. The sign's so big, there's barely room for the NSF logo, but that's what happens when you're the largest of the NSF's eleven divisions.

Leading us past another reception desk and around the corner to a sitting area that has all the charm of a hospital waiting room, she doesn't say another word. On our left and right, the walls are covered with science posters: one with a row of satellite dishes lined up under a rainbow, another with a shot of the Pinwheel Galaxy from the Kitt Peak National Observatory. Both are meant to calm anxious visitors. Neither one does much of a job.

Over my shoulder, the elevator doors open in the distance. I spin around to see who's there. If we can find the premier neutrino expert in the country, so can Janos. Back by the elevators, a man with thick glasses and a rumpled sweater steps into the hall. From the way he's dressed, it's clear he's just a local.

Reading my relief, Viv turns back toward the waiting area, which is surrounded by half a dozen closed doors. All are numbered *1005*. The one directly in front of us has the additional label *.09*. Only the National Science Foundation assigns rooms with a decimal designation.

"Doctor Minsky?" Marilyn calls out, knocking lightly and turning the knob.

As the door slowly opens, a distinguished older man with puffy cheeks is already out of his seat, shaking my hand and looking over my shoulder. He's searching for Cordell.

"The Congressman should be here shortly," Marilyn explains.

"He said we should start without him," I add.

"Perfect . . . perfection," he replies, finally making eye contact. Studying me with smoky gray eyes, Minsky scratches slightly at the side of his beard, which, like his wispy, thin hair, is more salt than pepper. I try to smile, but his stare continues to bear down on me. That's why I hate meeting with academics. Social skills are always slightly off.

"I've never met you before," he finally blurts.

"Andy Defresne," I say, introducing myself. "And this is—"

"Catherine," Viv says, refusing my aid.

"One of our interns," I jump in, guaranteeing that he'll never look twice at her.

"Dr. Arnold Minsky," he says, shaking Viv's hand. "My cat's name was Catherine."

Viv nods as pleasantly as possible, checking out the rest of his office in an attempt to avoid further conversation.

He's got an upholstered sofa, a matching set of end chairs, and an outstanding view of downtown Arlington outside the plate-glass windows that line the entire right side of his office. Forever the academic, Minsky goes straight to his desk, which is covered with meticulous size-order stacks of papers, books, and magazine articles. Like his work, every molecule is accounted for. As I take the seat directly across from him, Viv slides into the chair that's next to the window. It's got a perfect view of the busy street out front. She's already searching for Janos.

I check the walls, hunting for anything else that'll give me a read. To my surprise, unlike the usual D.C. ego shrine, Minsky's walls aren't covered with diplomas, famous-person photos, or even a single framed newspaper clipping. That's not the commodity here. He's done proving he belongs.

Still, every universe has its own currency. The walls on both sides of Minsky's desk are covered with built-in bookcases, floor to ceiling, filled with hundreds of books and academic texts. The spines are all worn, which I quickly realize is the point. In Congress, the golden ring is fame and stature. In science, it's knowledge.

"Who's that with you in the photo?" Viv asks, pointing to a tasteful silver frame of Minsky standing next to an older man with curly hair and a quizzical expression.

"Murray Gell-Mann," Minsky says. "The Nobel Prize winner . . ."

I roll my tongue inside my cheek. Stature plays everywhere.

"So what can I help you with today?" Minsky asks.

"Actually," I say, "we were wondering if we could ask you a few questions about neutrinos . . ."

65

Y OU SAW THEM?" Janos asked, holding his cell phone in one hand and gripping the steering wheel of the black sedan with the other. The morning traffic wasn't bad, even for Washington, but at this point, even a moment's delay was enough to get him raging. "How'd they look?" he demanded.

"They're lost," his associate said. "Harris could barely get a sentence out, and the girl . . ."

"Viv."

"Angry little thing. You could see it in the air. She was ready to take his head off."

"Did Harris say anything?"

"Nothing you don't know."

"But they were there?" Janos asked.

"Absolutely. Even went up to the boss's office—not that it did them any good," the man said.

"So you took care of everything?"

"Everything you asked."

"And they believed it?"

"Even the Dinah stuff. Unlike Pasternak, I see things through to the end."

"You're a real hero," Janos said wryly.

"Yeah, well . . . don't forget to tell your boss that. Between the loans, the surgeries, and all my other debts . . ."

"I'm well aware of your financial situation. That's why—"

"Don't say it's the money—screw money; it's more than that. They asked for this. They did. The snubs . . . the shrug-offs . . . People think it goes unnoticed."

"As I was saying, I completely sympathize. That's why I approached you in the first place."

"Good, because I didn't want you to think every lobbyist is in it for the cash. That's a hurtful stereotype."

Janos was silent. In many ways, his colleague was no different from the shiny sedan he was driving—overhyped and barely adequate. But as he reasoned when he first picked out the car, some things are necessary to blend in in Washington. "Did they say where they were going next?" Janos asked.

"No, but I have an idea . . ."

"So do I," Janos said, making a sharp right and pulling into the underground parking garage. "Nice to see you," he called out as he waved to the security guard outside the employee lot. The guard threw a warm smile back.

"Are you where I said?" his colleague asked through the phone.

"Don't worry where I am," Janos shot back. "Just focus on Harris. If he calls back, we need you to keep your eyes and ears wide open."

"Ears I can help you with," Barry said, his scratchy voice raking through the phone. "It's the eyes that've always been a bit of a problem."

66

Now what's this for again?" Dr. Minsky asks, unbending a paperclip and tapping it lightly on the edge of his desk.

"Just background," I say, hoping to keep the discussion moving. "We've got this project we're looking at—"

"A new neutrino experiment?" Minsky interrupts, clearly excited. It's still his pet issue, so if there's some new data out there, he wants to play with the toys first.

"We really shouldn't say," I reply. "They're still in the early stages."

"But if they're—"

"It's actually someone who's a friend of the Congressman," I interrupt. "It's not for public consumption."

The man has two Ph.D.s. He gets the hint. Congressmen do favors for friends every day. That's why the real news on Capitol Hill is never in the newspapers. If Minsky wants any more favors from us, he knows he has to help us with this.

"So neutrinos, eh?" he finally asks.

I smile. So does Viv—but as she turns her head slightly, glancing out the window, I can tell she's still searching for Janos. We're not gonna outrun him without a head start.

"Let me do it like this," Minsky says, quickly shifting into professor mode. He holds the unbent paperclip up like a tiny pointer, then motions downward, from the ceiling to the floor. "As we sit here right now, fifty billion—not million—fifty *billion* neutrinos are flying from the sun, through your skull, down your body, out the balls of your feet, and down through the nine floors below us. They won't stop there, though—they'll keep going past the concrete foundation of the building, straight through the earth's core, through China, and back out to the Milky Way. You think you're just sitting here with me, but you're being bombarded right now. Fifty billion neutrinos. Every single second. We live in a sea of them."

"But are they like protons? Electrons? What are they?"

He looks down, trying not to make a face. To the educated man, there's nothing worse than a layperson. "In the subatomic world, there are three kinds of particles that have mass. The first and heaviest are quarks, which make up protons and neutrons. Then, there're electrons and their relatives, which are even lighter. And finally come neutrinos, which are so incredibly lightweight there are still some doubters out there who argue they don't have mass at all."

I nod, but he knows I'm still lost.

"Here's the significance," he adds. "You can calculate the mass of everything you see in a telescope, but when you add all that mass up, it's still only ten percent of what makes up the universe. That leaves ninety percent unaccounted for. So where's the missing ninety percent? As physicists have asked for decades: Where's the missing mass of the universe?"

"Neutrinos?" Viv whispers, accustomed to being a student.

"Neutrinos," Minsky says, pointing the paperclip her way. "Of course, it probably isn't the full ninety percent, but a portion of it . . . they're the leading candidate."

"So if someone's studying neutrinos, they're trying to . . ."

". . . crack open the ultimate treasure chest," Minsky says. "The neutrinos that we're swimming in right now were produced at the big bang, at supernovas, and even, during fusion, at the heart of the sun. Any idea what those three things have in common?"

"Big explosions?"

"Creation," he insists. "That's why physicists are trying to figure them out, and that's why they gave the Nobel to Davis and Koshiba a few years back. Unlock neutrinos and you potentially unlock the nature of matter and the evolution of the universe."

It's a nice answer, but it doesn't get me any closer to my real question. Time to be blunt. "Could they be used to build a weapon?"

Viv looks away from the window; Minsky cocks his head slightly, picking me apart with his scientist's eyes. I may be sitting in front of a genius, but it doesn't take one to know something's up.

"Why would someone use it as a weapon?" he asks.

"I'm not saying they are—we just . . . we want to know if they can."

Minsky drops the paperclip and puts his palms flat against his desk. "Exactly what type of project is this for again, Mr. Defresne?"

"Maybe I should leave that for the Congressman," I say, trying to defuse the tension. All it does is shorten the fuse.

"Maybe it'd be best if you showed me the actual proposal for the project," Minsky says.

"I'd love to—but right now it's confidential."

"Confidential?"

"Yes, sir."

The fuse is on its last hairs. Minsky doesn't move.

"Listen, can I be honest with you?" I ask.

"What a novel idea."

He uses the sarcasm as a mental shove. I purposely twist in my chair and pretend he's got control. Rope-a-dope. He may have twenty years on me, but I've played this game with the world's best manipulators. Minsky's just someone who got an A in science.

"Okay," I begin. "Four days ago, our office got a preliminary proposal for a state-of-the-art neutrino research facility. It was hand-delivered to the Congressman at his home address." Minsky picks up his paperclip, thinking he's getting the inside poop.

"Who did the proposal? Government or military?" he asks.

"What makes you say that?"

"No one else can afford it. You have any idea how much these things cost? Private companies can't pull that kind of weight."

Viv and I exchange a glance, once again rethinking Wendell, or whoever they really are.

"What can you tell me about the project?" Minsky asks.

"According to them, it's purely for research purposes, but when someone builds a brand-new lab a mile and a half below the earth, it tends to get people's attention. Because of the parties involved, we want to make sure that ten years from now, this won't be coming back to haunt us. That's why we need to know, worst-case scenario, what's the potential damage they can do?"

"So they're going with an old mine, huh?" Minsky asks.

He doesn't sound surprised. "How'd you know?" I reply.

"It's the only way to get it done. The Kamioka lab in Japan is in an old zinc mine . . . Sudbury, Ontario, is in a copper mine . . . Know what it costs to dig a hole that deep? And then testing all the structural support? If you don't use an old mine, you're adding two to ten years to the project, plus billions of dollars."

"But why do you have to be down there in the first place?" Viv asks.

Minsky looks almost annoyed by the question. "It's the only way to shield the experiments from cosmic rays."

"Cosmic rays?" I ask skeptically.

"They're bombarding the earth at all times."

"Cosmic rays are?"

"I realize it must sound a little sci-fi," Minsky says, "but think of it like this: When you fly from coast to coast on an airplane, it's the equivalent of one to two chest X-rays. That's why the airlines regularly screen flight attendants to see if they're pregnant. We're being bathed in all sorts of particles right now. So why put your science underground? No background noise. Up here, the dial in your wristwatch is giving off radium—even with the best lead shielding, there's interference everywhere. It's like trying to do open-heart surgery during an earthquake. Down below the earth's surface, all the radioactive noise is shut out, which is why it's one of the few places where neutrinos are detectable."

"So the fact that the lab's underground . . ."

". . . is pretty much a necessity," Minsky says. "It's the only place to pull it off. Without the mine, there's no project."

"Location, location, location," Viv mutters, glancing my way. For the first time in three days, things are finally starting to make sense. All this time, we thought they wanted the mine to hide the project, but in reality, they need the mine to get the project going. That's why they needed Matthew to slip the mine in the bill. Without the mine, they have nothing.

"Of course, what really matters is what they're doing down there," Minsky points out. "Do you have a schematic?"

"I do . . . it's just . . . it's with the Congressman," I say, smelling the opening. "But I remember most of it—there was this huge metal sphere filled with these things called photomultiplier tubes—"

"A neutrino detector," Minsky says. "You fill the tank with heavy water so you can stop—and therefore detect—the neutrinos. The problem is, as neutrinos fly and interact with other particles, they actually change from one identity to another, making different neutrino 'flavors.' It's like a Jekyll-Hyde type of affair. That's what makes them so hard to detect."

"So the tubes are just for observation purposes?"

"Think of it as a big enclosed microscope. It's an expensive endeavor. Only a few exist in the world."

"What about the magnet?"

"What magnet?"

"There was this narrow hallway with a huge magnet and these long metal pipes that ran the entire length of the room."

"They had an accelerator down there?" Minsky asks, confused.

"No idea—the only other thing was this big crate labeled *Tungsten*."

"A tungsten block. That definitely sounds like an accelerator, but—" He cuts himself off, falling unusually silent.

"What? What's wrong?"

"Nothing—it's just, if you have a detector, you don't usually have an accelerator. The noise from one . . . it'd interfere with the other."

"Are you sure?"

"When it comes to neutrinos . . . it's such a developing field . . . no one's sure of anything. But up until now, you either study the existence of neutrinos or you study their movement."

"So what happens if you put a detector and an accelerator together?"

"I don't know," Minsky says. "I've never heard of anyone doing it."

"But if they did . . . what's the potential application?"

"Intellectually, or—"

"Why would the government or military want it?" Viv asks, getting to the point. Sometimes, it takes a kid to cut through the nonsense. Minsky's not the least bit thrown. He knows what happens when the government digs its nails into science.

"There are certainly some potential defense applications," he begins. "This doesn't require an accelerator, but if you want to know if a particular country has nuclear weapons, you can fly a drone over the country, get an air sample, and then use the 'quiet' of the mine to measure the radioactivity in the air sample."

It's a fine theory, but if it were that simple, Wendell— or whoever they are—would've just requested the mine from the Defense subcommittee. By trying to sneak it through Matthew and the Interior subcommittee, they're playing dirty—which means they've got their hands on something they don't want public.

"What about weaponry . . . or making money?" I ask.

Lost in thought, Minsky twirls the tip of his paperclip through the edge of his beard. "Weaponry's certainly possible . . . but what you said about making money . . . you mean literally or figuratively?"

"Say again?"

"It goes back to the nature of neutrinos. You can't just see a neutrino like you see an electron. It doesn't show up under the microscope—it's like a ghost. The only way to see them is to watch their interactions with other atomic particles. For example, when a neutrino hits the nucleus of an atom, it generates a certain type of radiation like an optical sonic boom. All we can see is the boom, which tells us that the neutrino was just there."

"So you measure the reaction when the two things collide," Viv says.

"Exactly—the difficulty is, when a neutrino hits you, it also changes you. Some say it's because the neutrino is constantly shifting identities. Others hypothesize that it's the atom that gets changed when there's a collision. No one knows the answer—at least, not yet."

"What does this have to do with making money?" I ask.

To our surprise, Minsky grins. His salty beard shifts with the movement. "Ever hear of transmutation?"

Viv and I barely move.

"Like King Midas?" I ask.

"Midas . . . Everyone always says Midas," Minsky laughs. "Don't you love when fiction is science's first step?"

"So you can use neutrinos to do alchemy?" I ask.

"Alchemy?" Minsky replies. "Alchemy is a medieval philosophy. Transmutation is a science—transforming one element into another through a subatomic reaction."

"I don't understand. How do neutrinos . . . ?"

"Think back. Jekyll and Hyde. Neutrinos start as one flavor, then become another. That's why they tell us about the nature of matter. Here . . ." he adds, opening the top left-hand drawer on his desk. He rummages for a moment, then slams it shut and opens the drawer below it. "Okay, here . . ."

Pulling out a laminated sheet of paper, he slaps it against his desk, revealing a grid of familiar square boxes. The periodic table. "I assume you've seen this before," he says, pointing to the numbered elements. "One—hydrogen; two—helium; three—lithium . . ."

"The periodic table. I know how it works," I insist.

"Oh, you do?" He looks down again, hiding his smile. "Find chlorine," he finally adds.

Viv and I lean forward in our seats, searching the chart. Viv's closer to tenth-grade science. She jabs her finger at the letters *Cl*. Chlorine.

| 17 |
| Cl |

"Atomic number seventeen," Minsky says. "Atomic weight 35.453(2) . . . nonmetallic classification . . .

yellowish-green color . . . halogen group. You've heard of it, right?"

"Of course."

"Well, years back, in one of the original neutrino detectors, they filled a hundred-thousand-gallon tank with it. The smell was horrific."

"Like a dry cleaner's," Viv says.

"Exactly," Minsky says, pleasantly surprised. "Now remember, you only see neutrinos when they collide with other atoms—that's the magic moment. So when the neutrinos plowed into a chlorine atom just right, the physicists suddenly started finding . . ." Minsky points down to the periodic table, pressing his paperclip against the box next to chlorine. Atomic number eighteen.

17 Cl	18 Ar

"Argon," Viv says.

"Argon," he repeats. "Atomic symbol *Ar*. Seventeen to eighteen. One additional proton. One box to the right on the periodic table."

"Wait, so you're saying when the neutrino collided with the chlorine atoms, they all changed to argon?" I ask.

"All? We should be so lucky . . . No, no, no—this was one little argon atom. One. Every four days. It's an amazing moment—and completely random, God bless chaos. The neutrino hits, and right there, seventeen becomes eighteen . . . Jekyll becomes Hyde."

"And this is happening right now in the air around

us?" Viv asks. "I mean, didn't you say neutrinos are everywhere?"

"You couldn't possibly see the reactions with all the current interference. But when it's isolated in an accelerator . . . and the accelerator is shielded deep enough below the ground . . . and you aim a beam of neutrinos just right . . . well, no one's come close yet, but think about what would happen if you could control it. You pick the element you want to work with; you bump it one box to the right on the periodic table. If you could do that . . ."

My stomach twists. ". . . you could turn lead to gold."

Minsky shakes his head—and then again starts laughing. "Gold?" he asks. "Why would you ever make gold?"

"I thought Midas . . ."

"Midas is a children's story. Think of reality. Gold costs what? Three hundred . . . four hundred dollars an ounce? Go buy a necklace and a charm bracelet, I'm sure it'll be very nice—nice and shortsighted."

"I'm not sure I—"

"Forget the mythology. If you truly had the power to transmute, you'd be a fool to make gold. In today's world, there are far more valuable elements out there. For instance . . ." Minsky again stabs the periodic table with his paperclip. Atomic symbol *Np*.

$$\boxed{\begin{array}{c} 93 \\ Np \end{array}}$$

"That's not nitrogen, is it?" I ask.

"Neptunium."

"Neptunium?"

"Named after the planet Neptune," Minsky explains, forever the teacher.

"What is it?" I ask, cutting him off.

"Ah, but you're missing the point," Minsky says. "The concern isn't *what is it?* The concern is *what it could be . . .*" With one final jab, Minsky moves his paperclip to the nearest element on the right.

93	94
Np	Pu

"Pu?"

"Plutonium," Minsky says, his laugh long gone. "In today's world, it's arguably the most valuable element on the chart." He looks up at us to make sure we get it. "Say hello to the new Midas touch."

67

SCRUBBING HIS HANDS in the fourth-floor men's room, Lowell stared diagonally down at the front page of the *Washington Post* Style section that lay flat across the tile floor and peeked out from the side of the closest stall. It was nothing new—every morning, a still-unidentified coworker started the day with the Style section, then left it behind for everyone else to share.

For Lowell, who usually never read anything but the newspaper clips his staff prepared, it was a ritual that stumbled headfirst across the fine line that separated convenience from bad hygiene. That's why, even though the paper was right there, he never reached down to pick it up. Not once. He knew what others were doing when they read it. And where their hands had been. *Disgusting,* he'd long ago decided.

Of course, some things took precedence. Like checking the *Post*'s infamous gossip column, *The Reliable Source,* to make sure his name wasn't in it. He'd meant to look this morning, but time got away from him. It had been barely three days since he last saw Harris. He'd counted at least four reporters in the restaurant that night.

So far, everything was quiet, but any one of them could've tattled about the meeting between him and Harris. For that alone, it was worth taking a peek.

Using the tip of his shoe to pin down the top corner of the paper, Lowell slid the section out from under the stall. The back page was wet, making it stick slightly as he tried to pull it toward him. Lowell tried not to think about it, focusing instead on using the side of his foot to wedge open the front page. But just as he nudged his foot inside, the door to the bathroom swung open, smashing into the wall. Lowell spun around, pretending to be busy by the hand dryer. Behind him, his assistant darted inside, barely able to catch his breath.

"William, what's—?"

"You need to read this," he insisted, shoving the red file folder toward Lowell.

Watching his assistant carefully, Lowell wiped his hands against his slacks, reached for the folder, and flipped it open. It took a moment to scan the official cover sheet. Lowell's eyes went wide—and within thirty seconds, the gossip column didn't matter anymore.

68

"HOLD ON," I SAY. "You're telling me people could smash some neutrinos against some . . ."

"Neptunium . . ." Minsky says.

". . . neptunium, and suddenly create a batch of plutonium?"

"I'm not saying they've done it—at least not yet—but I wouldn't be surprised if someone was working along those lines . . . at least on paper."

He's speaking with the calmness of someone who thinks it's still theoretical. Viv and I know better. We saw it with our own eyes. The sphere . . . the accelerator . . . even the tetrachloroethylene . . . That's what Wendell's building down there—that's why they wanted to keep it so quiet. If word got out they were trying to create plutonium . . . there's no way it'd make it through the process.

"But no one can do that yet, right?" Viv asks, trying to convince herself. "It's not possible . . ."

"Don't say that in these halls," Minsky teases. "Theoretically, anything's possible."

"Forget whether it's possible," I say. "Assuming you

could do it, how feasible is it to pull it off? Is neptunium even accessible, or is it just as hard to find?"

"Now that's the vital question," Minsky says, knighting me with his paperclip. "For the most part, it's a rare earth metal, but neptunium-237 is a by-product from nuclear reactors. Here in the U.S., since we don't reprocess our spent nuclear fuel, it's hard to get your hands on. But in Europe and Asia, they reprocess massive amounts."

"And that's bad?" Viv asks.

"No, what's bad is that global monitoring of neptunium only began in 1999. That leaves decades of neptunium unaccounted for. Who knows what happened during those years? Anybody could have it by now."

"So it's out there?"

"Absolutely," Minsky says. "If you know where to look, there's lots of unaccounted-for neptunium that's there for the taking."

As the consequences hit, I squirm in my seat, wiping my sweaty hands against the sides of the seat cushion. Minutes ago, I was pretending to be uncomfortable. I'm no longer faking it. Whatever branch of the government Wendell Mining really is, the news isn't gonna be good.

"Can I just ask one question?" Viv says. "I heard what you said—I know it's possible, and I realize you can get neptunium—but for one second, can we just talk about the likelihood? I mean, studying neutrinos—that's a small field, right? There can only be a handful of people who are even capable of putting something like this together . . . So when you add that all up, and you look around the neutrino community, wouldn't . . . wouldn't you know if something like this were going on?"

Minsky again scratches at his beard. His social skills are too off to read Viv's panic, but he understands the question. "Have you ever heard of Dr. James A. Yorke?" he finally asks. We both shake our heads. I can barely sit still. "He's the father of chaos theory—even coined the term," Minsky continues. "You've heard the metaphor, correct?—that a butterfly flapping its wings in Hong Kong can cause a hurricane in Florida? Well, as Yorke puts it, that means if there's even one butterfly you don't know about, it's impossible to predict the weather on a long-term basis. One tiny butterfly. And, as the man says, there'll *always* be one butterfly."

The words collide like a sack of doorknobs. I talked Matthew into flapping his wings . . . and now Viv and I are swirling through the hurricane.

"It's a big world out there," Minsky adds, staying with Viv. "I can't possibly account for everyone in my field. Does that make sense, Miss— I'm sorry, what was your name again?"

"We should get going," I say, hopping to my feet.

"I thought the Congressman was on his way?" Minsky asks as we head for the door.

"We've already got what we needed."

"But the briefing . . ."

It's amazing, really. We just dropped poorly hid hints about a government project that could create plutonium, and he's still worried about face time. God, what's wrong with this town? "I'll be sure to tell him how helpful you were," I add, whipping the door open and motioning Viv outside.

"Please send him my best," Minsky calls out.

He says something else, but we're already up the hallway, running for the elevators.

"So where're we going?" Viv asks.

The one place Janos thinks we'll never go. "The Capitol."

69

I DON'T UNDERSTAND," William said as he raced down the circular stairwell. "Where're we going?"

"Where do you think?" Lowell asked, leading them past the sign for the first floor and continuing toward the basement.

"No, I mean *beyond* the parking garage. Where we going after that? Shouldn't we tell someone?"

"Tell them what? That we know who really owns Wendell? That they're not who they say they are? Sure, they're linked to Janos, but until we get the rest, it doesn't do us any good. There's nothing to tell."

"So where does that leave us?"

"Not *us*," Lowell said. *"Me."* Leaping down the last few steps and shoving open the door to the basement, Lowell plowed into the parking garage. He didn't have to go far. Deputy Attorney General gets a spot right in front. If he wanted, he could've been in his car within four seconds. But he still paused, searching to make sure Janos wasn't waiting for him.

The silver Audi was empty.

With the push of a button, Lowell unlocked the car and slid inside.

"What're you doing?" William asked as Lowell tried to shut the driver's door.

"I'm going to see a friend," Lowell said, starting the engine.

It wasn't a lie. He'd known Harris for over ten years—since they both worked in Senator Stevens's office. That was why Janos came to him in the first place.

He'd already tried Harris at work, at home, and on both his cell phones. If Harris was in hiding, there was only one place he'd be—the one place he knew best. And right now, finding Harris was the only way to get the rest of the story.

"Why don't you at least bring some backup?" William asked.

"For what? So they can interrogate my friend? Trust me, I know how Harris thinks. We want him to talk, not panic."

"But, sir . . ."

"Good-bye, William." With a hard tug, Lowell slammed the door and punched the gas. The car peeled out of the spot. Refusing to overthink it, Lowell reminded himself who he was dealing with. If he showed up with armed agents at the Capitol—even forgetting the scene it would make—there's no way Harris would ever go for that.

Switching on the radio, Lowell lost himself in the mental massage of talk radio. His grandmother used to love talk radio, and to this day, Lowell still used it to, in his grandmother's words, *catch his calm*. As the car was filled with the top news stories, Lowell finally took a breath. For one full minute, he forgot about Harris, and Wendell, and the rest of the chaos circling through his head. But as a result, he missed the black sedan that was trailing a few hundred feet behind him as he pulled out of the parking garage and into the daylight.

70

TRUST ME, I know how Harris thinks. We want him to talk, not panic."

"But, sir . . ."

"*Good-bye, William.*"

Tucked back among the rows of cars and hidden by nothing more than a nearby parking spot, Janos watched the exchange from the front seat of his black sedan. The crinkle in Lowell's forehead . . . the desperation on his face . . . even the slant on his assistant's shoulders. Lowell asked William to stay quiet, but he was still protesting. Janos narrowed his eyes, focusing intensely on William's slouched shoulders. From this distance it was hard to get a read. The creases in his white, wrinkled button-down said he was still wearing his shirts twice to save cash. But his brand-new belt . . . Gucci . . . Mom and Dad bought that. The kid's from cash—which means he'll follow his boss's directions.

"I told you Lowell wouldn't sit still . . . he won't focus on anyone but himself," Barry said through the cell phone.

"Quiet," Janos warned. He didn't like talking to

Barry—the paranoia was always too much, even if it was a perfect button to push. Still, he had to admit, Barry was right about Lowell.

In the distance, Lowell slammed the car door shut. His tires howled as he pulled out of his parking spot. For a few seconds, William lingered, craning his neck as he watched his boss disappear . . . then finally headed back toward the stairs.

With a twist of his wrist, Janos turned the key in the ignition. The sedan coughed awake, but Janos quickly looked down, putting his open hand on the dashboard. Typical, he thought. Bad idle. The cam needed more lift.

"You should've called me in earlier," Barry said in his ear. "If you came to me before you went to Pasternak—"

"If it weren't for Pasternak, Harris would've never been in the game."

"That's not true. He's more jaded than you think he is. He just wants you to think—"

"Keep believing that," Janos said, giving Lowell just enough of a lead. As the silver Audi turned the corner, Janos hit the gas and slowly pulled out after him.

"Any idea where he's headed?" Barry asked.

"Not yet," Janos said, leaving the parking lot and turning onto the street. Directly in front of him was a classic orange Beetle. Four cars ahead of that, Lowell's Audi wove in and out of traffic. And a mile or so beyond them all, at the end of Pennsylvania Avenue, the dome of the Capitol arched toward the sky.

"I wouldn't worry about it," he said to Barry. "He's not going very far."

71

NEXT GROUP, PLEASE! Next group!" the Capitol police-
man calls out, waving us toward the visitor's entrance on
the west front of the Capitol. Shuffling behind the
twenty-person group of high-schoolers armed with
Future President baseball caps, Viv and I keep our heads
down and our government IDs hidden beneath our shirts.
On average, the west front handles four million visitors a
year, making it a constant crowded mess of map- and
camera-wielding tourists. Most days, staffers avoid it at
all costs. That's exactly why we're here.

As the group shoves its way inside, I'm once again reminded that the Capitol is the only building in the world
with no back—both the west front (overlooking the Mall)
and the east front (overlooking the Supreme Court) claim to
be the true front. Mostly, it's because, with so many self-
important people in one place, they all want to think their
wonderful view is the best. Even the north side and south
side get into the act, calling themselves the *Senate entrance*
and *House entrance.* Four sides of a building, and not one
of them is the back. Only in Congress.

Lost amid the tour groups, we're in the one place

where no one checks our ID or looks at us for more than a second. With this many people moving, all we can do is blend in.

"Put all cameras and phones on the X-ray," one of the guards says to the group. It's a simple request, but the students turn it into the final moments on the *Titanic*. Talking, bitching, moving—everything a fuss. As the kids make their usual scene, Viv and I slip through the metal detector without a second glance.

We stay with the group as they make their way under the grand domed ceiling of the rotunda and directly below to the Crypt, the circular room that now serves as an exhibition area for blueprints, drawings, and other historical Capitol documents. The guide explains that the rounded shape of the Crypt structurally supports not only the rotunda but also the Capitol dome directly above it. On cue, the entire group crane their necks up to the ceiling—and Viv and I slip out to the right, through the doorway next to the Samuel Adams statue. Racing down a wide set of sandstone stairs, I reach into my shirt and pull out the chain with my ID. Behind me, I can hear Viv's jingling around her neck. From tourists to staffers in one minute or less.

"Narcs . . ." Viv whispers as we hit the bottom step. She motions to our far right. Up the hallway, two Capitol police are headed our way. They still don't see us, but I'm not about to take a chance. Grabbing Viv's wrist, I twist around the marble banister and tug her to the right, off the main hallway. A freestanding sign reads, *No Tours Beyond This Point.* I blow past it so fast, I almost knock it over. I've been back here before—it's still open to staff. The hallway dead-ends at a black wrought-iron gate with a slight arch on top.

"Isn't it amazing?" I ask Viv, shoving some pep in my voice.

"Incredible," she says, following my lead. Behind the gate, under a rectangular glass case, a long black cloth is draped over what looks like a coffin. The plaque on our right, however, tells us it's the wooden catafalque that supported the bodies of Lincoln, Kennedy, LBJ, and everyone else who has ever lain in state in the Capitol.

Over my shoulder, the click-clack of boots on the floor lets me know the Capitol cops are just about to pass. Trying to look like staffers but feeling like prisoners, Viv and I hold tight to the bars, staring into the tiny concrete cell. Located at the direct center of the Capitol, the small, dank room was originally designed to be a tomb for George and Martha Washington. Today, their bodies are at Mount Vernon, and this room is just for storing the catafalque. I shut my eyes. The Capitol police are getting closer. I try to stay focused, but even without Washington's remains, this crouched little space still smells like death.

"Harris, they're coming . . ." Viv whispers.

Back in the hallway, the footsteps are right behind us. One of them stops. There's a crackle through his radio. Next to me, I can hear Viv praying.

"Yeah, we'll be right there," one of the cops says.

The footsteps pick up—there's no doubt they're getting closer—and then, just like that, they're gone.

As usual, Viv's first to react. Spinning around, she slowly checks back toward the hallway. "I think we're okay," she says. "Yeah . . . they left."

Refusing to turn around, I still cling to the bars.

"Harris, we should hurry . . ."

I know she's right—we're almost there—but as I

stare at the dark black shroud . . . watching it drape lifelessly over the almost hundred-and-fifty-year-old coffin
stand . . . I can't help but feel that, if we're not careful,
the next bodies around here are going to be our own.

"You sure this is the way?" Viv asks, running in front of
me even though I'm supposed to be leading.

"Keep going," I tell her as she follows the hallway to
the right, weaving us even deeper through the sand-
colored corridors of the concrete basement. Unlike the
rest of the Capitol, the halls down here are narrow and
cramped, a labyrinth of random turns that's taken us past
garbage rooms, paint storage, HVAC equipment, and
every type of repair shop from electrical to plumbing to
elevator care. Worst of all, the further we go, the more the
ceiling seems to shrink, the headroom eaten up by air
ducts, water pipes, and random wiring. When I used to
bring Matthew down here, he would bitch because he'd
have to duck to get around. Viv and I don't have that
problem.

"You swear this looks familiar?" Viv asks as the ceiling gets lower.

"Absolutely," I tell her. I don't blame her for being
nervous. In the more heavily trafficked areas, there're
signs on the walls to make sure Members and staff don't
get lost. I glance up at the spider web of cracks along the
walls. We haven't seen a sign for at least three minutes.
On top of that, as we go deeper, the hallway seems to fill
up with stacks of discarded equipment: broken file cabinets, antique upholstered chairs, industrial-sized spools
of cable wire, rolling garbage bins, even a stack of old
rusted pipes.

We haven't seen another human being since we passed the last sign for the elevator. Indeed, the only hint of life is the hum of machinery from the surrounding mechanical rooms. Viv's still ahead of me, but with a final sharp right, she stops. I hear her shoes skid across the dusty floor. As I turn the corner behind her, the furniture and wiring and pipes are stacked higher than ever. It's not hard to read her thoughts. Like any other bad neighborhood, the further we go, the less we should be walking alone.

"I really don't think this is right," she insists.

"You're not supposed to."

She thinks I'm being glib. I'm not.

Rushing forward, I pass half a dozen closed doors on my right and left. Most of them, like ninety percent of the doors throughout the Capitol, have a sign out front that tells you exactly what's inside. *Electrical Substation. Senate Daily Digest.* Even one that says *Designated Smoking Area.* One is unmarked. That's the one I go for—room ST-56, the nondescript, unlabeled door that's halfway down the hall on my left.

"This is it?" Viv asks. "It looks like a broom closet."

"Really?" I ask, reaching into my pocket and pulling out a set of keys. "How many broom closets do you know that have a double set of deadbolts?"

Stabbing the keys into their respective locks, I give the doorknob a sharp twist. The door is heavier than it looks—I have to put my entire shoulder against it to get it open. As it gives way, I jab the light switch with my fist and finally give Viv a good look at what's inside.

The first thing she notices is the ceiling. Unlike the air-duct limbo stick they force you under in the hall, the ceiling inside rises up at least twenty feet over the long, spacious room. Against the warm burgundy walls, there's a chocolate brown leather couch, flanked by matching Empire mahogany dressers. Above the couch, a collection of antique toy sailboats is mounted to the wall. Adding to the men's-club feel, there's also a twelve-foot fish—I'm guessing a marlin—up on the left-hand wall, a bag of golf clubs just inside the door, and on the right side of the room, an enormous 1898 nautical map of the Atlantic Coast from the Chesapeake Bay to the Jupiter Inlet.

Viv looks at the room for a total of thirty seconds. "Hideaway?" she asks.

I nod and grin.

Some people say there are no more secrets in Washington. It's a nice, quotable statement. But it clearly comes from someone who doesn't have a hideaway.

On the stepladders of power, some Members of Congress have great committee assignments. Others have great office space for their staff. A few get preferential parking right outside the Capitol. And a very few get personal drivers to make them look extra important. Then, there are those who have hideaways.

They're the best-kept secret in the Capitol—private sanctuaries for a Senator to get away from staff, lobbyists, and the dreaded tour groups who want just-one-quick-photo-please-we-came-all-this-way. How private are they? Even the architect of the Capitol, who manages the entire building, doesn't have a full list of who's in each one. Most aren't even on the floor plan, which is just how the Senators like it.

"So what does Stevens use this for?" Viv asks.

"Let me put it to you like this . . ." Over her shoulder, I point to the round light switch on the wall.

"A dimmer switch?" Viv asks, already disgusted.

"Had it installed his first week in here. Apparently, it's a popular option—right after power windows and power brakes."

She can tell I'm trying to keep things calm. It only makes her more nervous.

"So how do you know the Senator won't come down here any minute?"

"He doesn't use this one anymore—not since he got the one with the fireplace."

"Wait . . . he has more than one hideaway?"

"C'mon, you really think they keep this stuff fair? When LBJ was majority leader, he had seven. This is just a spare these days. There's no way he'd—"

My eyes stop on the hand-carved coffee table. A set of keys with a familiar key ring sits on top.

There's a loud flush of a toilet. Viv and I spin left, back by the bathroom. The light's on under the door. Then it goes black. Before either of us can run, the bathroom door swings open.

"Don't look so surprised," Lowell says, stepping out into the room. "Now do you want to know what you've gotten yourself into or not?"

72

"WHAT'RE YOU DOING?" I ask, my voice already booming through the small room.

"Take it easy," Viv says.

"Listen to her," Lowell says, trying to sound concerned. "I'm not here to hurt you."

He nods at Viv, trying to make it look like she's taking his side. He's been Deputy Attorney General too long. All he's got now are old tricks. He taught me that one the first year I worked for him in the Senator's office.

"How'd you get in here?" I ask.

"Same as you. When I was chief of staff, they gave me a key."

"You're supposed to give it back when you leave."

"Only if they ask for it," Lowell says, pretending to be playful. Strike two. He may've been a great friend, but that disappeared the moment he sent me running out of that restaurant.

"I know what you're thinking, Harris—but you don't understand the position I was in. He threatened my family . . . came to my daughter's playground . . . even smashed my head when I tipped you off that night," he says, showing me the Band-Aid on the back of his head.

Now he's going for sympathy. Strike three and he's out. "Fuck you, Lowell! You understand me? *Fuck you!* The only reason Janos was there that night was because you *told him! You set it up!*"

"Harris, please . . ."

"So what's the next dart you'll jab in my neck? Did you tell him I'd be hiding here, too, or is that what you're saving for dessert?"

"I swear to you, Harris—I'm not working with him."

"Oh, and I'm supposed to believe you now?"

"Harris, let's just go," Viv says, grabbing my arm.

"Do you even realize how stupid it was to come here?" I ask. "You think Janos didn't follow your every step?"

"If he did, he'd be standing here right now," Lowell points out. It's a fair point. "Now can't you just listen for a second?" he begs.

"Whattya mean, like trust you? Sorry, Lowell, we're all sold out of that this week!"

Realizing he's getting nowhere, he studies Viv and sees his new target. "Young lady, can you . . . ?"

"Don't talk to her, Lowell!"

"Harris, I'm fine," Viv says.

"Stay away from her, Lowell! She's not part of—" I cut myself off, fighting to stay in control. *Don't lose it,* I tell myself. I bite the inside of my cheek just to kill the rage. We're running out of time. I open the door and point Lowell toward it. "Good-bye, Lowell."

"Can't you just—?"

"*Good-bye.*"

"But I—"

"Get out, Lowell. *Now!*"

"Harris, I know who they are," he finally blurts.

Watching him carefully, I check the pitch of his eyebrows and the anxious tilt of his neck. I've known Lowell Nash most of my professional life. No one's that good a liar. "What're you talking about?" I ask.

"I know about the Wendell Group . . . or whatever they call themselves. I had them put through the system. At first glance, they're as solid as Sears—registered in Delaware, doing a furniture-importing business—but when you dig a little deeper, you see they're a subsidiary of a corporation in Idaho, which has a partnership in Montana, which is part of a holding company that's registered back in Antigua . . . The list kept going, layer upon layer, but the whole thing's a front."

"For the government, right?"

"How'd you know?"

"You could see it in the lab. Only a government would have that kind of cash."

"What lab?" Lowell asks.

"In the mine." From the look on his face, this is all brand-new. "In South Dakota . . . they've got an entire lab hidden in an old gold mine," I explain. "You could tell from the machinery that the experiments—"

"They were building something?"

"That's why we—"

"Tell me what they were building."

"This is gonna sound nuts . . ."

"Just say it, Harris. What were they making?"

I look at Viv. She knows we don't have a choice. If Lowell were in on it, he wouldn't be asking the question.

"Plutonium," I say. "We think they're creating plutonium . . . from the atomic level up."

Lowell stands there, frozen. His face goes pale. I've seen him nervous before, but never like this.

"We have to call someone . . ." he stutters. His arm flies into his jacket pocket, reaching for his cell phone.

"You can't get a signal down here."

Seeing I'm right, he scans the office. "Is there a . . . ?"

"On the dresser," I say, pointing to the phone.

Lowell's fingers pound across the digits, dialing his assistant. "William, it's me . . . Yeah," he says, pausing a moment. "Just listen. I need you to call the AG. Tell him I'll be there in ten minutes." He again stops. "I don't care. Pull him out of it."

Lowell slams down the phone and races for the door.

"It still doesn't make sense," Viv calls out. "Why would the U.S. government build plutonium when we already have plenty? All it can do is get in the wrong hands . . ."

Lowell stops and turns. "What'd you say?"

"I-It doesn't make—"

"After that."

"Why would the U.S. government—?"

"What makes you think it's *our* government?" Lowell asks.

"Pardon?" I ask.

Viv's just as confused. "I thought you said . . ."

"You have no idea who owns Wendell, do you?" Lowell asks.

The room's so silent, I hear the blood flowing through my ears. "Lowell, what the hell is going on?" I ask.

"We traced it back, Harris. It was well hidden: Idaho, Montana—all the states that make it harder to do a good corporate records search. Whoever set it up knew all the magic tricks. After Antigua, it bounced to a fake board of directors in Turks and Caicos—which was no help, of course—but they also listed a registered agent with a local address in Belize. Naturally, the address was fake, but the name . . . it went to the owner of a government-owned concrete company in, of all places, Sana'a."

"Sana'a?"

"Capital city of Yemen."

"Yemen? You're telling me Wendell Mining is a front for Yemen?" I ask, my voice cracking.

"That's where the records run—and do you have any idea what happens if they start making plutonium and selling it to whoever's got the fattest money clip? Know how many lunatics would line up for that?"

"All of them."

"All of them," Lowell repeats. "And if even one of them gets close . . . we've gone to war for far less than that."

"I-It's impossible . . . they gave money . . . they were on the wish list . . . all the names . . ."

"Believe me, I've been looking for a single Arabic name on the list. These guys usually only hire their own, but the way they're hidden . . . I'm guessing they brought in someone over here to put on a public face and grease the right pockets—some CEO-type so it all looks clean. We're looking at this guy Andre Saulson, whose name is on one of Wendell's bank accounts. The name's probably fake, but one of our boys noticed the address matches an old listing we had for someone named Sauls. It'll take some time to confirm, but he fits the mold. London School of Economics . . . Sophia University in Tokyo. We looked at him a few years back for art fraud—he was supposedly trying to move the

Vase of Warka when it was snatched from Iraq's National Museum, which is probably how the Yemenis found him. Very high-end scams. Yemen brings him in for credibility, then Sauls hires Janos to flatten out the speed bumps, and maybe even another guy to help them maneuver through the system . . ."

"Pasternak . . . That's how they got into the game."

"Exactly. They bring in Pasternak—he may not even know who they really are—and now they've got one of the best players in town. All they have to do is get their gold mine. You have to give them credit. Why risk the wrath of inspectors in the Middle East when you can build your bomb right in our own backyard without anyone thinking twice? Set it up right, and Congress will even give you the land for free."

My stomach plummets. I can barely stand up.

"W-What do we do now?" Viv asks, her whole face already shiny with sweat.

We're not just out of our league—we don't even know what sport they're playing.

Running back toward the hallway, Lowell's already in rescue mode. "Lock the doors behind me—both bolts. Time to ring the king."

I've heard the term before. Once he gets to the Attorney General, they're calling in the White House.

As Lowell disappears from the room, Viv notices his keys on the coffee table. "Lowell, wait . . . !" she calls out, grabbing the key ring and following him outside.

"Viv, don't!" I shout. Too late. She dashes into the hallway.

As I run for the door, I hear Viv scream. I step out into the hall just as she backs into me. Up the hallway, barely around the corner, Janos presses his forearm against Lowell's neck, pinning him to the wall. Before I can even react, Janos pulls his black box from Lowell's chest. Lowell's body convulses slightly, then drops lifelessly to the floor. His body hits with two dull thuds—first his knees, then his forehead—echoing through the empty hallway. It's a sound that'll never leave me. I look down at my friend. His eyes are still open, staring blankly at us.

Janos doesn't say a word. He just lunges forward.

73

*R*UN!*"* I shout to Viv, yanking her by the shoulder and pushing her further up the hallway, away from Janos.

As Janos barrels toward me, he lets out a smirk, trying to intimidate. He expects me to run. That's why I stay put. This lunatic's killed three of my friends. He's not getting a fourth.

"Keep going!" I call to Viv, making sure she has enough of a lead.

From the angle Janos is coming from, he can't see what I'm looking at: Just inside the door of the hideaway, the Senator's leather golf bag leans against the wall. I reach for the clubs, but Janos is moving too fast.

Just as my hand grabs a shiny nine iron, he plows into me, slamming me backwards into the threshold of the doorway. My back lets out a loud crack, but I still don't let go of the club. Pinning me like Lowell, he stabs the black box at my chest; I knock his arm aside with the tip of the club. Before he realizes what's happening, I ram my head forward, head-butting him as hard as I can in the nose. Same place I hit the scientist in the mine. *The sweet spot,* my uncle called it. Sure enough, a trickle of blood runs down from Janos's left nostril, across the top of his lip. His hound-dog eyes widen the slightest bit. He's actually surprised. Time to take advantage.

"Get . . . off!" I shout, seizing the moment and shoving him backwards. Before he can get his balance, I hold up the golf club like a baseball bat and rush straight at him. Sometimes the best chess is played fast. As I swing the club, he protects the black box, cradling it close to his chest. He thinks I'm going high. That's why I go low, arcing the club downward and smashing him as hard as I can in the side of his knee.

It's like hitting a boulder. There's a loud crack, and the club vibrates in my hands. I still don't let go. At the last second, he rolls with the impact, but it's enough to send his leg buckling beneath him. Like before, he barely lets out a grunt. I'm not impressed. Feeling good, I move in closer for another swing. That's my mistake. As he falls to the ground, he never takes his eyes off my club. Before I can even wind up again, he yanks the nine iron from my hands. He's so fast, I barely see it happen. It's a quick reminder I can't beat him head-on. Still, I got what I wanted. Behind me, Viv's turned the corner. Now we've got a head start.

Janos slams against the concrete floor. I turn and sprint as hard as I can up the hallway. As I turn the corner, I practically plow into Viv.

"What're you doing?" I ask, sidestepping around her. She falls in step right behind me. "I said to run."

"I wanted to make sure you were okay." She's trying to sound strong. It's not working.

Behind us, the golf club scrapes against the concrete floor. Janos is getting up. As he starts running, the echoes of his footsteps are off beat. He's definitely limping—but the beat's getting quicker. He's shaking it off.

Frantically scrambling past the stacks of old furniture scattered on each side of us, I search the hallway for help. Down here, most of the doors are locked and unmarked.

"What about that one?" Viv asks, pointing to a door that's marked *Sergeant At Arms*. I lunge for the doorknob. It doesn't twist. Damn. Locked.

"This one, too," Viv says, trying a closed door on our right. I hear her panting over my shoulder. We're running out of hallway, and unlike last time, the Capitol police are too far away. We have a short lead, but it's not enough— not unless we do something quick.

Up ahead, on our left, there's a loud mechanical hum. It's the only door that's open. The sign on it reads:

Danger
Mechanical Equipment Space
Authorized Personnel Only

I look over my shoulder to see how we're doing. Down the hallway, Janos tears around the corner like a wounded tiger. He's got the golf club in one hand and the black box in the other. Even with the limp, he's already charging fast.

"Move . . ." I say, tugging Viv toward the open door. Anything to get us out of his line of vision.

Inside, the concrete room is narrow but deep—I can't even see the end of it—filled with row after row of buzzing ten-foot-tall industrial air-handlers, exhaust fans, and air compressors, all of them interconnected by a crisscrossing jungle of spiral ductwork that snakes out in every direction like the tendrils of a 1950s robot. Overhead, gas lines, copper tubing, and electrical work combine with the various pipes and ducts as they weave their way across the ceiling and block what little fluorescent lighting the room already has.

By the door, there's a wall full of circular glass pressure gauges that haven't been used in years, as well as two rolling garbage cans, an empty box of air filters, and an empty, filthy mop bucket with a few random tools stored inside. Behind the garbage cans, a dark green army blanket sits crumpled on the floor, barely covering a row of six metal propane tanks.

"Hurry . . . C'mere . . ." I whisper to Viv, clutching her shoulder and tugging her toward the tanks.

"What're you—?"

"Shhhh. Just duck." Shoving her downward, I grab the blanket and drape it over her head.

"Harris, this isn't—"

"Listen to me."

"But I—"

"Dammit, Viv—for once, listen," I scold. She doesn't like the tone. But right now, she needs it. "Wait till he runs past," I tell her. "When he's gone, go get help."

"But then you're—" She cuts herself off. "You can't beat him, Harris."

"Go get help. I'll be fine."

"He'll kill you."

"Please, Viv—just get help." Our eyes lock, and she stares straight through me. When Viv first saw me speaking to her page class, and then heard about the Lorax story, she thought I was invincible. So did I. Now I know better. And so does she. Realizing what I'm asking, she starts tearing up. After everything we've been through, she doesn't want to leave.

Kneeling down, I give her a tiny kiss on her forehead. "Viv . . ."

"Shh," she says, refusing to listen. "Say a prayer with me."

"What? Now? You know I don't believe in—"

"Just once," she pleads. "One little prayer. My last favor."

With no choice, I lower my head. Viv's is already down. She grabs my hands as I close my eyes. It doesn't do any good. My mind's racing too fast, and then . . . as the silence seeps in . . . *God, please take care of Viv Parker. That's all I ask. I'm sorry for everything else . . .* My brain empties, and my eyes stay shut.

"Now was that so bad?" Viv asks, breaking the quiet.

I shake my head. "You're an amazing person, Vivian. And you're gonna make a great Senator one day."

"Yeah, well . . . I'm still gonna need a great chief of staff."

It's a sweet joke, but it doesn't make it any easier. I haven't felt this bad since my dad died. I feel the pregnant lump at the center of my throat. "I'll be fine," I promise, forcing a smile.

Before Viv can argue, I pull the blanket over her head, and she disappears from sight. Just another hidden propane tank. Convincing myself she's safe, I go for the tools, searching for a weapon. Needle-nose pliers . . . electrical tape . . . a tape measure . . . and a box of industrial razor blades. I grab the razor blades, but as I flick open the box, the blades are gone. Needle-nose pliers it is.

Darting deeper into the room, I clang the pliers against the side of every metal machine I pass and make as much noise as possible. Anything to keep Janos moving past Viv. I keep telling myself this is the best way to protect her. Stop the ride and let her off. As I turn the corner behind an enormous air-conditioning unit, there's a scraping sound back by the door. Italian shoes skid to a stop.

Janos is here. Viv is hidden. And I'm ducked behind a metal grille that comes up to my chin. I pound the grille, pretending to hit it by accident. Janos starts running. *C'mon, Viv,* I say to myself, mouthing a final silent prayer. *Now's your chance . . .*

74

THE SCRATCHY, STAINED army blanket reeked from a mixture of sawdust and kerosene, but as Viv ducked her head between her knees and shut her eyes, the smell was the last of her worries. Tucked underneath the olive green cloak, she could hear the scratching of Janos's shoes as he entered the room. From the noise Harris was making—banging on what sounded like sheet metal in the distance—she figured Janos would run. And for a few steps, he did. Then he stopped. Right in front of her.

Holding her breath, Viv did her best to remain motionless. Instinctively she opened her eyes, but the only thing she could see was the tip of her right foot sticking out from underneath the blanket. *Was it covered up, or was that what Janos was looking at?* As a slow grumble rippled through the air, Janos pivoted slightly, bits of concrete grinding beneath the tips of his shoes. Knowing better than to move, Viv gripped her knees, digging her nails into her own shins.

"Hurry . . . !" Harris whispered in the distance, his voice echoing down the concrete hall.

Janos stopped, twisting back toward the sound.

Viv knew it was Harris's lame way to distract, but as Janos started running, it was clearly working.

Counting to herself, Viv was careful not to rush it. *Don't move an eyebrow until he's long gone.* Once again, she held her breath—not just to hide, but to take in every sound. The rumble of the air-conditioning units . . . the buzz of the overhead lights . . . and most important of all, the light rasp of Harris's footsteps fading in the distance . . . and the gnawing, quick shuffle of Janos's shoes as he gave chase right behind him.

Even when they were out of earshot, Viv still took another few seconds, just to be safe. Finally peeking out from below the blanket, she scanned the entryway. Nothing anywhere. Just some garbage cans and her fellow propane tanks. With a sharp snap, she whipped the blanket off her shoulders and sent it flying toward the trash.

Scurrying for the door, Viv burst out into the hallway and followed it back around to the left. "Help!" she cried. "Someone . . . we need help!" As before, the piles of discarded office furniture were the only things to hear her call. Mapping her way back to the Capitol police, she raced for the short staircase up on her left—but just as she turned the corner, she smacked flat into the chest of a tall man in a crisp pinstriped suit. The impact was hard—her nose collided with his magenta Zegna tie, pressing it against his chest. To Viv's surprise, the man managed to backstep and roll with it. Almost as if he heard her coming.

"Help . . . I need help," Viv said, her voice racing.

"Take it easy," Barry replied, his glass eye staring just off to the left as he put a hand on her arm. "Now tell me what's going on . . ."

75

RUSHING THROUGH THE twisting aisle between two adjacent air compressors, I listen carefully for Janos, but the churning of the equipment drowns out every other noise. At the entrance it was noisy; back here it's deafening. It's like running through rows of revving eighteen-wheelers. The machines back here are all oversized dinosaurs. The only good part is, if I can't hear him, he can't hear me.

At the end of the aisle, I follow the path around to my right. To my surprise, the room keeps going, a labyrinth of ductwork and ventilation machinery that never seems to end, each room bleeding into the next. On my left, there's a section of oval tanks that look like industrial water heaters. On my right, there's an even bigger rectangular compressor with a giant motor on top. There are three different paths, which can take me in any direction: right, left, straight. To the untrained eye, with machine next to machine and all the ductwork blocking a clear line of sight, it's easy to get lost and turned around. That's why there's a faded yellow line painted across parts of the floor. I'm guessing that's what the maintenance people use to get in and out. I use it to the same effect, but instead of sticking to the line and giving Janos an easy trail to follow, I purposely avoid it, always picking a random path.

Halfway up the aisle, I crouch under a section of duct-work and follow the adjacent aisle even deeper into the dark room, which is looking more and more like a true cellar. Mildewed brick walls . . . damp, mud-caked floors . . . and not a window in sight. The cracked plaster ceiling runs low like a cave, then arches twenty feet upward to black, unlit peaks.

The further I go, the more the machinery thins out, and the quieter it gets. A cool draft blows against my face, giving me flashbacks to the wind tunnels in the gold mine. There must be an open door somewhere in the distance. On both sides of me, stacks of intertwining duct-work still block my view, but I can hear the pounding of heavy footsteps. Janos is getting closer. The sound echoes on my right, then my left. It doesn't make sense. He can't be in two places at once.

I spin around to follow the noise. My elbow crashes into one of the ducts, sending a metallic gurgle reverberating through the room. I shut my eyes and duck low so fast, my knuckles hit the concrete. Then I hear the metallic rumble echo behind me. Way behind me. Raising an eyebrow, I glance up at the dark arches of the ceiling. A high-pitched whistle rushes overhead. Huh. Down on my knees, I flick a finger against the duct. There's a light ping on impact, followed by an echo of the ping about thirty feet over my shoulder. It's like the sound equivalent of a hall of mirrors.

When the Capitol was first built, air-conditioning didn't exist, so when the Congressmen complained about the stifling temperatures in the Senate and House

Chambers, an elaborate system of natural air tunnels was built underground. From outside, air would flow though subterranean tunnels, weave its way up into the building, and from there, snake through internal tunnels that resemble stone-lined air-conditioning ducts, eventually bringing cool air into the building's cavernous rooms that didn't have the benefit of exterior windows. To this day, while it's obviously been updated, the system is still in place, collecting fresh air that's fed directly into the air-conditioning units, then pumped through the still-existing ducts and a few remaining passages.

I quickly realize I'm not just in the cellar. The way the wind whips around me . . . the echoing sound . . . I thought the air tunnels were running above and below me. But as I look around at the rounded curves of the walls . . . This entire room is one giant tunnel. I've been standing in it the entire time. That's the breeze I feel on my face. And that's why all the air-conditioning units are here. The subterranean tunnels burrow up from below us, empty into this room, and feed all the machines fresh air. Glancing up at the dark arches in the ceiling, I see they're not dead ends at all. Beyond the darkness are the passageways that run up through the Capitol. This is the hub that feeds the spokes of the building. Like air-conditioning ducts, the tunnels are all interconnected. That's why Janos's footsteps echoed on my left and right. Tap the metal grille on your right and you'll also hear it from behind. It's a good thing to know—especially right now.

Crouched down, I run between two parallel sets of air ducts and hear Janos's footsteps in three different directions. All three of them are getting louder, but because of the whistling of the air tunnel and the faint churning of the machines, it's still impossible to tell which set of footsteps is coming first. The only good thing is, Janos is having the same problem.

"We've already got help coming!" I shout, hearing it echo behind me. "Capitol police are on their way!" I'm headed toward the left side of the room. With the help of the echo, Janos should hear it from the right. It's not the greatest trick in the world, but right now all I need is to stall. Buy some time and let Viv ride in for the rescue.

"Did you hear what I said, Janos?! They're on their way!" I add, hoping to confuse him as my voice bounces back and forth through the room.

Once again, he stays silent. He's too smart to answer. That's why I decide to get personal.

"You don't strike me as a fanatic, Janos—so how'd they get you to sign up? Something against the United States, or was it purely a financial decision?"

There's a sharp skritch as he pivots and backtracks. The sound's coming from behind him. He's definitely lost.

"C'mon, Janos—I mean, even for a guy like you, there's gotta be some limits. Just because a man has to eat, doesn't mean you lick every piece of gum off the sidewalk."

The footsteps get louder, then softer as he second-guesses. Now he's annoyed.

"Don't get me wrong," I continue, stooping underneath a section of air vents and hiding behind one of the oval water heaters. "I understand life is about picking sides, but these guys . . . Not to stereotype, but I've seen you, Janos. You're not exactly from their nest. They may want *us* dead now, but you're not too far down the list."

The footsteps get slower.

"You think I'm wrong? They'll not only put a knife in

your spine, they'll know exactly which two vertebrae to stick it between to make sure you feel every single inch of the blade. C'mon, Janos, think of who we're talking about . . . This is Yemen—"

The footsteps stop.

I lift my head, staring back across the room. Unreal. "They didn't tell you, did they?" I ask. "You had no idea."

Again, silence.

"What, you think I'm making it up? It's Yemen, Janos. You're working for Yemen!" I sneak out from behind the water heater and curve back in Janos's direction, still crouching low. With a light tap, I hit another machine with the pliers. The more I keep moving, the harder it is to trace me. "How'd they hide it from you, anyway? Let me guess: they hired some CEO-type to make it look like an American company; then that guy goes out and hires you. How'm I doing? Hot? Cold? Feet on fire?"

He still won't answer. For once, he's actually off balance:

"Didn't you ever see *The Godfather*? The hired guns don't ever get to meet the real boss."

The last part's just to get him raging. I don't hear a footstep anywhere. He's either taking it in or trying to follow the sound of my voice. Either way, there's not a chance he's thinking straight.

Hunched over and staying completely silent, I weave behind a ten-foot-tall blower fan that's encased in the dustiest metal grille I've ever seen. Connected to the grille is a long aluminum duct that runs a good twenty feet across the room, back toward the door. In front of me, the blades of the fan spin slowly, so when I time it just right, I can see through the length of the duct, out the other side. I take a peek, and almost swallow my tongue when I see the back of a familiar salt-and-pepper crewcut.

Dropping down low, I squat beneath the grille of the fan. From where I'm crouched, I have a clear view that runs along the underside of the long duct. There's no mistaking the Ferragamo shoes on the other end. Janos is dead ahead, and from the way he's standing there, frozen in frustration, he has no idea I'm behind him.

Gripping the needle-nose pliers in my sweaty fist, I keep to my squat and get ready to move forward. Within three seconds, I talk myself out of it. I've seen enough *Friday the 13th* sequels to know how this one ends. The man's a killer. All I have to do is stay hidden—anything else is a bad-horror-flick risk. The thing is, the longer I sit here, the better the odds of him turning around and staring straight at me. At least this way, I've got surprise on my side. And after what he did to Matthew, and Pasternak, and Lowell . . . some things are worth the risk.

Crouched down and steeling myself with one last deep breath, I slowly chicken-walk forward. One hand skates lightly against the side of the metal vent; the other holds tight to the needle-nose pliers. I duck down even lower to check underneath the length of the vent. Janos is still at the far end, struggling to pinpoint my location. From this section of the room, the rumble of the machines makes it harder than ever. Still, I take it as slow as possible, being cautious with every step.

I'm about ten feet away. From my current angle, Janos's upper body is blocked by the length of the vent. I can see the tip of his right shoulder. Moving in a bit closer, I get the back of his head and the rest of his arm. Less than five feet to go. He's looking around—definitely lost. In his right hand is the black box, which looks like an old Walkman. In his left is the Senator's nine iron. If I'm right, those are the only weapons he's got. Anything else—a knife or a gun—he'd never get through the metal detector.

He's just a few feet away. I grit my teeth and raise the pliers. The wind whips through the tunnel, almost like it's picking up speed. Below my feet, there's a slight crackle. A stray piece of plaster snaps in half. I freeze. Janos doesn't move.

He didn't hear it. Everything's okay. Counting to myself, I shift my weight, ready to pounce.

I'm so close, I can see the stitching on the back belt loop of his slacks, and the overgrown stubble on the back of his neck. I almost forgot how big he is. From down here, he's a giant. I tighten my jaw and raise the pliers even higher. On three: one . . . two . . .

Springing upward, I jack-in-the-box straight at him and aim the pliers at the back of his neck. In a blur, Janos spins around, holding the neck of the golf club and swatting the pliers from my hand. They go flying across the room. Before I can even react, he's got his other arm up in the air. In one quick movement, it arcs downward. And the black box stabs directly at my chest.

76

"HURRY . . . WE HAVE to get help!" Viv insisted, tugging on the sleeve of Barry's jacket.

"Relax, I already did," Barry said, scanning the hall-way. "They should be here any second. Now where's Harris?"

"There . . ." she said, pointing back to the machinery room.

"What're you pointing at? The door?"

"You can see?" Viv asked.

"Just outlines and shadows. Take me there . . ." Grabbing Viv's elbow, he rushed forward, forcing her toward the door.

"Are you nuts?" Viv asked.

"I thought you said he was in there with Janos."

"I did, but—"

"So what would you rather do—stay out here and wait for the Capitol cops, or get in there and maybe save his life? He's alone against Janos. If Harris doesn't get help now, it's not going to matter."

"B-But you're blind . . ."

"So? All we need right now are bodies. Janos is

smart—if two people walk in, he's not risking a confrontation. He'll run. Now you coming or not?"

Lost in the rush, Viv trailed Barry slightly as he tapped his cane through the hallway. Looking over her shoulder, she once again checked for the Capitol police. Barry was right. They were running out of time. Picking up speed, she quickly led him forward. She wasn't leaving Harris alone.

Halfway up the hall, they passed Lowell's lifeless body, still sprawled against the ground.

Viv glanced up at Barry. His eyes stared vacantly ahead. He couldn't see it.

"Lowell's dead," she said.

"Are you sure?"

She looked back at the frozen body. Lowell's mouth was wide open, lost in a final, soundless scream. "I'm sure." Turning back to Lowell, she added, "Was he the one who called you?"

"What?"

"Lowell. Was he the one who called you? Is that how you knew to come?"

"Yeah," Barry said. "Lowell called."

Barry's cane collided with the base of the door. Viv reached out for the doorknob. As she pushed the door open, a cool burst of air brushed against her face.

"How's it look?" Barry whispered.

Peeking inside, she made sure it was clear. Nothing had changed. The mop bucket. The propane tanks. Even the army blanket was right where she'd left it. Further back in the room, though, she heard a deep, guttural grunt. Like someone in pain.

"Harris . . . !" she cried, tugging Barry into the room. As fast as she moved, he held tight to her elbow. She thought about leaving him behind, but Barry was right about one thing: There was still strength in numbers. "You sure you can keep up?" she asked as they rushed forward. To her surprise, even with Barry's weight, it was easier to run than she thought.

"Absolutely," Barry said. "I'm right behind you."

Viv nodded to herself. He'd obviously done this before. But just as she turned away from Barry and focused back on the room, she felt his grip tighten around her elbow. At first, it was just an annoyance, but then . . .

"Barry, that hurts."

His grip got tighter. She tried to pull her arm free, but he didn't let go.

"Barry, did you hear what I—?"

She turned to face him, but he was already in midswing. Just as Viv spun toward him, Barry backhanded her across the face. The punch was wild, catching her just above the mouth. Her top lip split open, and as she fell off balance to the floor, she could taste the thick sourness of her own blood.

She put her palms out to stop her fall, but it didn't help. Crash-landing on her knees, Viv scurried on all fours to get away.

"What, now you're suddenly quiet?" Barry asked. He was right behind her.

"Harris . . . *Harris* . . . " she tried to scream. But before she could get the words out, Barry wrapped his arm around her neck and pulled as tight as he could. Viv coughed uncontrollably, unable to breathe.

"I'm sorry—did you say something?" Barry asked. "Sometimes I don't hear so good."

77

JANOS'S BLACK BOX comes lunging at my chest. My eyes are focused on the two fangs on the end of it. They're going straight for my heart—the same place I saw him stab Lowell. Twisting, I try my best to slide out of the way. Janos is ruthlessly fast. I like to think I'm faster. I'm wrong. The needles miss my chest, but they still punch through my sleeve, sinking deep into my biceps.

Pins and needles come first, shooting down my arm and rippling across my fingertips. Within seconds, the jolt begins to burn. A rancid stench that reminds me of burnt plastic fills the air. My own flesh and muscle burning.

"Rrruhh!" I shout, thrashing violently and shoving Janos in the shoulder with my free arm. He's so focused on protecting the black box, he almost doesn't notice as I snatch the golf club from his other hand. Enraged, he raises the box for another pass. I swing wildly, hoping to keep him back. To my surprise, the tip of the club catches the edge of the box. It's not a direct hit, but it's enough for Janos to lose his grip. The box whips through the air, eventually crashing on the ground and cracking open.

Wires, needles, and double-A batteries scatter across

the floor as they roll under a nearby air-handler. I glance back at Janos. His unforgiving eyes tear me apart and are darker than I've ever seen them before. Moving toward me, he doesn't say a word. He's had enough.

I once again raise the golf club like a bat. Last time, I surprised him. The problem is, Janos doesn't get surprised twice. I swing the club at his head—he sidesteps it and hammers the knuckle of his middle finger into the bone on the inside of my wrist. A jolt of pain seizes my hand, and my fist involuntarily springs open, dropping the club. I try to make a fist, but I can barely move my fingers. Janos is having no such problem.

Jabbing at me like a precision boxer, he drills the tip of his knuckle straight into the dimple on my upper lip. The hot burst of pain is unlike anything I've ever felt, and my eyes flood with water. I can barely see. Still, I'm not here to be his piñata.

Barely able to close my hand, I lash out with a sharp punch. Janos leans left and grabs my wrist as it passes his chin. Taking full advantage of my momentum, he pulls me toward him, and in one quick movement, lifts my arm up and digs two fingers deep into my armpit. There's a bee sting of pain, but before it even registers, my whole arm goes limp. Still not letting up, Janos holds tight to my wrist. He shoves it even farther to his left, then uses his free hand to ram my elbow to the right. There's an audible snap. My elbow hyperextends. As my muscles continue to tear, it's clear that whenever the feeling comes back, my arm isn't gonna work the same way again. He's picking me apart piece by piece—systematically short-circuiting every part of my body.

Kneeling slightly, he lets out a throaty grunt and spears me with another jab that hits me right between my groin

and belly button. The entire bottom half of my body convulses backward, sending me stumbling toward his corner of the room. As the back of my calves collide with a
two-foot-tall section of vents, momentum again gets the
best of me. Tumbling backwards, I trip over the vents and
crash flat on my ass behind an enormous air-conditioning
unit that's easily the size of a garbage truck. On the side
of the machine, a spinning black rubber conveyor belt
chugs to life—churning fast, then suddenly slowing
down, its short cycle complete. But as Janos thunders toward me, leaping over the vents and landing with a
booming thump, his eyes aren't on the conveyer belt . . .
or even on me. Whatever he's looking at is directly over
my shoulder. Still on the floor, I spin around and follow
his gaze.

Less than twenty feet away, a curving, corroded brick
wall marks the edge of the air tunnel—but the focus of
Janos's attention is what's right below it: a dark open hole
that's wider than an elevator shaft, and from the looks of
it, just as deep. I've heard about these but never seen one
for myself. One of the subterranean tunnels that runs up
from under the building. Here's where the fresh air comes
in from—underground, below the entire Capitol . . . and
feeding from one of the few fresh air-intake areas. Some
people say the holes run down hundreds of feet. From the
yawning echo that whistles past me with a burst of fresh
air, that doesn't sound too far off.

Next to the hole, a rectangular metal grate is propped
upright, leaning against the wall. Usually, the grate serves
as a protective cover, but right now, the only thing on top
of the hole is a thin strip of yellow and black police tape
with the word *Caution* on it. Whatever they're doing
down there, it's clearly under construction. Of course, the

Capitol takes its usual safety precautions: two yellow plastic *Caution—Wet Floor* signs are balanced right on the edge. The signs couldn't keep out a sneeze—which is what Janos is counting on as he leans down and grips me by the collar of my shirt.

Lifting me to my feet, he shoves me backwards toward the hole. My legs feel like they're filled with oatmeal. I can barely stand. "D-Don't do this . . ." I beg, fighting for my footing.

As always, he's stone silent. I try my best to stay on my feet. He again slams me in the chest. The impact feels like a sonic boom. I fight to hold on to his shirt, but I can't get a grip . . . Stumbling backwards, I fly directly toward the hole.

78

WITH HIS ARM LOCKED tight around Viv's neck, Barry clenched his teeth and leaned back, squeezing as hard as he could. As Viv fought for air, Barry could barely contain her. From the span of her shoulders, she was bigger than he'd remembered. Stronger, too. That was the problem with judging by shadows—you never really knew until you got your hands on someone and felt for yourself.

Viv's body squirmed and thrashed in every direction. Her nails dug into Barry's forearm. Still gasping for a breath, she coughed a spray of saliva across his exposed wrist. *Filthy,* he thought. It only made him pull tighter, tugging her close. But just as he did, Viv reached over her shoulder and clawed at his eyes.

Protecting his face, Barry turned his head to the side. That's all Viv needed. Reaching back, she grabbed a clump of his hair and pulled with everything she had.

"Aaahh . . . !" Barry roared. "Son of a—!" Leaning forward to stop the pain, he was up on his tiptoes. Viv bent down even further, making him feel every inch of her height. Barry was finally off balance. Throwing her weight backward, she launched herself toward the brick wall behind her. Barry's back smashed hard into the bricks, but he still didn't let go. Stumbling out of control, they plowed into the collection of propane tanks, which tumbled like bowling pins. Barry tried to tug Viv back, but as they continued to spin, Viv pushed off even harder. Flying backwards toward a nearby boiler, she felt her full weight crash into Barry as the tip of an exposed pipe drilled into his back, grinding into his spine.

Howling in pain, Barry crashed to his knees, unable to hold on any longer. He could hear Viv's shoes scuff against the concrete. She scrambled deeper into the room. Not far. Just enough to hide.

Rubbing his back, Barry swallowed the pain and looked around the room. There wasn't much light, making most of the shadows muddy blobs that seemed to float in front of him. In the distance, he heard a series of raspy grunts and nasally groans. Harris and Janos. It wouldn't take Janos long to finish that, which meant Barry just had to focus on Viv.

"C'mon—you really think I can't see you?" he called out, following the scratch of her shoes and hoping the bluff would draw her out. Up high, he could make out the edges of the air-handlers, but down toward the floor, the details faded fast.

To his left, there was a scraping of rock against concrete. Viv was moving. Barry turned his head, but nothing flashed by. It was the same muddy blob as before. Had it moved? *No . . . stay focused. Especially now,* Barry told himself. Once he got Viv . . . when they pulled this off . . . He'd been at the bottom—this was his turn at the top.

A second later, he heard a high-pitched clink behind

him. One of the propane tanks. He turned to chase the
sound, but the pitch was too high. Like a pebble against
metal. She'd thrown a rock.

"Now you're testing me?" he shouted, spinning back to
the machines. He was trying to sound strong, but as he
scanned the room—left to right . . . up and down—the shadows . . . no . . . nothing moved. Nothing moved, he insisted.

All around him, machines hummed their flat, droning
symphony. On his right, the furnace flame flicked on,
belching up a loud whoosh. On his left, a chugging compressor finished its cycle, clicking into oblivion. The
wind whistled straight at him. But still no sign of Viv.

Searching for the panting rise and fall of her breathing, Barry isolated each sound—every clink, hiss, sput-
ter, creak, and wheeze. As he stepped further into the
room, it definitely got harder to see, but he knew Viv
was scared. Off balance. This was when she'd make a
mistake.

The problem was, the deeper Barry went, the more the
sounds seemed to dance around him. There was a clang
on his left . . . or was that his right? He paused midstep,
freezing in place.

A brush of fabric wisped behind him. He spun back toward the door, but the sound stopped just as quick.

"Viv, don't be stupid . . ." he warned as his voice
cracked.

The room was dead silent.

There was a tiny snap, like a stick when it's thrown in
a campfire.

"Viv . . . ?"

Still no response.

Barry again turned toward the back of the room, scan-

ning the outline of every machine. The blob was un-
changed. Nothing moved . . . nothing moved . . .

"Viv, are you there . . . ?"

For a moment, Barry felt a familiar tightening at the
center of his chest, but he quickly reminded himself there
was no reason to panic. Viv wasn't going anywhere. As
long as she had that fear, she wouldn't take the chance by
trying something—

A loud screech tore across the floor. Shoes clunked at
full gallop. Behind him . . . Viv was running for the door.

Barry spun around just in time to hear the mop bucket
slam into the wall. There was a sharp grinding of metal
against concrete as she picked up one of the empty
propane tanks. Barry assumed she was moving it to get to
the door, but by the time he caught sight of her, he was
surprised that the mass of her shadow wasn't getting
smaller. It was getting larger. She wasn't running away.
She was coming right at him.

"Take a good look at this one, asshole . . ." Viv
shouted, swinging the propane tank with all her strength.
She held tight as it collided with the side of Barry's head.
The sound alone was worth the impact—an unnatural
pop, like an aluminum bat smacking a cantaloupe.
Barry's head jerked violently to the side, and his body
quickly followed.

"Did you see that? That bright enough for you?" Viv
shouted as Barry fell to the floor. She'd been picked on
since the first day they moved into their house on the
edge of the suburb. Finally, there was a benefit to all the
fistfights.

He reached for her leg, but his world was already spinning. Viv dropped the propane tank on his chest. With the
wind knocked out of him, he could barely move. "You

really thought you had a chance?" she screamed as streams of spit flew from her mouth. "You can't see! What'd you think—you could beat me because I'm a girl?!"

Looking up, Barry saw Viv's long shadow standing over him. She lifted her foot over his head, ready to stomp down. It was the last thing Barry saw as the world went dark.

79

STUMBLING BACKWARD TOWARD the open hole at the end of the air tunnel, I don't waste time trying to slow myself down. Using everything that's left, I spin to the side and try to turn myself around.

By the time I can see the depth of the pit, I'm only a few steps from the rim. But at least I'm moving fast. My foot touches down on the edge of the hole, and I use the speed to take a huge diagonal leap to my right. Inertia carries me most of the way. I just barely clear the corner of the hole—which is good—but now I'm headed straight for a brick wall—which is bad.

Putting my palms out, I slam into the wall at full speed. My arms take most of the impact, but as my full weight hits, my elbow gives way. The pain's too much. Janos tore it up pretty bad. Collapsing to the floor, I roll over onto my back, prop myself up on my good elbow, and glance over at the open pit. Stray pebbles and flecks of dirt tumble into the mouth of the hole. I listen to see how long it takes till they hit bottom, but before I realize what's happening, there's a tight tug on the front of my shirt. I look up just as Janos tries to yank me up.

In full panic and unable to fight, I scootch on my rear end, trying to crab-walk away. His grip's too tight. Holding me with his left hand, he uses his right to backhand me across the forehead. Again, he knows exactly what he's aiming for. His knuckle slices open my eyebrow. The blood comes fast, rushing down the side of my face and blinding me even worse than before. He's trying to take the fight out of me, but as the impact knocks me back on my ass, I lash out with the only thing I've got left. Kicking upward and aiming between his legs, I plant the toe of my shoe deep into his testicles.

Janos grits his teeth to hide the grunt, but there's no mistaking the damage. Bent over, he grabs tight at his crotch. More important, he finally lets go of my shirt. Scrambling backwards, all I need are a few seconds. But it's still not enough. Before I can even get to my feet, Janos picks himself up and plows straight at me. From the look on his face, all I did was make him mad.

Behind me, I bump into the side of the air conditioner, which dead-ends perpendicular to the wall. I'm all out of running space.

"You don't have to do this," I tell him.

As always, he's silent. His eyes tighten, and a thin sneer takes his lips. From here on in, he's doing this for himself.

Gripping my ear, Janos squeezes hard and twists it back. I can't help but lift my chin. He tightens his grip, and I'm staring at the ceiling. My neck's completely exposed. Winding up for the final blow, he . . .

. . . snaps his head to the left and staggers off balance. A loud hollow thud echoes through the air. Something clipped him in the back of the head. The amazing part is, at the last second, he managed to roll with it—almost as if he sensed it was coming. Still, he was skunked pretty hard—and as he holds his head and lurches sideways toward the brick wall, I finally see what's behind him. Gripping the nine iron I dropped earlier, Viv readies the club in perfect batting stance.

"Get the hell away from my friend," she warns.

Janos looks over in disbelief. It doesn't last long. As he locks on Viv, his forehead furrows and his fists constrict. If he's in pain, he's not showing it. Instead, it's all rage. His eyes are black—two tiny pieces of charcoal in sunken sockets.

Lunging forward like a rabid dog, he flies at Viv. She swings the club with clenched teeth, hoping to put another dent in his head. I tried the same thing earlier. She doesn't have a chance.

Catching the club in midswing, Janos twists it sharply, then jabs it forward like a pool cue toward her face. The blunt end of the club stabs her right in the throat. Teetering backwards, Viv clutches her neck, unable to breathe. From sheer momentum, she manages to rip the golf club from his hands, but she can't hold on to it, and it drops to the floor. Janos doesn't need it. As Viv violently coughs, he blocks the path out and moves in for the kill.

"S-Stay back," she gasps.

Janos grips the front of her shirt, pulls her toward him, and in one blurred movement, swipes his elbow into her face. It catches her in the eyebrow, just like mine—but this time, even as the blood comes, Janos doesn't let up. He jabs his elbow forward and tags her again. And again. All in the same spot. He's not just trying to knock her out . . .

"Don't touch her . . . !" I shout, hurtling forward. My arm's so swollen, I can't even feel it. My legs are shaking,

barely able to hold me up. I don't care. He's not taking her, too.

Ignoring the pain, I rush in, slamming him from behind and wrapping my arm around his neck. He swipes his hand back over his own shoulder, trying to take my head off. The only chance we have is two against one. It's still not enough.

Viv tries to scratch at his cheek, but Janos is ready. Lifting up both feet, he kicks her directly in the face. Viv flies backwards, slamming into the metal side of the air conditioner. Her head hits first. She sinks, unconscious. Refusing to let up, Janos whips his head back, smashing me in the nose. The loud pop tells me it's broken.

Letting go of Janos, I stumble backwards, my face a bloody mess.

Janos doesn't slow down. He marches right at me . . . a walking tank. I take a swing with my left hand, and he blocks the punch. I try to raise my right, but it sags like a tube sock full of sand. "P-Please . . ." I beg.

Janos pummels me again in the nose, unleashing a sickening crunch. As I continue to stumble, he glances over my shoulder. Like before, he's got his eyes on the open hole.

"Don't . . . please don't . . . !"

He shoves me backwards, and I crash to the ground, hoping it'll at least stop me from moving. Just as I look up, he clutches my shirt and tugs me to my feet. The hole's right behind me. Unlike before, he's not giving me any extra running space.

Janos pulls me in for one last shove. My right arm's dead. My head's on fire. The only thing my brain processes is the smell of black licorice on his breath.

"You can't win," I stutter. "No matter what you do . . . it's over."

Janos stops. His eyes narrow with his smirk. "I agree," he says.

His hands burst forward, plowing me in the chest. I go reeling toward the hole. Last time, I made the mistake of trying to grab his shirt. This time, I go for the man himself. Stealing his own trick, I reach out, grip Janos's ear, and hold tight.

"What're you—?!" Before he can even get out the question, we're both heading for the hole.

My foot slides down the edge. I still don't let go. Janos's head jerks forward. As I slip down, sliding off the edge, Janos grabs my arm, trying to ease his own pain. I continue to hold tight. He crashes down on his chest. It slows our descent, but I'm already moving too fast. The lower half of my body's already in the hole . . . and slipping quick. As I slide, bits of gravel bite at my stomach. The concrete does the same to Janos's chest. He's following me, headfirst. As we continue to skid, he lets go of my arm with one hand and struggles to backpedal, clawing at the concrete; I kick at the inside walls of the hole, searching for a foothold to stop our fall. Janos shuts his eyes, digging in with everything he has. There's a huge vein running down the front of his forehead. His face is tomato soup. He's not letting me take his ear with me. And then, out of nowhere . . . we stop.

A final cloud of dirt and dust rolls off the edge of the floor, landing on my face. I'm dangling by my left arm, which is the only part of me not in the hole. My armpit's on the edge, which holds most of my weight, but my hand grips on to Janos's ear with whatever strength I have left. It's the only reason he's holding my wrist. Flat on his

chest, and realizing we've stopped, he continues to hold
tight. If he lets go, I'll definitely plunge down the hole,
but I'll be taking part—if not all—of him with me.

Thanks to the pressure on his ear, Janos can barely
pick his head up. His cheek is pressed against the concrete. But not for long. Twisting slightly, he glances my
way—making sure I can't get out. From inside the hole,
my chin and arm sit just above the edge. He's ready to
send me the rest of the way down.

"Janos, don't . . . !"

Trying to break my grip, he squeezes my wrist and
shifts his position. He's too off balance. We slide down
again, deeper into the hole, then come to another sudden
stop. Instead of my armpit, I'm down to my elbow, which
now holds part of my weight. Janos is still on his stomach. His cheek's in the dirt, and the way his body's
turned, one of his shoulders is already over the edge. My
eyes barely peek above the rim. I still refuse to let go. I'm
gripping his ear so tight, it's turning purple. If I go down
holding on to him, he'll follow fast.

Below my feet, the tiny plink of fallen rocks echoes from
below. No question, it's a long way to the bottom. Ignoring
the risk, Janos digs his fingers into the underside of my
wrist. The pain is indescribable. I can't hold on any longer.
My pinkie slides off his earlobe. He pulls his head back, trying to tug himself free. My ring finger slips off next. He's
almost there. The way he's gripping my wrist, it feels like
he's about to puncture my skin. I rake at the concrete with
my free hand, but I'm down too far. There's no way to get
a handhold. The pain's too much. I have to let . . .

"Janos, you drop him and you'll race him to the bottom," a familiar female voice warns. She puts a foot on
his hip, threatening to shove him down.

Janos freezes . . . and grabs my arm. My weight's no longer on his ear, but I still hold tight to it. He doesn't even try to turn his head toward the voice. I don't blame him. As close as he is to the edge, one wrong move, and we're both going down.

I look over Janos's shoulder. Viv's on her feet, the golf club cocked in the air.

"I'm serious," Viv says. "You let him go, and I'll tee your head up and knock you to Nashville."

80

THAT'S IT . . . HOLD him tight," Viv says to Janos as he grips my wrist. She thinks he's listening, but as he lies there flat on his chest, he's still just trying to protect his ear and buy some time.

"Viv, watch him carefully!" I call out. My feet continue to dangle over the pitch-black hole, but I can see it in the dark crinkle between his eyebrows. Even with the pain, he's plotting his final move.

"Exactly . . . just like that," Viv says, nine iron arched above her shoulder. "Now pull him up."

Janos doesn't move. He's clutching my wrist and keeping me afloat, but only because I've got his ear.

"Did you hear what I said?" Viv asks.

He still doesn't budge. Even though he's supporting most of my weight, he can't support all of it. I keep up the pressure on his ear. His cheek is close to the concrete, and his head is cocked awkwardly toward the hole. His face is an even deeper shade of red than before. Janos is holding me, but the pain's starting to burn. Closing his eyes, he presses his lips together, then breathes through his nose. The crinkle between his eyebrows fades, but not by much.

"Janos . . ."

"Drop the club," Janos barks.

"Pardon?" Viv asks. In her mind, he's in no position to make demands.

"Drop the golf club," he repeats. "No fucking around, Vivian. Put it down, or I let Harris go."

"Don't listen to him!" I shout.

Viv stares downward, trying to get a better read.

"You'll hear him scream the whole way down," Janos says. "Think you can handle that?"

Her mouth opens slightly. For anyone, this is tough. For a seventeen-year-old . . .

"You think I'm joking?" Janos asks. He digs his fingers back into my wrist.

I scream out in pain.

"Harris . . . !" Viv shouts.

Janos lets up, once again just holding my wrist.

"Harris, you okay?" Viv asks.

"T-Take his head off," I tell her. "Swing away."

"Do it and I drop him!" Janos warns.

"He's gonna drop me anyway," I add.

"That's not true," she says, refusing to believe it. "Just bring him up!" she yells at Janos. "I want Harris up here *now!*"

In spite of the pain that comes along with it, Janos slowly shakes his head side to side. He's done negotiating. I don't blame him. The instant I'm back on level ground, he risks getting kicked into the hole himself. Not only that, but it's back to two against one.

Dangling by my arm, I feel reality settling in. There's no way he's bringing me up—which makes my decision that much easier.

"Viv, listen to me!" I shout. "Hit him now while you have the chance!"

"Not so smart, Vivian," Janos warns, his voice unflinchingly calm. "You do that and Harris plummets with me."

"Viv, don't let him get into your head!"

Too late. She's studying him, not me.

"I need you to focus! Are you focusing?" I shout. She turns my way, but her stare is vacant. She's frozen by the choice. *"Viv, are you focusing?!"*

She finally nods.

"Good . . . then I need you to comprehend one thing. No matter what you do, I go down in the end. Either Janos drops me on his own, or you smash him, and Janos and I go down together. Do you understand? I go down either way."

My voice cracks as I say the words. She knows it's true—and she's smart enough to catch the consequences: She's seen how fast Janos moves. If she doesn't take him out now, he'll be all over her in an instant.

I feel Janos's grip tightening around my wrist. He's ready to dump me and make a jump for Viv.

"Do it now!" I shout.

"C'mon, Vivian—you really ready to kill your friend?" Janos asks.

With the nine iron poised in the air, Viv stares down—her eyes dancing from Janos to me, then back to Janos. She's only got a few seconds to decide. She pulls the club back. Her hands begin to shake, and the tears roll down her cheeks. She doesn't want to do it, but the longer she stands there, the more she realizes there's no other choice.

81

HIT HIM, VIV! Hit him now!" I shout.

Viv's got the club up in the air. She still doesn't swing.

"Be smart, Vivian," Janos adds. "Regret is the worst burden to bear."

"Harris, you sure?" she asks one last time.

Before I can answer, Janos squeezes my wrist, trying to break my grip. I can't hold on to his ear any longer.

"D-Do it!" I demand.

With his back to Viv, Janos stays focused on my wrist, digging his fingers in deep. He doesn't even bother looking back at her. Like all gamblers, he's playing the odds. If Viv didn't swing by now, she's not swinging at all.

"Viv, please . . . !" I beg.

Her whole body's shaking as the tears come even faster . . . She starts to sob, completely overwhelmed—but the golf club's still up over her head.

"Harris . . ." she calls out. "I don't want to—"

"You can do it," I tell her. "It's okay."

"A-Are you . . . ?"

"I swear, Viv—it's okay . . . I promise . . ."

With one last stab, Janos jams his finger into my wrist.

My grip pops open—but just as I slip, sliding down into the hole, he doesn't let me fall. Instead, he grabs my fingers, crushing them together. A wide smile takes his face. He likes being in control . . . especially when he can use it to his advantage.

I dangle by my arm, watching Viv carefully. "Please . . . please do it!" I beg.

Viv swallows hard, barely able to speak. "J-Just . . . God forgive me," she adds.

Janos stops. He hears something in her voice. Twisting slightly, he turns toward her.

Their eyes lock, and Janos checks again for himself. The rise and fall of her chest . . . the way she keeps readjusting her grip . . . even the way she keeps licking her bottom lip. In the end, Janos lets out a small, almost inaudible laugh. He doesn't think she has it in her.

He's wrong.

I nod at Viv. She sniffles up a final noseful of tears and mouths the word *Bye*. Turning back to Janos, she plants her feet.

C'mon, Viv—it's him or you . . .

Viv pulls the club back. Janos again laughs to himself. And all around us, the air-handlers continue to chug. It's a frozen moment. And then . . . as a drop of sweat leaves her nose . . . Viv puts all her weight behind the club and swings away. Janos immediately lets go of my hand and turns to pounce on her.

Janos expects me to fall back and drop to my death. But he doesn't see the tiny foothold I've been balancing on for the past few minutes—a manmade divot that's dug into the interior wall of the hole. The tip of my shoe grips the two-inch ledge. I flex my leg. And before either of them realizes what's happening, I leap upward just

enough to grab Janos by the back of his shirt. Lunging at
Viv, he's totally off balance. That's his mistake—and the
last one he'll make in our little chess match. In any sport,
especially politics, nothing works better than a good dis-
traction. Barely able to hold the edge of the hole with my
right hand, I yank him backwards with my left. He has no
idea what's happening. I give him a sharp tug toward the
hole, duck down, and let gravity do the rest.

"What're you—?!" He never gets the words out.
Tumbling out of control, Janos plummets backwards into
the mouth of the hole. As he passes, he clutches at my
shoulders . . . my waist . . . my legs . . . even the sides of
my shoes. He's moving too fast to get a handhold.

"*Nooo . . . !*" he screams, his final word echoing upward as he plunges and disappears in the darkness. I hear
him bounce off one of the interior walls . . . then another.
There's a raw, scraping sound as he ping-pongs back and
forth the whole way down. The screaming never stops.
Not until the muted thud at the bottom.

A second later, a shrill siren wails from the depth of
the hole. I'm not surprised. It's the air intake system for
the entire Capitol. Of course it's alarmed. Capitol police
won't be far behind.

As the siren continues to howl, I clutch the concrete
ledge and struggle to catch my breath. I peer downward,
studying the depth of the darkness. Nothing moves.
Except for the alarm, it's a perfectly still black pond. The
more I look at it, the more mesmerizing it gets.

"Harris, you okay?" Viv asks, kneeling down toward
the edge.

"Get away from the hole!" a deep voice screams.
Behind her, three Capitol policemen storm into the room,
their guns aimed at both of us.

"Stewie, I need a lockdown on all vents!" the tallest officer barks into his radio.

"It's not what you—!"

In an eye blink, the other two officers grip my armpits and haul me out of the hole. Tossing me facefirst on the ground, they try to cuff my hands behind my back. "My arm . . . !" I scream as they bend it back.

"You're hurting him!" Viv shouts as the tall officer pins her down and puts her own set of cuffs on. "His arm's broken!"

Both our faces are dripping with blood. They're not listening to a word.

"Vents are going down," a man's voice squawks through the radio. "Anything else?"

"We got a body in the hallway and an unconscious guy up here!" the officer with the radio adds.

"Barry tried to kill me!" Viv yells.

Barry?

"We were attacked!" she says. "Check our IDs—we work here!"

"She's telling the truth," I stutter, barely able to pick my head up. My arm feels like it's snapped in half.

"So where's the attacker?" the shortest officer asks.

"Down there!" Viv shouts, flat on her chest and pointing with her chin. "Check the hole!"

"H-His body . . ." I add. "You'll . . . You'll find his body . . ."

The short officer motions to the tall one, who lifts the walkie-talkie to his lips.

"Reggie, you there yet?"

"Almost . . ." says a deeper voice that comes simultaneously from the radio and the opening of the hole. He's down at the bottom. "Oh, man . . ." he finally adds.

"What you got?" the officer with the radio asks.

"There's some bloodstains down here . . ."

"I told you!" Viv shouts.

". . . all the explosive sniffers are crushed . . . the trail keeps going . . . and from the looks of it, he ripped the grating clear off the safety gate . . ."

Oh, no.

"That's a forty-foot drop," the officer with the radio says.

"Oh, he definitely did himself some damage," Reggie says through the radio. "But I'll tell you right now . . . I don't see a body."

I lift my chin off the ground. My arm's the least of my worries.

"Jeff, make sure maintenance locks down those vents, and get Reggie some backup," the shorter officer says to the one with the radio. "And Reggie . . . !" he adds, leaning over the edge of the hole and shouting as loud as he can, ". . . get outta there right now and start following that blood! He's hurt, with at least a few broken paws. He couldn't have gotten far."

82

THEY STILL HAVEN'T FOUND him. They never will.

I'm not surprised. Janos was hired for a reason. Like any great magician, he not only knew how to keep a secret—he also knew the value of a good disappearing act.

It's been seven hours since we left the depths of the Capitol basement and air tunnels. To double-check that the air system wasn't compromised, they evacuated the entire building, which hadn't been done since the anthrax scares a few years back. They moved us, too.

Most people know that if the Capitol is under a full-on terrorist assault, the bigwigs and hotshots get relocated to a top-secret off-site location. If the attack's on a smaller scale, they go to Fort McNair, in Southwest D.C. But if the attack is minor and containable—like a gas canister thrown in the hallways—they come here, right across the street, to the Library of Congress.

Standing outside the closed doors of the European Reading Room on the second floor, I sink down to sit on the marble floor. My shoulder eventually rests on the leg of one of the enormous glass display cases that line the hallway and are filled with historical artifacts.

"Sir—please don't sit there," a nearby FBI agent with silver hair and a pointed nose says.

"What's it make a difference, huh?" my lawyer, Dan Cohen, threatens as he rubs a hand over his own shaved head. "Don't be an ass—let the poor guy take a seat." An old friend from my Georgetown Law days, Dan's a half-Jewish, half-Italian matzoh-ball-meatball of a guy stuffed into a cheap, poorly tailored suit. After graduation, while most of us went to firms or to the Hill, Dan went back to his old neighborhood in Baltimore, hung out an honest-to-God shingle, and took the cases most lawyers laugh at. Proudly tracing his family tree back to his great, great-uncle, gangster Meyer Lansky, Dan always liked a good fight. But by his own admission, he no longer has any connections in Washington. That's exactly why I called him. I've had enough of this town.

"Harris, we should go," Dan says. "You're falling apart, bro."

"I'm fine," I tell him.

"You're lying."

"I'm fine," I insist.

"C'mon . . . don't be a jackass. You've been through five and a half hours of interrogation—even the agents said you should take a break. Look at you—you can't even stand."

"You know what they're doing in there," I say, pointing to the closed doors.

"It doesn't matter . . ."

"It *does* matter! To me it does. Now just give me a few more minutes."

"Harris, we've been waiting here two hours already—it's almost midnight; you need to get your nose set, and a cast for your arm."

"My arm's fine," I say, readjusting the sling the paramedics gave me.

"But if you—"

"Dan, I know you mean well—and I love you for it—but just be humble for once and acknowledge that this is one part of the problem you can't fix."

"Humble?" he asks, making a face. "I hate humble. And I hate humble even more on you."

Glancing down between my knees, I see my reflection in the marble floor. "Yeah, well . . . sometimes it's not as bad as you think."

He says something else, but I'm not listening. Sunk down, I take another look at the closed doors. After everything I've been through, this is the one thing I care about right now.

Forty minutes later, I can feel the thump of my heartbeat pumping down the length of my arm. But when the doors to the reading room open, every ounce of pain is gone . . . and an entirely new one takes its place.

Viv walks out of the room with two bandages over her eyebrow. Her bottom lip is cut and swollen, and she's holding a baby blue ice pack to her other eye.

I climb to my feet and try to make contact, but a double-breasted suit quickly steps between us.

"Why don't you leave her alone for a bit," her lawyer says, putting his palm against my chest. He's a tall African-American man with a bushy caterpillar mustache. When we were first taken in, I told Viv she could use Dan, but her parents quickly brought in their own attorney. I don't blame them. Since then, the FBI and the lawyer have made sure Viv and I haven't seen, heard, or spoken to each other. I don't blame them for that either. It's a smart move. Distance your client. I've never met this lawyer before, but from the suit alone, I can tell he'll get the job done. And while I'm not sure how Viv's family can afford him, considering all the press this'll get, I don't think he's worried. "Did you hear what I said, son? She's had a long night."

"I want to talk to her," I say.

"Why? So you can mess her life up even more than you have already?"

"She's my friend," I insist.

"Mr. Thornell, it's okay," Viv says, nudging him aside. "I can . . . I'll be fine."

Checking to be sure, Thornell decides to take her cue. He steps about two feet away. Viv gives him another look, and he heads back to the display cases, where Dan and the other FBI agent are. For now, we've got the corner of the gilded hallway all to ourselves.

I look over at Viv, but she avoids my gaze, dropping her eyes to the floor. It's been eight hours since we've last spoken. I've spent the past three trying to figure out exactly what I wanted to say. I don't remember a single word.

"How's your eye?" "How's your arm?" we both ask simultaneously.

"I'll live," we both reply.

It's enough to get a small smile out of Viv, but she quickly pulls it down. I'm still the one who got her in this mess. Whatever she's feeling, it's clearly taking a toll.

"Y'know, you didn't have to do what you did in there," she finally says.

"I don't know what you're talking about."

"I'm not a moron, Harris—they told me what you said . . ."

"Viv, I never—"

"You want me to quote 'em? That you forced me into this . . . that when Matthew died, you threatened me into helping you . . . that you said you'd 'break my face' if I didn't get on the private jet and tell everyone I was your intern. How could you say that?"

"You're taking it out of context—"

"Harris, they showed me the statement you wrote!"

I turn to the classical murals on the wall, unable to face her. There are four murals, each one with a woman soldier in ancient armor, representing a different stage in a nation's development: *Adventure, Discovery, Conquest,* and *Civilization.* They should have another one labeled *Regret.* My answer's a whisper. "I didn't want you to follow the ship down."

"What?"

"You know how these things go—who cares if we saved the day? I made bets on legislation . . . misappropriated a corporate jet . . . and arguably contributed to the death of my best friend . . . Even if you were there for the very best reasons—and believe me, you were the only innocent in the whole crowd—they'll take your head off just because you were standing next to me. Assassination by association."

"So you just twist the truth and take the fall for everything?"

"Believe me, Viv—after what I sucked you into, I deserve far worse than that."

"Don't be such a martyr."

"Then don't be so naive," I shoot back. "The moment they think you were acting on your own is the exact same moment they put you on the catapult and fire you."

"So?"

"Whatta you mean, *So?*"

"I mean, *So?* So what if I lose my job? Big whoop. It's not like they gave me the scarlet letter. I'm a seventeen-year-old page who lost her internship. I wouldn't quite consider it the end of my professional career. Besides, there are more important things than a stupid job—like family. And friends."

Staring me down with one eye, she holds the ice pack to the other.

"I agree," I tell her. "I just . . . I just didn't want them to fire you."

"I appreciate that."

"So what happened in there?" I ask.

"They fired me," she says nonchalantly.

"What? How could they—?"

"Don't look at me like that. At the end of the day, I still broke the cardinal rule of being a page: I went off campus without authorization and stayed overnight without permission. Worst of all, I lied to my parents and the principal, then flew off to South Dakota."

"But I told them—"

"It's the FBI, Harris. They may be hard-asses, but they're not complete idiots. Sure, maybe you can force me on a plane, or to run an errand or two, but what about getting me to the motel, and to the mine, then down the shaft, and into the lab? Then we gotta catch the return flight back. You're a lot of things, Harris, but *kidnapper*'s not on the list. You really thought they'd believe all that crap?"

"When I told it, it was flawless."

"Flawless, huh? *Break my face?*"

I can't help but laugh.

"Exactly," she says. Viv pauses, finally taking the ice pack off her face. "I still appreciate you trying, though, Harris. You didn't have to do that."

"No. I did."

She stands there, refusing to argue. "Can I ask you one last thing?" she says, motioning to the ground. "When we were down there with Janos . . . and you were stuck in the hole . . . were you standing on that little ledge the entire time?"

"Just toward the end . . . my foot stumbled on it."

She's silent for a moment. I know what she's after.

"So when you asked me to swing the golf club . . . ?"

There we go. She wants to know if I was really willing to sacrifice myself, or if I just did it to distract Janos.

"Does it matter?" I ask.

"I don't know . . . maybe."

"Well, if it makes you feel any better, I'd have asked you to swing either way."

"That's easy to say now."

"Sure is, but I didn't find the foothold till the last second, when he broke my grip."

She stops as the consequences sink in. It's no lie. I would've done whatever it took to save her. Foothold or not.

"Take it as a compliment," I add. "You're worth it, Viv Parker."

Her cheeks rise uncontrollably. She has no idea what to say.

Up the hallway, a cell phone starts chirping. Viv's lawyer picks it up and puts it to his ear. Nodding a few times, he closes it and looks our way. "Viv, your parents just checked into their hotel. Time to go."

"In a sec," she says. Sticking with me, she adds, "So still no word about Janos?"

I shake my head.

"They're not gonna find him, are they?"

"Not a chance."

"Think he'll come hunting for us?"

"I don't think so. FBI told me Janos was paid to keep things quiet. Now that the word's out, his job's over."

"And you believe them?"

"Viv, we've already told our story. Security cameras got pictures of him entering the Capitol. It's not like they need us as witnesses or to identify him. They know who he is, and they have everything they need. There's nothing gained now by putting bullets in our heads."

"I'll remember that as I check behind every closed shower curtain for the rest of my life."

"If it makes you feel better, they said they'd assign security detail to both of us. Besides, we've been sitting here for eight hours. If he wanted us dead, it already would've happened."

It's not much of a guarantee, but in a warped way, it's the best we've got. "So that's it? We're done?"

I look back to my lawyer as she asks the question. After a decade on Capitol Hill, the only person standing in my corner is someone who's paid to be there. "Yeah . . . we're done."

She doesn't like that tone in my voice. "Look at it this way, Harris—at least we won."

The FBI agents told me the same thing—we're lucky to be alive. It's a nice consolation, but it doesn't bring back Matthew, or Pasternak, or Lowell. "Winning isn't everything," I tell her.

She gives me a long look. She doesn't have to say a word.

"Ms. Parker—your parents . . . !" her lawyer calls out.

She ignores him. "So where do you go from here?" she asks me.

"Depends what type of deal Dan cuts with the government. Right now, the only thing I'm worried about is Matthew's funeral. His mom asked me to give one of the eulogies. Me and Congressman Cordell."

"I wouldn't sweat it—I've seen you speak. I'm sure you'll do him justice."

It's the only thing that anyone's said in the last eight hours that's actually made me feel good. "Listen, Viv, I'm sorry again for getting you into—"

"Don't say it, Harris."

"But being a page . . ."

". . . paled to what we did these last few days. Just paled. The running around . . . finding that lab . . . even the stupid stuff—I took a shower in a private jet!—you think I'd trade all that so I could refill some Senator's seltzer? Didn't you hear what they said at page orientation? Life is school. It's *all* school. And if anyone wants to give me crap about being fired, well . . . well, when's the last time they jumped off a cliff to help a friend who needed it? God didn't put me here to back down."

"That's a good stump speech—you should save it."

"I plan to."

"I'm serious what I said before: You're gonna make a great Senator one day."

"Senator? You got a problem with a giant, black woman President?"

I laugh out loud at that one.

"I meant what I said, too," she adds. "I'll still need a good chief of staff."

"You got a deal. Even I'll come back to Washington for that one."

"Oh, so now you're leaving us all behind? What're you gonna do—write a book? Join the law practice with your guy Dan? Or just kick back on a beach somewhere like at the end of all those other thrillers?"

"I don't know . . . I was thinking of just heading home for a bit."

"I love it—small town boy goes home . . . they give you the victory parade . . . everyone chows on apple pie . . ."

"No, not Pennsylvania," I say. For the better part of a decade, I've been convinced that success in the big leagues would somehow bury my past. The only thing it buried was me. "I was actually thinking about staying around here. Dan said there's a junior high school in Baltimore that could use a good civics teacher."

"Hold on a second . . . you're gonna teach?"

"And that's so bad?"

She thinks about it a moment. A week ago, like any other page, she would've said there were bigger things to do with my life. Now we both know better. Her smile is huge. "Actually, that sounds perfect."

"Thank you, Viv."

"Though you know those kids'll eat you alive."

I grin. "I hope so."

"Miss Parker . . . !" her lawyer bellows for the last time.

"Be right there . . . Listen, I should run," she tells me, offering a quick hug. As she wraps her arms around me, I can feel her ice pack on my back. She squeezes so tight, my arm starts to hurt. It doesn't matter. The hug's worth every second.

"Knock 'em dead, Viv."

"Who, my parents?"

"No . . . the world."

She pulls away with that same toothy grin she had when we first met.

"Y'know, Harris . . . when you originally asked me for help . . . I had such a crush on you."

"And now?"

"Now . . . I don't know," she teases. "I kinda think I should get a suit that fits." Walking backwards up the hallway, she adds, "Meanwhile, know what the best part of being a teacher is?"

"What?"

"The annual class trip to Washington."

This time, I'm the one with the toothy grin.

"Y'like that, don't you, King Midas?" she adds.

Turning around, she puts her back to me and heads for her lawyer. "I'm serious about that chief of staff job, Harold," she calls out as her voice echoes down the long hallway. "Only eighteen years until I reach the age requirement. I'll expect you there bright and early."

"Whatever you say, Madame President. I wouldn't miss it for the world."

83

London

Have a nice evening, Mr. Sauls," the driver said as he opened the back door of the black Jaguar and held an umbrella over his boss's head.

"You, too, Ethan," Sauls replied, climbing out of the car and heading to the front door of the exclusive six-story apartment building on central London's Park Lane. Inside, a doorman behind a burled-walnut welcoming desk waved hello and handed Sauls a short stack of mail. Getting on the elevator, Sauls spent the rest of the ride flipping through the usual assortment of bills and solicitations.

By the time he stepped into his well-appointed apartment, he'd already picked through the junk mail, which he quickly tossed in a ceramic trashcan just beside the antique leather-top secretary where he threw his keys. Heading over to the hall closet, he hung his gray cashmere overcoat on a cherry-wood hanger. Passing through the living room, he flipped a switch, and recessed lights glowed to life above the built-in bookcases that lined the left side of the room.

Eventually making his way to the kitchen and breakfast nook that overlooked Speaker's Corner in Hyde Park, Sauls went straight for the shiny, black-paneled refrigerator, where he could see his own reflection in the door as he approached. Grabbing a glass from the counter, he pulled the fridge open and poured himself some cranberry juice. As the door slapped shut, he was once again staring at his own reflection in the refrigerator door—but this time, there was someone standing behind him.

"Nice address," Janos said.

"Nnnnuh!" Sauls blurted, spinning around so fast he almost dropped his glass.

"Don't scare me like that!" Sauls shouted, clutching his chest and setting the glass on the counter. "God . . . I thought you were dead!"

"Why would you think that?" Janos asked as he stepped in closer, one hand stuffed into the pocket of his black overcoat, the other clenching the brushed-metal tip of an aluminum cane. He lifted his chin a bit, highlighting the cuts and bruises along his face—especially where the bones were crushed in his cheek. His left eye was cherry bloodshot, a fresh scar was stitched across his chin, and his left femur was shattered into so many pieces, they had to insert a titanium rod into his leg to stabilize the bones and keep the muscles and ligaments from being a flaccid sack of blood and tissue. Three inches down, the only things holding his knee together were the Erector Set pins that ran through his skin and straight into the fragments of bone. The fall was worse than he'd ever let on.

"I've been trying to contact you—there's been no answer for a week," Sauls said, stepping backwards. "Do you even know what's going on? The FBI seized it all . . . They took every last thing from the mine."

"I know. I read the papers," Janos said, limping forward. "By the way, since when'd you get a private driver?"

"What're you—? You followed me?" Sauls asked, backing up even further.

"Don't be paranoid, Sauls. Some things you can spot from your bedroom window—like my car that's parked in front. Did you see it out there? The iris blue MGB . . ."

"What do you want, Janos?"

". . . model year 1965—first year they changed to the push-button door handles. Hard to shift with the nails in my leg, but really a beautiful car . . ."

"If it's money, we paid you just like we said . . ."

". . . unlike that old Spitfire I used to have, this baby's reliable . . . dependable . . ."

"You did get the money, didn't you?"

". . . some might even say *trustworthy*."

Backed up against the kitchen counter, Sauls stopped.

One hand still in his pocket, Janos fixed his eyes on his partner. "You lied to me, Marcus."

"I-I didn't! I swear!" Sauls insisted.

"That's another lie."

"You don't understand . . ."

"Answer the question," Janos warned. "Was it Yemen, or not?"

"It's not how you think . . . When we started—"

"When we started, you told me Wendell was a private company with no government ties."

"Please, Janos—you knew what we were doing down there . . . We never hid—"

"A private company with no ties, Marcus!"

"It's the same result either way!"

"No, it's not! One's speculation; the other's suicide! You have any idea how long they'll hunt us for this? Now who signed the damned check—was it Yemen or not?"

"Janos . . ."

"Was it Yemen or not?"

"Just please calm down and—"

Janos pulled out a gun from his pocket and shoved it against Sauls's forehead. He pressed it forward, digging the barrel against his skin. "Was. It. Yemen. Or. Not?"

"P-Please, don't . . ." Sauls begged, the tears already welling up in his eyes.

Janos pulled back the hammer on the gun and put his finger on the trigger. He was done asking questions.

"Yemen!" Sauls stuttered, his face scrunched up as he shut his eyes. "It was Yemen . . . Please don't kill me . . . !"

Without a word, Janos lowered the gun, sliding it back in his pocket.

As the gun left his forehead, Sauls opened his eyes. "I'm sorry, Janos . . . I'm so sorry . . ." he continued to beg.

"Catch your breath," Janos demanded, handing Sauls the glass of cranberry juice.

Sauls desperately downed the drink, but it didn't bring the calm he was searching for. His hands were trembling as he lowered the glass, which clinked against the counter.

Shaking his head, Janos pivoted on his good leg and turned to leave. "Good-bye, Sauls," he said as he made his way out of the kitchen.

"S-So you're not gonna kill me?" Sauls asked, forcing a petrified smile.

Janos turned and held him with a midnight stare. "Who said that?"

A long, pregnant pause passed between the two men. Then Sauls started to cough. Slightly at first. Then harder. Within seconds, his throat exploded with a wet, hacking wheeze. It was like a backfire from an old car. Sauls grasped at his neck. It felt like his windpipe had collapsed.

Janos stared at the empty glass of cranberry juice and didn't say a thing.

Between coughs, Sauls could barely get the words out. "You little motherf—"

Again, Janos just stood there. At this point, a black-box-induced heart attack was too much of a calling card. A temporarily swollen windpipe, however, was just another choking accident in the kitchen.

Clawing at his own throat, then clutching at the counter to stand up, Sauls fell to his knees. The juice glass shattered across the black and white floor. Janos left before the convulsions started.

It was time for a vacation anyway.

Epilogue

STARING THROUGH THE glass partition at D.C.'s Central Detention Facility, I can't help but listen to the one-way conversations around me. *Rosemary's doing fine . . . Don't worry, he's not gonna use your car . . . Soon, they said soon, sweetie . . .* Unlike the movies, the visitors' hall here doesn't have walled-off partitions on my right and left for extra privacy. This is D.C. Jail on a D.C. budget—no perks allowed. The result is a chorus of chattering voices, each one attempting to keep it low, but pitched loud enough so they can hear themselves over all the noise. Add the unnatural hum of the prisoners' voices as they seep through the glass, and we've got all the makings of a giant, enclosed phone booth. The only good news is, the people in the orange jumpsuits are on the other side of the glass.

"Here he comes," the guard by the door calls out to me.

As he says the words, every visitor in the room, from the black woman with blond hair to the well-dressed man holding the Bible in his lap, imperceptibly turns their head to the left. This is still Washington, D.C. They all want to know if it's someone worth looking at. To me, it is.

With both his arms and legs in shackles, Barry shuffles forward, his cane replaced by the guard who holds his biceps and guides him toward the orange plastic seat across from me.

"Who?" Barry asks as I read his lips.

His guard mouths my name.

The moment Barry hears it, he pauses, then quickly covers it up with a perfect grin. It's a classic lobbying trick—pretend you're happy to see everyone. Even when you can't see.

The guard lowers Barry into the seat and hands him the receiver that's hanging on the glass. Around his wrist, there's a nametag that looks like a hospital bracelet. There're no shoelaces in his sneakers. Barry doesn't seem to be bothered by any of it. Crossing one leg over the other, he tugs on the pant leg of his orange jumpsuit like it's his regular two-thousand-dollar suit.

"Pick up," the guard yells through the glass, motioning for me to grab the receiver.

An ocean of acid churns through my stomach as I lift the chipped receiver to my ear. I've been waiting two weeks for this call, but it doesn't mean I'm looking forward to it.

"Hey," I whisper into the mouthpiece.

"Man, you sound like crap," Barry sings back, already trying to act like he's inside my brain. He tilts his head as if he can see my every expression. "Really, though—like someone kicked you in the face."

"Someone did," I say, staring straight at him.

"Is that all you're here for?" he asks. "One last potshot?"

I continue to stay silent.

"I don't even know how you can complain," he adds.

"You seen a newspaper recently? The way the press is reading it, you're coming through just fine."

"That'll change when the gambling part gets released."

"Maybe yes, maybe no. Sure, you won't get another government job—and you'll probably be a pariah for a few years, but that'll pass."

"Maybe yes, maybe no," I volley back, trying to keep him engaged. Anything to keep him talking.

"What about Senator Stevens?" Barry asks. "He feeling the regret yet for giving you the boot?"

"He didn't have a choice."

"Spoken like a true staffer," Barry says.

"You telling me I'm wrong?"

"You're definitely wrong. He knew you'd make a deal with the government—that's all the cover he needed. Instead, you spend over a decade slaving away for the man, and he drop-kicks you when you need him most? Know how bad that looks for him? Mark it right now— that's gonna cost him reelection."

"He'll be fine."

"As I said, spoken like a true staffer."

"Ex-staffer," I shoot back.

"Don't bitch to me," Barry says. "I mean, look at it this way . . . at least you have your shoelaces." He twirls the ankle that's up on his knee. He's trying to play it cool, but back by his waist, he's picking at his wristband.

"By the way, did you see the piece in today's *Post*?" he adds. He smiles wider, but he's scratching even harder at the wristband. There's only so long he can wear the brave face. "They actually called me a *terrorist*."

I once again stay quiet. He's definitely taking the public fall. Even though Lowell's office was able to find Sauls's name and trace it back to Wendell, it took weeks to prove what really went on. Today, with Sauls dead and Janos missing, they need a neck for the noose—and right now, Barry's it.

"I heard you hired Richie Rubin. He's a good lawyer," I point out.

He smells the small talk a mile away—he used to be in the business of it. Now he's annoyed. The smile disappears fast.

"What do you want, Harris?"

There we go . . . a full two minutes to get back to reality. The man's no dummy. He knows how I feel—I wouldn't piss down his throat if his lungs were on fire. If I'm sitting here, I need something.

"Let me guess," Barry says. "You're dying to know why I did it . . ."

"I know why you did it," I shoot back. "When you have no loyalty, and you're so damn paranoid, you think the world's against you—"

"The world *is* against me!" he shouts, leaning toward the glass. "Look where I'm sitting! You're telling me I'm wrong?!"

I shake my head, refusing to get into it. Whatever perceived slights he thinks he's the victim of, they've clearly whittled away at his reality.

"Don't judge me, Harris. Not all of us are lucky enough to lead your charmed life."

"So now it's my fault?"

"I asked you for help over the years. You never gave it. Not once."

"So *I* made you do all this?"

"Just tell me why you're here. If it's not me, and it's not to catch up—"

"Pasternak," I blurt.

A wide smile creeps up his cheeks. Sitting back in his seat, Barry crosses his arms and tucks the receiver between his chin and shoulder. Like he's putting the Barry mask back on. He's no longer fidgeting with his wristband. "It's gnawing at you, isn't it?" he asks. "You and I . . . we always had the competitive friendship. But you and Pasternak . . . ? He was supposed to be your mentor. The one person you turned to when you had an emergency and had to break the glass. Is that what's got you tossing and turning all night—wondering how your personal radar could be so completely wrong?"

"I just want to know why he did it."

"Of course you do. Sauls bit his bullet . . . I'm on my way to biting mine . . . but Pasternak—that's the one that'll frustrate you the rest of your life. You don't get to punch him, or yell at him, or have the big final confrontation scene with the bittersweet ending. It's the curse of being an overachiever—you can't handle a problem that can't be solved."

"I don't need it solved; I just want an answer."

"Same difference, Harris. The thing is, if you expect me to suddenly scratch your back . . . well . . . you know how the cliché goes . . ."

Forever the lobbyist, Barry makes his point clear without ever saying the actual words. He's not giving any info unless he gets something in return. God, I hate this town.

"What do you want?" I ask.

"Nothing now," he replies. "Let's just say you owe me one."

Even in an orange jumpsuit and behind six inches of glass, Barry still needs to believe he has the upper hand.

"Fine. I owe you one," I tell him. "Now what about Pasternak?"

"Well, if it makes you feel any better, I don't think he knew who was really driving the train. Sure, he took advantage of you with the game, but that was just to get the mining request in the bill."

"I don't understand."

"What's to understand? It was an unimportant request for a defunct gold mine in South Dakota. He knew Matthew would never say yes to it—not unless he had a good enough reason," Barry says. "From there, Pasternak just took the game and put in the fix."

"So Pasternak was one of the dungeon-masters?"

"The what?"

"The dungeon-masters—the guys who pick the bets and collect the cash. Is that how the mine request got in the game? He was one of the guys who ran it?"

"How else would it get there?" Barry asks.

"I don't know . . . it just . . . all those months we were playing . . . all the people we were betting against— Pasternak was always trying to figure out who else was in on it. When the taxi receipt would come in, he'd go through each one, hoping to read handwritings. He even made a list of people who were working on particular issues . . . But if he was a dungeon-master . . ." I cut myself off as the consequences sink in.

Barry cocks his head to the side. His cloudy eye's staring straight at me; his glass eye's off to the left. Out of nowhere, he starts to laugh. "You're kidding me, right?"

"What? If he were a dungeon-master, wouldn't he know all the other players?"

Barry stops laughing, realizing I'm not in on the joke. "You don't even know, do you?"

"Know what?"

"Be honest, Harris—you haven't figured it out?"

I try my best to act informed. "Of course—I got most of it . . . Which part are you talking about?"

His foggy eye looks right at me. "There is no game. There never was one." His eye doesn't move. "I mean, you know it was all bullshit, right? Smoke and mirrors."

As his words creep through the receiver and into my ear, my whole body goes numb. The world feels like my personal gravity's just doubled. Sinking down—almost through—the seat of my orange plastic chair, I weigh a thousand pounds.

"What a punchline, huh?" Barry asks. "I almost fell over when they first told me. Can you imagine—all this time spent looking at coworkers, trying to figure out who else is placing bets, and the only people actually playing the game are you and Matthew?"

"Two minutes," the guard behind Barry announces.

"It's brilliant when you think about it," Barry adds. "Pasternak talks it up; you believe him because you trust him . . . then they send in a few pages, fill out some taxi receipts, and you guys think you're in on the biggest secret Capitol Hill has to offer. It's like those flight simulator rides at Disney World, where they show the movie on-screen and shake your car a bit—you think you're flying up and down a roller coaster, but you really haven't moved an inch."

I force a laugh, my body still frozen.

"Man, just the thought of it," Barry adds, his voice picking up steam. "Dozens of staffers placing bets on unimportant legislation without anyone knowing? Please, what a dream—like anyone here could even keep their mouth shut for longer than ten seconds," he teases. "Gotta give Pasternak his credit, though. You thought you were playing a great joke on the system, and the entire time, he's playing the joke on you."

"Yeah . . . no . . . it's definitely amazing."

"It was humming like clockwork, too—until everything with Matthew. Once that happened, Pasternak wanted out. I mean, he may've signed up to convince you—that's part of any lobbyist's job—but he didn't want to hurt anyone."

"That's . . . That's not what I heard," I bluff.

"Then you heard wrong. The only reason he put this together was for the exact same reason anyone does anything in this town: Ever have a small country for a client? Small countries bring in small fortunes, which small businesses are in desperate need of—especially when billings are down thirty-six percent this year alone. After the first year of failing to get the gold mine transferred, Pasternak eventually decided to go with the more inventive backdoor. Say hello to the Game—the most harmless way ever to sneak an earmark into a bill. But then Matthew got curious, and Janos came in, and, well . . . that's when the train jackknifed off the tracks . . ."

The guard looks over at us.

We're almost out of time, but Barry doesn't show the slightest sign of slowing down. After all this time in jail, he's finally having fun.

"You gotta love the name, too—the Zero Game—so melodramatic. But it *is* true: In any equation, when you multiply by zero, you always wind up with nothing, right?"

I nod, dumbfounded.

"So who told you anyway?" he asks. "FBI, or did you figure it out yourself?"

"No . . . myself. I . . . uh . . . I got it myself."

"Good for you, Harris. Good man."

Stuck in my seat, I just sit there, looking at him. It's like finding out a year of your life has been a staged production number. And I'm the only putz still in costume.

"Time," the guard says.

Barry keeps talking. "I'm so glad you—"

"I said, *Time,*" the guard interrupts. He pulls the receiver from Barry's ear, but I still hear his final thought.

"I knew you'd appreciate it, Harris! I knew it! Even Pasternak would be happy for that—!"

There's a loud click in my ear as the guard slaps the phone in its cradle. He pinches the back of Barry's neck and yanks him from his seat. Stumbling across the room, Barry heads back to the steel door.

But as I sit alone at the glass partition, staring through to the other side, there's no question Barry has it right. Pasternak said it the first day he hired me. It's the first rule of politics: The only time you get hurt is when you forget it's all a game.

About the Author

BRAD MELTZER is the author of the *New York Times* bestsellers *The Tenth Justice, Dead Even, The First Counsel,* and *The Millionaires.* A graduate of the University of Michigan and Columbia Law School, he currently lives in Maryland with his wife and son. When he was nineteen, he was an intern on Capitol Hill.

To find out more about *The Zero Game* and the author, please visit www.bradmeltzer.com.

1

Six minutes from now, one of us would be dead. That was our fate. None of us knew it was coming.

"*Ron, hold up!*" I called out, chasing after the middle-aged man in the navy-blue suit. As I ran, the smothering Florida heat glued my shirt to my chest.

Ignoring me, Ron Boyle darted up the tarmac, passing Air Force One on our right and the eighteen cars of the motorcade that idled in a single-file line on our left. As deputy chief of staff, he was always in a rush. That's what happens when you work for the most powerful man in the world. I don't say that lightly. Our boss was the Commander in Chief. The President of the United States. And when he wanted something, it was my job to get it. Right now President Leland "The Lion" Manning wanted Boyle to stay calm. Some tasks were beyond even me.

Picking up speed as he weaved through the crowd of staffers and press making their way to their assigned cars, Boyle blew past a shiny black Chevy Suburban packed with Secret Service agents and the ambulance that carried extra pints of the President's blood. Earlier today, Boyle was supposed to have a fifteen-minute sit-down with the President on Air Force One. Because of my scheduling error, he was now down to a three-minute drive-by briefing sometime this afternoon. To say he was annoyed would be like calling the Great Depression *a bad day at the office.*

"Ron!" I said again, putting a hand on his shoulder and trying to apologize. "Just wait. I wanted to—"

He spun around wildly, slapping my hand out of the way. Thin and pointy-nosed with a thick mustache designed to offset both, Boyle had graying hair, olive skin, and striking brown eyes with a splash of light blue in each iris. As he leaned forward, his cat's eyes glared down at me. "Don't touch me again unless you're shaking my hand," he threatened as a flick of spit hit me in the cheek.

Gritting my teeth, I wiped it away with the back of my hand. Sure, the scheduling hiccup was my fault, but that's still no reason t—

"Now, what the hell's so damn important, Wes, or is this another vital reminder that when we're eating with the President, we need to give you our lunch orders at least an hour in advance?" he added, loud enough so a few Secret Service agents turned.

Any other twenty-three-year-old would've taken a verbal swing. I kept my cool. That's the job of the President's aide . . . a.k.a. the body person . . . a.k.a. the buttboy. Get the President what he wants; keep the machine humming.

"Lemme make it up to you," I said, mentally canceling my apology. If I wanted Boyle quiet—if we didn't want a scene for the press—I needed to up the ante. "What if I . . . what if I squeezed you into the President's limo right now?"

Boyle's posture lifted slightly as he started buttoning his suit jacket. "I thought you— No, that's good. Great. Excellent." He even painted on a tiny smile. Crisis averted.

He thought all was forgiven. My memory's way longer

than that. As Boyle triumphantly turned toward the limo, I jotted down another mental note. Cocky bastard. On the way home, he'd be riding in the back of the press van.

Politically, I wasn't just *good*. I was great. That's not ego; it's the truth. You don't apply for this job, you're invited to interview. Every young political gunner in the White House would've killed to clutch this close to the leader of the free world. From here, my predecessor had gone on to become the number two guy in the White House Press Office. *His* predecessor in the last White House took a job managing four thousand people at IBM. Seven months ago, despite my lack of connections, the President picked me. I beat out a senator's son and a pair of Rhodes scholars. I could certainly handle a tantrum-throwing senior staffer.

"Wes, let's go!" the Secret Service detail leader called out, waving us into the car as he slid into the front passenger seat, where he could see everything coming.

Trailing Boyle and holding my leather shoulder bag out in front of me, I jumped into the back of the armored limo, where the President was dressed casually in a black windbreaker and jeans. I assumed Boyle would immediately start talking his ear off, but as he passed in front of the President, he was strangely silent. Hunched over as he headed for the back left seat, Boyle's suit jacket sagged open, but he quickly pressed his hand over his own heart to keep it shut. I didn't realize until later what he was hiding. Or what I'd just done by inviting him inside.

Following behind him, I crouched toward one of the three fold-down seats that face the rear of the car. Mine was back-to-back with the driver and across from Boyle. For security reasons, the President always sat in the back right seat, with the First Lady sitting between him and Boyle.

The jump seat directly across from the President—the

hot seat—was already taken by Mike Calinoff, retired professional race car driver, four-time Winston Cup winner, and special guest for today's event. No surprise. With only four months until the election, we were barely three points ahead in the polls. When the crowd was that fickle, only a fool entered the gladiator's ring without a hidden weapon.

"So she's fast, even with the bulletproofing?" the racing champ asked, admiring the midnight-blue interior of Cadillac One.

"Greased lightning," Manning answered as the First Lady rolled her eyes.

Finally joining in, Boyle scootched forward in his seat and flipped open a manila folder. "Mr. President, if we could—?"

"Sorry—that's all I can do, sir," Chief of Staff Warren Albright interrupted as he hopped inside. Handing a folded-up newspaper to the President, he took the middle seat directly across from the First Lady, and more important, diagonally across from Manning. Even in a six-person backseat, proximity mattered. Especially to Boyle, who was still turned toward the President, refusing to give up his opening.

The President seized the newspaper and scrutinized the crossword puzzle he and Albright shared every day. It had been their tradition since the first days of the campaign—and the reason why Albright was always in that coveted seat diagonally across from the President. Albright started each puzzle, got as far as he could, then passed it to the President to cross the finish line.

"Fifteen down's wrong," the President pointed out as I rested my bag on my lap. *"Stifle."*

Albright usually hated when Manning found a mistake. Today, as he noticed Boyle in the corner seat, he had something brand-new to be annoyed by.

Everything okay? I asked with a glance.

Before Albright could answer, the driver rammed the gas, and my body jerked forward.

Three and a half minutes from now, the first gunshot would be fired. Two of us would crumble to the floor, convulsing. One wouldn't get up.

"Sir, if I could bend your ear for a second?" Boyle interrupted, more insistently than before.

"Ron, can't you just enjoy the ride?" the First Lady teased, her short brown hair bobbing as we hit a divot in the road. Despite the sweet tone, I saw the glare in her leaf-green eyes. It was the same glare she used to give her students at Princeton. A former professor with a PhD in chemistry, Dr. First Lady was trained to be tough. And what Dr. First Lady wanted, Dr. First Lady fought for. And got.

"But, ma'am, it'll just take—"

Her brow furrowed so hard, her eyebrows kissed. "Ron. *Enjoy the ride.*"

That's where most people would've stopped. Boyle pushed even harder, trying to hand the file directly to Manning. He'd known the President since they were in their twenties, studying at Oxford. A professional banker, as well as a collector of antique magic tricks, he later managed all of the Mannings' money, a magic trick in itself. To this day, he was the only person on staff who was there when Manning married the First Lady. That alone gave him a free pass when the press discovered that Boyle's father was a petty con man who'd been convicted (twice) for insurance fraud. It was the same free pass he was using in the limo to test the First Lady's authority. But even the best free passes eventually expire.

Manning shook his head so subtly, only a trained eye could see it. First Lady, one; Boyle, nothing.

Closing the file folder, Boyle sank back and shot me the kind of look that would leave a bruise. Now it was my fault.

As we neared our destination, Manning stared silently through the light green tint of his bulletproof window. "Y'ever hear what Kennedy said three hours before he was shot?" he asked, putting on his best Massachusetts accent. *"You know, last night would've been a hell of a night to kill a President."*

"Lee!" the First Lady scolded. "See what I deal with?" she added, fake laughing at Calinoff.

The President took her hand and squeezed it, glancing my way. "Wes, did you bring the present I got for Mr. Calinoff?" he asked.

I dug through my leather briefcase—the bag of tricks— never taking my eyes off Manning's face. He tossed a slight nod and scratched at his own wrist. *Don't give him the tie clip . . . go for the big stuff.*

I'd been his aide for over seven months. If I was doing my job right, we didn't have to talk to communicate. We were in a groove. I couldn't help but smile.

That was my last big, broad grin. In three minutes, the gunman's third bullet would rip through my cheek, destroying so many nerves, I'd never have full use of my mouth again.

That's the one, the President nodded at me.

From my overpacked bag, which held everything a President would ever need, I pulled out a set of official presidential cuff links, which I handed to Mr. Calinoff, who was loving every split second in his folded-down, completely uncomfortable hot seat.

"Those are real, y'know," the President told him. "Don't put 'em on eBay."

It was the same joke he used every time he gave a set away. We all still laughed. Even Boyle, who started scratching at his chest. There's no better place to be than in on an inside joke with the President of the United States. And on July 4th in Daytona, Florida, when you'd flown in to yell, "*Gentlemen, start your engines!*" at the legendary Pepsi 400 NASCAR race, there was no better backseat in the world.

Before Calinoff could offer a thank-you, the limo came to a stop. A red lightning bolt flashed by us on the left—two police motorcycles with their sirens blaring. They were leapfrogging from the back of the motorcade to the front. Just like a funeral procession.

"Don't tell me they closed down the road," the First Lady said. She hated it when they shut traffic for the motorcade. Those were the votes we'd never get back.

The car slowly chugged a few feet forward. "Sir, we're about to enter the track," the detail leader announced from the passenger seat. Outside, the concrete openness of the airport runway quickly gave way to rows and rows of high-end motor coaches.

"Wait . . . we're going out on the track?" Calinoff asked, suddenly excited. He shifted in his seat, trying to get a look outside.

The President grinned. "Did you think we'd just get a couple seats in front?"

The wheels bounced over a clanging metal plate that sounded like a loose manhole cover. Boyle scratched even more at his chest. A baritone rumble filled the air.

"That thunder?" Boyle asked, glancing up at the clear blue sky.

"No, not thunder," the President replied, putting his own

fingertips against the bulletproof window as the stadium crowd of 200,000 surged to its feet with banners, flags, and arms waving. "Applause."

"*Ladies and gentlemen, the President of the United States!*" the announcer bellowed through the P.A. system.

A sharp right-hand turn tugged us all sideways as the limo turned onto the racetrack, the biggest, most perfectly paved highway I'd ever seen in my life.

"Nice roads you got here," the President said to Calinoff, leaning back in the plush leather seat that was tailor-made to his body.

All that was left was the big entrance. If we didn't nail that, the 200,000 ticket holders in the stadium, plus the ten million viewers watching from home, plus the seventy-five million fans who're committed to NASCAR, would all go tell their friends and neighbors and cousins and strangers in the supermarket that we went up for our baptism and sneezed in the holy water.

But that's why we brought the motorcade. We didn't *need* eighteen cars. The runway in the Daytona Airport was actually adjacent to the racetrack. There were no red lights to run. No traffic to hold back. But to everyone watching . . . Have you ever seen the President's motorcade on a racetrack? Instant American frenzy.

I didn't care how close we were in the polls. One lap around and we'd be picking out our seats for the inauguration.

Across from me, Boyle wasn't nearly as thrilled. With his arms crossed against his chest, he never stopped studying the President.

"Got the stars out too, eh?" Calinoff asked as we entered the final turn and he saw our welcoming committee, a small mob of NASCAR drivers all decked out in their multicolor, advertising-emblazoned jumpsuits. What his untrained eye didn't notice were the dozen or so "crew members" who were standing a bit more erect than the rest. Some had backpacks. Some carried leather satchels. All had sunglasses. And one was speaking into his own wrist. Secret Service.

Like any other first-timer in the limo, Calinoff was practically licking the glass. "Mr. Calinoff, you'll be getting out first," I told him as we pulled into the pit stalls. Outside, the drivers were already angling for presidential position. In sixty seconds, they'd be running for their lives.

Calinoff leaned toward my door on the driver's side, where all the NASCAR drivers were huddled.

I leaned forward to block him, motioning to the President's door on the other side. "*That* way," I said. The door right next to him.

"But the drivers are over *there*," Calinoff objected.

"Listen to the boy," the President chimed in, gesturing toward the door by Calinoff.

Years ago, when President Clinton came for a NASCAR race, members of the crowd booed. In 2004, when President Bush arrived with legendary driver Bill Elliott in his motorcade, Elliott stepped out first and the crowd erupted. Even Presidents can use an opening act.

With a click and a thunk, the detail leader pushed a small security button under the door handle which allowed him to open the armor-lined door from the outside. Within seconds, the door cracked open, twin switchblades of light and Florida heat sliced through the car, and Calinoff lowered one of his handmade cowboy boots onto the pavement.

"And please welcome four-time Winston Cup winner . . . Mike Caaaalinoff!" the announcer shouted through the stadium.

Cue crowd going wild.

"Never forget," the President whispered to his guest as

Calinoff stepped outside to the 200,000 screaming fans. *"That's* who we're here to see."

"And now," the announcer continued, "our grand marshal for today's race—Florida's own . . . President Leeeee Maaaaanning!"

Just behind Calinoff, the President hopped out of the car, his right hand up in a wave, his left hand proudly patting the NASCAR logo on the chest of his windbreaker. He paused for a moment to wait for the First Lady. As always, you could read the lips on every fan in the grandstands. *There he is . . . There he is . . . There they are . . .* Then, as soon as the crowd had digested it, the flashbulbs hit. *Mr. President, over here! Mr. President . . . !* He'd barely moved three steps by the time Albright was behind him, followed by Boyle.

I stepped out last. The sunlight forced me to squint, but I still craned my neck to look up, mesmerized by the 200,000 fans who were now on their feet, pointing and waving at us from the grandstands. Two years out of college, and this was my life. Even rock stars don't have it this good.

Putting his arm out for a handshake, Calinoff was quickly enveloped by the waiting crowd of drivers, who smothered him with hugs and backslaps. At the front of the crowd was the NASCAR CEO and his surprisingly tall wife, here to welcome the First Lady.

Approaching the drivers, the President grinned. He was next. In three seconds, he'd be surrounded—the one black windbreaker in a Technicolor sea of Pepsi, M&M's, DeWalt, and Lone Star Steakhouse jumpsuits. As if he'd won the World Series, the Super Bowl, and the—

Pop, pop, pop.

That's all I heard. Three tiny pops. A firecracker. Or a car backfiring.

"Shots fired! Shots fired!" the detail leader yelled.

"Get down! Get back!"

I was still smiling as the first scream tore through the air. The crowd of drivers scattered—running, dropping, panicking in an instant blur of colors.

"God gave power to the prophets . . ." a man with black buzzed hair and a deep voice shouted from the center of the swirl. His tiny chocolate eyes seemed almost too close together, while his bulbous nose and arched thin eyebrows gave him a strange warmth that for some reason reminded me of Danny Kaye. Kneeling down on one knee and holding a gun with both hands, he was dressed as a driver in a black and bright yellow racing jumpsuit.

Like a bumblebee, I thought.

". . . but also to the horrors . . ."

I just kept staring at him, frozen. Sound disappeared. Time slowed. And the world turned black-and-white, my own personal newsreel. It was like the first day I met the President. The handshake alone felt like an hour. Living between seconds, someone called it. Time standing still.

Still locked on the bumblebee, I couldn't tell if he was moving forward or if everyone around him was rushing back.

"Man down!" the detail leader shouted.

I followed the sound and the hand motions to a man in a navy suit, lying facedown on the ground. Oh, no. *Boyle.* His forehead was pressed against the pavement, his face screwed up in agony. He was holding his chest, and I could see blood starting to puddle out from below him.

"Man down!" the detail leader shouted again.

My eyes slid sideways, searching for the President. I found him just as a half dozen jumpsuited agents rushed at the small crowd that was already around him. The frantic agents were moving so fast, the people closest to Manning were pinned against him.

"Move him! *Now!*" an agent yelled.

Pressed backward against the President, the wife of the NASCAR CEO was screaming.

"You're crushing her!" Manning shouted, gripping her shoulder and trying to keep her on her feet. "Let her *go!*"

The Service didn't care. Swarming around the President, they rammed the crowd from the front and right side. That's when momentum got the best of them. Like a just-cut tree, the crush of people tumbled to the side, toward the ground. The President was still fighting to get the CEO's wife out. A bright light exploded. I remember the flashbulb going off.

"*. . . so people could test their faith . . .*" the gunman roared as a separate group of agents in jumpsuits got a grip on his neck . . . his arm . . . the back of his hair. In slow motion, the bumblebee's head snapped back, then his body, as two more pops ripped the air.

I felt a bee sting in my right cheek.

"*. . . and examine good from evil!*" the man screamed, arms spread out like Jesus as agents dragged him to the ground. All around them, other agents formed a tight circle, brandishing semiautomatic Uzis they had torn from their leather satchels and backpacks.

I slapped my own face, trying to kill whatever just bit me. A few feet ahead, the crowd surrounding the President collided with the asphalt. Two agents on the far side grabbed the First Lady, pulling her away. The rest never stopped shoving, ramming, stepping over people as they tried to get to Manning and shield him.

I looked as the puddle below Boyle grew even larger. His head was now resting in a milky white liquid. He'd thrown up.

From the back of the President's pile, our detail leader and another suit-and-tie agent gripped Manning's elbows, lifted him from the pile, and shoved him sideways, straight at me. The President's face was in pain. I looked for blood on his suit but didn't see any.

Picking up speed, his agents were going for the limo. Two more agents were right behind them, gripping the First Lady under her armpits. I was the only thing in their way. I tried to sidestep but wasn't fast enough. At full speed, the detail leader's shoulder plowed into my own.

Falling backward, I crashed into the limo, my rear end hitting just above the right front tire. I still see it all in some out-of-body slow motion: me trying to keep my balance . . . slapping my hand against the car's hood . . . and the splat from my impact. Sound was so warped, I could hear the liquid squish. The world was still black-and-white. Everything except for my own red handprint.

Confused, I put my hand back to my cheek. It slid across my skin, which was slick and wet and raw with pain.

"Go, go, *go!*" someone screamed.

Tires spun. The car lurched. And the limo sped out from under me. Like a soda can forgotten on the roof, I tumbled backward, crashing on my ass. A crunch of rocks bit into my rear. But all I could really feel was the tick-tock tick-tock pumping in my cheek.

I looked down at my palm, seeing that my chest and right shoulder were soaked. Not by water. Thicker . . . and darker . . . dark red. *Oh, God, is that my—?*

Another flashbulb went off. It wasn't just the red of my blood I was seeing. Now there was blue . . . on my tie . . . and yellow . . . yellow stripes on the road. Another flashbulb exploded as knives of color stabbed my eyes. Silver and brown and bright green race cars. Red, white, and blue flags abandoned in the grandstands. A screaming blond boy in the third row with an aqua and orange Miami Dolphins T-shirt. And red . . . the dark, thick red all over my hand, my arm, my chest.

I again touched my cheek. My fingertips scraped against something sharp. Like metal—or . . . is that bone? My stomach nose-dived, swirling with nausea. I touched my face again with a slight push. That thing wouldn't budge . . . *What's wrong with my fa—?*

Two more flashbulbs blinded me with white, and the world flew at me in fast-forward. Time caught up in a fingersnap, blurring at lightspeed.

"I'm not feeling a pulse!" a deep voice yelled in the distance. Directly ahead, two suit-and-tie Secret Service agents lifted Boyle onto a stretcher and into the ambulance from the motorcade. His right hand dangled downward, bleeding from his palm. I replayed the moments before the limo ride. He would've never been in there if I hadn't—

"He's cuffed! Get the hell off!" A few feet to the left, more agents screamed at the dogpile, peeling layers away to get at the gunman. I was on the ground with the rest of the grease stains, struggling to stand up, wondering why everything was so blurry.

Help . . . ! I called out, though nothing left my lips.

The grandstands tilted like a kaleidoscope. I fell backward, crashing into the pavement, lying there, my palm still pressed against the slippery metal in my cheek.

"Is anyone—?"

Sirens sounded, but they weren't getting louder. Softer. They quickly began to fade. Boyle's ambulance . . . *Leaving . . . They're leaving me . . .*

"Please . . . why isn't . . . ?"

One woman screamed in a perfect C minor. Her howl

pierced through the crowd as I stared up at the clear Florida sky. *Fireworks . . . we were supposed to have fireworks. Albright's gonna be pissed . . .*

The sirens withered to a faint whistle. I tried to lift my head, but it didn't move. A final flashbulb hit, and the world went completely white.

"Wh-Why isn't anyone helping me?"

That day, because of me, Ron Boyle died.

Eight years later, he came back to life.

ONE BEST-SELLING THRILLER WRITER

The World's Greatest Super Heroes®

BRAD MELTZER

Justice League of America®

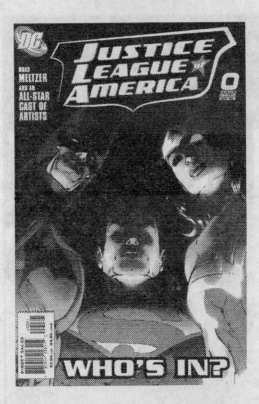